Justice of the Heart

Justice
of the Heart

E. Arnot Robertson

New York
The Macmillan Company
1958

© *E. Arnot Robertson* *1958*

First Printing

Printed in the United States of America

Library of Congress catalog card number: 58–12440

Author's Note

I have called the island where more than half this book is set, Zanzibar, because it is meant to be Zanzibar, which would be obvious, whatever I called it, to anyone who had ever been there: nowhere else is in the least like Zanzibar. This would make any pretense that the background should be considered "an imaginary island off the east coast of Africa" even more useless, as well as more irritating, than usual. I assure the reader, however, that none of the characters can be met in Zanzibar, but only in several of the other thirty-three British protectorates and colonies.

Contents

Contents

Justice of the Heart

1
Lunch Party

No one, thought Louise, trying to listen to the conversation going on around her, has ever written adequately of the boredom of love. Of its ecstasies and torments, yes, indeed: these have been superbly captured. But not the obstinate unreality of any scene which cannot hold the one essential figure, where other forms and faces become fully visible for a second or two only, on first meeting, and then fade back into unreality. Not the difficulty of paying enough attention to irrelevant voices to hear what they are saying.

She made a more determined effort: this was an interesting Cambridge lunch party, even amusing in its way. There were all sorts of invisible human strings stretching across and around the table, moving people to behave and talk in an animated manner.

Opposite her was the empty chair where her cousin Dorothy, daughter of the house, ought to have been sitting. What new, obsessive entanglement was keeping her away? Louise had intercepted, earlier in the meal, a worried glance between the parents, who were to her, Uncle Arthur and Aunt Rose. Certainly she would listen, and take part herself, instead of remembering continually that this was the first time since her husband's death that she had come back to the house from which she had been married.

People were being wonderfully characteristic of themselves, and that was always enjoyable. It had to be. At the farther end of the table her uncle, Master of one of the Colleges, was being humble about his high classical distinctions to a group of visiting scientists from various foreign universities, who probably thought little of his achievements in any case—a likelihood, Louise knew, which could never cross his mind.

"When one realizes the amount of research the previous Master managed to get through here . . . ashamed of my own indolence." Gross modesty from a man with bulky proofs of scholarship in his published work, prominently displayed on a shelf all by itself in the room where they had recently drunk sherry. If the visitors were unaware of his new, almost scandalous translations of Ovid, and of other, more obscure authors, that was their loss, shared by no one who mattered in the academic field.

At the nearer end of the table sat the Master's wife. Aunt Rose was effusively thanking a Belgian physicist for the lovely flowers on the table which, by the look on his face, he had not given her, but now felt awkwardly that he ought to have brought with him, as a tribute to the hostess. He had no chance to explain her error before she turned away and beamed, with surprised pleasure, at the visitor placed between Louise and herself, who had accepted and consumed a second helping of her chocolate pudding. Used as she was to the appetites of the few gifted undergraduates, mostly scholarship boys, who were occasionally admitted to the Master's table, his wife was not accustomed to this. Rose Farrant's chocolate pudding for official occasions was well known throughout the University.

"Just a little more, Mr. van . . . er?" she said to the young Dutchman beside Louise. A hospitable spoon waved above the remains of the gray-brown, glutinous slab.

"Thank you!" he said in alarm. The spoon descended, scooping up a generous lump. "Thank you, thank you!" he repeated. Courtesy and international misunderstanding had already forced him to swallow all he could manage. Inexorably the spoon was emptied on his plate. He looked wildly round the table.

Louise roused herself and leaned forward, smiling at her aunt. "Continental 'thank you,' meaning 'no,' Aunt Rose, darling! As in France, I'm sure he's had enough. It was as delicious as ever. But filling." She turned to the Dutchman. "You don't want this, do you?"

He shook his head, dumb with gratitude for the moment. Louise whipped his plate away and swiveled in her chair, to lean with her arm over the back, holding out the plate so that her cousin Dorothy, who had just come into the room, was forced to take it and put it down on the sideboard, in order to get by to her own place. If Dorothy could have avoided being helpful in this way, or any way, certainly she would have done so, Louise judged by her expression. Louise knew that look of old: through no inclination of hers, the cousins had been much together in childhood. Dorothy was furious for some reason, and this meant that, if possible, everyone should be made to atone for it.

Half an hour late for lunch, and still in riding clothes, the young woman mumbled something about not noticing the time as she sat down, acknowledging introductions curtly. "Hallo!" she said to Louise. They had met once or twice in London, when Aunt Rose had almost dragged them together, after Louise became a widow, but it was three years since they had seen each other under this roof.

Louise began to talk to the reprieved Dutchman, to cover any awkwardness he might feel. "I had the same sort of thing happen to me once in Holland, only the other way round. I said, 'Thank you,' meaning 'yes,' when I wanted more of something, so of course I didn't get it."

"You *wanted* some more? Of Dutch cooking?" he said, as though this confirmed his suspicion that everyone present was mad.

"Well, yes. Just that once," Louise told him. Putting him at ease seemed a somewhat thankless task. "You consider your own national cooking so poor, then?"

"Please?"

"You think your food is as bad as ours?" Everyone was talking hard, except Dorothy, so that she could say this to him conspiratorially.

"Oh, not that. But bad, yes," said the Dutchman, and grinned broadly, becoming suddenly quite a different person. "From what I have met so far, when eating is good in this country, it is very good. When it is not— Now, I have the right word for it if I can think it. During the war I was with a British spy who was dropped in Walcheren Island. From him I have what English I know. Ah, yes, it is ———— awful," he said, using an obscenity startling in that company.

Dorothy burst out laughing. Thank goodness, thought Louise: this would lighten the gloom when the guests had gone and she, urgently invited by her aunt for the week end, would have to stay on. She slid a glance left and right along the table: no one else appeared to have heard. She agreed heartily with the Dutchman.

"How fortunate I am," he said, "that Amsterdam and my government have lent me to your East Africa, so from now on I will live mostly in the island of Pemba," and they talked of other things, with difficulty, because of the scantiness of his English. His true love was Austria, he conveyed to her; and his hobby, climbing. But there were fewer problems for the botanist in Europe than in tropical places; or rather for the kind of botanist he was, a specialist in mold diseases in trees.

Another brief but less anxious look, intercepted by Louise, had passed between the parents at the sound of Dorothy's laughter; as though they, too, were reassuring one another, This will make things easier!

Not at the time but a few minutes later, when she was congratulating herself on giving all her attention to the Belgian scientist, Louise realized that there had been something more in that last consultation of eyes—a hint of complicity, perhaps—which struck apprehension into her. Was it possible that after all this time she had been urged to come down to Cambridge, lovingly bullied rather than invited, for a particular purpose? In order that when everybody else had left, they might consult her about Dorothy?

In a small, closed society forever buzzing with University gossip, it would not be surprising if at last the Farrants had come to suspect what nearly all their world knew, but on the whole refrained from discussing openly, because Arthur Farrant was greatly respected—the emotional mess which their daughter was making of her life: more exactly, it had been a series of emotional messes, so far.

If so, Louise thought in panic, she must get out of the family conference, somehow—anyhow. Nothing she could say would help these people's difficult relationship with their daughter. The truth as Louise knew it could only hurt them, not make them wiser, for they would not understand it. Indeed, describing color to the blind would be scarcely harder than making plain, to a couple as nearly sexless as she judged these two to be, the twisted, self-thwarting motives which impelled the luckless creature whom they had unaccountably produced between them from one unsatisfactory experience to another. Particularly, Louise was unwilling to distress her aunt, of whom she was fond; much fonder than of her uncle.

How mysterious marriages were! These relatives had taken her in when her own parents died. She had spent ten years in their house as a girl; but how little she knew of them! Giving up the pretense of being more than a spectator at this feast, Louise considered again the incongruous pair at the ends of the table. Outside the Farrants' household, people wondered that such a gentle, quiet-voiced, sensitive-seeming man, who was almost everyone's idea of what a don should be, could put up as amiably as he did with an incompetent, garrulous and supremely tactless woman. Mrs. Farrant's tactlessness was as famous as her chocolate pudding. It had an ingenuousness so well intentioned that it was sometimes endearing; but only sometimes, and only to people who were not personally affected by it. Colleagues of her husband who were proud of their Scottish blood were likely to be assured by Rose Farrant that they need not worry, it did not show, no one would guess. To other dons' wives, aged about thirty-six, she said with the air of insincerity which clings to such a statement that they hardly looked a day over thirty-five. There was a story, probably apocryphal, thought Louise, but characteristic, that she had once reproved some scandalmongers who were discussing another Master's son, when the lad had left his public school under a cloud, by saying with her devastating, bright charity that she was sure it would turn out to be "a cloud no bigger than a man's hand," which in fact it did.

Yet when Louise's husband was killed, during the war, her aunt's bumbling kindness was more acceptable than her uncle's delicate wariness. Mrs. Farrant had rushed up to London, where Louise worked, on hearing the news, to beg and indeed badger her niece to come back to Cambridge and live with them again. Louise had never even considered returning permanently. Afraid, however, lest she should accept, and his comfort be disturbed by her sad presence, her uncle had managed to get a note to her by special messenger before his wife arrived. It must have taken considerable organization, in wartime, for an apparently unworldly man, to enable him to forestall the invitation which, knowing his wife, he was sure that she would press on the stricken girl. He had told Louise, for whom the world had suddenly stopped, that he respected her sorrow and was sure that she would prefer not to come back to his house, "full of memories, as it must be," until "the worst is over for you." He had been fond of her while she had been under his roof, finding her useful, as well as more congenial than his own daughter, but anxiety rather than sympathy breathed from every hurried line of his letter. Grief, it seemed, was only bearable to him in translation.

Since that day, Louise had learned to accept that most angels who fear to tread, refrain because of possible discomfort to themselves; but she had been younger then, and more vulnerable. It was this note which had kept her away for so long, rather than the associations of the house. For anyone who walks with sorrow, in the cold, gray world of the boredom of love—of love cut off but still possessing—surroundings make some difference, naturally, but not very much. Memory can reign anywhere. She had returned here today—arriving just before lunch, relieved to learn that there were other guests expected—only because Aunt Rose had begged so persistently, and the invitation had coincided with forty-eight hours' leave from her job on a newspaper, when an assignment had fallen through unexpectedly.

Was the worst over for her by now? She could not have said. The first rough havoc of grief is not necessarily the most damaging. Outwardly she was composed enough, a detached and self-assured young woman, older in manner than her years warranted: she was twenty-six. Inwardly she was aware of being desiccated. This drying up in her of the springs of joy had at any rate made her an acute observer of other people's lives; she had become an excellent journalist. Certainly her uncle, at least, appeared to think her fully recovered: Arthur Farrant had greeted her with playful reproaches for her neglect of him. For one reason or another he had not been able to run up to London to see her with his wife and daughter, but in the three years since he and Louise had met, he did not appear to have changed at all.

Time stood wonderfully still in Cambridge, she thought. Had he managed to forget entirely that extraordinary communication of his? These were the real secrets about human beings, the questions they could never be asked, no matter how intimate the curious might be with them. Had he even realized when he wrote it that he was virtually forbidding the desperate girl the only home where she had any human right to be? Louise and her husband had been married for so short a time, during the war, that they had never established a home of their own: she had lived in a small hotel, where he could come to her on leave from his ship. And now, for her, home was wherever her portable typewriter happened to be. It was upstairs, at the moment, in the bedroom which had been hers when she was part of this household: and Arthur Farrant looked pleased.

Affable, always self-deprecating, he was telling stories against himself and his kind—classicists and literary purists in general—to the scientists down his end of the table, with what amounted in him to gusto. Louise's reporting eye noted how monstrous excessive humility could be, with its inference of great talent not put to full use. Compared with other men, what had he got to be so humble about? The wonder, to her, was that a generous-hearted woman, his wife, had not only put up with his self-centered pretentiousness for many years, but loved and admired him unreservedly.

He quoted gaily to his guests Hilaire Belloc's Latin-hating Oxford don who, in order to confine himself to words of Anglo-Saxon derivation, was forced to describe the impenetrability of matter as "the unthoroughfaresomeness of stuff."

"But," the Dutchman muttered in Louise's ear, "matter is not impenetrable, so why should anyone need to say that? I do not understand!"

"No—well—it's just—" All at once Louise found herself exceedingly tired, and was glad that he did not insist on an explanation, but went on talking.

"From what you said of eating in Holland I am hoping," he said, "that as you have been there on one visit, some day you will come again?"

"Some day, almost certainly. But I can't say when. As a newspaper woman I go where I'm sent, and I'm not often sent abroad." For a second her mind flashed back to her work. A temporary foreign job, which might lead on to something more permanent, was in fact open at the moment: it would be assigned to someone in her department, on the feature editor's staff. She had almost decided not to try for it. As usual, there were so many personal strings attached: office intrigue, the inevitable jealousy of a particular colleague if she fought all-out to get herself appointed, as she probably could if she went over his head to the editor. She was not a fighter by nature: better let it go.

"But perhaps you will be," said the Dutchman. "And then you will come back to Holland. Please, I would like to give you my card, in case."

"From what you said, though, I thought you wouldn't often be there, in future?"

"Oh, sometimes I shall go home for a little. To Walcheren Island, where I have sisters. If you come—you have been so kind—"

She noted with mild amusement that she had made what her aunt would call "a conquest," merely by removing a plate, and thought how easy her work would be—it was largely interviewing— if sympathy could always be established so easily. She gave him her name, which he had not taken in on introduction—Louise Downes —along with the vague promise of meeting again, if possible, distributed freely and inattentively by all journalists, as a polite social formula: she was accustomed to leaving half-formed friendships behind, day after day. She took his card, knowing that she would throw it away at the first opportunity—Karel van Epp, it said, of the Department of Mycology, Amsterdam University, with a private

address in Veere—and when they had said goodbye, thought no
more of him for several years; except, occasionally, as the man
who had actually got through two helpings of the Farrants' chocolate
pudding.

2

"Hurrah for Lou Flap"

As soon as the visitors had left, it became clear that Louise's suspicion was justified: Dorothy disappeared, after returning a curt, "I don't know," to her mother's timid question about supper, and Louise was invited back into the room where they had drunk sherry: "to have a little talk, dear."

Her aunt said anxiously, "It's such a long time since your uncle and I have had the chance! Although—you know—we understand. Very sensible of you to make a new world for yourself." On all sides it was to be assumed, from now onward, for convenience' sake, that up to the present Louise had felt unable to face the memories in the house, and that this was the sole reason for her absence. Study

10

of the growth of legends in families would be a fascinating form of anthropology, she thought.

"Oh, but I must give Anna a hand first," she said. "Just for auld lang syne. And tell her she's still the same old miracle worker she used to be."

"But you know she prefers to do everything herself."

"She says she does. I've never believed it. Anyway, she'd be hurt if I didn't go to see her, as soon as I could." It was always possible to get round Aunt Rose by suggesting that someone, somewhere, might be hurt. The Farrants' cantankerous old Swedish maid could indeed work miracles if allowed to do everything herself, ordering, cooking and washing up, for the Master's unavoidable entertaining at home; but they were not necessarily desirable miracles. An arrangement by the Cambridge colleges allowed Fellows, living out, to have excellent food, cooked and served from their kitchens, sent over in special containers. Anna would have none of it. "Everything sure to be half-cold," she objected. "I don't hold with twice-warmed food." Long ago the Farrants had given in. Whatever she provided, owing to the difficulty of getting everything ready at once, single-handed, was almost bound to be not half-cold but congealing on its dish. On this occasion, Louise was grateful to her for her slow-ness: spread between the two of them, washing up was made to last three-quarters of an hour.

Cornered after this, Louise pleaded a filler for the feature page which must be typed in time to catch the afternoon post to London, and hoped they would not point out that, this being Saturday, it would get there just as quickly if she took it back with her on Sunday evening: it could not be delivered anywhere before Monday morning. In any case, had the urgency been real, she would have telephoned her work. They did not think of this. She had actually brought a small job to do, as a protection against ghosts, but there was no hurry about it, an interview for the Wednesday arts page. She escaped to her bedroom and, unable to manage anything which needed concentration, tapped out over and over again, at varying speeds, "Now is the time for all good men to come to the aid of the party," altering the rhythm occasionally with the exercise about the quick brown fox. Her uncle, she knew, was due to dine in Hall: if she could stave off confidences till then there was a chance of

Dorothy turning up to save the evening from becoming a tête-à-tête with Aunt Rose, and the next day she could announce suddenly that she must leave by an earlier train than the Farrants had expected. ". . . jumps over the lazy dog."

Getting up to reach for a cigarette, she caught sight of herself accidentally in the dressing-table mirror, and looked away quickly. She had avoided seeing herself in this particular mirror ever since she arrived: it had reflected the excited face of a girl in a not very becoming little hat, bought locally in a tremendous hurry because a sailor had arrived on leave saying, "We've just time to get married," and she had insisted on being married in Cambridge, to please Aunt Rose. Deliberately Louise made herself look again, to break the spell over everything in the room. (The last time I touched this . . . the last time I saw that . . .) Nowadays her face was slightly thinner: she knew better how to manage her thick, heavy fair hair, wearing it drawn back sleekly, instead of fluffed out round her face; and how to dress for her tall, bony elegance. She had always been elegant rather than pretty, and in these days was beautifully dressed —because it was the sensible thing to be in her job. It paid her, and she took a careful interest in her clothes for no other reason. Otherwise, she thought wonderingly, staring back at her image, Uncle Arthur was justified in considering her, outwardly at least, as little changed as she thought him. "Now is the time for all good men—"

The Farrants hovered about downstairs, waiting for her. When she emerged at last, with a sheaf of typescript in her hand, saying that she must rush out and get stamps and the right-sized envelope ("No, no, thank you. Too small! They don't like it folded"), they both insisted on coming with her to the post office and stationers in Silver Street. Almost everyone they met on the way was an acquaintance, who said something like, "So you've got your niece back! How nice!" In between encounters, Louise talked briskly of Fleet Street matters, creating a frivolously impersonal atmosphere, in which no serious problems could be raised.

They had changed after all, her uncle and aunt, in the past three years, she discovered. They seemed to her diminished, pathetic people, for whom it was impossible to feel anything but pity. Uncle Arthur, bereft of an audience, was without even enough scholastic bounce left in him to go on being self-critical.

"How are you sleeping, these days, dear girl?" he asked solicitously, as though insomnia had always been Louise's trouble.

"Very well indeed," she said. "That is, just as usual."

"Louise always has been a very good sleeper, don't you remember, dear?" his wife prompted him gently. "Didn't we tease her about the way she could just drop off in a chair, or on the lawn, any time!"

"I'm so thankful to hear that. So very thankful," he said, addressing his conversation only to Louise, ignoring his wife's contribution. "It must be a great help, in a life as busy as yours, the knack of sleep. I wish I had it."

Dorothy's description of her father, given in a moment of more than usual irritation, sprang into Louise's mind: "Always trying to cash moral checks at a bank of benevolence, he is. One where he has no credit." Really, Arthur Farrant and his daughter deserved each other: Louise was remotely tempted to let him have the talk he wanted. But there was Aunt Rose, small, anxiety-ridden, protectible, squeezing her arm on the excuse of being shepherded across the road to the post office, murmuring, "We have missed you so! Busy or not, you've got to come and see us more often, now you've—you know—broken the ice."

More and more extraordinary, Louise reflected, became the fact that in matters of University politics, business concerns and everything touching the prestige of the college, her uncle had proved himself shrewd, tolerant but forceful, and was regarded by nearly everyone in Cambridge who ought to know as one of the most effective Masters of his time.

The Farrants were claimed by yet another acquaintance just outside the post office, a Fellow of the college. Louise was able to slip in alone, buy some stamps, and deposit the Lazy-Dog rubbish in the litter basket by the door, with a crumpled newspaper on top to conceal it in case her uncle or aunt followed her in; but they stayed outside, chatting. Letters could be posted from inside the building. "Gone!" she said cheerfully on emerging. "That's one weight off my mind."

From Silver Street, with the other don persuaded to come too, it was easy to divert the party through the flowery autumn blaze of the Backs. A perfect September afternoon abetted her. By taking a

small detour they could pass through the College gardens, overlooked
by the Fellows' rooms. Teatime was approaching, and Cambridge
was always hospitable.

Crushing down her own particular association with the showering
of golden leaves on this exquisitely tended grass—on the still water
where the ducks were parading their late broods—on graveled paths
and weathered bridges—Louise spun the time out by asking eagerly,
"Couldn't we just go through John's? And I must see Trinity and
King's College Chapel again. Oh, look! There's Clare!" she said, as
though astonished that this centuries-old garden should be exactly
where she had left it. In the end, tea in College was offered. Mrs.
Farrant looked harassed, Uncle Arthur definitely put out, but Louise
accepted with alacrity. "Can I have buttered toast, out of the special
muffin dishes, sitting in your window seat? It's so long since I
looked out on a properly kept lawn."

When they reached the Master's house it was almost time for
Arthur Farrant to leave it again for Hall. No important discussion
could begin now. Louise accepted a glass of the excellent College
sherry with the feeling that it had been well earned. Drink, Anna
allowed the College servants to bring over, so that there was a
startling contrast between the quality of liquids and solids offered
to guests in this house. But for once supper was a pleasant meal.

Dorothy came in for it after all, and in a smiling mood. The
mental storm of the morning had blown itself out, after breaking
over someone else's head. From her cousin's gay talk, Louise
gathered that a new bosom friend with whom Dorothy often rode,
an undergraduate from one of the women's colleges, had let her
down that morning by not turning up at the stables as arranged.
In the afternoon Dorothy had sought her out, there had been a
tremendous row, and a reconciliation, and after this Dorothy was so
pleased with everything that her pleasure even extended to seeing
Louise. There was something touching, almost innocent, in her
satisfaction.

In this state of mind she renewed a silly childhood joke which
the cousins had shared, the turning into literal French of some English phrase ("Oh, vous voudriez, voudriez-vous? N'êtes-vous pas une
une!) and the reverse ("Fitch me the peace, my old!"). Nothing
could have annihilated the years quicker for Louise: it seemed as if

she had never escaped from watching the sadly similar disintegration of all the friendships into which Dorothy had rushed too enthusiastically. This one had reached the middle of the pattern, which started with the unsparing pursuit of the other person, followed by the first defection, the swift anger, and the temporary coming together again, always taken by Dorothy as a real closing of the breach. And soon, any time now, would begin the final stage, the growing reluctance of the quarry to meet and suffer further reproaches.

"Dorothy has so many girl friends," said her mother, greatly daring, basking in the rare warmth of the atmosphere, "I say she should collect a few young men for a change!" Dorothy's eyes turned expressionlessly to Louise, and as expressionlessly, Louise met them and then looked away.

Unwisely feeling safe, Louise went early to bed, pleading her ability to put away long stretches of sleep, when she could get them, which was not often with her job. Only the ghosts particular to her bedroom remained to be faced that day, she believed. To keep them at bay she looked round for books. No more than minor changes had been made in the room since it was permanently hers. Close-packed at the back of a cupboard were not only the books of her adolescent reading, acquired while she lived in this house, but her baby books, mostly picture books, which she had brought with her from her parents' home, when she came here at twelve years old. Already, at that age, she must long have discarded such books as reading matter: they had been taken by a lonely and frightened child for the comfort to be had from old possessions: it was unlikely that she had opened them for eighteen years. But leafing through them now she discovered that she could recite by heart the caption to every picture, and almost every page of the text. "Lou Flap" was there, dear Lou Flap with his splendid recurrent line, " 'Hurrah for Lou Flap!' cried Lou Flap." This was the right reading for the moment. The well remembered smell of the binding— there were moldy biscuit crumbs between the pages where the small Louise had stored provision for the night—carried only the bearable nostalgia of all time out of reach; no sharp and special reminders.

She got into bed with "Lou Flap," to be astonished again, not this time by her word-perfect familiarity with most of the story, but by the strangeness of paragraphs which her eyes must have learned to skip, neatly, through many rereadings. She could have sworn that she had never seen these distasteful passages before. They were always those in which a moral was embedded: so much for the efforts of authors to elevate the young. She was not conscious of having avoided them with care. In the description of a house on fire, with children asleep in it, a horror piece vivid enough to foster nightmares for weeks, every phrase was a cherished old friend. ("And the flames crept, mutter-mutter, up the stairs. Would they never wake? Or waking, find every escape closed to them?") But the next chapter gave an account of a mother and child, saved at the last moment, standing by night in the falling snow, watching all their worldly goods disappear in smoke, with the mother drawing the crying child toward her and saying, "Hush, darling! Nothing should make us sad, except a sense of sin." This dispiriting speech, and the whole scene in the snow, seemed entirely new. It was while Louise was reading it again with incredulous pleasure that a knock sounded on her door, and her aunt came in before she could answer.

"I saw your light," Aunt Rose said breathlessly. With Lou Flap in her hand, it was impossible for Louise to pretend that she was on the edge of sleep. She put the book aside with nervous resignation, and moved to let Mrs. Farrant sit down on the bed. Even then it was some time before her aunt could bring herself to the point of the visit.

"Your uncle is so delighted to see you again! I think he's been just a tiny bit hurt that you didn't find time to come before—although of course he's just the best person to understand that work must come first."

Living by herself, Louise had forgotten the swiftness with which these monstrous pretenses and evasions could be erected and demolished again at will in family life, without open agreement. So now it was not only her unwillingness to face the past, but her selfish absorption in a career, which was to be responsible for keeping her away from Cambridge for so long. Yet at some period in these last three years, probably soon after it was written, Aunt Rose must have come to suspect (if she did not actually know) that a letter from her husband had been the real barrier between Louise

and this house. Otherwise she would have badgered the girl into
coming down long before this.

"I expect Uncle Arthur's pretty busy himself," Louise said, accepting the new shape of their relationship.

"Oh, he is!" Aunt Rose seized upon this opening, putting off
the bad moment. "He's been up till all hours, lately, revising two
books of his for reprinting or something. A new edition, I think.
And he's very dissatisfied with them. But then you know he always
is, about his own work. Nothing's ever good enough, by his standards. For himself, that is. There's some quotation about men like
him—scholars—only picking up pebbles on the seashore of knowledge—"

"Yes. I've heard him quote it."

"He says this revising has made him realize that all his work has
been inadequate. His whole life's work! And he's sure at last that—
I must get this right—it's either that people ought only to trans-
late dead authors, or—no, only the living, that's it. Because after all,
the living have a chance of saying if they don't think the work
does them justice. But it isn't fair on the dead, he says, because who
is he that better men should be forced to live on, only through
what he calls his limited understanding?" Mrs. Farrant looked pink
and pleased with her unusual accuracy.

She must have heard this disclaimer of merit a great many times
to have got it so nearly correct, in his own words, Louise realized,
and felt another gust of pitying affection for her aunt.

"Really, his modesty"—she said obligingly, suppressing the rest of
the sentence—"goes beyond all decency."

"Isn't it absurd?"

"But he still *is* translating dead authors, isn't he?"

"Oh, well, of course, when Latin and classical Greek are your
special province—"

"—the authors are bound to be dead? Yes. Of course." Try as she
would, Louise could not think of anything more to say. How much
nicer Lou Flap was than Uncle Arthur. Mrs. Farrant made her heroic
effort.

"We're so worried about Dorothy! Somebody said—we don't know
what to believe. We don't feel we can talk it over with anyone who

lives here. We thought, perhaps you, really more in the world than we are— Oh, Louise, do you think she's drinking?"

"Drinking?" Louise was astounded. "No. I don't. My opinion's not worth much because I've hardly seen her for years. But I can't remember that drink ever did matter to her particularly. And I'm as sure as anyone can be that it doesn't now."

"We wondered if that could be what's wrong. She seems so queer, sometimes. I mean, depressed. The way people are supposed to feel after—after excess. Before she took up with this girl, Elaine someone, she went up to Town a lot, and she often came back so unhappy and moody."

"But she was always like that. Here or in London," Louise said, taking Aunt Rose's hand in hers. "Dorothy is just—a difficult person." It would be impossible to find a truer understatement, she thought, about this temperamentally passionate but physically frigid woman, a year younger than herself, who had been flinging herself, from the age of seventeen onward into shabby adventures of all kinds, in search of the sensations experienced by others and denied to her. Drink, and drugs too, she might well have tried by this time —Louise simply did not know—but they would give her even less of an illusion of belonging, the satisfaction which Dorothy craved. She was not likely to be seriously addicted to either; at least not yet, while human relationships remained a more promising hunting ground.

"Oh, if you think that's all it is!—I mean, nothing new—I'll be so thankful."

"Look, Aunt Rose, darling, I'm certain it's 'nothing new,' as you say. Sometimes moody people can get moodier than usual, can't they, without it meaning anything? I work among a pretty hard-drinking set." (Sympathy for this kindly, uncomprehending and now tormented woman brought tears pricking at the back of Louise's eyes.) "From the little I've seen of Dorothy today, I'd say she certainly isn't taking too much, steadily. I don't mean that at a party she never by any chance has a drop more than she should. Believe me, people nowadays don't worry very much about that. You and Uncle Arthur shouldn't either. She's far from being what people mean when they talk about 'someone who drinks.' "

Parallel with compassion, in Louise, ran a strong desire to laugh at the pompousness of her own voice, chasing the red herring of drink as her cousin's trouble, but compassion won again when the older woman said gratefully:

"I knew if I could talk to you, I'd feel better. I told Arthur so."

Mrs. Farrant got up from the bed, kissed her, said automatically, "Don't read too late, will you?" in the habit of years, and moved toward the door. There she paused, and said waveringly, "It was something we heard."

"People are awfully malicious. Good night, Aunt Rose."

"You don't think—please tell me quite honestly"—clenching her hands round one another, Mrs. Farrant said with supreme courage —"she goes with men?"

"No," Louise told her with relief. "I'm absolutely convinced she doesn't."

"Oh, thank you! Good night, dear."

Strange indeed was family life, in which it was possible for people perched, like Arthur Farrant, on the edge of the ancient world, to remain ignorant that for years his daughter's brief, scarring affairs had all been with women. Or possibly he half-realized, and it was only his wife who could not, must not know.

When she had the room to herself again, fierce loneliness took Louise, the sudden incalculable loneliness, like a beast in the jungle, always waiting to spring, which had stalked each day and night of the last three years. Lately she had imagined that it seemed a little less eager to pounce on any unguarded moment; but now the approach of tears, though they had been not for herself but for someone else, had weakened the defense against emotion which she had been struggling to put up all day. She lay and cried, as she had not cried for a long time, for the young, laughing and tender lover whom she had walked out of this room to marry. (I have managed not to think of you for a whole hour or more. You would be glad of this for my sake, so I want to tell you. But you are no-where to tell.)

The stair halfway down the flight gave its particular squeak, which she recognized: and then another squeaked. Someone was coming up who moved more quickly than Aunt Rose. Louise switched off her bed lamp, that no light should show under her door, but Dorothy walked straight in. Louise had just time to throw up an arm over her eyes before the main light was turned on by the switch near the door.

"Turn that out. Hurts my eyes."

"All right." The room was again in saving darkness. "Put yours on over the bed, then."

"No, and don't sit down and start talking, either. I'm tired." Her voice, husky with tears, sounded as though she had just been awakened. For once, she was thankful for Dorothy's complete absorption in her own concerns. She would notice nothing.

"You've got to tell me—I know they wanted to discuss me— what do they think?"

"That you're a fool. Same as I do." It was a distraction to find that contact with Dorothy, who had never had any manners, still had the effect of reducing her own to the same level. She had control of herself again now. "Oh, not a fool for wanting whatever you can't help wanting, but for the way you go about getting it."

"Welcoming, aren't you!"

"Why should I be? You never were." If not a fighter by nature, she could be made one by Dorothy, for the time being: many people reacted in the same way. When Louise first came to this house her cousin, jealous, had done everything possible in the boundless cruelty of childhood to make life miserable for her. Between them, in private, there had never been even a pretense of affection, and yet there had always been this mutual respect of straight speaking. That was something else which had not changed. The tradition had been founded in hours of disturbing confidences given by Dorothy, talking in the darkness, curled up on the foot of Louise's bed—the kind of exhibitionist, childish confidences of which Louise was determined not to receive an adult version tonight. They had always been one-sided revelations; by nature and upbringing, Louise herself told no one of anything which was of real importance to her. It had been a luxury to her eventually, when she married someone she trusted, to speak without thinking beforehand what could be made of her words, by careless or spiteful repetition. Perhaps this was almost the greatest freedom she had known, in marriage—freedom from that particular kind of caution.

Dorothy could tell anything to anyone, except her parents. In her shut-in, reticent childhood, Louise had not wanted these confidences, but they had held a frightening fascination. Years later,

when she had become a newspaper reporter, her work proved to
her that fantastic adventures did indeed happen to pathologically
cold young women, like Dorothy, searching without scruple for someone or something able to make them share what others prized:
Louise interviewed them, able to print little of what they said,
when they had enraged men they associated with by their unre-
sponsive, insatiable curiosity, and were genuinely astonished by the
vicious assaults they provoked. They came her way mainly through
police channels, when they had got themselves into situations where
they unwittingly courted murder on top of rape, and escaped by
accident. They were the pathetic raw material of front-page stories.
But to glimpse their world before she was capable of seeing it in any
sort of perspective had been horrifying, though in those early days
Dorothy quested and experimented only on the fringes of it. The
memory of her cousin's voice saying lightly one night, "I'm the
sort that's found doubled up in a trunk in some frowsy boarding-
house, in the end," could still give Louise a shiver, for though the
words had been a joke, as spoken, Dorothy's bravado had held a
sediment of dread: and the dread, the frank appraisal of the girl's
worth in her own eyes, sorted so ill with the decorous insincerity of
Arthur Farrant's house. Now, if Dorothy wanted an honest report,
Louise felt by old association that she was entitled to it, in her own
terms.

"What have they heard?" Dorothy asked.

"I don't know. Something. But you're lucky, they didn't quite
take it in."

"What did she ask you?"

"If I thought you drank, or had men!"

"How funny. So you could say no with a clear conscience. Did
you?"

"I said no."

"Ought I to thank you?" There was a defensive sneer in the
voice.

"Why should you? Everything I said was for your mother's sake."

After a pause, "Why do you dislike me so much?" Dorothy asked
dispassionately. "I've never bothered you. Not even when I first
went queer."

"That's nothing to do with my not liking you—whether you're

queer or not. You aren't kind, that's all. A lot of people of your sort are, unusually kind. But you never were. And I don't think anything else really matters."

Dorothy laughed heartily, as she had laughed at lunch. "That doesn't sound adequate as a reason!"

"But it is. The only worth-while thing about you is that you don't want your people to get hold of what you're like. And a good deal of that is for your own convenience, isn't it?"

"Oh, yes, about fifty-fifty."

"—that, and your peculiar form of sincerity!"

"Blast you!" Dorothy was suddenly angry, her voice shot with misery. "You're so lucky, what right have you got to judge anyone?"

"I'm not judging. You've a right to do what you like, only not to hurt people in doing it, more than you can help." There was no response from the darkness. After a few seconds Dorothy went out, leaving Louise, more disturbed than she had been all day, to lie awake and wonder. Lucky? Had she been? Was she now? It was more than three years since she herself had thought so.

Falling in love in wartime, unwillingly, helplessly, foreseeing the price—a marriage shadowed by fear, with agony in every parting, and then the expected end, made harder to accept by circumstances which neither Dorothy nor anyone else but Louise herself had ever known—was that conceivably to be called being lucky?

Perhaps after all life had been openhanded; she had loved and been loved, and from the height of that good fortune, had no right to look down and set up standards. It was untrue to say that she had not judged her cousin: every opinion was in some sense a judgment, though not necessarily a final one. And opinion was always colored by the holder's own luck, or lack of it.

For once her talent for sleep deserted her. After long wakefulness she dozed off, and was roused by the pigeons murmuring in the trees round the house, at dawn. Before she slept again, she could say to the crowding memories in the room, Yes! I have been lucky, in some ways!

One other thing was decided that night: she would not come back to the Farrants' house again. After this renewal of contact with Cambridge she would be expected by her aunt to appear more and more often. It would be easier to save Mrs. Farrant's feelings if Louise could go abroad. She would do her utmost to get the chance which she had more or less relinquished in her mind.

Looking back, long afterward, it seemed extraordinary that so much had depended on a strip of light showing under her door while she reread "Lou Flap."

3

"Les Eperons Chauds"

War opened in the office on Monday morning.

Louise walked into the feature editor's room, prepared to fight for the job she wanted, and found him wrangling on the telephone with a well-known outside contributor from whose copy he had, in his own words, "subbed the purple." He motioned to her to sit down, beaming at her briefly. He had a disconcerting trick of carrying on abusive conversations in a loud voice while welcoming, by a series of switched-on grimaces, anyone with whom he was not irritated at the moment. Her courage oozed away while she waited. She was gentle and courteous by nature: so far it had always seemed easier to let this man, who was neither, have his own way. He was her immediate boss on the paper, and she was almost sure that he

24

had earmarked for himself the pleasant little expedition abroad.

All feature editors who fancy themselves as writers are a burden to those who work for them. Apart from their tendency to rewrite everything and refrain from naming the original author, there is the fact that they go into conference with the editor in chief every morning, taking with them ideas, put up by their subordinates, which they can bring forward as their own if they intend to use them personally. This one had less shame than most of his kind.

Louise was not reassured by the smile he gave her while lambasting the other writer's choice of rich, ripe adjectives: it was warmer than usual. A week-end drinker, he tended to be surly to everyone on Monday mornings unless he had an end to gain. As he put down the receiver, on a contemptuous quotation from the lushest passage he had cut, he ran on affably without pause: "I've got a series for you, my girl. By-line stuff. 'What Did the Money Do for Them?'"

"Oh, not that again!" said Louise boldly.

All trace of smile was wiped away. "What d'you mean, 'Not that again'? You don't know what I want."

"Don't I? Interviews with people who've won fortunes by chance. In which I'd be expected to back up the paper's campaign against football pools and lotteries and big cash prizes by finding they've frittered the money away, and done themselves a bit of no-good, all round. So now, after a few years of luxury, they're really much worse off than all our hard-working readers who've never won anything."

"And why not? Why shouldn't ordinary, decent people have that much consolation?"

"Because it isn't true. When MacAlister tried this series, two years ago, you wouldn't run the result. Rightly, from the policy point of view—he told me about it. Nine out of ten of the winners he talked to had invested the money quite sensibly, given their children a nice start in life, or bought the little tobacconist's shop they'd always wanted. And never looked back. Very satisfactory but non-moral."

"Are you suggesting I'd expect you to falsify the findings?"

"Yes," said Louise, wondering at herself, but the tone of the talk with Dorothy in the darkness still lingered in her mind. "Anyway, that idea was originally put up by Mac. Not by me. Nor you. So if anyone is to try it again, Mac should be given the chance. But you

never do give him his chance, do you, if you can help it, because
he's the same kind of journalist as you are? Good on descriptive
stuff. Maybe he could dig up the tenth man again, the one he
interviewed two years ago who wasn't the better for getting five
thousand pounds without working for it. Just to make the readers
happier."

He did not know how to take this new, bland insolence from her,
and switched the smile on and off again.

"Well, all right, if that's how you feel about it. How did you like
the way I ran that story of yours on Saturday? Good position, eh?
Gave you quite a spread."

She noted thankfully that he was willing to placate this truculent
stranger. If she failed to get away from the London office, she would
have to go on working with him: she must press hard, but not beyond that delicate point of no return, verbally, after which reconciliation would become impossible.

"Why wasn't my name on it? Or Mac's on that Spanish story,
which was much more important?"

"Look here, what's come over you? It's my business to decide
whether I by-line the stuff on my page or not!"

"Was this the reason, in Mac's case—" She could feel her hands
beginning to shake. Although she was fighting for herself in the long
run, the means to her object, for the moment, was fighting for justice
to a colleague, and it was always regrettably hard to maintain the
full pitch of indignation when the person chiefly wronged was someone else. "—You didn't want to draw the Old Man's attention to
the fact that one of your staff speaks workable Spanish, which you
don't, just when you'd suggested combining a project of Mac's
with ten days' leave still due to you—the Gibraltar project, which
you discussed in conference as your own— Oh, yes, you did!" (Louise
had checked her guess with the editor's secretary, who took in cups
of tea to the morning conference, and gathered far more than most
of the staff ever realized. She and Louise were close friends.) "A
pleasant free holiday you were hoping for in Gibraltar—quite a
nice place for a short stay, I'm told. That way, you said, the project
would cost the paper hardly anything—and well you know the Old
Man's weakness for piddling little economies."

"That's a damned nasty accusation."

"And a damned nasty act. MacAlister's a family man and hard up. Paid leave means something to him, very little to you. What about that other proposition, one of mine? The Norwegian witch trial, being held in a village at the same time as the Nobel prize-giving in the capital? That was accepted, wasn't it? Well, who covers it?"

"The foreign editor's affair. We've men on the spot, I suppose."

"Not now, we haven't. Our Trondheim man's ill, and you know that, too. You also put up this idea as your own, didn't you, in case the Gibraltar story folded?"

"If you think so, why don't you see the Old Man about it?" He was white with anger, and incautious.

"Good. I've been waiting for that." She picked up his telephone and put through a call to the editor's secretary. "Hello, Laura. This is Louise. Speaking from the feature editor's room. He suggests I should see the editor. Yes. Thanks. As soon as he's free. I'll wait in the reporters' room. Yes, I'm with the feature editor now! Goodbye. All my working life," she said, replacing the phone on his desk, "I've accidentally gone over people's heads to get information. Not meaning to offend them. And they've protested that of course they didn't mind for themselves—that's what everyone always says—it was the dignity of their department they were concerned about. For years I've wanted just one person to say honestly, 'I don't give a damn about my department, it's me you've by-passed, and that's what I mind!' Well, you'll be in a position to say that soon, and I do hope you will?"

"If you go to the Old Man about this, not another word will you get on to this page!"

"Nonsense," said Louise, walking to the door. "You know, and I know, I'm the most reliable interviewer we've got. But you didn't think I knew." This, she felt, was just about the point of no return. If only he would help her now—

He said unpleasantly as she was going out, "I suppose you're going to tell him you talk Norwegian as well as Mac speaks Spanish?" She turned back.

"No, not a word. Except 'Skål!'—which is probably enough, in Norway. Though of course I realize that on other foreign jobs, if I land them, it'll be a handicap that my French is nothing like as good as yours."

He was taken off guard: "How do you know I talk French?"

"Because the last time I met you coming out of the Press Club—
you won't remember, you were very drunk, and I was just passing by
—you were telling a man from *Paris Soir*, very earnestly, that 'les
Eperons Chauds de Tottenham' had almost no chance at all, you
thought, 'contre les Boulevardiers de Bolton.' "

They eyed one another guardedly, and then he suddenly roared
with laughter. "That's a lie. A bloody good lie!"

"Yes, it is, isn't it?" she agreed. "Actually I wasn't near enough
to hear what you were saying to him, but it sounded very fluent."

"Come back, Louise. You know, there's something about you. I
don't know what it is, and I wish you hadn't got it, because I'd like
to get you sacked. But there it is, you have it. 'Les Boulevardiers de
Bolton'—Sounds so much less scruffy than the Bolton Wanderers.
I suppose if I'd been having a few with Yves Latour, their New York
chap, instead of their London man, you'd have said we were discussing 'les Chausettes Blanches, et les Géants de New York'—tell
you something interesting about Yves—" In a moment, while she
worried lest the editor's call should be going through to the reporters'
room, he was detaining her with an involved, self-congratulatory
story about what he and Yves had said to Charles (de Gaulle) in the
last world war, about Willie (Maugham) as a secret agent in the
first. He had to an extreme degree the journalist's weakness for using
the Christian or pet names of the prominent men whom he had met
only on duty. "As I said to 'Dickie' Mountbatten—" slipped out casually. Probably in this case, she thought, he had not even had professional contact: it would indeed put her beyond forgiveness were she
to make fun of him for that particular foible. She listened with a
return of her usual cool politeness, escaping as soon as she could.

"Reconsider this little scrap of ours, will you?" he said as they
parted. "You'll have to see the Old Man now you've asked to, but
you can easily find some other reason besides Norway."

"No," said Louise.

The reporters' room was full of the usual uproar of typewriters,
telephones and the chatter of cheerful young men, giving Louise
to wonder, not for the first time in years of helping to produce one,
how a daily newspaper ever emerged at all from the frantic, apparently aimless chaos of its birth. She sat down to wait before a spare

typewriter, slipped in a sheet of paper and headed it *Conversation Piece:*

> *Now as I said to Dickie Mountbatten*
> *When Larry and Willie were there—*

It was like trying to kill time, nervously, in her bedroom in Cambridge. She could settle to nothing until the editor's summons came. In any case, she could never write seriously in this room. A special feature writer, talented or not, is usually better paid than a good all-round reporter, but is not made of such stout mental material: Louise had always admired an ability to concentrate which she herself did not possess. She came to the office when she was wanted, but wrote in her own flat. These young men lived and worked—producing twenty words to her one: simple, readable if not distinguished prose—in the midst of unending distraction.

In front of her two of them were consulting together over shorthand notes, probably the House of Commons special staff, while beside them, oblivious of their conversation, another typed with two fingers, in bursts of enormous speed, with short, sighing pauses in between, during which he banged his teeth alarmingly hard with a pencil. If they were his own teeth, Louise would have expected the enamel to flake off, and if they were not, it seemed still more extraordinary that they stood such treatment: she found it hard to drag her attention away.

> *And the talk, of an intimate pattern,*
> *Was racy, allusive and rare—*

Next to her the jolly, spotty youth who collected theatrical gossip was singing, as a compliment to her, to the tune of "Billy Boy," a jingle she had launched during the previous Christmas festivities, "Are you happy in your work, Spreading dirt, spreading dirt? Are you happy in your work of spreading dirt?"—while he rearranged and pasted together a handful of scribbled paragraphs.

"Up-stick!" protested the man beyond him, and Louise's neighbor obligingly fell to a loud, wordless humming, while the protestor imitated to an audience of sports writers the exquisite refinement of one of the girls on the telephone board. Asked to get his opposite number on the *Daily Express* she had languidly inquired, "Mr. *Who*, shall I say, wishes to speak to Mr. *Whom?*"—"Now there's education for you! Preposition taking the accusative case. One of these days I shall get a rise and buy me some."

On Louise's other side, MacAlister was working on a routine piece about the Board of Trade's Import List for the current year. He had nodded to her gloomily as she came in. She was interested to find that for once she was feeling positively fond of him—stolid, humorless creature as he had always seemed to her, with an unenviable gift for producing the appropriate sentiment on public occasions. (Mac could be trusted to find the acceptable thing to say, every time, about young royalty.) How unfailingly it worked, the psychological law by which everyone conferring a benefit knew affection for the receiver, even if the benefit existed mainly in the intention of the giver, as in this case; whereas benefactors were as automatically resented, by those on the receiving end. Still, he could not know that she had spoken up on his behalf, Louise reflected, and so had no reason to dislike her. She was quite sorry now that she had started a slogan which had caught on in the office, by saying defiantly, "Mind you, some of my best friends are Scots!" whenever he became patriotic. It always puzzled him.

> *But perhaps it'd sound a bit silly*
> *To some, if I started to tell—*

"Listen to this, Louise," said MacAlister. "Pickled goatskins are on the Import List! How's that to make the imagination boggle? What can we be doing with them? And elk hair. It says here we import that. Also llama wool, smelling salts—who uses them nowadays?— and both rum and imitation rum. What on earth would we want with imitation rum, when we get the real thing from our own colonies, and if we don't buy enough from them, we have to pay subsidies?"

"I don't know, Mac. What do we do with it?"

> *—What I actually said before Willie,*
> *And Larry, and Dickie as well—*

"No, I'm asking you. All it says here is that we get it. From overseas. 'Brought into the United Kingdom under General License' —You'd never believe what's in the list. Dolls' eyelashes. Wouldn't you think we could make those ourselves!"

"Oh, I would." She altered two lines to improve the scansion.

"Sesame oil. Whatever's that? You know, I think I can make half a column, easy, out of this. Funny stuff. The thing about Government pamphlets is what they don't explain. What would you guess sesame oil was for?"

"Our politicians. They put a little dab behind each ear before talking with the Russians."

> For I shouted, "Hallo there!" to Dickie,
> And though I'm not easy to flatten,
> The silence grew more and more sticky—
> I got no reply from—

"Then we haven't been using much lately," chipped in the man on MacAlister's other side, the writer of a police court column. "Glad to hear we're importing some now."

"Blanc-mange powder! Now here's a weird thing. Seems we both import and export that. It's in both lists. Fancy our buying the muck to bring into the country, anyway."

"Fancy."

"And having got it in, fancy being lucky enough to find anyone to take it off us again. At a profit, I suppose, or we shouldn't do it, should we?"

"Probably not."

"What are you on?" he asked, finally becoming aware of lack of attention. He came and stood behind her, reading the jingle in the typewriter. " 'Pattern' is a terrible cockney rhyme for 'Mountbatten'!"

"I know, but there aren't many, and I've used 'flatten' later. Anyway, it's only nonsense," she said. "I'm waiting for a phone call."

"Is it about our unrespected feature editor?"

"Of course."

"Frankly, I'm not a lover of light verse, but I can see this has point. What are you going to do with it?"

"Nothing at all. Throw it away when I get the message I want."

"It would put the cat among the pigeons, wouldn't it?"

"If he saw it, you mean? Oh, yes, and far too cruelly. Much as I dislike him at times, I don't want to jolt him where it could hurt permanently. And this might."

"A lot he cares where he jolts other people!"

"Yes, but *I* don't want to do it to him. Apart from not wanting to say goodbye to my job."

A messenger came in with something for her. However, it was only the letter she had known she would get, today or tomorrow, from Cambridge.

"Thought I'd catch you sooner at the office. . . . Let you know . . . like a tonic to your uncle. . . . Such a comfort to me, too. Wonderfully reassuring . . . the very next week end you possibly can."

Dear, dear Aunt Rose, selectively blind, and sweet: she deserved to have a much nicer family, Louise thought, but might not have known so much loving satisfaction in trying to protect them from themselves if she had.

"How are you going to end this?" asked MacAlister, and watched while she typed,

> *But there's no one can prove it was hooey,*
> *And surely the thought that—*

Someone called, "Phone for you, Louise!" This time it was the awaited message: the Old Man would see her in a few minutes' time.

She pulled the sheet of paper out of the machine, crumpled it into a ball and tossed it on to the mass of spoiled paper bulging out of a basket.

"Wait a minute. How much more of it is there?" asked Mac-Alister.

She ran impatiently through the last verse for him—

> *"But there's no one can prove it was hooey,*
> *And surely the thought that will stick,*
> *Is that I can refer to Lord Louis*
> *(Except in his presence) as Dick."*

The ball of paper had bounced off the other rubbish and opened out a little. She picked it up, squeezed it tighter, and pushed it well down toward the bottom of the basket, burying it carefully before going away, anxiously rehearsing her request to the editor under her breath.

The next time she saw the sheet of paper it had been smoothed out and was lying on the feature editor's desk, with the last lines typed in, almost correctly. Whoever had put it there had not added her name, but everyone on the editorial side of the paper knew that Louise Downes had a knack of turning out this sort of thing, to amuse herself and others: it was signed in every line. "Are You Happy in Your Work?" saw to that.

She had believed that everyone in the reporters' room was her friend. From vicarious shame, she could never bring herself to speak of the incident to MacAlister, nor learned for certain who was responsible.

Once or twice, in everyone's life, it is of value as an experience— as a swift and bitter education—that the ground should shake under- foot, through some unexpected betrayal, great or small. But not too often.

For the moment, though, she did not know what was to be made of a trivial joke, and went resolutely up to the Old Man's office. The second battle for her newly chosen way could hardly be more unpleasant than the first.

4
The Voices

Few of her carefully planned arguments were needed in the editor's room.

He said, as soon as he heard what she wanted, "Well, you've been doing some sharp work recently. With occasional lapses. With occasional appalling lapses. Yes, I think you're about ready to hear Voices. I might try you out on this Norwegian assignment. I'm not sure yet."

"'Voices'?"

He swiveled round in his chair, kicking away some of the froth of the morning's papers lying discarded at his feet; his own early editions and those of his rivals. A large, hairy, frowning man, he looked like a suspicious Teddy bear.

"Angelic-journalistic Voices. Young woman, you are trying to humor me in my dotage. There's none of my staff, I fancy, who hasn't heard about my Voices."

"You aren't in your dotage, and I'm not really young. Getting toward thirty." She said this with satisfaction, as much to please herself as him. How long youth could seem—contrary to what everyone expected—to someone who was presumably not yet in the middle of life! Perhaps in ten years' time, or in twenty years', nothing would matter so much. "And anyway, you haven't told me yourself!"

"Very well. I shall be humored."

Certainly everyone on the paper, down to the printer's devils, knew about the Old Man's Voices, but personal regard as well as tact prompted anyone who had not heard about them from him to seek to be told direct. It was a measure of Louise's lack of personal ambition that she had not yet had the story from him.

Few successful editors, who have much in common with successful headmasters, are both liked and respected by those serving under them. This was the exception; in his own day as an active journalist, one of the magical figures which Fleet Street threw up in numbers in the 1920's—the men who, between the wars, made the news; who did not so much report it as live in the midst of modern history: crises happened where they were. Under the battered Teddy bear charm he was shrewd and unjust and ruthless; his crotchets and peculiar acts of vision were retailed with admiration by the men and women whom he overworked, goaded on to greater professional competence by a nice mixture of praise and pained surprise, and kept ludicrously short of cash on all small assignments. Toward any expense sheet which could legitimately go over a hundred pounds, he acted with careless generosity: it was unlikely to be questioned whatever the figure. (A hundred pounds was the largest sum of money he had been able to envisage in his own hard-up youth.) None of them, unless driven to it by financial stress and his exasperating meanness over unimportant things, ever wanted to work for anyone else. Even his meanness was unpredictable: he was rumored to be the original editor of the famous legend of Fleet Street, through which "Upstick" had become a local synonym for "Stop it" or "Shut up," so cleaned of its original offense by time that it could be used in any writing company. One of his correspondents, sent to

Geneva when this editor had recently taken over the paper, was said to have wired back a long dispatch in plain English, and been told to use cable-ese, to save telegraph bills. The luxury of letting its men file their stories in full had been the paper's speciality in former days. Another dispatch came into the office from Geneva, variously described as starting, "Before me, the placid blue of Lac Leman, its depths reflecting—" and, "From where I sit, with the evening sun gilding the tips of the Dent du Midi—" The rebuke ran "Unwant upwrite scenery use cableese or inturn assignment"; the reply came, "Upstick job arsewards." The correspondent was retained and, alone among the staff, allowed for the rest of his days to send his dispatches at any length in ordinary language.

In Louise's generation of journalists, no one had ever had the nerve to ask this deceptively cuddly-looking old bear how much of the myth was true: it may all have been. Everyone on his staff loyally maintained that it was.

"When you become a reasonably able journalist," he said, "—presuming, of course, that this happy change ever occurs to you—the transition will happen suddenly, from one day to the next. You will begin to hear Voices. They come, as to Joan of Arc, at unexpected moments. And must be obeyed." It was quite a long time since anyone but this man had spoken to Louise as though she had learned little more than the rudiments of her trade.

"For instance?" she asked.

"You do want to get to Norway, don't you! Well, I was a cub reporter listening to a Midlands mayor fairly covering himself and the Town Council with bouquets, in a speech about the whacking big sum raised by their unceasing labors, and so on, in order to buy up the slum property which had long been a disgrace to the dignity of their town. As soon as the slums had been cleared away, worthy buildings would arise on the site— You know the sort of thing. I was half asleep because the mayor had given round copies of his speech beforehand, and they'd let even the cub reporters share a good lunch. It was a whacking big sum too. The angel Voices woke me up, whispering, 'Find out who owns the slum property, to be bought with all that money. And don't be put off by the name not being the same as the mayor's. *Find out the relationship between them.*' The answer was, brothers-in-law. We stopped the deal. Little

country rag with no circulation, entirely written by the proprietor
and me! But we stopped the deal. That's what the Press can do. And
the Voices."

"Was that your first scoop?"

"Yes, and it's a long time ago. But it isn't seeing the scoop in
print that's pleasant—by that time the fun's over. It's the excitement
of hearing the Voices, and getting the salt taste again. I wish I could
get it nowadays. The taste that comes into the back of your throat,
or ought to, just before you go into battle against skulduggery in
high places. Best flavor in the world. You know, I'm not sure about
you and this job. You have your uses elsewhere—of a sort. I'm
going to get on the blower to the feature editor, and if he says he
wants you on that page, you can't go." He reached for the telephone. "What terms are you on with him at the moment?" There
was little he did not know about the temperaments of his staff.

"At the moment, not too bad," said Louise despondently. It
seemed a waste of the Old Man's time, for him to ask the feature
editor's view, after that placatory "Reconsider this, will you?"
Naturally the man would not want her to go: why had she over-
charmed herself back into favor with "les Eperons Chauds"! A
less winning remark, she thought ruefully, would have done far
better.

"That you, George? How d'you feel about sparing Downes for a
few days?"

The reply from the feature editor took much longer than the
simple question seemed to warrant. The Old Man's eyebrows shot
up toward the worn fluff on his forehead as he listened. He pushed
back the phone at last.

"You appear to have overestimated your popularity," he said
dryly. "The explanation is somewhat cloudy, but I gather it has
to do with his being for years a close friend of Sir Laurence Olivier,
who always calls him Bertie. How odd, when his name's George!
Perhaps Olivier mistakes him for someone else, and always has. In
any case, he says that if he never sees you again, that will be excellent,
and one or other of you has got to get out of this office. As I have
no intention of losing either, you will go to Norway. And mind you,"
he went on, holding up his hand as she started to thank him, "I
shall expect to hear, if not the full echo of the Voices in your stuff

as yet, at least something more pungent than the maunderings I recognized as yours in the paper last Saturday. Seven lines before you came to the nub. Insufficiently localized. No indication of age, class or community setting for the principal figure. Really, Louise, really! I was amazed. What do you imagine we can do with you, when you come back from Norway, if this tiresome feud is still on? Whatever it's about, and don't tell me. I've heard plenty."

"Well, you could send me out again on that story down there—it's what I'd really like to cover," she said, prodding with her toe the account she had read, on the way to the office, of a newspaper row in Zanzibar. Little space had been given to it: a colored journalist was said to have libeled the British Resident, and gone to jail. Her own paper had not carried the story, but by now the editor could have been expected to have skimmed through the London Press and a few of the big provincials; he had probably seen it in another paper. She was relieved by her easy victory, knew just what the rebuke was worth, and did not for a moment expect him to take her last remark seriously.

But, "That?" he said, peering down over his desk at the litter around it. "Nothing like important enough for us to send anyone out specially. Has no interest here, really, and could be covered from Nairobi if it had. Anyway, you're not sufficiently experienced. Off you go, see the foreign editor, get an imprest—don't imagine you can squander money on this trip, though!—pick up something frankly disgusting which George says you left on his desk, and remember the Voices. It should be apparent, I think, even to someone capable of writing as you did for the Saturday page, that hearing them is really a matter of subconscious attention. As an example, I am now going to say to you, at random, the word "Martinique." You are probably unaware of having heard it in the last six weeks. But you *will* be aware, in the next six weeks, that you are hearing it again and again. Because, and only because, you will be listening for it."

"Yes," said Louise gratefully, "I know how that happens," and dutifully kept her ears open for references to Martinique.

No one, in fact, mentioned Martinique to her for many months, nor did she come across the word in print. Instead, Zanzibar kept cropping up, unexpectedly.

5

The Flowers in the Desert

After all, the witch trial in the remote Norwegian village, and the Nobel prize-giving in Oslo, provided nothing like such a contrast in civilization as Louise and everyone else had expected. The suspect-witch was judged to be no such thing: the national jealousies and smiling recriminations among the prize-winners' wives, over the relative status of their husbands, proved slightly shocking to someone new to the reporting of international gatherings. On the whole, the participants in the witch trial showed the greater sense and dignity.

Louise enjoyed most of the trip thoroughly, accustomed herself to the local habit of eating three light breakfasts, nicely spaced out, and then meat and two vegetables at four in the afternoon, and,

although she heard no inspired Voices as yet, managed to send back
enough printable stories, with an edge of wit on them, to convince
the editor that he had made no mistake in giving her this assignment.
It was in the train from Oslo to Trondheim, on the way to the island
where the witch trial was to be held, that Zanzibar was mentioned
to her for the first time after her interview with him.

This train started every evening at seven o'clock, reached Trondheim the next morning shortly after eight, and had for years and
years started and arrived at these times, according to the attendant
who made up her sleeping berth. Each day, he added, speaking
sadly as though this were an unalterable act of God, the foreigners
who used this train almost as much as the Norwegians kicked up a
fuss—"Oh, my, the fuss they kick!"—because there was no restaurant car. And no food to be bought at the stations where the train
stopped during the night. "We Norwegians," he confided to her,
"are not much interested in making money."

"So I've noticed already. It struck me as one of the nicest things
about this delightful country."

"We often say, someone should go down with hard-boiled eggs
to sell on the platforms. They would in Italy; the Italians all say
so. Because of the poor foreigners who have embarked for thirteen
hours before they know about no food. But then, because we are
Norwegians, we think how much nicer it is to stay warm in our
houses, and not make the extra *kronen* from the eggs. Especially
now, in autumn, and again in winter."

"Especially then, of course. What's that extraordinary noise?"

"Oh, my," he said. "It is the entire Scala opera company from
Milan. Going to sing in Trondheim. That is what made me think of
Italians. They have discovered about the restaurant car."

Bel canto distress raged up and down the corridor. Being Italian,
the members of the troupe had not thought of eating an evening
meal before seven o'clock. "But this is uncivilized. It is intolerable.
How can they expect us to give a performance after what will be,
for us, thirty hours of starvation? Nothing since midday. Oh, what
if there is time for a meal in Trondheim before the show: you cannot treat a voice like this, starve it and then overfeed it, and ask it
to sing well." And later, over and over again at the stops along the
line, they repeated in full, tragic, carrying voices, to anyone who

would listen, "If this were Italy, or any reasonable place, there would at least be *gelati*, there would be something—but something!—to be bought through the windows when we stop."

"Oh, my, this is worse than mostly!" said the attendant, coming into Louise's compartment and closing the door. "Would you like some biscuits? I have a packet. I think, each time, I must bring more. But then I forget." They ate in amiable conspiracy, carefully clearing away the crumbs afterward. The other occupant of the two-berth couchette, one of the singers, was out in the corridor, swelling the chorus of complaint. When the attendant left, Louise opened the window before leaving the compartment herself, to air away the guilty smell of biscuit. All down the train, one touch of Latin excess was making kin of Nordic strangers. People sidled up to one another, muttering out of the corners of their mouths, "You English?"

"Nei, jeg er Norsk."

"Jolly good. I say, I've got some ham in my compartment—"

In half an hour, by an entirely spontaneous segregation, there were no English, Americans or Norwegians in the corridor, except a knot of Spanish-American businessmen, plaintively calling out to one another to know where everyone had got to. Near midnight, Louise found herself sitting on the bunk of a huge, golden-bearded owner of a smoked salmon, beside two other Norwegians with whom, as she had guessed, "Skål!" was the only word she really needed. They drank aquavit by turn from a tooth-glass: it gave her a headache but was, she accepted, a fitting initiation to the life of a roving correspondent. Outside, the hungry Italians prowled.

Creeping back to her own compartment when the party broke up eventually, she tried to breathe in continuously and not out at all, while climbing into the top bunk, watched with silent accusation by the woman below. Fumes of aquavit and salmon must have come drifting down; in a few minutes her companion said in bitter French, "Never have we been treated like this. And it is not only these Norwegians, who are from the Stone Age. No wonder you people are having trouble in all your colonies, my sister writes from Zanzibar! The things she says—!"

What happened in Zanzibar, that far-off tropical British protectorate, was of more concern to the rest of the world, then, than her editor chose to believe: Louise would have liked to hear more,

but further conversation was bound to be awkward. Pleasantly
ashamed, she pretended to have fallen sound asleep instantly, and in
the morning, to understand no French or Italian. It seemed, on the
whole, the kindest course for both of them.

"Kind"—"kinder"—"kindest." Such words figured very seldom, she
found, in the talk of the international journalists with whom she
came in contact later, in Oslo, when the awards were made for
outstanding contributions toward peace. These men and women
were the established figures of her new world, not the newspaper
giants of her editor's generation, but correspondents with names
widely enough known to allow them to afford generosity of spirit:
they were no longer fiercely climbing to success nor yet, in most
cases, clinging precariously to eminence. They were well informed,
perceptive, and within the limits set by their papers' editorial policies,
honest. Between themselves they were admirably free with money,
and to a lesser degree, with other help. But the strength of disin-
terested kindness, as a motive, was something they tended to over-
look. That ordinary people in the countries they visited—not politicians, perhaps, but private citizens—often acted as they did for no
more ingenious reason than kindness was an idea which could not
easily occur to the members of this polyglot crowd. There was always a more subtle explanation to be found for human behavior.

The Palace Hotel in Oslo; the Scribe in Paris; the Miramar in
Berlin: for the next two years she was to hear what was really the
same conversation, carried on by much the same voices, in various
languages which she gradually picked up by listening. She was good
at listening, and grew better. Interesting, swift and funny talk, it
was strikingly devoid of any understanding of kindness.

Yet the practiced hands at the game of seeing all, reporting half,
and feeling as little as possible (this was a Swedish correspondent's
description of their job) were pleasant to her from the first, sensing
with the acuteness which they could turn on to their own concerns
as well as on to the outside world, that this newcomer had arrived
among them to stay.

There were occasional exceptions. Of these the Swede, Einarsen,
was the most persistently irritating. He gave her the first detailed
account she heard of what had actually happened at the trial of a
journalist in Zanzibar, but it took a good deal of prising out of him,

while she fended off other topics, his favorites. All she had seen in print so far had been the short paragraph to which she had pointed on the editorial floor; and then she had picked it out because Zanzibar had a lovely sound, and was at least a thousand miles from the London office, and from Cambridge. But because the story touched on Press freedom, the men who wrote the newspapers were more closely concerned with it than their editors. Einarsen knew all about it.

"Dignity and reticence," he said. "That's what the British love. Justice comes a bad third. And dignity and reticence have won over public opinion from justice again—six months ago, now, and the wretched little man is still in prison, I believe. Dignity and reticence on the side of the British Resident; complete lack of both on the colored man's, so what could he hope for—up for throwing dirt at that dignity? It's a very small protectorate, you know: nobody cares much. You and the Sultan, your puppet, run it together. Just like the French in Morocco—till the Moroccans turned nasty. Oh, dear, the deplorable French, who aren't dignified or reserved either, are they? Serve them right to lose Morocco: such bad luck, isn't it, that they're your nearest neighbors at home? Instead of the Germans, who are really more congenial to nine out of ten of your people, in peacetime anyway, don't you agree?"

"Do stop trying to get a rise out of me, and tell me about this little man in Zanzibar. What his name is, to begin with, so I can think of him as a person."

"Falla bin Mahomet, always called—by himself—Falla Lufa. That's the name he writes his editorials under. He's an Arab. Or claims to be an Arab. Most colored people there do, if they can. Falla Lufa—Full o' Love: once the British can give a nickname like that, they don't have to bother any more. He's a clown. Clowns don't really suffer; they only bleed sawdust."

This seemed to Louise so uncomfortably near the truth that she said nothing. Einarsen had been trying to get to bed with her since their second meeting. He tried his luck with all personable women colleagues, and yet could never take a refusal as meaning no more than that the woman did not want to go to bed with him: it was always an insult to his manhood, his race, his opinions and everything he stood for. He could not speak to Louise, who had at last

convinced him that she meant no when she said no, without looking round constantly for some means to annoy her; and for the moment, till someone else attracted him, he could not keep away from
her.

"Isn't it a little surprising, even to you, that an Arab should get a
rough deal in a courthouse which no doubt had a Union Jack flying
over it? (But think what he was up against: if it hadn't been for
that—!) What has formed your country's policy abroad, over the last
fifty years, not only in little places like Zanzibar, but all through
the Middle East? Your Foreign Office, do you suppose? So largely
Catholic and homosexual—neither conducive to dignity and reticence?
Oh, dear, no. The unshakable British preference for Arabs as against
Jews. For Arabs are essentially dignified—all, that is, except Falla
Lufa, who is unfortunate in that way. While Jews are so awfully
voluble, they never know when to shut up, do they? Why do you, as
a race, go on liking the Turk? Even after World War One—even
after Gallipoli—'Johnny Turk, he's a gentleman'; that's what the
English have always said. In truth, he's a cruel type, and they don't
care for cruelty, do they, when they actually have to witness it? But
he is so dignified, the Turk! And why—this is what may really
count most in the history of the next fifty years!—why don't they
like Americans? And never will? Just because of those noisy and un-
restrained elements which didn't come over in the *Mayflower*.
Americans, except of British stock, are not dignified or reticent, do
you think? Sometimes not even then."

"For an intelligent man, you do have difficulty in sticking to the
point," she said. "Which was about an Arab pressman serving a jail
sentence in Zanzibar! On the international line you're talking dangerous rubbish, because it's mainly rubbish, with a very tiny grain of
truth in it, which is what makes it dangerous. Look, I must go back
to the hotel now. I've got a story to file." If she stayed with him, he
would go on picking at the sore she had made in his mind, oblivious
of the charming world around them, and in the end he would
succeed in making her oblivious too.

They were walking through that astonishing park in Oslo, full of
statues which appear to be the work of a mad sculptor with a
masterly knowledge of anatomy, bent on illustrating the theme of
what to do with a woman and child in the long winter evenings.

Around them, more than life-sized bronze males tossed female nudes aimlessly over their backs, while balancing an unconcerned baby in the crook of one knee. Sparkling autumn frost had made the air sweet and jeweled the cobwebs which the spiders had hung, occasionally with surprising effect, as though they were less broadminded than the Norwegian populace. The Oslo citizens had brought their children to play there, in droves, for education and relaxation in one. The towheaded children, with their summer tan still on them, were pleasant to look at, and so were the statues, in their fashion. She would come back, she thought, when she had got rid of him. But Einarsen was not easy to shake off. "Hell hath no fury like a woman scorned" was all too plainly written by a man, Louise decided: how few men, even of considerable analytical capacity, like this one, could avoid becoming grotesquely petty toward any woman who had wounded their vanity. This was one aspect of man which probably no other man fully realized.

"So you don't care for even one grain of truth about your own people?"

"I mind what you think, when you're wildly generalizing about them, as much as that child over there minds seeing its mother bowled around like a hoop!"

"But I think you should listen to this, before filing your wholly imaginary story!"

"I'll listen if it's about Zanzibar." She must remember to tell her editor, when the opportunity arose, of the way his prophecy had worked sideways. "I want to know what actually happened there to get the man into jail."

"All right. There's a small, pompous paper, written in the vernacular. One of several in the place, I understand. The editor's also the printer, and writes nearly all of it himself—that sort of little publication. You'd say, wouldn't you, no sensible government could bother to take it seriously? But in an editorial, Falla Lufa became carried away by his own vehemence. A good white friend of his, called Storr, had got sacked from the police—we carried the story quite fully in my paper: it suited our anti-imperialist policy!—and a drunken enemy of his, called Hilbery, had been promoted into Storr's job. (We had to be very discreet, suggesting the bottle!) Falla Lufa is never discreet: that's why he is where he is, while cautious

men go free. He worked himself up to a—a frothy peroration—"
Einarsen's command of foreign languages was fantastic, like his
memory: it was sad that in personal matters he rarely used either
of them with any advantage to himself. " 'I accuse!' came into
every sentence. 'I accuse the Police Authorities of partiality—Because a white officer has chosen to be the friend of the colored—has
committed the grave fault of associating with those who would be
called "niggers" by his successor—he must go! I accuse the Resident
of knowingly permitting this persecution, and the power behind the
Resident I accuse—' It didn't mean a thing, of course. But 'Bringing
the Person of the Resident into Ridicule and Contempt'—that's the
wording of your Colonial law, do you recognize it? And 'the power
behind the Resident'—why, that can only refer to the Throne. Trial
for sedition, and they have Falla Lufa where they want him, put
away for being a nuisance. Now he is finding out if the police
authorities running the prison, drunk or sober, are, or are not, partial
to 'niggers'!—Poor chap."

"But that's a dreadful story. Dreadful!" said Louise, really moved.

"Well, they are your people, not mine. The Resident, as I said, is
no doubt dignified and reticent. He doesn't throw silly accusations
about like Falla Lufa. He just waits till the law is on his side, and
then hits hard. What are you going to do about it?"

"I?" she said. "I don't know."

He looked at her and laughed. "You're very English, aren't you?
Why don't you say, 'Nothing'? Because that's what you are going to
do. You wouldn't really like Falla Lufa from near to. The colored,
they're like us. Like the Jews. Not dignified or reticent enough."

"I do wish that once—just once!" said Louise, exasperated, and
more exasperated because she was giving in to his desire to see her
so—"you would accept the fact that a woman can dislike you as a
man, not as a Jew. So far as I'm concerned you don't represent a
breed or a principle, or anything except one fellow human being I
don't happen to want to get any closer to than we are at present.
After all, the world is fairly stuffed with men, Jews and non-Jews,
with whom I don't want to go to bed. Admittedly, they haven't
shown any sign of wanting me to, the vast, vast majority of them,
but I still shouldn't if they did. Now can you take it that, to me,
you're one of that vast, vast, raceless majority?"

To her distress, he crumpled. "I know," he said without rancor, "we're always making the same mistake. It's so hard for us, as Jews, to accept that sometimes people just dislike us as human beings."

She hesitated, realizing that at this moment she could make a valuable friend of him, but a weariness inside her urged withdrawal. She insisted that it had not been merely an excuse, her reference to a story waiting to be filed, although in fact this was a lie on top of a lie, told to save embarrassment. She went away, and thereafter avoided Einarsen as much as she could, but the thought of Falla Lufa—he had become much more real, having a name—worked on in her mind.

He and Zanzibar next cropped up in conversation in North Africa, several months later, at a moment when she particularly did not want to hear about anyone's troubles. The desert was in flower, between Derna and Benghazi, in the breath-taking transformation of arid sand into crowding blossom which followed the short spring rain.

The flowering of the desert could never be predicted: it had come that year early in February. Whenever it came, it lasted only three or four days. No one had warned her that this spectacle, on which she came by chance, is always one of the most heart-lifting and—in its transience—one of the most heartbreaking experiences of beauty in all the world.

For Louise, the excitement of it came as a reward for six weeks of arduous work in grim surroundings. As soon as she returned from Norway, she had been sent out to an assignment in Germany, and then another in France, because the feature editor remained adamant that he would not have her back on his page, and the editor in chief equally resolved to keep her on the paper. Her factual dispatches were accurate, and she had developed what was almost a habit of turning off a sudden, happy phrase which made them more memorable than her competitors'. Rare indeed was the correspondent who could make the readers not only think but laugh, at times. From the south of France, not because her style was suitable but because she was handy, she was sent on to cover the unveiling of an Allied war memorial in Tobruk, without returning to London between jobs: the foreign editor who arranged this was pandering to his chief's incurable desire to save something under seventy pounds in plane fare. This economy cost the paper, in the end, the sort of money about which he did not think twice; but it also paid handsomely, in prestige. Waiting about in Cyrenaica, with several empty days in hand, Louise fell in with the American Air Force, which was to be represented at the dedication: the detachment sent for the job had also arrived too soon: she became friendly with one particular aircraft crew and persuaded them to give her a lift into Homs. Widespread riots had broken out, centered on the town, and civilian entry was barred officially.

As the only foreign journalist who got in before the barrier became efficient, Louise had done excellently for her paper, smuggling out, though she was trapped in the town herself, reports which were incidentally extremely amusing about the behavior of prominent citizens under stress. (Throughout their association, she and her editor shared the same view of civic dignitaries—that with few exceptions they were a self-selected subspecies of humanity.)

Agency messages covered the dedication in her absence, and were more than adequately written up in the office by MacAlister, with emotional phrases which she could not have used: she read them with discomfort in the files, many weeks later. The lost young men commemorated by the much saluted and consecrated pillar would have laughed wryly, she knew, at the speeches of the old men, beribboned and garrulous, their survivors, talking into microphones for all the world to hear, about the ungrudging sacrifice of the dead. They had been young, the dead, and afraid while they lived for all that they had to lose— So much to lose, she remembered. Of course they had grudged dying. She was glad to have missed the ceremony, even though the alternative was more actively unpleasant. She had been, at the time, among the shouts of a hostile native crowd, within range of flying stones and undiscriminating police baton charges. Her reputation as a traveling correspondent was more or less settled by her reports from the main trouble areas in Tripoli, into which she made her unauthorized way, one after the other: physically, this was not difficult to do, once she was past the check points; all it took was persistence and nerve. Pledging her paper's credit freely when cash ran out, she bought decrepit vehicles, one after the other, to get her stuff through despite the taking over, by the military, of all ordinary lines of communication; and later abandoned them wherever they happened to be when petrol failed. Transport was at a premium, the prices were lunatic; that would be all right, she knew. Here was an expense account after the editor's own heart, including at one place a donkey, which might have been fed on platinum. In fact the donkey seemed older and more decrepit than the cars, and Louise made certain that it was mercifully destroyed when she had finished with it. To be quite sure of this she had to stand and watch: she had no intention of letting it fall back into Italian-Arab hands, after the things that her sickened eyes had seen in the streets.

And on her way back, eastward along the coast, the desert bloomed for her unexpectedly, first with a thin scum of green left on the sand when the rain ceased, and presently, as the sun burned down again, with small, gay flowers unfolding while she watched. Within hours, the matted surface of blossom stretched on all sides to the horizon, broken only by the track over which she was driving, and on its edges too the flowers trespassed, filling every rut and gully formed by the rain, almost hiding it as they had already hidden the desert.

Along this fantastic road she was driven by a bristling-mustached British major in an Army jeep, talking endlessly of his domestic worries.

"Not as if I'd ever pretended to be a brainy type," he said plaintively. "My wife knew that when she married me. But I never minded her going in for things like literary competitions—whole thing seems so unfair, somehow. Think I shall probably emigrate to the Colonies when I'm through with the Service out here. Place I've always had a fancy for is Dar-es-Salaam. Know why—know what the name means?"

"No. Do tell me," said Louise reluctantly. He was so friendly and unhappy. He had given up three days' leave to drive her back to Tobruk, where mail and clean clothes awaited her, plainly in order to pour out into a stranger's ears the things that he could not tell anyone with whom he was in daily contact. All traveling journalists become accustomed, but not always hardened, to being used as confessionals: for this purpose they have the great recommendation of being almost as transient as the desert flowers.

"Means 'Peacehaven'!" he said. " 'Dar—es—Salaam. Haven—of—peace.' I was brought up at Peacehaven. The English one. Know it?"

"Good heavens. Yes," she said, as noncommittally as possible.

"Nice place. No slums."

"You mean, Dar-es-Salaam has no slums?" she asked, recalling the sprawling bungalow town outside Brighton.

"Oh, they're frightful," he said, lurching the jeep so that she had to clutch for support. "Sorry, it's this peculiar road. Can't see where it begins or ends. But of course the Europeans don't live in that part. I was in Dar before the war. Not too bad then, life in the Colonies and such. Even now they're about the last places where a man can remain more or less a gentleman on £500 a year. I might make it Zanzibar this time—I've got a brother in the copra business—but I don't much care for the way things are being handled out there now, from what I've heard." He gave her a résumé of the arguments in favor of a firm hand with the natives, which she had listened to several times; in Italian, in Homs; and before that in French, on the Riviera. It was surprising how little the phrases differed in any language, down to the literal translation of the words, "Really happier that way."

Alongside the jeep's wheels the flowers were almost visibly striving and jostling one another for space in which to live their few hours, in a lovely ferocity of growth. A deep red clover-like bloom, massing in clumps which attracted all the bees in the vicinity, strained upward to overtop myriads of blue, yellow and speckled trumpet flowers, desperately depriving them of the service of the matchmakers, the pollen carriers, for this flower withered the soonest. Already, on the third day after the light rain, a few patches by the track were paling into ripeness, and deserted by the bees. And there the trumpet buds rose in triumph, pushing through the seeding clover, to burst open at the touch of the sun in a peal of wild, fresh color. In four days these desert flowers would all have completed their life cycle of springing up, blossoming, seeding and dying. If only she could shut out the major's voice! She would have given much to have been allowed to live, for a little while, only with her eyes. By instinct, the bees knew how short their harvest must be, and worked furiously, but where had they sprung from, in this parched land, to meet the sudden flowering, that every clover tuft still in blossom was being rifled?

"Newspaper fellow called Full o' Love or something got chucked into prison in Zanzibar, and now he's out and stirring up trouble. In the old days he'd have been shoved back again, pronto."

"Then I think they must have let him go before his sentence actually ran out! Good."

"Oh, you know something about that? Don't see anything good about it. You people who write for the papers are always making trouble," he said morosely, and swung back to his own concerns. "If it hadn't been for one damned brainy publication—" and out came the story he had brought her all the way to hear. It was no less pathetic for being utterly ridiculous. His wife had won an Honorable Mention in a competition in one of the intellectual weeklies. Louise took the *New Statesman* and the *Spectator* when she was in London, and vaguely remembered a jolly contest for the best Verbal Boomerangs—damning sentences of self-praise like, "I know no one's indispensable, but the fact remains, I was away when it happened," "Isn't it silly, my daughter and I are always being taken for sisters?" and "I'm bringing up my boys to be useful in the house, then they won't miss me *quite* so much when I'm gone."

"First I knew about it," he said, "some people came in to bridge and congratulated her, and she said, 'Yes, I know.' Didn't think till some time later it was funny she hadn't told me. They had quite a bit of fun about it; I felt rather out of things. Asked her what her entry was, but she couldn't remember. D'you know, it was several days before I realized there was something fishy there, and then it came to me all of a sudden. Very queer that she could remember all the other prize-winners, and not what she'd sent in. After a bit I went along to the office of the periodical or whatever you call it, and looked up the back numbers. Felt as if I was spying, you know, but I'd got to see. And there was her name, and 'They thought the world of me in the R.A.F.' Perfectly certain I never said anything of the kind."

"But you were in the Air Force?" asked Louise, aching for his deep and stupid hurt.

"During the war. Transferred to the Army when they wouldn't

let me fly any more. Sight of one eye not so good after a crash."

"But I'm sure they did think the world of you in the R.A.F."

He went crimson. "That's not the point. It simply isn't the sort of thing one could ever have said. Not to anyone," he insisted stiffly. "That's what's so unfair," and any comfort Louise tried to give him was offered in vain.

"Have you tackled your wife about it? Does she know what you feel?" Poor, gallant little man. The desert glowed and its strange plants rushed through their rage of living scarcely noticed.

"No, and I'm not going to say anything, either. I certainly shan't write about it. She always says my letters are like telegrams. You can't explain all that in a telegram— Well, I suppose you newspaper people spread yourself that way, but I can't. She's gone back to her people while I'm out here. Probably I'll just write and say I've decided to go to Dar; what about it? And she certainly won't want to join me out there. Funny thing, you know, all your shoes mildew in the northeast monsoon weather. Suppose you spill something on your clothes here, and send them to the cleaners, so there isn't a stain left: not a thing to be seen: and then take them out to Dar. Next November (that's when the monsoon starts) there it'll be, neatly outlined in mold. The old stain. Not the sort of thing that'd appeal to her. And not enough brainy people around, either. So I expect that'll be that. Don't know why I'm telling you all this. Feel I've made rather a fool of myself."

"No, you haven't. Indeed, you haven't. But even if you had, you won't be seeing me after tomorrow, in Tobruk, so it wouldn't matter, would it? Do think of that if it's any satisfaction. What I feel is this, though I see how wounding the whole incident must have been, isn't it in some ways too small a thing to be allowed to mess up two lives?"

"Oh, I don't know," he said, with the sudden insight of very simple people, "I expect marriages have often gone to pieces over smaller things than that."

"Yes, I suppose they have," she said, and realized that all she could do for him was to let him talk, round and round the subject, and tell her about it, in one way and another, over and over again. Perhaps the kindest thing one could ever do for most people was just to listen to them, really to listen, so that they felt less alone. She shifted deliberately in her seat, turning toward him, asking more questions, ignoring the desert flowers.

The colors had faded from the ground long before the jeep reached Tobruk, while they were still not far from Derna. Under a blasting wind the seeds dropped back into the sand, burned dry once more by the sun and ready to hold them dormant in its heat for another year. And all the bees disappeared, within an hour or two, as mysteriously as they came.

What remained in Louise's mind from the coastwise journey was an absurdly touching human story, the discomfort of three insect-ridden nights in Arab hotels (but at least they had been quieter than in the riot centers) and a glimpse of splendor, of a miracle which she had not fully seen. That, and the chance-gleaned knowledge that Falla Lufa was out of prison and making trouble again—good luck to him.

At Tobruk a mixed reception awaited Louise in what had once been the Italian officers' club, and was temporarily a Press head-quarters. News of unrest had brought the vultures flying in, but they had been forced to pick up what they could from a distance. Einarsen was among them. Because she had slipped through the controls ahead of the rest, Louise was subjected to the sort of good-natured attack from her colleagues which was the real badge of success in this company.

She brought Major Deane into the club with her, in order to give her sad little escort a drink and a meal, as the least she could do in return for his kindness, before he started back to Derna to spend the rest of his pointless leave alone. He went away to the men's room to wash, and Einarsen cornered her. "How many U.S. flyers did you have to sleep with, to get that oh-so-useful lift?" He corrected himself; one of his self-lacerating moods was working up. "Or how many did you sleep with anyway? Maybe you like them? So often tall, blond and Nordic, like yourself. How many, eh?"

"Plenty," she said, tired from the journey and off guard. "You should remember, I sleep for choice with everyone except Swedes, people with aunts in Leicestershire, and left-handed men from Bagh-dad. Anything for the job." This was unwise, in a community where everything was repeated, and subtly altered by translation. For many months to come evidence kept cropping up that word had flown

round among her colleagues of what she had said; or at least part of
what she had said. She had lightheartedly admitted, in a semiprivate
conversation (there being no really private talks between journalists at work) to sleeping with almost anyone who could help her
professionally. Oddly, this improved her relations with the other
women journalists, who were on the whole inclined to be chaste.
Thereafter, whenever she succeeded where they failed in getting
difficult interviews, concessions or news, they referred to the reason
and felt superior instead of resentful. But the men considered it
unethical. They were used to women competitors taking unfair ad-
vantages when they could, but not to their talking about it as
blatantly as Louise was reported to have done. Between them, she
was credited with a ruthless ambition which was as far as possible
from her real nature. Still, to be thought efficient at any price was
not unhelpful in the work she did: no one, even of the few who
had not welcomed her to start with, tried any longer to stand in her
way. She had come too quickly along the road to eminence.

Spruced up, with his mustache bristling jauntily but his spaniel-
eyes as mournful as ever, Major Deane came back to the bar, and
Louise introduced him, unavoidably, to those of her colleagues who
were standing nearest, Einarsen and the representative of a left-wing
English paper. What actual remark of his started a fierce argument
she did not know; badinage from all sides was claiming her attention.
Almost certainly it had to do with the riots, which had started not
far from where he was stationed with AMGOT: the origins were
complex, but one factor had certainly been the rumor that the Italians were to be allowed back as rulers. He could be expected in such
circumstances to say something complacent about British colonial
rule in the old days. The two correspondents turned on him aggressively. Exploitation. Oppression disguised as nursemaid protection. The angry men whose trade was words ran rings round any
arguments he could muster. Quite soon they had Deane looking like
a particularly foolish little bull tormented by skillful picadors. Distressed that her guest should be humiliated like this, Louise tried to
stop or divert the unequal argument. Major Deane was slow and
flustered; the other men, sharper witted as well as more widely read,
showed no pity. Louise herself knew too little about colonial questions at that time to be effective. Vehemence turned personal. The

major fell back on talk of expediency, which played into their hands. Hypocrisy! Louise could not imagine how two such verbally competent men, thoroughly irritated though they might be, could go on pressing their advantage over someone so obviously unaccustomed to treating his thoughts as weapons. The spectacle of the unequal contest was highly embarrassing. Eventually a long-distance telephone call—the summons no correspondent can resist, for it might be his editor—took the Englishman out of the bar, and Louise finally succeeded in shutting up the seething Einarsen, and getting Major Deane away to a table for two, where they were still within earshot of the others, but not actually alongside them.

Still uncomfortable about the scene, she accompanied Deane out to his jeep afterward, to apologize to him beyond the hearing of her colleagues and supposed friends.

"Fancy that small argy-bargy before dinner gave our critics something to think about, don't you?" he said, with honest satisfaction, before she could begin. He got into his vehicle, started the engine, let it roar and then quiet down again, to allow him to say, "Yes, I 'hae me doots' if those two fine fellows will be quite so keen, next time, to throw mud our way! Glad I had a chance to talk to them. I enjoy a bit of a set-to like that. No quarter given either side. Well, it was nice meeting you, too." He drove away leaving her staring after him with thankful amazement, unwilling to return to the company and the bright, quick, merciless conversation of her colleagues.

It was a reluctance which grew with time.

6

The Circus

"My *toe* hurts, Betty. My *toe* hurts, Betty. My—"

In the trees along the Walcheren canal the pigeons cooed, for Dutch pigeons, with really remarkable English accents. They might have been in Cambridge.

Louise laughed at herself for noticing this; and thought how insular she had remained, after two years of covering foreign assignments. A few minutes ago, drinking with other correspondents in the main square of Middelburg, she had caught herself feeling slightly supercilious toward a woman who chattered to her dog in Dutch, as though the creature could be expected to understand. But perhaps all travelers felt the same about animals and birds in countries other than their own? She must find out from someone who would know whether French people, on holiday in Britain, were surprised by the Gallic mooing of local cows. When the journalists inevitably met for more drinks in the same square later in the evening, it would be something to talk about apart from the frustration of their present job. Meanwhile it would be pleasant to put a little extra distance between herself and those colleagues.

She had a letter from Aunt Rose in her handbag, and an hour in hand before she need see again, at the official evening briefing, the faces opposite which she had sat over drinks not only, by now, in Oslo, Berlin, Paris, Cannes and Tobruk, but also in Trieste, Madrid, Geneva, Athens and other cities—for so many days, indeed, if all the hours were added together, that as a foreground their features tended to make the background of any new foreign town strongly resemble the one in which the owners of the faces had last fore-gathered.

She walked on briskly beside the canal, toward Veere, consciously enjoying the Dutchness of the flat landscape, and the way the Groot Kirk in the distance floated in the vast, pale yellow autumn sky. It was nice being alone. Einarsen was busily chasing someone else, and had been for some time; Louise was not even his last exaspera-tion but one: this was a blessed relief.

She had come to Holland to report—or to try, like the others, to find something to report about—a conference of foreign ministers' deputies. These were striving to agree on an agenda which their principals might discuss, elsewhere, in due course. Every evening, the representative of whichever conferring nation had the turn of duty that day would call the Press together, and convey failure in optimistic terms of "useful exploratory discussions . . . some further advances in understanding." The agenda progressed slowly back-ward: they would definitely not be discussing, now, the stockpiling of atomic armaments, nor the Middle East, nor several other im-portant topics round which the conference had originally been planned.

Meanwhile there was the letter from Cambridge still unread and burning a hole in her compassion. Half a mile or so from the town she slowed up to a stroll and opened it. "Such a long time, dear . . . Your uncle quite well, but so much looking forward to seeing something of you soon . . . and I, too . . . a bit worried . . .

Dorothy. Although she seems more settled in her ways" (Aunt Rose
had always been adept at making vague statements which could be
given various meanings) "she has now taken up work on one of
those magazines which seem to need a lot of money to keep going.
We don't altogether care for the people who run it. So plausible."
("Plausible," to both Arthur Farrant and his wife, as to many people,
meant "implausible." Dorothy's co-workers must be exceptionally
implausible, Louise supposed, for that couple to have seen through
them.) "We should so value your advice—"

Bicycle bells jangling behind her made Louise jump smartly for
the grass verge between the canal and the path. She had been long
enough in Holland, by this time, to respect the lethal rights of
Dutch workers pedaling homeward at the end of the day, or indeed
of any Dutch cyclist at any time. These people, she supposed, must
almost have been born on wheels. Close by her, among a large,
chattering group, swept a man with one small child perched on
his handlebars and another, slightly older, behind him on the carrier,
facing backward and holding a miniature spare bicycle, on which
both children had probably ridden to school. Over his shoulder was
balanced a plank. Two other men had a ladder between them, and
one of them also had a child clinging to his waist and sitting sideways on the crossbar. Women were cheerfully burdened too, with
their families or enormous string shopping bags, or a combination
of the two. The riders wove in and out at relentless speed. A charge
of Walcheren cyclists, loudly exchanging gossip, and apparently not
looking where they were going, was a happy but awe-inspiring
sight. A man near the front of the group swerved round, risking
grave probability of injury, in Louise's view, and threaded his way
back, stopping beside her unhurt.

"So you have come back to Holland! Now what are you running
away from this time?"

"What—"

"I am Karel van Epp," he said, at her startled expression.

"I know. I recognized you. It wasn't that, but what you said—"

"And you never let me know you were coming." He spoke re-
proachfully, smiling at her. "See the enormous coincidence that we
have met again!"

"It isn't, really." She was talking to gain time, and get command of herself again. Of course, that remark of his had been only a chance shot in the dark, a pleasantry to someone who was almost a stranger. "If you do my sort of job, it's more surprising when you don't meet someone you know, wherever you go. In fact it rarely happens to me nowadays. A much less probable thing is that I was reading a letter from my relations in Cambridge just before you came by."

"Ah, the uncle—he is being as modest as ever?"

An astonishing young man, she thought. He had taken in more than she had imagined of the atmosphere of the Master's house. "As outstandingly modest as ever!" she agreed.

He laughed, less at what she had said than with sheer pleasure at seeing her again. "Well, then, for me it is a big coincidence to meet you, but for you it is not even a little one to meet me! I am sure this is true, but not how it can be."

"You're a scientist," she said, smiling back. "You ought to be able to reconcile it with the laws of probability."

"I will manage even this if you will come to the circus with me tonight!"

"The circus?"

"We have a little traveling one passing through Middelburg. Part of what we call *kermis*. Fireworks, acrobats. No big performing animals, no dogs acting like human beings. I am sure you cannot like animals made to do human things, which they do badly, because it is undignified for them, and so for us, watching them."

"You're quite right, I don't like them."

"Then you see we are exactly the people to go to this special little circus together, because I don't, either."

"But I can't," she said. "I wish I could. I'm not on holiday. I'm over here to work—supposed to be working, anyway. There's a Press conference this evening."

"Perhaps no one will say anything interesting at it."

"That's more than likely, but I'm still expected to be there."

"Oh, not tonight! I have two tickets for the circus, and now the friend who was coming with me is ill. When I saw you I was cycling to Veere, to see if my sister there would like to come instead. But I am sure she will be enmeshed with her family."

" 'Enmeshed,' " Louise repeated irrelevantly. "Hasn't your English improved!" Standing there in an open-necked shirt and worn Austrian *Lederhosen,* in place of the sober dark suit he had been wearing when she had met him, he seemed so young and cheerful that he made her feel suddenly irresponsible too. The pigeons were cooing again, loudly, from the trees on the other side of the water, where they had been frightened by a second knot of reckless cyclists, riding three abreast with linked arms, singing.

"That comes from living in the Zanzibar Protectorate. Where we are very, very British indeed. When we are not Arab or Indian or African, of course. And sometimes even then— Oh, yes! I now know that I said something terrible to you at that lunch! When my English was—well, you remember how it was."

"You couldn't have been more helpful," Louise assured him. "As things turned out, you made a difficult family situation quite a lot easier by that remark."

"Good. You must explain this to me sometime. But now, in gratitude, you will come to the circus?"

She had a mental picture of her colleagues as she had recently left them, and as they would be again tonight, killing time in the square. Though Einarsen was looking elsewhere, he chose by instinct women who could be relied on to reject him, and remained prickly as ever in defeat. Having achieved in the morning a rather public snub from the current object of pursuit, a French agency reporter, he would be ready by nightfall to take vicarious revenge. Louise would not be the butt; ever since the baiting of Major Deane at Tobruk, however, she had loathed having to witness even the mildest degree of this childish indecency. Opportunity for baiting would inevitably be provided by a popular male, or semi-male, writer for the women's periodicals, who had unaccountably been brought out from London as a stunt, by a Continental broadcasting company, to write personal gossip about this abortive conference. His highly colored daily bulletins sent shivers through the regular newspaper men and women, who could not resist listening to them out of morbid curiosity to know how luscious he could get. This intruder was capable of describing anyone he believed to be reasonably honorable—even a foreign minister's deputy—as "steel-true and blade-straight"; he earned far more money than the accredited correspondents, and would be roasted during the evening by Einarsen, who had managed to get hold of the script of his last talk, containing references to "the saber cuts of Saxon speech."

And talking imperviously through everything said by everyone else would be the head of a German syndicate, who had the curious gift of the contra-Midas touch. Whatever he handled which had been gold hitherto turned rapidly to dross. He knew more about the intricate international situation of the moment than anyone else, but as soon as he started to speak of some aspect which concerned them all, none of the journalists could go on caring. This gift was unfortunately common, Louise had begun to find, among conscientious pressmen. The religious woman from a Polish paper, who believed Louise's spurious reputation for sexual go-gettery, would be drinking in the square too, wanting to share remorse and experience in a low but carrying voice.

"I should love to come to the circus!" Louise said. "I know this is unwise—it's generally considered the short route to being recalled —but I'll wire my paper there's nothing to report. And for once I'm not going to concoct anything. There's time for them to take the routine agency stuff."

"Fine. First, we eat. At once. Very nicely, because you are being so brave!"

"Oh, do we? What about your views on Dutch food?"

"So lucky, there is a little Javanese restaurant in the town. Not smart at all. Unless you mind, it won't matter that I look as if I am going to sing opera, at any minute, in these funny leather pants. Do you mind? I won't sing. But if I dressed up for you properly we should hardly have time to eat enough of this worthy Javanese food."

"No, I don't mind." It was absurd how rapidly her spirits were rising at the thought of not seeing any of her colleagues for several hours, perhaps not until the next day's conference. "No chocolate pudding, this time!"

"No, thank God, no chocolate pudding! Then from the restaurant," he said disarmingly, "I can send a boy along to the *kermis* to buy our tickets."

"But I thought—"

"Yes, I know. I just wanted you to come! For you, as a journalist," he went on, before she could say anything, "it is most important,

I think, to see the Dutch people at their most Dutch. That is, while watching fireworks. Do you know, we are the only people in the world who can look at a rocket going up, and then at a rocket coming down, without saying, 'Ooh—aah!'?"

"What do you say?"

"Nothing! We wait in pleased silence for the next. You'll see."

"Very good of you to go to such lengths for my education," she said, and they started walking back toward the town. "Tell me something I was puzzling about just before you turned up. Do Dutch pigeons seem to you to have English accents? Here, it seems to me, they're saying what I've always heard them say in Cambridge, and I think they were making me a bit homesick, which doesn't make sense, because I'm a person without roots."

A motor barge passed on the canal, towing two lighters festooned with washing, and the setting sun turned them into golden flags, the splendid, fluttering flags of a brief, stolen freedom.

He listened gravely while she explained that, to her, the Middelburg pigeons articulated clearly, "My toe hurts, Betty," but assured her that they spoke pure Dutch. "High Dutch. Not Walcheren-talk. Perhaps that's why you didn't recognize that what they actually say is, '*Ik zoek een kermis*'—'I want to go to the circus'—and then '*Ja!*' It's like the birds among the clove plantations on Pemba and Zanzibar."

"They talk Dutch, too?"

"Certainly they do. Just as well, or I would forget my own language. You should come and hear!"

"It's what I'd like to do. I want to go to Zanzibar for a particular reason. But there's no chance of it, I'm afraid."

"Oh, I shall hope there may be, only you don't know of it yet. Look, when we met, you said you couldn't tell when you might come to Holland again. And now you are here! Then, a few minutes ago, you said you couldn't come to the *kermis*, but see, you are coming. So one day, when I have come in on the boat from Pemba—that's Zanzibar's other island, where I live. 'El Huthera' it's called, too, which is 'The Green One,' and it is very green, and even more beautiful than Zanzibar—well, just before I land, I will notice on the quay a figure with honey-colored hair, and say to myself, 'Why, that is like Miss Downes' (Miss Downes? Mrs. Downes?)."

"Mrs. Downes."

"I thought, but was not sure, that you were married. I think of you only as 'Louise Downes' because that is what you said, and since then I have read what you have written, and seen your name like that, as a shape, not as a Miss or a Mrs. But that day, anyway, it will be you. Do you know one of the most exciting things possible? To see someone you are very, very pleased to see when they don't see you. That can be quite wonderful. What is this thing you want of Zanzibar?"

"There's a little editor-journalist fellow, called Falla Lufa, who seems to have had a raw deal. I'd like to look into it. See what can be done by an outsider, with nothing to lose or gain, to put things right. Tell the world about it, if necessary. But my editor doesn't see eye to eye about Falla Lufa's importance. As I heard, the authorities clamped down on him for writing and printing one highfalutin sentence he probably didn't mean, about the Resident and the power behind the Resident. Maybe you can tell me more about it? They put him in prison and then let him out again."

"And have now put him back again. Just before I came away."

"Oh, no! Have they? Why?"

"I can't tell you. I was in Pemba when he was sentenced this time. Pemba's twenty-five miles from Zanzibar, but sometimes you would think it was a thousand. I just knew there was such a man, and he was in bad with the authorities again. I was leaving on holiday—I didn't go into it."

"How queer this is! People in various parts of the world have mentioned him to me, feeling strongly about him. Thinking he's suffered shocking injustice. Or else that he's been too lightly handled, as a troublemaker. And now you, actually living in Zanzibar territory, don't feel much about it either way!"

"When you see something close to," he said, "it hardly ever looks the same shape as from far away. It is not a question of bigger or smaller, but quite a different shape."

For the rest of the walk, to the one-room restaurant tucked away in a back street, Karel talked as he wheeled the bicycle beside her of the two islands lying off the Tanganyika coast; of Fort Jesus at Mombasa, built and so named by the Portuguese two hundred years ago, and useful to the slavers in the worst days of the trade in "black ivory"; of the famous carved doors of Zanzibar, still studded with great brass nails traditionally put there to prevent elephants from butting them

open; and, with infectious pleasure, of his own work, research on the
diseases of the island's chief crops, focused for the time being on
combating a blight known as "die-back" among the clove trees.

Over the succulent dinner, with the gaiety between them dropping
away suddenly, she asked him, "Why did you say that, about my running away?"

"Because that's how you seemed to me when I met you. Sad.
Very sweet and kind. A little afraid. Running away from people.
From living. From everything except work. And now, this evening, I
have made you run away from work, too, for a bit—I wonder if I
ought to have done that?"

"I don't think you need worry, it won't be for long! 'Afraid,' you
said. Why, did you think? What was I afraid of?"

"Of being touched, I supposed. Though you were so far away already, no one could have reached you."

"But we didn't talk very much, for you to get that impression. We
couldn't."

"No, and if I had tried—if I had talked better English then, and
could at least have tried—you would have run away into being amusing, wouldn't you? Your way of escape, when anything comes too
near."

Startled again, she did not speak.

He said: "As I told you, I have read quite a lot of what you have
written, since we met. We get the English papers in Zanzibar, naturally. When I go there from Pemba, I stop for a meal at the Asian
Club or the English Club. It happens, they both have your paper. So
I have seen your name, and said, 'Now she has run away from Tripoli
to Greece! And now from Trieste to Spain! What a long way—but
only in miles, really.' You know those books we are given as children?
Where you go through a forest on a sleigh and the wolves are after
you? You must throw something to the wolves to delay them. Well, I
always saw you throwing jokes to the wolves. Very successfully. And
elegantly. Good, nice-mannered jokes. And of course I always wondered what would happen if one of the wolves had no proper sense of
humor, and didn't stop to let you run on."

"I still don't understand how you knew—realized something
about me I didn't know myself."

"Look, how does one know about people, more than they tell? I can't say, but it happens all the time. Not only in Cambridge! A man, any man who isn't a fool, can go into a room full of people, and see a woman who isn't looking his way, and know she's open to him. She had come there looking for someone, and he'll do, if he takes the trouble to make her notice him. But if the meeting happens—oh, perhaps three days later, and in that time she's found someone who pleases her well—why then, the signs aren't out, saying 'Come and fetch me,' and he can know that too, without talking to her about anything important. I could be sure you weren't available; certainly not to me, and I thought probably not to anyone. It seemed a waste. Because there are not so many people who are charming as well as intelligent."

"It worried me when you talked of my running away," she said slowly. "Because I see now that it's true! I've done it for years. More or less continuously. I think I half knew I was doing it, but only half. And that's because each time there's been a different and apparently excellent reason for whatever I did."

"That I would also have guessed."

"When we met in Cambridge I was running away, hard, from being involved in other people's lives. I was anxious not to be responsible for them in any way. But it looked like something more creditable—not wanting to hurt the person I was fond of in that household. And the same when I got myself out of the London office into a roving job—the motive looked nicer than it was. Being a foreign correspondent, which lets me run and run, getting away from everything with a good conscience before I can be made to take sides—well, most people would say it was a particularly interesting way of earning a living—"

"But you didn't choose it for that reason, I think?"

" 'Choose it'? I fought for it with everything I'd got, just because I suppose part of me knew it meant a perpetual warding off. A good journalist isn't personally biased—that's what we say. It's only by looking at the over-all pattern like this, I can see how much of my time I've spent running away!"

"Not always, surely?"

"I meant, in the last five years. Since the war. This evening, before you came along, a bit of my mind was thinking quite happily about pigeons, but the rest was getting ripe to repeat the pattern. I was growing sick of this job. Almost ready to drop it in favor of trying something else. I realize, now, the stage before another retreat for me is always dissatisfaction with something on the surface. Something I can admit not liking to myself. Like rootlessness. Lately I've grown so consciously tired of that. And traveling to places which ought to be wonderfully different from each other, but look awfully alike from the Press bar. Making literally thousands of acquaintances every year and no friends, because there isn't time." She glanced round the tiny restaurant, hazy with cigar smoke, where they were the only all-European couple. The superb food was served on one long, bare table by the proprietor, a vast, balding Dutchman, with his monkey-like Javanese wife cooking on three braziers in a recess—a woman so withered that she might have been any age. Helping them was the un-likely product of their flesh, a young girl and boy of delicate beauty and grace, who drifted about with plates and glasses like exquisite leaves moved by a highly benevolent wind. "Do you know, this must be the first time for months and months that I've eaten a meal with someone who has nothing to do with my gang or my work," she said wonderingly. "And in spite of my gloomy talk, I'm enjoying it very much."

"Oh, for the hollow in the stomach I would always recommend Javanese food," he said. "But for the hollow in the heart—the thing people run away from—I don't know!"

"Nor I, of course. Or I suppose I shouldn't be here."

Silently, the lovely Eurasian boy laid the circus tickets, fetched by some other, unseen member of the family, beside them on the table. Every slow, grave, trivial movement he or his sister made seemed part of some secret rite in the service of beauty.

"You'd still like to go?" van Epp asked, picking up the tickets. "You would not rather stay and talk?"

"No, of course I'd rather go," Louise answered almost brusquely, moved by one of those gusts of obscure anger which wise people care-fully examine, but she was too deeply disturbed to be self-critical. Why should he imagine that she might prefer to tell him more about herself, she who—unlike Dorothy, or the Polish woman journalist with religious fervor, or Major Deane among the desert flowers, or practically everyone, everywhere—was not given to making confi-dences? What business was it of his if, for a long time now, she had been spiritually running away—avoiding contacts and entanglements? At the same time, it was a shaking discovery.

"All right." He paid the bill. The Eurasian boy carried away the money as though it were in a chalice, not on a chipped plate.

"If that's the result of miscegenation, I'm for it, aren't you? Especially in this country!" Louise said, looking after him, with a vague inclination to annoy van Epp by recognizing the ungainliness of the Dutch. In Walcheren Island the plain girls tended to wear national costume, as the only way of attracting attention, and their bare arms bulging out of tight, short sleeves were usually of an unappealing tomato color. Even prettier girls, in ordinary European dress, were regrettably broad-based and heavy-boned.

"Especially in this country," van Epp agreed, unruffled. "It works well between us and the Javanese. Not so well with other mixtures, in other places. Out where I work, considering the number of Indians living among the Arabs, there isn't such thorough interbreeding as you might expect: those races don't much like each other. When the mixing has gone on for some time, the results are mostly very ugly. But a first-generation cross between a pure strain of Arab and a pure strain of Indian—well, that produced the most beautiful human being I have ever seen."

They went out into the darkness which had fallen while they ate. "You will have to share my bicycle as far as the fairground," he said. "It's on the other side of the town."

"Thank you, no; I've seen how you ride!"

"But you are in Holland. And there is no other way of getting you there in time. Now I am sorry I have no carrier, but you sit facing me on the handlebars—"

"Not me."

"You can put your hands on my shoulders and shut your eyes."

"There are trams in this town. And several taxis because I've already been in two. I'll walk anywhere you like, gladly. But I don't cycle."

"You don't need to cycle—"

"Or share a cycle with you or any of your wheel-happy countrymen!"

"If we wait for a taxi, you will miss the fireworks, and the trams go nowhere near. It is too far to walk—anyway, no one ever walks here."

"Too bad. In no circumstances—"

Laughing, he swooped and picked her up—Louise was tall but light—put her on the handlebars and rode off with her triumphantly. "You see, it is quite easy to balance this way. If I need to ring the bell, I will call '*Wagele!*' That means, 'Wriggle,' " he told her.

For the first minute or so, while they swerved into a side street, and then zigzagged at speed over what felt like cobbles, through a number of alleys, Louise kept her eyes shut and held on tightly. When she opened them cautiously they were darting down a lane of prim old houses with huge lanterns above the doors and mirrors sticking out from the walls, to let the inhabitants spy without being seen, and decide whether or not to answer a knock. Almost at once, this began to seem a very suitable way to observe a charming medieval Dutch town, which now looked totally unlike the view from any Press bar she remembered. To fit in with the step-gabled houses, squinnying down disapprovingly through their mirrors, she should have been riding pillion on a horse, she supposed, but at least this was an accepted local manner of traveling.

By the time they struck into the magnificent sixteenth century Grootplatz, Louise had gathered enough courage to let go of van Epp with one hand, and wave it affably at the other correspondents; the bicycle passed close to their table, slowing down to let the cross-traffic go by. Einarsen's face as he recognized her was a pleasure to see, and that of the Polish woman even more so. Facing backward, Louise could keep them all in sight long enough to try a formal bow from the waist, like an actor acknowledging applause, when they gesticulated at her enthusiastically. The skirt of her slim black suit was well up above her knees, and wisps of her long hair, generally worn sleek and coiled, were blown forward in a mane over her face. Her movement made the bell cluck faintly, and the machine wobble, as it shot forward again into the milling herd of other cyclists.

"I have not said, '*Wagele*'!" van Epp protested.

There, beside Einarsen, was the alien contributor to women's magazines, no doubt thankful to the sight of Louise for a brief pause in the remorseless questioning about "the saber cuts of Saxon speech." The "subbing of the purple" was always a painful business for a journalist, most painful of all when it came too late. On his other side the Polish woman looked entranced. For lack of Louise as a compan-

ion, she must have been listening, for what would certainly have
seemed like hours, to the German bore, seated next to her: he alone
was not staring after the bicycle; he was drawing a map on the table
with large, energetic gestures as he talked on. It had become nice
again, very nice indeed, Louise thought, to be going to the circus.

And it became nicer still when they arrived at the fairground.
There were stalls and fortune-telling booths and shooting galleries
outside the circus tent: Karel van Epp was proved right about the
fireworks, a Dutch crowd, full of children, could stolidly observe
golden stars streaking across the sky and exploding into a rain of green
and blue sparks, without showing any sign of appreciation. Rockets
hissed up and appeared to hang motionless for exultant seconds: several more elaborate ones gave birth to cascades of snakes. Set pieces
went off splendidly, but no murmur arose from the watchers until the
show was over. Then they exchanged opinions as they moved toward
the circus tent. "A better show than last year," van Epp translated to
her as the gist of them.

The circus was packed: they could not have got in without tickets
bought beforehand. The tumblers and trapeze acts were efficient, and
received mild applause. Toward the end came the special turn, for
which the earlier numbers were more or less a warming up of the
audience. Almost incredibly, someone had booked a troupe of English
trick cyclists for this itinerant show; or perhaps they became popular
whenever the circus moved out of Holland.

They came on with a fanfare, doing handstands on their saddles
and other stylish things, and were received in silence: a deader silence,
it seemed to Louise's sympathetic ears, than the reception accorded to
the rockets. They rode round the arena, skillfully taking their cycles
to pieces and putting them together again on the way, balancing on
one wheel, upside down and in a variety of positions, working the
pedals with their hands, and the audience looked on in kindly patience, waiting for them to do something interesting.

"This is awful!" Louise muttered, and tried clapping what appeared to her a more-than-human feat of mechanical *haute école*,
and all the nearby heads turned at once in her direction, trying to
make out why she had clapped. She stopped, feeling that she was only
making things worse for the unfortunate performers.

In vain they exerted themselves further, in defiance of gravity, probability and, it seemed, safety: the audience fidgeted slightly, feeling it high time the show started. And grew at last bewildered, getting an inkling that what was going on in the arena was meant to be entertainment. Doggedly, the gifted troupe ran through their repertoire. To Louise, aware of that odd national solidarity which grows so easily abroad, this turn seemed to be going on forever. Finally the cyclists piled themselves into a despondent pyramid of wheels and bodies and rode slowly out of sight, in the same wooden hush. Louise had neither the heart nor the effrontery to clap again, alone. There was a slight stir of surprise in the audience, before the Middelburghers settled down to wait hopefully for the next and last turn. This consisted of back-chat, in faulty Dutch, van Epp told her, between two mediocre French clowns, who were relatively well received.

"Well, now you know us even better than I hoped you would, through the fireworks!" her escort said, grinning, and took her out to get some beer.

"I certainly could do with a drink! I feel I need it almost as much as those wretched cyclists must. That was very funny, but how awful for them!" Now that the turn was over, Louise could laugh unreservedly. "I wouldn't have believed it if I hadn't seen it, and I wouldn't have missed seeing it for anything. Thank you!"

They found an unoccupied bench by the canal, and carried over to it bottles of lager from a stall in the *kermis*. The idea of bringing this troupe to Holland, and the faces of people wondering what Louise could be applauding, grew funnier and funnier to them, looking back on the circus.

"But pity—" he said, when they had turned serious again. "That's something which sorts out people. Into those who enjoy it and those who don't. You don't, I think, in the ordinary way."

"Pitying, or being pitied, do you mean?"

"Both. Deep down, you resent them, don't you?"

"Of course. Either way, human dignity is destroyed. Doesn't everyone resent having to pity, or being pitied, for any important reason? Not just 'What a pity Holland doesn't appreciate trick cyclists'?"

"Heavens, no. For many people, pity fills the hole in the heart nicely. Feeling sorry for other people—that is superior. Or having others feel sorry for them—that is—what shall I call it?—cozy!"

Beside her, he was no more than a darker blur in the darkness; a companionable voice, slightly hesitant, with which it was pleasant to discuss anything, drinking cool Dutch lager beside black water, with the jolly, strident music of a steam organ going on in the background. Afterward, it seemed to Louise that there had been no warning at all of the breaking of a dam in her mind. The conversation, easy and enjoyable, was one she might have held with any one of five or six of her closer acquaintances.

"You must have interviewed so many peculiar people in these last years," he said, "have you never met stranger satisfaction than that?"

"I suppose so—yes! There were two old ladies I was sent to talk to, the last time I was in England. They'd gone bankrupt, with great self-respect. Because, as they pointed out to me, they simply couldn't have lived on less food, with less shelter, so it wasn't their fault that they owed a lot of little debts to the local tradesmen. Except for one item of expenditure, which they didn't think at all remarkable, either. But it was why the editor wanted an interview. Every week, for over two and a half years—this came out in the bankruptcy court— they'd come to London from Lancashire to see Ivor Novello in *The Dancing Years*. Those names mayn't mean anything to you, but he was a romantic actor with a refined profile, appearing in a musical comedy he wrote which ran and ran. I saw it once and was very bored. To see it more than once would have seemed to me an excruciating bore. But to pay to see it, when money was terribly short, well over a hundred times—"

"They never went to anything else?"

"Never. I asked them. I gathered they would have considered that an extravagance, on their income. As well as a kind of infidelity. But he was a necessity. So they'd nothing to reproach themselves with. Oh, and another contented person I talked to with great interest was a man who wanted sewage, specially of human origin, put straight back on the land, instead of being wasted in the sea or neutralized by chemicals. Lucky man, he'd got a cause which he could rely on to remain lost, and knew it, so he could go on campaigning for it vigorously all his life. We're breaking an essential life cycle at our peril, he said, with our present methods of disposal—look how cancer's increasing. And polio. He seemed thoroughly pleased by the increase; it proved how right he was."

Van Epp said, "I would like to hear you interview someone who is

called 'the uncrowned queen of Zanzibar.' A Mrs. Corryman. She
will not speak to me, nowadays. Once I was talking of the difference
in education between our countries (you would think that was a
harmless subject, wouldn't you?) and I told her, in Holland we are
always taught St. Augustine was a colored man. Not an Arab or an
Indian—those are the races she approves, if they don't mix in the
wrong way, and go to bed with Europeans—but an African."

"I didn't know he was, but I'm delighted to hear it. I can think of
several people I must tell, when I get the chance. The most startling
person I've ever talked to, for the paper, was a cheerful little woman
whose husband had been awarded the George Cross after his death;
he'd been killed fighting against bandits in Malaya. Nice-seeming,
very ordinary housewife, in a nice-seeming, very ordinary suburban
home. She'd just arrived back in England with her two children when
I saw her. I found it an awkward interview, the sort I used to dislike.
One of the best things about being a roving correspondent abroad
is that one's never required to ask people such impertinent personal
questions as at home. But the odd thing is that there, people hardly
ever resent them. She didn't. We got all the proper things said. She
gave me a cup of tea. When I was going she added in a matter-of-fact
voice, 'Well, miss, thanks for coming. And I'm glad they got the
bastard.' I thought I couldn't have heard her say that, but I knew I
had. I suggested, 'Do you mean, they caught the man who killed your
husband?' though I'd heard the bus he was driving was ambushed,
and the attackers got away. She said, 'No, I mean Ted.' That was her
husband. No explanation. And then she shut the door behind me."

Before van Epp could comment, a flock of cyclists swept by, as
noisily as in the earlier evening. There was silence for a few seconds
between the two on the seat. When the cyclists had passed, Louise
heard her own voice saying, "I don't know why I should talk as if
she had no right to judge the dead. Who am I to judge her? I was
with another man at the moment my husband was killed. The night
of the raid on Saint-Nazaire. In bed with him, you understand. I
don't even know his name. I was drunk at the time."

Panic and horror took her. She had not said that. She could not
have said that. She had told no one. The dam had held too long to
break now.

The blur in the darkness did not move or speak, but waited.

Her voice said again, involuntarily it seemed, "I was drunk, you see. That's how it happened." She got up, striving for control, and in a moment said in her normal, cool, distant tone, "Will you take me back to the town, now? I don't know what made me say that. I don't want to give you the history of something that happened a long while ago, five years ago, and concerned only three people, anyway. One's dead, as you gather, and to the other man the whole incident didn't matter; we were both drunk. London in wartime. Please let me go now. It's been a most interesting evening, what with one thing and another—"

"No," he said. "If I let you run away again like this, I shall be one more thing you will avoid, if you can, for the rest of your life. If there is ever a chance of our meeting again, you will not let it happen. I don't want that. This is quite selfish. I am not one who thinks confession 'does good.' Not to people like you, who look at their reasons for doing things, as a rule. But I hope to see you again. So what you have said is either too much or too little. Sit down. You must tell me more now."

"No. Please—"

He caught her by the arm, not roughly but with weight behind the grip, and forced her back on to the bench. "Why did you get drunk?" he said curtly.

"To get away—" She stopped and could not go on.

He said, "It would not be like what I know of you. The little I know. You would always find it hard to let go, to lose control of yourself, I think. In drink, in love. For that reason, you could be a cold woman, but I don't think you are. Well, why did you?"

"To get away for a bit from being afraid. To try to get away. Because I couldn't bear it alone any more. Not fear at that pitch." It became easy to go on talking in the darkness once the dam had finally broken.

"Fear for your husband? You were in love with him—you still are, I believe?"

"Yes. His leaves were the worst times. Although of course I longed for them. Apart from everything else, I knew then that he was safe for twenty-four hours, anyway. Leave was always very short in the Light

Coastal Forces, but it came round quite often. At least, oftener than in the other services. We seemed to be always saying goodbye. There was never time to get in the least used to being apart. For me, that is. Saying goodbye and thinking, 'Perhaps this time—' We always knew, almost for certain, that he'd be out the night after he got back. Channel patrol. 'E. boat Alley.' Pitcher to the well. He sent me cards when he could, when he hadn't time to write more. Lots of couples arranged that, cards written beforehand about receiving a parcel or somebody's birthday; it was the posting that mattered. For me, terror had been mounting up before his last leave, and that one was the worst of all. There was so much pretending for both of us. He didn't tell me anything particular lay ahead, but we both knew that the other knew there was something that wasn't being told. What you said about people knowing things without words —people in love do that most of all. I realize, now, he must have had some idea about the Saint-Nazaire raid coming. Probably not exactly when or where, but some idea. I still don't understand how more women didn't go mad during the war, just from the waiting."

"I shan't pity you," said the voice in the darkness, "whatever you tell me. It's what a woman is for, isn't it, in war and at all such times —to wait till she's wanted, and then pretend? As much as necessary. To make things easier."

"Yes. Oh, yes. And my job helped a little, as a sort of distraction. I don't think I told you what I did in the early part of the war, before I became a journalist? Funny, in a way." Her voice lightened, getting away from the personal horror. "When I knew he was going to get short leave, pretty often, I found myself a job in a ministry, so as to be in London and free in the evenings, for him to come to me when he could. Not at all an important job, just censoring civilian letters going overseas. I was only supposed to look for place names, troop movements, mention of ships—that sort of thing—and cut them out. Actually, because I didn't care if I lost the job or not, I used to look for openings like, 'Now you know me, Son, never one to make trouble. But when I think of you in that tanker, and your Ethel and this Canadian carrying on here—' Mainly letters from mothers. And then I'd tear the whole thing up. I destroyed quite a number of inflammatory letters from mothers. In any future war, mothers should be prevented from the start, by Service regulation, from writing to sons who can't do anything about their home life except worry from a distance. Nowadays, whenever I'm in England for a little while, and see grim-faced women of the right age in trains or buses, I often wonder, Are you one of those I wronged technically?"

"What a habit it is of yours, this running away! You are trying to do that again, aren't you?"

"I suppose so."

"Well, why did it happen, this thing that is still an agony in your mind? Go on. About you, not the job."

"When he left, that time, I was fairly all right the first night. Fairly —I told you, things had been worse than usual. Then no card came, the day after. Then no card the next day. They must have been doing what they usually did before these big raids, holding the men who were going out of any communication with the shore, but of course the best security plans get defeated by people like us, with arrangements to post meaningless cards. 'Thanks for the cake' just said 'I'm all right': but if it didn't come, that said something too. I lost whatever courage I had—not much—the third evening. I got back to my room after work and still found nothing. I'd been telling myself all day, It'll be there. I went out so as not to be alone in the place where we'd been together, and met two people I knew, and drank with them in a pub till they wanted to go home, and then I stayed on and drank by myself, putting off going back to that room. I can just remember talking to someone I didn't know, and being glad I needn't drink by myself any more. And saying, 'Yes, you can come back with me. Why not?' It was something to do. A way of not thinking. That's how it happened, do you understand, that I was with someone else, at the moment he died?"

"Yes, I understand. And so would he."

"Of course. Anyone who was kind would understand, and he was kind. Very kind."

"Don't you see a man wouldn't even mind, particularly? Not in those circumstances, even if he could have known?"

"I know that. If he'd lived and I'd told him—I shouldn't have done that, naturally, because it's only selfishness to want to share that sort of thing—part of him would have been quite glad I found any way out of so much misery and terror that night. Just any way out."

"And this sort of thing happened all the time in war. Everywhere. You must know that, too."

"I know that," she said again, as though this had no bearing on what they had been saying. "There was an incident at Norwich, just afterward. Very soon afterward, that's why I remember it specially. Because as you say, this sort of thing happens all the time in war. A small hotel got a direct hit during an air raid. R.A.F. crew, some of them married, were there with women who weren't their wives. They were all killed. Next of kin were notified that the bodies of Flight Lieutenant and Mrs.—whatever the name was—had been found, because they'd registered like that, of course. So the wives heard. I hoped —there wasn't anything I could do, I didn't know any of them—I hoped so very much they realized that probably those women their men had gone with, that last night, really didn't matter to them at all. A way of escape from strain, when there'd got to be some relief. Women don't easily realize that, but I know it's true."

"But if you know that—you who can think—you cannot possibly believe you touched his chance of living or dying, that night, by what you did?"

"No, of course I don't believe that. What I did made no difference to him. Then or at any time. Only to me. 'For the dead know not anything. Also their love and their hatred is now finished. . . . Neither have they any part for ever of anything that is done under the sun.' The most surprising passage to find in, of all places, the Bible, in Ecclesiastes. I think it's true. Except that for me there is nothing 'done under the sun' in which he hasn't a part, forever, and there's a blotting out of the sun, because this thing happened."

"There's neither sense nor justice in that," van Epp said. "Not to my mind."

"Oh, 'justice'! 'To your mind'— Can't you realize that you're only speaking with your mind, and they've very little in common, the justice of the mind and the justice of the heart? I can look with sensible eyes at what I did that night, and say—and mean—and believe —'It really doesn't matter. Not to him, so why should it matter to me? I ought to be able to put it out of my mind.' My mind, you see! But that isn't the justice of the heart, which is stupid and enduring. I've tried, all right. I've even tried going to bed with someone else.

Quite casually. As a sort of exorcism. It didn't work. I suppose I should have known it couldn't. Not an affair gone into in a deliberate casual way. And there was no other way I could manage any sort of contact. Not an experiment I'd want to repeat! The justice of the heart is pretty thorough, as well as stupid and enduring. Now can I go?"

7

Exchange of Cables

" 'Along the sky the line of the Downes, So noble and so bare—!' "
This was from Einarsen, whose knowledge of English literature was
as wide as his command of languages, and as unprofitable to him personally. "My dear, where did you pick him up?"

"Or where did he pick you up?" This, with a giggle, was from the
outsider, greatly daring. After the uncomfortable evening he must
have spent, it could be nothing but balm, to the writer for women's
magazines, to share a sour chuckle with his tormentor: for a few
precious seconds, he belonged.

"Such a worker, our Louise!"—"But she missed the Press conference."—"The one Press conference where somebody actually said
something, finally!" This was envy in the ascendant, masquerading as

78

good-natured chaff, offered by several voices. Satisfaction was plain among the group of fellow journalists, milling round the foyer of the hotel where most of them were living, at the thought that the reliable, distant Louise Downes, the too consistently successful Louise Downes, had slipped badly, professionally at last. "In fact we can only hope the evening was well worth missing what you missed for it?"

"I was at the circus," said Louise, raising unbelieving laughter. "Will someone please tell me what happened at the Press conference?"

She was told the more willingly because the cable office, which the rest of them had dutifully besieged in time, would have closed long ago, in this small Dutch town. Even if Louise could get through to London by telephone without delay, she would be too late for the early editions of her paper. An official spokesman had unexpectedly announced complete agreement on the time and place of the all-important meeting of ministers, to discuss the still undecided agenda.

This was "hard news"; not of headline quality, as complete agreement on the agenda would have been; but to have missed it was inexcusable in her position, sent out specially to cover the conference. She had indeed, it seemed, ignored the first soft whisper of the Voices. And the Voices, which had prompted her to say, "But I can't, I'm working," in reply to van Epp's invitation, had treacherously refrained from warning her again when she wavered.

"My dear, if you could have seen yourself! Looking so wonderfully smug, too." This was from a younger journalist, whom Louise had helped unobtrusively on a few occasions. *Et tu, Brute.* "We tried to stop you, but no, on you went." The Press briefing must have finished about half an hour before Louise and van Epp rode through the square—no one had attempted to stop her: colleagues had made friendly-derisive signals, and she had gestured back in the same spirit. None of her witty lines, repeated appreciatively by this crowd as part of their clique language, had given so much pleasure as her failure, tonight.

If she had minded—as at any other time she would have minded very much—that she had let down her editor as well as herself by her dereliction, how maddening they would have been, these pleased voices. There was so much gloating in their cumbersome fun. "Your friend with the Tyrolean trousers, does he yodel?" "Ça te va, envélo!

Ah, les jolies cuisses!" But tonight she could not greatly care.

Even so, whatever the circumstances, it is always bound to be shattering to confidence, for those who have walked with the praise of their fellows in their ears, to discover how many people dislike them in secret, concealing this only while all goes well with them. She remembered a dictum of the Old Man's, when he sent her off to Trieste as a reward for doing well in Athens: "There's no wind colder than the draft from the rats' passing, when they rush from a sinking ship! You'll find that out one day. And it'll make you wiser. But not nicer." MacAlister, reading over her shoulder in the reporters' room, came unbidden into her thoughts.

"Is he not very handsome?" asked the Polish woman wistfully.

"Who?"

"Your friend with the bicycle."

"No, I don't think so. Not very, only rather. Just pleasant looking," said Louise, returning from afar and considering van Epp critically in this way for the first time. He was of the dark, lean, Spanish-looking type of Dutchman found in those parts of Holland, like Walcheren Island, where some of the ships of the beaten Armada ran ashore while the local men were away at war; the crews were, in the main, hospitably received. Compared with the Eurasian boy and girl in the Javanese restaurant, he could hardly be considered good looking at all. He had a nice mouth.

"Suppose you explain where you were really going on that bicycle?" Einarsen came back to the attack.

"Suppose you all mind your own business," said Louise, smiling steadily, and went off to try the telephone, for her paper's sake, not her own. As she expected, there would be delay, she was told. All the outgoing lines from the town were blocked for an hour and a half; busy foreign ministers' deputies were presumably reporting back to their own countries. In an hour and a half's time she would have lost the late editions, she could not even make the Stop Press column. She went up to her room to do what she had decided on doing before she met the journalists assembled for a cannibal feast in the foyer— to type out her resignation on a cable form: it could go off early in the morning.

"Listen," van Epp had said at the end of her story. "There is not much point, is there, for you, in going on as you are? Stop avoiding things which in the end you can't escape. Go straight toward something for once. I am not interested in this Falla Lufa case, but you are. Then come out to the Protectorate and see about it."

"I can't afford that," she told him, trying to keep her head in this wholly unreasonable atmosphere. "I can't just drop one job before I've another in view. I'm dependent on what I earn."

"You will manage it if you want to," he had said. "If you really want to, and don't find another excuse for disengaging yourself. With a good English joke!"

A curious sense of elation took her as she began to write.

When she had done, prompted by the professional habit of years and unwilling to think of the future, or the past, she envisaged what must be happening now in the London office of the paper.

There would have been time for the bare news-agency report to get there, but waiting for amplification from the special correspondent on the spot, the news editor would certainly go on holding space for her until the last minute. He was a man with a glum distrust of unconfirmed agency reports, because he had once been seriously led astray by one: possibly, sensing that something was amiss, he might have decided not to run the item at all. Usually, to the fury of correspondents, news editors tended to correct stories filed by their own staff by what the agencies said, rightly or wrongly: not this man. Luck was running against her, she noticed, indifferently. Tomorrow, the paper would be beaten to an important piece of information by its competitors. According to the standards of her craft, she had treated her editor, who trusted her, exceedingly badly, and his anger would be justified, to the point of getting rid of her. Her resignation was likely to cross with his cable sacking her, she thought. And if, against all reason, he were prepared to give her another chance, she would still not take it.

Doors began opening and banging in the hotel, and agitated voices rose from the foyer and the corridors. All the correspondents accredited to the conference were being notified, by messages hurriedly scribbled out in four languages, of an official correction. Owing to a fault in translation, an objection had been recorded as an agreement. (Later, the Ethiopian bloc made clear their determination to attend no conference while the return of the Italian colonies remained on the agenda.) The spokesman at the Press briefing had been mis-

taken in announcing a unanimous decision; nothing was settled. A
retraction must be filed as soon as possible. Meanwhile the cable
office stayed shut. Any inconvenience caused to messieurs/mesdames,
the correspondents, was regretted. Sitting by herself with her head in
her hands, Louise began to shake with what she believed to be
laughter, and found herself in exhausted tears.

Her paper and *The Times* were alone among the London national
dailies in not carrying the misstatement the next morning; the foreign
Press and the provincials were nearly all trapped too. Her news editor had in the end yielded to his prejudice against unsupported agency
stuff: no one discovered how *The Times* escaped.

She sent off her resignation, and it crossed with the Old Man's
elated message of congratulation to her on avoiding the pitfall which
had caught so many. Her action began to look appallingly rash by
daylight, but she reaffirmed the resignation, putting in a condition.
She was prepared to stay with the paper if she could go to Zanzibar to
follow up what had always seemed to her a promising story—she
stressed the Press freedom aspect of the Falla Lufa case in a wily
manner, and hinted at important recent developments.

She received within two hours a strongly worded reminder that not
only had this request already been turned down, but the paper's
correspondent in Nairobi would have handled any new twist in the
story, had this been worth reporting: the message ended with an offer
of more pay. Her salary was already high enough (and had been so
ever since her Tripoli days) for the thought of an increase not to hurt
the editor's reluctance to part with small sums.

The detached part of her mind was annoyed that he should have
taken her resignation, at this moment, as a form of blackmail. She
sent back as close a repetition of the famous telegram from Geneva as
she thought the more puritanical Dutch cable office likely to accept;
and in reply was told to take three months off, without pay but on a
small retaining fee, "As unhope you permanently overkick trace-
minded."

Her knees shook somewhat when she considered her finances, to
see if she could follow her inclination to refuse even this slight control of her activities: the retainer was small enough. Relinquishing her
salary had brought her down to the level where the Old Man turned
fanatically economical again: moreover—and this probably had some-

thing to do with the size of the offer—she had an enemy at court, close to the top, in these days. The former feature editor had moved up, and become assistant editor. He had never forgiven her for "Conversation Piece." He could be relied on to back up, by his advice, the editor's instinct for parsimony in certain circumstances.

But over the past two years she had saved almost nothing of what she earned; there had seemed no object in saving: the money went out as it came in. She dressed more and more expensively, because this meant that she could bother less and less about what she wore, and she had always lived in whatever comfort her succession of jobs allowed: she was a lavish spender, an "easy touch" in a fraternity which borrowed freely. On her own present resources, she could hardly manage to reach Zanzibar. Living there on the meager monthly sum suggested by the paper would probably be one long, anxious contrivance. It was impossible to guess now how long she would want to stay. A carefully worded proviso in the retainer—this was surely the assistant editor's inspiration—debarred her from writing for any other publication while she was in receipt of it.

Walking nervously by the canal, considering her next move, she watched the same motor barge as on the previous evening passing in the opposite direction, still with washing fluttering from the rigging of the tows; but in the flat noon air this looked far less like the beckoning flags of freedom than a squalid display of domestic rags and underclothing. The pictorial Old Master effect brooded yet over the luminous hollow of the landscape, but the sustaining magic of anger and despair had departed from it with the night.

No pigeons cooed now along the banks, to break the oppressive, waiting silence which closed round her when the barge had passed. There was a dearth of other traffic, on land and water; the gay cyclists were no doubt at work. She had rarely felt more alone. It was unfortunate, she thought, that gestures could scarcely ever be followed up in the careless spirit of their making. Soberly she went back to the cable office and accepted the retainer.

After a session with the town's travel agency she rang, with some diffidence, the telephone number in Veere which Karel van Epp had given her, to let him know that she was leaving for England by the night boat from the Hook. (A fleeting idea shot through her mind that he might insist on coming to see her off. As things were, it would be rather a heart-sinking embarkation for her, by herself.) A cargo steamer, touching at all the small East African ports and taking a handful of passengers, was due to sail in three days' time from South-ampton.

After the sudden intimacy of the evening she was reluctant to hear his voice again, but when they talked, briefly, she was mildly hurt—once more, the remoter part of her brain seemed to be func-tioning independently of the practical side, which was far too deeply troubled to be hurt—to find that he seemed remarkably unimpressed by the disruption he had brought into her life, outwardly so well ordered.

"So soon? Good. Remember I said, just after we met this time, perhaps you are coming to Zanzibar but you don't know it yet? Well, now you will be there, before I get back to somewhere near by. I think I told you, Pemba is twenty-five miles more north? I have still six weeks of my leave in Europe, and always I spend the last bit in Austria, climbing with friends, so I will not be seeing you again for about seven weeks. It is really very quick, only two days, going out by air."

But unfortunately, she thought, it also costs considerably more than by sea, and money had begun to matter, out of all proportion to speed or comfort.

"Would you consider renting me your flat, or whatever you live in out there, till you need it again? Because the agency man seemed to think I'd find it hard to get anything but a hotel room—though I don't know why he should be an authority on that—and I've had enough of living in hotels." She would not say, "I don't yet know if I can afford a hotel," lest he should feel an obligation to lend her his place: but at the moment, whatever obligation he felt was apparently not toward her.

"Yes, I am afraid it is very hard to find anything private. Nearly im-possible for Europeans who are not on Government contracts. But I'm sorry, I cannot do what you ask. I'm really sorry. You might as well know why I cannot do it, because you are sure to be told soon enough, by the Mrs. Corryman who does not talk to me on account of St. Augustine. And for other reasons—"

"Oh, probably I shan't meet Mrs. Corryman, so never mind," she interrupted. "It was just an idea. It doesn't matter." She did not want to be told.

"Not meet Mrs. Corryman? That will be impossible, even for as much as two days after you arrive—white, Mem-class and unprotected! Looking back, you will sadly think this is the funniest joke you ever made. Now for one reason, between Pemba and Zanzibar the communication is not good. Very slow, and you wouldn't want that. A dear old steamer, with a great high yellow funnel, goes wheezing backward and forward with very mixed cargoes, mostly goats and Moslem pilgrims. But the real objection is that I have lent it to a girl, half-Indian, half-Arab, who is used to sharing it anyway. Only I can't see her sharing it with you, or any other woman!"

"No. Of course not. Why should she?" Louise was distantly surprised again that she could be so easily taken aback by the people of Holland—shocked on various levels—first by the assumption of the woman who talked Dutch to her dog, and now by the decent frankness of this man, to whom she herself had said too much. Why should things not be as he indicated? She remembered, "But a first-generation cross . . . a pure strain of Arab and a pure strain of Indian . . . the most beautiful human being I have ever seen." Why not?

"Suppose you ever need anything, though, for any reason," he persisted, "before I get back, then tell her. Cochi, she is. You will run across her too, in Zanzibar, I expect, though not in the same places as Mrs. Corryman! Tell her I say you are to have it. When you hear what Mrs. Corryman calls 'such a surprising public school accent, coming from a dark face,' you will know you have met Cochi. She's a queer girl."

"I see. Thanks. So this is why your English has greatly improved!" said Louise, and managed creditably, she thought, listening to it with a critical ear, a man-of-the-world laugh worthy of Einarsen, before she rang off, feeling desolate.

8

A Poster of Cambridge

In London she had no leisure for worrying over what she had done.

To placate Aunt Rose, who wanted her to collect clothes from her London flat while staying in Cambridge, Louise agreed to lunch with Uncle Arthur and his family at Waterloo on the day she left England. The flurry of packing and preparation went on until the last hour. In the short time available she managed to find a tenant for the three rooms in the Temple which she had always left unoccupied, extravagantly, on previous trips; to be inoculated against various things; to consult her bank manager, who did nothing to cheer her; and to transfer to Zanzibar the alarmingly small sum of money of which she could dispose when all her bills were paid. She rushed to meet her relatives in the station restaurant, trying to think of convincing ex-

86

cuses for traveling to Africa by boat. For years, as they knew, she had considered flying the ordinary way of getting anywhere; she was a miserably bad sailor, and unfortunately they knew that, too. She had no intention of explaining anything: let them take it for granted that she was off on another assignment for the paper.

Uncle Arthur arrived for the meal in splendid form: no lies were required from Louise to satisfy him. He had come up to Town not only to see her off but to read a paper to a learned society in the afternoon; and apart from asking her anxiously if she were sleeping all right, and saying, "So thankful, dear girl! That's capital. Simply capital!" when she told him she was, he showed no curiosity about her concerns. Through the first part of lunch he talked of the kindness of the society in inviting him to make the principal contribution to the meeting: were there not other, better qualified classicists, he suggested, who could have done justice to the donnish-waggish theme, "The Decent Obscurity of a Foreign Tongue"? "I thank God that even in these days," he said, laughing, "a nodding acquaintance with Latin and Greek—or shall we in the circumstances say a *winking* acquaintance?—is hardly a rarity!" He made statements on subjects about which, if he did not know, then no one did, and qualified them with something like, "But of course that's only my opinion. I may very well be wrong!" He seemed more conscious than ever of how little he had accomplished beyond the achievements of everyone else in his own line. The face of Karel van Epp appeared to Louise's inner eye, wearing a sardonic grin.

They ate sitting alongside a travel poster of Cambridge, newly issued by the publicity department of the railways; it gave them something to talk about during the second part of the meal, when Arthur Farrant withdrew from them mentally to think over his paper. The other two tried to impress on Louise how much things had changed there since she was last in Cambridge, and everything they said suggested that all was exactly the same, even to Dorothy's behavior. She came late and left early, explaining that she had just had a straight talk about fair shares of work with the head of the bookshop by which she was now employed. This was a woman with whom she also shared a flat for five nights a week in Hampstead, and for the remaining two they both came down to Cambridge: they were at present almost inseparable. And her friend had taken the talk wonderfully, Dorothy reported; the air had been cleared, they were better friends than ever. Dorothy was obviously longing to hurry back to Cambridge—it was Saturday—to savor the brief *rapprochement*.

When she had gone, Aunt Rose said apologetically, "It's not this young woman, of course; it's the men she gets to know through the bookshop that I can't like. They look so *intense*. I went up to that Hampstead place of hers the other day, and there were two of them outside the Underground station, one selling a Communist paper, and the other something to do with the Roman Catholic Church. But unless you read the placards they were holding, you couldn't guess which was which. Not from the faces; I tried. I think they were both friends of hers. I felt I ought to go up to them and say, 'Do tell me what you're being fanatical about?' "

"Dear Aunt Rose, I wish you had!"

"They can't be a *good* influence, can they?"

"On Dorothy? I'm sure they can't be anything else," said Louise, and turned the conversation to other acquaintances, connected with the College: but nowadays it was hard to think of enough people after whom she could inquire.

The time for the departure of the boat-train came near. In the pauses in the conversation an inner commentator nagged at Louise: You are throwing away years of work, and a great deal of luck. Such luck may not come to you again. (Whatever anyone else thought, she had always held that her career had been about seventy per cent luck, and only thirty per cent the ability to make use of that luck.) There is still time to pull back, said the commentator. There is no need to catch that train.

Arthur Farrant rose to say goodbye. He reached for his wallet and then chuckled (Louise had already settled the bill): "D'you know, I was just going to say what I always did when you were going off to school? 'Well, I expect you can find a use for this!'—and tip you half a sovereign!"

"Thank you, I can still find a use for it." Louise held out her hand firmly until, much amused, he gave her a ten-shilling note. In her schooldays the gift had not been as regular as he now liked to remember. This one would atone, at least in part, for some of those awkward occasions when it had been forgotten, and she had not cared to remind him about it. "Your ten shillings are going to stand me four drinks on board which I shouldn't otherwise buy," she said. They parted merrily. The commentator was silent. The tip stretched exactly as far as she had predicted.

The first drink, a brandy, helped to end her awful three days' sea-sickness, crossing the Bay of Biscay. The second, rum and orange, celebrated her first sight of the dolphin-escort, six or seven rippling great creatures, plunging in perfect unison, line-abreast, just in front of the bows, about a week later. She watched the precision of their movements, their remarkable station keeping, hour after hour, while she tried to forget the craving for cigarettes. She had given up smoking to save money, and the first week of deprivation, after her sickness ended, was by far the most trying period to her nerves that she had known for years.

Her last two drinks on board were of iced beer, because that was cheaper than spirits or brandy. She spun them out as long as she could, watching Zanzibar and the neighboring coastline rising slowly from the sea—changing from a cloud form to a certainty of land—growing feathered with an edging of mangroves and coconut palms—showing small white houses at last—and as the short dusk fell, sending lines of brilliance skimming toward her over the soft swell of the sea, the reflection of lights on shore.

The ship anchored out in the roadstead, waiting for morning and daylight before beginning to discharge her cargo into lighters, and landing her half-dozen passengers by motorboat. In the tideway the swell ran curving round the bow where Louise stood in the spice-scented darkness: scythes of brightness repeated and repeated the movement of cutting her away from the roots of the past. She was afraid: it must matter so much, what would happen to her in this town which she could see, and sense, but not yet enter.

For the past twenty-four hours the odor of pepper, nutmeg and cloves—the mingled spice smell which was never to take her unawares again without a tightening round the heart—had been drifting out from the land, growing stronger and stronger, till here it became over-powering, floating in waves on the air, as the light traveled over the sea, from the direction of the great go-downs along the harbor wharves.

Landfall is always moving: doubly so at night. Those intersecting lines of lights must indicate streets—soon these would mean something personal to her; but would it be good or bad? She had been told that many people from the town always came down to the harbor to look at any newly arrived ship. They would be there, now, unseen by her, enjoying the first coolness after the day's end—some of them friends shortly to be made; and a few, possibly, future enemies. Was Cochi among them? In which of those houses, whose glowing windows she could count, would she sit with them and listen or argue, happy or unhappy?

As soon as boats, sent out from the shore, landed the passengers the next morning, pestering guides fastened upon her and everyone else from the ship. Men plucked at her sleeves, hovered in front of her like giant gnats: the most brazen tried to wrest her two suitcases from her grip.

"Really, you might recognize someone who has lived here for three years!" she said testily, to one after the other, an inspiration based on the hope that every European face looked like every other European face to people uninterested in the faces of Europeans but only in their money. Residents such as Karel van Epp must be coming back all the time, and probably said something like that. Apparently they did: the guides melted away from her, concentrating on the other passengers.

She made for the heart of the Stone Town, the Arab quarter, to which the navigating officer had directed her from on board: he held out little hope that she would find a suitable hotel there, but it was a cheaper hunting ground than the European quarter on the edge of it. As if to prove her words to Karel van Epp—that wherever she went, more often than not she saw someone she knew—the first white man she met face to face in the narrow, twisting streets was Major Deane. He had come over, he told her, from Dar-es-Salaam, where he was living with his brother, on a weekly business jaunt. He seemed in no way surprised to recognize her. "You been here all the time?" he asked.

"All the time since when?" she said, mystified.

"Since we met in Tripoli. Drove you to Cyrenaica, remember? Thought you said then you were interested in something in Zanzibar. Forget what."

"Oh, yes, I did. I was—I still am interested. But I've only just arrived. Can you tell me if there's a very cheap hotel, anywhere in

Zanzibar? What I want most in the world is to put down these suitcases—"

They flattened themselves hurriedly against a wall as a man-drawn
cart dashed by, a big box on wheels with a single shaft, handled by
four shouting natives.

"Thought it a bit funny I hadn't seen you around. Explains it, of
course. If you've just arrived. Well, I got what I wanted, all right.
Niched in nicely in Dar, six months ago!"

"I'm so glad. You must tell me all about it sometime. Just at the
moment—"

They flattened themselves again as another man-handled cart clat-
tered round a corner, the end of the shaft missing them by inches.
The smell of sweating dark humanity after it had passed was suffocat-
ing. The airless Stone Town streets appeared to be all corners, too
sharp to be negotiated by any but these vehicles—called, he informed
her, homali carts, and peculiar to Zanzibar. "I say, there must be a
ship in."

"Yes, mine."

"Thought so. You can always tell. These homali chaps are paid
piece rates for unloading. They're like this whenever a ship's in. Bit
dangerous, really. Mind you come over to Dar and have a crack about
old times as soon as you can. Streets much wider there. That was a
funny business, wasn't it, when you and I waded into those com-
munist-minded fellows?"

"They weren't—" She stopped helplessly. What was the use of explaining that the representative of the British Left Wing paper was
an ardent Roman Catholic, and Einarsen gave liberally and regularly
to a fund for helping refugees from Iron Curtain countries? "I'd very
much like to see Dar-es-Salaam when I get the chance," she said.
"And, of course, to hear how you sorted out your own tangle. But just
now I must get rid of these suitcases. Each weighs a ton and they're
both getting heavier. I must find a small, cheap hotel, first, and then
from there, in the next few days, I hope to find a small, cheap, room
or rooms. Do you know of anything?"

"There's Mrs. Corryman!" he exclaimed. "She knows everybody
and everything. Regular Mrs. Fixit. I'll introduce you."

"No!" said Louise, stepped back and heard the warning yell too
late. The shaft of a homali cart took her in the small of the back, and

as she went down, falling forward, a wheel crunched over her left wrist.

For a few seconds there was no pain. The most frightening thing, she thought, looking up at the people gathering around her, was the fear on the faces of the men who had run her down. Then she was being lifted, and pain enveloped her, too intense to let her trouble about anything else. When it died down enough to let her think, she was installed in Mrs. Corryman's house, lying on Mrs. Corryman's own canopied bed, and Mrs. Corryman, a large, middle-aged woman with the face of a peremptory mare, was neighing at her reassuringly, telling her that she had nothing to worry about. Not a thing. One of the Sultan's own doctors had been sent for. "I've said he's not to send his assistant but to come himself. You needn't mind his being an Arab; he's a very good doctor. Some of them are. And I've sent a message to the police that these homali men are to be punished."

"No, no." Louise tried to sit up, fell back and beckoned with her sound hand to Major Deane, who was hovering about near the doorway of the enormous chintzy, frilly room, into which he had carried her suitcases. "You saw what happened," she appealed to him. "It was entirely my own fault. You saw that, didn't you?"

Mrs. Corryman patted her bruised shoulder, forcing Louise to stifle a cry. "Nonsense, dear. All those homali men are far too careless. They just race about regardless. Time some of them were made to show a bit more consideration for Europeans. But it's always the same with Africans."

"What will happen to them, Major Deane?"

"Depends what the police are feeling like, I suppose. Hilbery'll probably be in charge. Of course if the Sultan— No, wouldn't interfere. Political situation. Always very tricky. One of the reasons I don't like Zanzibar."

"You know I stepped back suddenly. They couldn't help it. Please tell that to whoever it is who might make trouble for those men!"

Mrs. Corryman was called from the room by an Arab servant, asking which bedroom he should get ready for "this other Mem."

"Oh, no," said Louise again, weakly. "I'm not staying." But Mrs. Corryman had bustled out, scolding as she went.

"I've already told you, Toma, the Picture Room. Why can't you listen? Now take these suitcases, and I'll give you the sheets—"

"Matter of fact," said Major Deane in a lowered voice, with his eye on the door, "won't make any difference what message she sent. Hilbery's a damn' good chap. Police officer who knows when to turn a blind eye, and when to come down like a ton of bricks. Won't do anything till those fellows are miles from Zanzibar. Probably in a friend's dugout already, streaking for the mainland."

"But that's most unfair. Why should they have to run out of Zanzibar because I got in the way of their cart?" She had received a glancing blow on the head as well as the wrist injury, and various bruises. She was considerably shaken. In her disturbed state it seemed to her particularly important that her stay here, in the interests of justice, should not start with wrong being done to other colored men on her behalf. "Please go to the police and explain that I say it was all my fault. Please go. Will you? In case they know whose cart it is."

"All right, all right," he said. "Don't know when I'll get all my errands done. Have to start back to Dar this evening. (And between you and me, never sorry to go.) What I stayed around for was in case you'd noticed some of the red flags in the town and were bothered about them—just about to explain when you took that crack. Did you notice?"

"Red flags? While I was being brought along here? Good heavens, no."

"Well, there are a lot. In fact, only two Union Jacks allowed in the place. One's in the Residency and I forget where the other is. But they aren't Communist, the red ones. Thought you'd better understand. It's the Sultan's flag. Plain red. Rather confusing, really."

"Oh. Yes. Thank you. But I wasn't worrying."

"She hasn't a thing to worry about. Not a thing!" said Mrs. Corryman firmly, hurrying back. "Now, my dear, where are you from, in England? I'm from Lyme Regis— Ah, here's Dr. Asaby arriving. I'll just have a word with him first." She trotted out again.

"You won't get away from here in a hurry," said Major Deane with morose satisfaction. "She's very hospitable. Mind you, I like seeing Europeans standing by each other in a black country. Come and inquire how you are, shall I, next time I'm around this way? Week's time?"

She really could not, Louise felt, go on saying "Oh, no!" ungratefully to almost everything, but the prospect of being still in Mrs.

Corryman's house in a week's time was not to be considered. There
was something about this room, although it was actually quite cool
compared with the heat in the streets, which made it seem suffocat-
ing: probably it was the amount of frilly upholstery, which went so
oddly with her hostess's appearance. A stable is expected to be bare.
"That's very kind of you," she said. "Very kind indeed. But give me
your address in Dar-es-Salaam; then I can let you know where I go
from here, before you come back to Zanzibar again."

"Letter wouldn't reach me in time," he said. "I'll just call here on
spec. Like to wait downstairs now to hear what the doctor says, then
I'll be off."

"And take my message to the police?"

"And take your message to the police."

"Thank you very much." Louise glanced at the door: there was no
sign yet of Mrs. Corryman bringing in the doctor. The preliminary
word, whatever it was about, was proving a long one. "Will you de-
liver a note, too, if I've time to write it? To the chief of police here.
This is on quite a different subject. Better on paper." She was already
sure that Mrs. Corryman would not fancy sending the letter she pro-
posed to write: it was wiser to make use of Major Deane while she
had him handy.

"All right." The nice little man sighed, but brought over to the
bed her handbag, in which she still carried writing material by habit.

"The chief of police—that's not this man you mentioned, Hilbery?"

"Lord, no. Hilbery's just a police officer. Has his failings like everyone else, but one of the best."

"You don't happen to know the name of the chief of police?"

He shook his head. Both of them kept glancing at the door, like
children concocting mischief in the absence of authority. Her right
hand and arm had escaped injury: he steadied the paper for her while
she wrote hurriedly, giving her address as "C/o Mrs. Corryman," asking to be allowed to see all the official documents relating to the arrest, imprisonment, release and re-arrest of Falla bin Mahomet,
known as Falla Lufa. "C/o Mrs. Corryman" was probably an excellent address for her purpose. As she had no desire for the actual care
which, she foresaw, was about to be forced upon her with hectoring
benevolence, her stay might as well be made as useful as possible.

"I say," Major Deane protested. "Can't help seeing— Is that wise? Raking things up?"

"I don't see why not," she said. "Anyway, as I told you among the flowers, I'm interested in him."

"Flowers? What flowers? Let sleeping dogs lie, my motto."

"It depends where they're lying," she began, but the doctor and Mrs. Corryman came in and Major Deane retired, taking the note, making elaborate signs of complicity at Louise from the doorway.

Dr. Asaby's verdict was comforting: two small bones fractured in the wrist, multiple bruising, but no displacement of the crushed bone, no damage that could not be relied on to put itself right in quite a short time. Pressed by Louise, he smilingly refused to be more definite about his understanding of "quite a short time." He was a charming, gentle-mannered man, but got at by Mrs. Corryman before he examined Louise, he agreed that she should stay where she was until he saw her again, in a day or so. For fear of delayed shock, he said, but Louise suspected that it was somehow for fear of Mrs. Corryman.

With sensitive hands he strapped up the wrist and set it in plaster, so that she could move her arm without serious pain: only a dull ache remained, and for this he dosed her heavily with aspirin.

"Well, now, for being so kind to my unexpected guest, I suppose I've got to forgive you for not turning up at my party last week!" Mrs. Corryman wagged a playful finger at the doctor, putting Louise in mind of a skittish shire mare flourishing her heels. "Half Zanzibar was here. Absolutely everyone I wanted except you! Now what excuse have you got?"

Dr. Asaby was unperturbed. "Dear madam, I was sadly prevented at the last moment by the most curious accident. Most curious. Before setting off to come to you, as I intended, I chanced to take a drink with the chief of police. Orange juice, of course, for you know I am a Moslem. And laughing at a witty remark he made, which I fear I have now forgotten, I broke the glass against my upper teeth by the backward jerk of my head. A small fragment of this glass embedded itself between two teeth. Try as I would, I could not dislodge it myself—"

While explaining in detail how he had sought the help of a colleague, who was unfortunately out at Mrs. Corryman's party, Dr. Asaby rose and moved toward the door. His lively eyes met and held Louise's

glance for a second before he bowed himself from the room. She was
left with the surprising impression that she had just had some kind of
covert understanding with the Sultan of Zanzibar's doctor.

"What puzzles me," said Mrs. Corryman when he had gone, "is
how anyone could laugh like that at something said by the chief of
police. He's not at all a witty man. Fond of a joke, I grant you. But it's
always the same joke, about only wanting to make everyone happy,
which you mightn't expect from a policeman. You can't call that
witty! By the way, dear, do you smoke? Naughty of me; I ought to
have asked you before."

"No, thank you." For the sake of a few free cigarettes now, much as
she would have liked one at the moment, Louise was not going again
through the misery of the first week of giving them up. "The chief of
police—" She threw out a piece of old ground-bait which nearly always gathered its fish. "Isn't that someone called O'Halloran? I remember hearing an uncle of mine talking about a friend of his called
O'Halloran, who was chief of police somewhere."

"Not here, dear. This one's a Colonel Callendar. And a very nice
man—after all, we can't all be witty, can we?" Mrs. Corryman
neighed again: she had a laugh which, like a small child's, reflected
satisfaction, not amusement; and the most astonishing teeth Louise
could remember seeing in a human face. In a horse's mouth their
length and squareness, and the curve between gum and tip, would
have seemed unremarkable. If anyone were looking at Mrs. Corryman
when she began to speak or smile or laugh, her general resemblance
to a horse made them appear appropriate: it was only if someone
glanced at her when her mouth was already open, as Louise did now,
that the effect was so startling; a smile or a laugh, being characteristi-
cally human, became odd indeed in conjunction with them. "Your
uncle must have known a chief of police somewhere else. Now who is
your uncle, because perhaps I know *him*? I know such hundreds and
hundreds of people. Not just in Zanzibar. Lyme Regis and all over
the place. Thousands, really."

But it appeared that the circles in which she and Arthur Farrant
moved had not intersected. Some people never deserved their good
luck, his niece thought darkly.

"No, no O'Hallorans in this territory, that I know of," said Mrs.

Corryman, going back to the bait and swallowing much more of it than Louise had expected. "In fact, no Irishmen among our police officers at all, which is odd, isn't it, when you think how the Irish are everywhere, in the police? Only what you might call an honorary one, dear Tom Hilbery—full of blarney and a great one for the girls, in his day. And we shan't have him with us long, unfortunately. Now, I don't mean 'unfortunately' at all! I hope I'm the last person to grudge anyone good fortune. He's inherited quite a bit of land and money from a cousin, so of course it'd be silly of him to stay on here as a policeman. Especially as he has his drawbacks, but we're all very fond of him."

Hilbery—retiring. Shaken as she was, Louise made mental notes. She recalled Einarsen's account: "A friend of his, called Storr, sacked . . . and an enemy of his, Hilbery, promoted into his place . . . the bottle."

"Between you and me," Mrs. Corryman went on, "though one daren't say this to everyone—and goodness knows I'm no snob—it's very pleasant to have someone who is definitely 'one of us' in the police. A great improvement that way on his predecessor!"

So Storr was not socially acceptable out here, thought Louise. Or not to the Old Guard. How did that affect the case?

"It's anybody's guess what we'll get next! But there, we mustn't go on chattering about the parish pump, till we've moved you into the Picture Room. And then I want you to tell me all about yourself, not just about your uncle. I call it the Picture Room because that's easier for servants and Arabs and Indians to understand, but actually, as you'll see, it's the Poster Room. I use it a great deal for entertaining, but it's got a great big Arab couch, and you'll be very comfortable there. I'm determined people shall know what a wonderful country England is to look at, not just in history. I invite all sorts of people to this house, not only whites, as you realized from hearing me talk to Dr. Asaby. So I have an arrangement with one of the railway informa- tion people in London to send me all the new posters, as soon as they're issued, and then I put them up on the walls and say, 'There, you see! There's nowhere like England.' Though as a matter of fact, the first thing that attracted me to Zanzibar is that in one way it *is* like Lyme Regis—so very, very green. I've never had better vegetables anywhere in the world since I left Lyme Regis than we grow in Zanzibar, when the May rains are over. I often see things out here that remind me of Dorset."

The massive dose of aspirin was beginning to work on Louise; she was growing sleepy.

"And Major Deane likes Dar-es-Salaam," she said, feeling that some response was expected of her, "because the name reminds him of Peacehaven in Sussex."

"A very good reason, too!" said Mrs. Corryman. "Now come along."

She shouted for the Arab manservant who had taken charge of the suitcases, and together they steadied Louise—who would have felt safer walking alone, bruised as she was—on her way down a long, many-angled passage and into another larger room, papered from near the floor almost to the ceiling with railway advertisements of beauty spots in the British Isles. Many of the pictures were artistically excellent, and unsuitable as they were to their background, the austere, noble proportions of an old-style Arab house, the gay colors harmonized well in the soft light coming through latticed blinds: Louise's first impression of her prison was pleasant. There, where she would be able to look at it from the bed without turning her head, was the new poster of King's College Chapel, seen from the Backs at Cambridge. "I'll send the cook to help you undress. She's the only woman servant I have," said Mrs. Corryman, shooing the man out before her.

"Oh, no," pleaded Louise again. "I want to lie down just as I am for a bit and go to sleep. It's the aspirin."

"Nonsense, you'll sleep much better in your night things. I've had them unpacked—and what pretty things! I can see you and I share a passion for hand embroidery."

Louise was left standing alone for a minute or two, giddily holding on to the back of one of the little gilt chairs in the room. There were, she realized at once, an ominous number of these, for an apartment which was otherwise bare of furniture except for the couch. It reminded her of several audience chambers in which she had spent unprofitable hours.

A stout little Arab woman arrived, giggling, abashed at first by her job, but so much interested by the difference in build between them that she overcame her shyness and measured each garment against

herself as they got it off, capering about to demonstrate that Louise's
stockings would have reached her hips, and the suspender belt could
not meet, by many inches, over her English-style apron. Toward the
end of the undressing, Mrs. Corryman strode in absent-mindedly,
whinnied, sending a gleam from her alarming teeth through the
gloom, said "Quite forgot you were in here!"—started to walk out
again, and then stopped. "Now I'm here, I'll just arrange the room
so as not to disturb you again for a bit. I've got quite a 'mixed
bag' of people coming in tonight. I nearly always have, as you know.
They'll cheer you up."

"But I want to sleep!" Louise almost wailed, while her hostess set
the chairs in groups.

"Oh, you'll have *had* your sleep. They aren't coming till late. For
sun-downers. And anyway, they're all women."

The time for sun-downers lasted, apparently, from shortly after six
o'clock until about half past nine. So many relays of refreshments
were brought in by Mrs. Corryman's servants that Louise felt as if an
endless supper party were taking place round her bed. She refused
something new to eat or drink, and acknowledged introductions, more
or less alternately. Struggling with the effects of a soporific insufficiently slept off, she tried to talk coherently to what seemed to be
scores of ever-changing women—white, whity-brown (Arab) and
brown (Indian). There were no Africans, though outside the windows Africa lay very close. Drums were throbbing in the native town,
and the drumming worked its way into Louise's head. In fact there
could not have been more than about fifteen people in the room at
any one time, for later she counted the chairs from which they were
constantly being called by their hostess to change places, in order to
talk in some other grouping, but for a few, rare moments Louise had
the firm impression that they were all sitting down together. Yet for
the rest of her stay in Zanzibar she kept running into people who
accosted her warmly and said, "We met, d'you remember, at Mrs.
Corryman's, your first night here? I was so interested in what you
told us—" Frequently there would follow the repetition of a statement so obviously inaccurate, or libelous, or both, about some figure
of the international scene, that Louise grew horrified by the evidence
of what her tongue could do while her mind wandered. But in the
meantime she was too hard put to it to form sentences which sounded

like sentences, against the handicap of drowsiness, to bother about
the effects of what she was saying.

Mrs. Corryman presented her colored guests with amiable asides
to them about Louise: "Her uncle is what we call 'Master' of one of
the Colleges at Cambridge. 'Master' meaning not like 'school-
master,' but Chief, or Head. Cambridge is this place, here. No, next
to it. That one's Worcester. And we think a great deal of our old
Universities. Learning, in England, ranks high, so he's considered
a very distinguished man."

Louise believed that she interrupted at this point to say, "He's
nothing of the sort. He's retively—relatly—" This was while de-
scending veil after veil of sleep could still be torn back by wild
efforts of politeness. Whether she actually tried the disclaimer or
only thought she did, Mrs. Corryman would not have heard it. As
more people came and went she dispensed questions to her guests
like canapés and coffee, turning away before they could respond.
"Now, Mrs. Downes, I'm sure everyone here is longing to know, is
this your first visit to Africa?"

Enunciating with greater care, to keep the slur of sleep out of
her voice, Louise obediently told the room at large, "I've been to
North Africa, but never to this part before." Mrs. Corryman, however, was giving instructions to the Arab servant, Toma, to bring in
more soft drinks. "Fetch some almost unsweetened lime for this
Mem. It'll be more refreshing for her that way." She hurried off to
reseat several people and make room for a new arrival. In the course
of time she worked round again to the bedside. "Well, Mrs. Downes,
we can hardly ask you yet what you think of Zanzibar, or is this
not your first visit hereabouts?"

"I've been to North Africa, but never—"

Mrs. Corryman, in a confidential whisper, was imparting information to someone in a sari, on the edge of Louise's field of vision,
a sari of such shrill yellow that Louise closed her eyes, spilling some
of the glass of lime juice which had been thrust into her hand by
Toma. Hardly sweetened at all, it tasted as if it could not possibly
be sticky; but in the bed, it was. She reopened her eyes and adjusted
a fixed mask of sociability. Wrist and head, and various bruises, but
particularly wrist and head, throbbed increasingly as the pain-killing

effects of the aspirin wore off, leaving only the sleepiness. In a little while her turn for another question came round again.

"Mrs. Loder, here, tells me you're a journalist. Naughty thing, keeping this from me! Do let us know, has your work—which must be so interesting!—ever led you to this corner of the globe before?"

"I have only—" The whole roomful of women must be wondering, she felt, when this tiresome newcomer would stop repeating facts about which no one cared in any case. But presumably they knew Mrs. Corryman's habits as a hostess.

On the rare occasions when she paused for a reply it was usually after a statement which suggested no easy comment. "Most people would call this a *soirée*," she observed to Louise, looking down upon her with proprietary satisfaction. "But I think *conversazione* is nicer. Mmm?" Her voice rose expectantly; she stood waiting with her head on one side. Major Deane's "You won't get out of here in a hurry!" rang like a knell in her guest's memory.

"Latin roots," murmured Louise indistinctly, wondering herself what bearing this had on the subject, and Mrs. Corryman smiled, nodded and went away.

Toward the end of the evening Louise longed to take another heavy dose of aspirin much as an alcoholic might long for a drink, but she had already been given three times more than she had ever taken before, at one time, and in these days she was always frightened of the effects of analgesics of all kinds. With her bruises protesting at every fretful shift in her position, and her head and wrist aching increasingly, she was at last able to take less and less part in the conversation: Mrs. Corryman had begun to talk about Lyme Regis. From there she went on to other parts of the world, judged by its standards. She appeared to have covered much of the earth's surface before electing to settle in Zanzibar; but she was one of the comparative travelers really anchored to one spot, constantly reminded by the savage, flaring tropical sunsets across one bay of the decorous pink-gray ending of day over another. Wherever she might go, Lyme Regis awaited her, in cliff scenery, wide sands, or a prodigality of green vegetables.

Louise's last conscious thought while the party lasted was of grudging wonder, almost of admiration: how had Mrs. Corryman

made herself such a power in Zanzibar without ever really leaving
Lyme Regis? The mask of social courtesy suddenly crumpled, and
Louise fell asleep, between one sentence and the next. She was
only half roused by the change in Mrs. Corryman's voice to that
most arresting conversational tone, a loud whisper: "There now,
I'm afraid we've tired her!" The guests were shushed and hustled
away. "No, no. Don't stop to thank me. Just let yourselves out.
She'll be better tomorrow. And come again. Come again."

Some time after they had all gone, Louise was roused by urgent
needs, struggled out of bed, felt her way down the dark, difficult
passage to a lavatory, and was violently sick of her unsweetened
lime juice, feeling considerably relieved thereafter.

9

"C/o Mrs. Corryman"

Mrs. Corryman was right; Louise was much better the next day—and needed to be, she thought, reading the communication from the Office of the Chief of Police which was brought in with her ample English breakfast: Zanzibar was no place for anyone at less than full strength, mental and physical.

Outside, the note was correctly addressed to her, by her full name, "Care of Mrs. Corryman": inside, in unpracticed typescript, it ran without a heading, "Why are we always at cross purposes? Why do you only ask for the moon? You know here we want to make everyone happy but still you cry for the impossible. It is too bad. No, no, no." The signature was illegible, but could not possibly be "Callendar."

Toma, the cook's husband, the grave elderly Arab servant who had shepherded her down the passage, waited beside her bed when he had opened the letter for her, to help her cut up bacon without using her damaged arm, and to spread butter and marmalade on the toast. "Today my wife work elsewhere, so I deal with this."

"You mean she's left Mrs. Corryman?" Louise was filled with envy.

"No. She just like to go away a little. Tomorrow she come back. Or next day." He looked closely at Louise's strapped and plastered wrist, clicked his teeth with respectful disapproval and observed, "Mem, you are a madcap."

The phrase delighted Louise into forgetting her envy: Toma, she discovered, had been to England twenty years previously as a stoker, and had picked up slang with which he enjoyed flavoring his conversation. It must have been already somewhat out of date when he learned it. Mrs. Corryman talked at him, as at all her staff, in simplified kitchen English, seldom taking in what they said in return, so that she probably remained unaware of the scope of his vocabulary.

"The Mem says to get up now, if it is not too much fag. Today she has lunch party downstairs."

"It is too much fag," Louise replied with determination.

"But Mem, proper white party. Not all this ragtag up here." He made a belittling gesture round the Picture Room, with its overmany little gilt chairs.

"Still too much fag. Would you explain to Mrs. Corryman I'm not well enough yet?"

If this lunch were planned to take place downstairs, she might be left in peace up here. The climate of Zanzibar is one of the most relaxing in the world; its effect on newcomers is to make them feel that a week of solid sleep could hardly be too much. This added to Louise's conviction that one social gathering of Mrs. Corryman's in twenty-four hours would be more than enough for her anywhere, whatever her condition.

She found out from Toma, with interest, that her hostess's mixed-color parties were deprecated more by the Arabs and Indians than he thought they could possibly be by the other Europeans. Louise felt guilty that, as a guest, however unwilling, she was encouraging

him to talk about his employer like this, but the chance of understanding more about local ways was too good to miss: she persisted,
and discovered that, surprisingly, the reason for this disapproval was
the exclusion of the Africans. Since Negroes were not invited,
some kind of selection was obviously exercised: in which case it appeared insulting to both Arabs and Indians to be asked to meet one
another, quite indiscriminatingly from the point of view of their
own class prejudices. But few people, he conveyed, cared to refuse
Mrs. Corryman's invitations, however comprehensive, when these
were issued to them personally.

He glanced toward the doorway, and lowered his voice. Everyone
in this household glanced frequently and apprehensively toward the
entrances: there were doors to the lavatories, bathrooms and Mrs.
Corryman's bedroom only. Elsewhere the curtains moved often in
the welcome breeze cleverly induced to blow through this well
built, cool house: there was no feeling of privacy. "Mem, you want
one-two rooms, where you live on your own? Nice and cheap?"

"Yes, I do! But how do you know?"

He shrugged, and did not answer such a foolish-seeming question
directly. "I go about. To some in Zanzibar I teach English."

"Do you, indeed! That's very"—she hesitated for a word—"en-
terprising of you."

"It has its uses," he said, though whether he meant the language
of the dominant race, or his circulation in Zanzibar, she did not
know. Later, Louise came to realize that almost every word spoken
by Europeans in the streets of the Stone Town, despite the clatter
of the homali carts, the shouting and the drumming, was overheard by the Arab women, secluded in the houses with grilles over
their windows, by which they sat, wistfully looking out at life—overheard, and if interesting, passed on. It was not yet twenty-four hours
since she had spoken to Major Deane about lodgings, half a mile
or so from this house. Certainly this process had its uses, but also,
she was never to forget, its sinister side. "I find this for you," he said,
"but mum's the word, eh?"

"Mum's the word! But can you find it at once, Toma? As soon as
Dr. Asaby says I can move? He's likely to look in tomorrow."

"This evening," he corrected.

"He said he'd try this afternoon, but it would probably be to-morrow morning. Depending on his other patients, and how busy he is."

"It will be this evening," he said with certainty. "And I tell you of something as soon as my wife is back."

"Toma, where are my clothes? And my suitcases?" She did not know when they had been taken out of the room: presumably while she slept.

"I cannot say." He spoke evasively. "My wife, she will know."

"But if Mrs. Corryman hoped I was going to get up this morning, somebody must have been going to produce my clothes?"

"Perhaps they are being cleaned?" he suggested. "From the mud when you fell? The Mem will have them. You will ask her when she comes." Plainly Louise would get no further with him on this subject.

There was scuffling in the passage, and two voices were raised in a language strange to Louise: Swahili, she supposed, noticing that whereas everywhere pigeons said, "My toe hurts, Betty," quite clearly, people quarreling in the common tongue of the mixed races of Zanzibar appeared to be insisting that "Hardly a macaroon remains in Penzance," to which the reply sounded like, "Nor can the Tudors get any coffee."

This exchange, or something similar, was repeated several times. Toma listened with an indulgent air, buttering her last piece of toast, giving no indication that the argument concerned her. "It is as well the Mem cannot understand," he told her at last, "for the talk is very bad. This Indian cannot take 'bugger-off' for an answer. They are all like that. So my fellow servant is telling him —" He gave her a translation of the phrase which she had heard as something about Tudors and coffee: it brought back, almost nostalgically, Karel van Epp in Cambridge. Then taking her tray with a bow, Toma went out and silenced the altercation with a few fierce words. There was quiet again; Zanzibar quiet, which had always a background of laughter and drumming, at all hours of the day or night.

Soon Mrs. Corryman bustled in. "Toma says you don't feel up to dressing? Oh, dear, that is a nuisance."

"I'm sorry."

"I was hoping to 'launch' you in Zanzibar this morning! Five of my nicest personal friends coming to lunch specially. I phoned them last night. You seemed in such good form at the party, till you suddenly fell asleep."

"Well, I'm afraid I'm not now."

"I hope some tiresome Babu clerk didn't disturb you, wanting to see you on business? No? Good. What a time to bother somebody about that, at breakfast! Anyway, the servants got rid of him."

"Oh, was he wanting to see me? Perhaps it was important."

"If so, he'll come back. You can depend on that. Very persistent, Indians. Let him come back at a reasonable hour. I suppose Toma told you his wife's gone, so perhaps you thought there'd be no one to help you dress, with that awkward arm? But that's all right, she's sent another woman to take her place. Zanzibar servants are always doing this when they want a holiday. You never know who'll be in your kitchen on any particular day. This is some relative—quite good, I've had her before. Better, from your point of view, she's taller. So won't you change your mind and have a try?"

"I'd rather stay where I am. Just till Dr. Asaby comes again. It's very hospitable of you to put me up—" Louise could not bring herself to use the more natural phrase, "It's very kind of you"—"and the width of this bed feels wonderful, after a narrow ship's bunk. So here I'll remain. For now."

"Oh, told you before, shan't dream of letting you out of the house till he says you're absolutely fit. But you know, these people I've asked to meet you will be terribly disappointed if you don't appear. I mean, it isn't as if it was a leg you'd broken."

"They wouldn't like me to come down and faint on them. I rather think I still turn giddy when I stand up." So far, that morning, Louise had not had the time nor the chance to find out if this were true.

"Most annoying of Lalla—that's Toma's wife—choosing today to go off! But that's the way it is out here, if you don't accept a substitute when servants turn restless, they don't come back at all. Makes me long for Lyme Regis sometimes. I can tell you."

"Though in Lyme Regis," Louise reminded her, "they wouldn't send a substitute."

"Oh, I daresay. What I meant was, if I'd still got Lalla in the kitchen—she's very good at canapés and cold stuff as you saw last night—we could have had lunch up here."

"Oh, no!" said Louise anxiously. "No. If you've arranged to lunch your friends downstairs, please do stick to that. I should hate to think you'd altered your plans because of me."

"Afraid we'll have to stick to it. This woman's only good for an ordinary meal, and you have to stand over her a bit even then—I'll tell you what!" In a whinny of satisfaction, Mrs. Corryman's lips fell back from her teeth as if the strain of keeping the flesh closed over most of their expanse while she talked had suddenly become too much. "We can have coffee up here!"

"Oh, n—"

"That's it. Then you can meet them: I hate disappointing people. We'll have your lunch sent up but I'll tell Toma not to put any coffee on your tray, because you'd rather have it hot with us."

"All right," said Louise weakly, adding with an effort, "Thank you. About my clothes and suitcases—I don't know where they've gone."

"Don't see what you want your clothes for if you're not getting up." Mrs. Corryman looked cross again. "Everything was taken away to be aired. You don't understand this climate." At some period during the previous evening, Louise noted, Mrs. Corryman had accepted that this really was her first visit to tropical Africa. Repetition, then, could sometimes make a fact strike home.

"Where have they gone?"

"Down in the airing cupboards. Anything leather, like shoes, mildews if it's left packed up. Mildews even when it isn't, in the wet monsoon. But thank God that's not yet awhile. Still, they're safer down in the airing cupboards, my dear. You've not a thing to worry about."

"But I'd like them back for a bit. As it isn't raining! I could mend my underclothes while I'm in bed."

"Don't look as if they need it. Anyway, Lalla can do anything like that for you later on. You can't sew with your wrist all strapped up."

"My fingers are all right for holding things, and I'm marvelous at threading needles with one hand," said Louise, who had hardly stopped a run in a stocking for years, paying an expensive laundry and cleaning service to look after repairs. "Could somebody please

bring all my things to me, this morning, so that I can sort them out
and see what needs doing?"

"Very well. Now I'm afraid I haven't time to stop here chatting,
with the new cook to supervise." She spoke as though her guest
had reproached her at the prospect of being left alone. "Of course,
I want to hear all about what's brought you to Zanzibar, but you
must tell us over coffee. We're 100 per cent white this time—did
Toma explain?"

"He said it was 'a proper lunch.'"

"Ha. He would. Arabs, they're the worst snobs. Expect you were
a bit surprised last night to see how I jumble 'em all up on occasion,
Arabs and Indians and us? Shocks a lot of people. But I do it on
principle."

"I thought so."

Mrs. Corryman sat down on an inadequate-looking gilt chair, and
forgot her pressing domesticities. "Someone's got to set an example
in accepting color. In the right way. Socially, yes, sexually, no, if you
follow? If we're going to keep up white prestige in Africa—and it's
our duty to everyone to do that. Everyone, white or colored, remember!—Well, this is the way it's got to be done. With people who
won't overstep the mark. That's the great thing. You're all right
with color, I say, if only you know where to draw the line."

"What about the Africans?"

"We're all Africans now! Of course, when I tell some people that,
just because we all live here, it upsets them more than anything.
Does them good. I give people jolts all round, you know!"

"There weren't any Bantus—Negroes—darkest Africans—whatever
you call them—at the party last night, were there?"

"No, that's the point. Still a very primitive lot round here. They
wouldn't understand, and they'd presume on any invitation. Arabs
and Indians don't. Or not often. We have far more trouble with the
foreign white element here than we do with the coloreds, because
they will go too far."

"With the Negroes?"

"With everyone. What I say is, people let us all down when they
let themselves down. Mind you, I don't expect white men to be
angels—know too much about them!" The teeth reappeared briefly.
It seemed almost incredible to Louise that Mrs. Corryman must at

one time have been married, presumably to a man, not a stallion. "I've no objection to fellows like Major Deane who *may*—don't say he *has*, mind you, but I wouldn't be surprised—have a little bit of something tucked away in Dar. Because he keeps it private if he has. I'm a woman of strong religious convictions; I don't pretend to like it. But I can make allowances for climate. There's a Dutchman in Pemba, though, who's set up house quite openly with a girl from an upper-class Zanzibar 'mixed' family. Well, what the 'mixed' think is upper-class, anyway! They have the most elaborate distinctions among themselves, the Indians and the Arabs and the half-and-halfs. I take no notice of that, of course; it seems so silly when they're all colored! But this girl being what she is, the whole affair becomes much worse as an example. Everyone knows her or of her; it simply can't be hidden, and I don't think he even tries—"

"Going back to the Indians and Arabs and their class distinctions —" said Louise. She was determined not to be told more about either Karel van Epp or Cochi, if she could help it—not by Mrs. Corryman. "Isn't there a danger that they may find our attitude more patronizing when we treat them as though they were all on the same level? More patronizing, I mean, than if we rated them as they rate themselves? I don't say this specially about your parties: I'm sure you're right in thinking plenty of people need shaking up about the color bar, here and elsewhere. But the English way of condescending to the local people, when we're abroad, does sometimes suggest, doesn't it, that the gap between them and us is so great anyway, it hardly matters who they are in their own eyes? This is only my impression of course. I haven't been here long enough to know if it's true."

As they were alone together, Mrs. Corryman actually heard what her guest said the first time. She stared at Louise blankly. "Don't understand what you mean."

"Well, suppose an admiral talked to a petty officer and a stoker, together, as if he couldn't imagine that the difference in rank between them could matter at all on board ship—don't you think the stoker would be just as horrified as the petty officer? And probably more uncomfortable?"

"But we aren't in the position of admirals here. More's the pity for the colored people! Make no mistake about that. This is only a protectorate: in a colony we could stop them being so nasty to each other. They are, you know, Arabs and Indians. That's why someone has to give them a lead, socially. They've no feelings of responsibility at all for other colored people.

"But mightn't they reasonably prefer being nasty to each other, to being stopped being nasty by us?"

"The Indians are like the Jews. All up and down the east coast of Africa. Shopkeeping. Getting people to work for them. In all the best trading jobs, which the Arabs want, naturally. So of course the Arabs hate them, because the Indians are like Jews without the advantage of Hitler."

"The advantage?"

"You must see Hitler was a great advantage to the Jews who didn't happen to be killed by him," said Mrs. Corryman impatiently. "He made anti-Semitism wrong, all over the world." She had Major Deane's knack, Louise discovered, of suddenly stating quite a profound truth, but the way she stated it made agreeing with her difficult. "People feel about Jews just the way they always did, but now they think they shouldn't. Anyway, they can't show it. Of course, that's an advantage to the Jews, and the Indians haven't got it. Everyone dislikes them openly, hereabouts."

"Oh, I see. But not the Arabs? Is that because they're less mercenary?

"The Arabs? Less mercenary? Did you see that huge, stinking old ditch between us and the Bantu shanty-town?" Mrs. Corryman said. "The one they're starting to fill in? Oh no, you haven't yet but you will! Centuries old, as old as this house which was built by the slave trader, Sheik Loair. Do you know what it used to be full of? Rotting bodies of black slaves who died on the way here in the Arab slave dhows. There's nothing to choose between them for the way they've always treated other people, but the Arabs are lazier and don't make so much noise about it. So people prefer them. And who put down the slave trade between Zanzibar and the Persian Gulf? The Royal Navy! What we have to consider sacred is our trusteeship of the future of the colored people."

She got up from the little chair, and with her head held invitingly on one side, waited for Louise's comment.

Nothing rose in Louise's mind on the topic of trusteeship. Trying to find something impersonal to contribute she fell back on a quotation. "What Tolstoi says that men have always held sacred is the means of preserving their power over other men."

"Well—!"

Louise was unprepared for the explosion that followed. Mrs. Corryman took this as a direct attack on British colonial administration, and on herself. It might have been on Lyme Regis, thought Louise regretfully, giving up the attempt to make herself heard against the other's vehemence.

"What a Russian says! As if they weren't imperialists . . . exploiting subject races . . . only not for the natives' good. If I'd known you had sympathies of that sort . . . Let me tell you . . . stopped tribal warfare . . . horrible practices, ritual murder, clitoridotomy . . . opened up the land . . . agricultural improvement . . . schools, churches, medicine. Mustn't waste another moment arguing if lunch is to be ready on time . . . and a great deal more I could say."

Mrs. Corryman swept out, giving an impression of arched neck and dilated nostrils, leaving Louise to recover from a feeling of having been kicked on the head; and then to hope that, unpleasant as the incident had been while it lasted, it might perhaps ease her departure in due course. As soon as this idea occurred to her, sleep —wonderful Zanzibar sleep, like a rising tide ready to float her away from the troubles of this peculiar morning—began to lap round her again, benignly. A struggle was necessary before she could seize the chance of being on her own, and force herself up and along the passage, on the way to the lavatory and the bathroom just beyond. Here she discovered her toothbrush waiting for her in a glass, and her washcloth disposed beside her soap on the washbasin, but no other sign of her possessions.

She had told the truth by accident, she found: standing up turned her a little giddy. Dr. Asaby had been right in expecting some delayed shock. She came back propping herself against the wall with her sound arm, and the delicious waves of sleep reached out to her as she sank back on to the couch.

The hours of the morning wore on, but her clothes and suitcases did not appear. She was half roused by a very soft, persistent knocking, almost a scratching, from the doorway. A worried-looking face, which she took to be an Indian's, poked round the edge of the curtain. "You see me?"

Memories of Western films, about other kinds of Indians, prompted Louise to murmur, "I see you."

"You see me *now?*"

She recognized one of the voices from the altercation in the passage. The waves of sleep receded. "Oh, yes. Do come in. I'm sorry you've had to call twice."

A clerkly little man slipped into the room, his top half dressed like a European, his lower half having shirttails almost to the knees, hanging outside his trousers. He, too, kept a harassed watch on the door, but this time, Louise realized, Toma and not Mrs. Corryman was the person feared.

"I wrote you the wrong letter," he said sadly. "I think."

"Was it from the Office of the Chief of Police?"

He brightened a little. "Then I addressed it rightly, and you got it. I am glad of that, at least. Lately I have made so many mistakes that sometimes I despair of ultimate advancement. Mistakes when I should have been doing my best—when I *was* doing my best. Only it is not a very good one. Everything is often so complicated."

For a second she wondered if he had learned his English from Toma, but his accent was more singsong. "What was in the letter you should have sent me instead of this?" she asked, handing him back the note beginning, "Why are we always at cross-purposes?"

"I don't know, I think," he said. "That is, not for certain. Because it is not yet written. But I expect the answer would have to be No. You see, I prepared the envelope, and was pondering about your letter, and some other letters, when your envelope went off with the messenger and the wrong letter inside. I have been so worried."

"I'm so sorry." He had a modest, mournful charm. No one could help feeling sorry for his distress.

"It is safer for me to say No. In the absence of authority. Then, later, authority can say Yes, and everyone is happy. As Colonel Callendar wishes."

"You are not"—it seemed unnecessary to ask, but courteous—"the regular secretary to the chief of police?"

"Oh, no!" he said, disturbed by the reflection on his office. "Colonel Callendar is a most efficient man, and naturally he has a most efficient secretary. I am filing clerk only. By a series of calamities, Colonel Callendar is the victim of appendicitis (very involved —he was flown to England at a moment's notice, yesterday), while his deputy and secretary are stricken, too, with illness, though less seriously. They have malaria. Caught on leave in Tanganyika," he added virtuously, "for we have stamped out this distressing and almost universal complaint in Zanzibar. I think."

"When will one of them be back? Have you any idea?"

"I have an idea, yes. But I am so often wrong."

"Just guess. That'll be better than nothing."

"In a week, then. Perhaps less. It must be very spurring to recovery for Colonel Callendar's secretary to know that I am alone in charge of the office. It was Colonel Callendar's style I tried to copy in my letter: he is a very pleasant, joky man. Constantly he says, 'I only want to make everyone happy.' Laughable, of course, in a policeman. But in a letter a joke is often not so prominent. You were not offended by the tone of my letter? Or if you were, you are not now, when you know it was a mistake?"

"I was never in the least offended. Just puzzled, at the time. Do tell me, unless this is indiscreet, what was the request you were refusing, in the letter which wasn't for me?"

"I think it will not matter if I tell you. Anyway, after the mistakes I have made it cannot make much difference—I am second-class filing clerk, you understand. I had hoped to become first-class this year, but now this may be postponed, I think. A shopkeeper, a fellow Christian, is always asking to register his sister-in-law as his daughter. I do not like a fellow Christian to ask such things."

"Why should he want to do this?"

"Because if she is a blood relation he can work her longer hours in the shop, with less pay. The labor regulations of Zanzibar," he said, and smiled cheerfully, "are very complicated. But just. I go now. Mrs. Corryman's Toma is not a considerate servant. Efficient, but not considerate. Thank you for your kind attention."

After he had moved cautiously into the passage his head came round the curtain again into the Picture Room, obscuring part of Loch Lomond. "You are a writing lady, I think, from your wish to read documents?"

"Yes, I am. How clever of you to guess!" He was unfairly disarming. Louise could understand perfectly how he survived in his job, even in a most efficient office. Nearly everyone must long to comfort him for his mistakes.

"After I have told you of my failings I am afraid you will not want me as a secretary, if by chance I am sacked?"

"I'm afraid not. But then, you see, I work straight onto a type-writer, and have nothing to file, so what could a secretary do?"

"I see now it would have been better if I had not tried to answer letters myself, but had said only about the unprecedented calamities. I will not send this on to the shopkeeper, but wait for someone to come back. I am conscientious in filing. And reliable, too."

"I'm sure you are."

"I will give you my name, in case you change your mind. Ralmi bin Saleh. I am a cousin of Falla Lufa, but I have nothing to do with him. He is a troublesome man. Stupid, too, for an Arab. Would you think I was Indian?"

"Aren't you?" Her ability to be surprised was exhausted for the moment. Certainly he looked in every way her idea of an Indian from India.

"Oh, no." He had gradually come back into the room entirely and stood haloed by the Illuminations at Blackpool. "I dress like this because Arabs are not polite to other Arabs who look like Indians but say they are Arabs. And Tamils—Indians—are not polite either if they think you are one of them pretending to be Arab. So it is better for me this way." He caught the high-pitched buzz of European women's voices making arrival noises, and began to sidle toward the doorway again. Downstairs the party was assembling, with those little cries of greeting and pleasure, rising shriller and shriller above the general buzz, which can sound strangely menacing. "But I am Arab, and all my family is Arab. All except my mother."

"And she is—"

"Tamil."

"Surely, in that case—" Louise had little hope of understanding his racial status, but intended to lead the talk round to Falla Lufa again and find out more about him. Ralmi, however, heard Toma approaching down the passage, and fled.

"When English ladies are high-spirited," said Toma, carrying in a lunch tray, "oh, how high-spirited English ladies can be!" He balanced the tray on two chairs beside the bed. "I bring this early because I must look after them down there. All is arranged for you to eat with one hand. Also I kill two birds with one stone, coming up with this now, for see, more letters have arrived for you. Shall I open them?"

There were two, both addressed to her "C/o Mrs. Corryman"; she recognized the handwriting on neither, but one bore an Austrian stamp, and she put it down again on the tray, with a mixture of apprehension and pleasure, to read when she was alone.

"No, I think I can manage, thank you," she said. "Oh, well, just open this other one, will you?"

It was a note from Major Deane which ran, "Just remembered second place where Union Jack may be flown in Zanzibar is of course the Courts of Justice. Done your errands. Hope you getting on fine. Off to my Peacehaven."

Louise had an incurable habit of snorting when she laughed aloud. She did this now: Toma, from near the doorway, made the clicking sound of disapproval with which he had informed her she was a madcap, and then put his hand before his face to hide non-existent shared amusement, out of immense Arab courtesy, before he left her.

She took up Karel van Epp's letter, hesitating to open it, and both pleasure and apprehension deepened. That he had written to her at all, after so markedly casual a goodbye, meant that when she had read whatever was waiting for her inside this envelope, inevitably their friendship entered a new phase, one less ordered by chance and circumstance. Here was choice, the deliberate reaching out of one human being to another. She was not sure, at the moment, that she wanted this change: between her and the large, square, foreign handwriting hovered the shadow of an unknown girl with "such a surprising public school accent, coming from a dark face."

She made herself begin on the excellent meal Toma had brought, with the envelope lying, protecting her still from its contents, beside her plate. She must remember that as soon as she was on her own there would be no more of this sort of luxury, duck-à-l'orange, with mounds of Zanzibar's famed green vegetables: and then suddenly she clawed the letter open and stopped eating.

There was anticlimax in the first few paragraphs: she had forgotten how single-minded and practical van Epp could be, as over "the impenetrability of matter."

"By now you must be well in tow, despite what you thought," he began, "so I fancy this will catch up with you about your fourth day in Zanzibar!" His letter had come quicker than he expected, but she was certainly "well in tow." "And by now I hope you will have seen your first clove trees in blossom and like them as much as I do." He went on to write in more detail than he had given her in Holland about the effects of die-back disease in the clove plantations. There appeared to be several tenable theories of its origin, which might be fungoid, or a virus carried by ants, entering through breaks in the bark at the time of harvesting; and its spread in recent years was seriously threatening the clove crop on which Zanzibar chiefly depended, much as banana disease had once threatened the West Indies; but Zanzibar, and Pemba too, were more completely dependent on this one valuable product. "If you decide to talk to me in Zanzibar you will have to listen to a lot about die-back," he wrote, "so you might as well learn something now."

She lay in bed and laughed at herself, silently, wryly.

What she had expected in his letter she did not know, but not this. Certainly not this!

Cochi, whatever she was like—"the most beautiful human being I have ever seen," he had said—was welcome to keep him.

10

"Tiresome Little Man"

The steady rise in the note of the female buzz from downstairs got Louise out of bed before she realized what had decided her action.

This was not fair, this was not in the contract: the lunch party was coming upstairs and it was not nearly time for coffee. Mrs. Corryman must be bringing her friends in for cocktails too. Slightly less giddy this time when she stood up, Louise fled down the passage and locked herself in.

From the Picture Room Mrs. Corryman's voice floated on the carrier tone of the buzz. "Such an interesting young woman, she is! Never mind, you'll meet her later on. I only thought it'd be nice for her to have a drink with us first." (So she had been wholly forgiven already, Louise deduced with disappointment: the fracas had achieved nothing!) "Oh, aren't these Arab servants tedious! Unless you're behind them all the time they do absolutely nothing. They sent up her lunch because I told them to, but look, they haven't straightened her bed or fetched the tray. She doesn't seem to have eaten much, but then one can't, in bed. We'll leave her the pawpaw, in case she fancies it later. Now you take the jug—careful— After you, dear! I'm afraid it's dark on these stairs, but as you know, I won't have electricity put into this old house. That's something Sheik Loair couldn't buy, with all the profits from his awful trafficking in human flesh, and I feel it'd be out of keeping."

"Well, so are your posters, come to that!" The note was dropping again, slowly, as the party negotiated the difficult stairs.

"Nonsense! He was a great collector of paintings, and he'd have loved these! Looked at all the places and wondered if he could sell them slaves."

When Louise ventured back the bed sheets had been twitched into neatness, and her lunch, on which she had been just about to start again, carried away, except for the fruit. Pawpaw tasted to her like solidified paraffin. Still, there would be coffee shortly. Van Epp's letter lay waiting, unfinished, the scattered pages tidied up with Major Deane's note placed on top.

"If you decide—" It was perceptive of him to realize that after talking too freely in Holland she might well—even though she had telephoned to him the next day—suffer from a reaction against him, which could grow strongly in an interval of weeks: she might not want to talk to him again.

"I am lucky," his second page went on. "For me, by the chance of what my work is, there is no hole in the heart. (You remember, eating Javanese food, how we spoke of the need of so many people today for something, some idea or some person, important enough to let them be devoted? And never mind—or not very much—if the thing or person is worth being devoted to, so long as it fills that hole?) Well, I have my thing. And of course I think it is worth while. The sight of healthy trees, heavy bearing, mostly because of the sun and the rain but just a little, too, because of me. There will always be enough tree diseases due to molds, at least in my lifetime, for me to have a fine supply of enemies."

Louise considered van Epp anew.

"You are lucky," Dorothy had said to her, years ago, and was right, because Louise had once been of the hale company of the devoted. She thought suddenly, her eyes looking through his curious writing into the emptiness of the years after the war, how quickly the mind becomes unappreciative of the absence of pain. Every part of her body was conscious and thankful that living, breathing—even moving, within limits—no longer hurt all the time: her wrist merely grumbled a warning occasionally. But she had not once been conscious of the hole in the heart since the night in which she decided to come to Africa, and she had not so much as noticed the lack of the familiar mental ache. The boredom of love was over. This letter, like its sender, was not to be underrated.

The arrogance of the last paragraph, however, made her snort again. "You are, just a little, spoiling my Austrian trip," he wrote. "And I am much annoyed with you because until now I have always enjoyed this more than anything else in my leave. I suppose it is because I see perplexities waiting for me in Zanzibar, or rather in Pemba, when I get back."

Jerked (largely at his suggestion) out of a world she had arduously learned how to manipulate—hard up—broken-wristed—practically a prisoner while recovering from concussion—she owed him little sympathy, it seemed to her, because his climbing holiday was slightly clouded for once. Nevertheless she accepted that this was, in some sense, a love letter. In some very odd sense indeed!—and the first which had been of the least importance to her since the pre-written messages about imaginary parcels and birthdays had stopped arriving, during the war. She lay thinking about this, surprised and a little amused.

The high-spirited ladies were approaching again, preceded by Toma with coffee. "Ah, *there* she is! Now, *dear* Mrs. Downes, we're all agog to hear what you're going to write about us in Zanzibar?" This was the recurring question for the European session.

Over and over again Louise heard herself explaining that she was not yet sure that she would be writing anything at all; nobody seemed to hear. Mrs. Corryman also wanted to know if she played bridge, and so did several of her guests. Louise did not. Another woman advised her, whatever else she did, to wear a cummerbund, which could make all the difference to newcomers in the tropics.

Louise promised to remember, and immediately forgot about this. And a Mrs. Loder, who had been at the previous party and revealed that Louise was a journalist, asked eagerly whether she had met a distant cousin who worked for a while on the *Manchester Guardian* before becoming curator of a museum in Scotland. By improbable chance, Louise had, and the conversation turned at once to whether she had met some other relative on the *Daily Mirror*, which she had not. Nor did she know an Oxford don who was the friend of someone else present. This passion for forging meaningless links, which were then dropped, proved to be one of the outstanding characteristics of polite white conversation in Zanzibar: it made expatriates feel cozy, and closed the ranks.

At this party, as at the previous one, no men were present. Mrs. Corryman appeared to believe that there could be nothing tiring, for a woman in bed, in talking to other women, but a man might be exhausting. For some time Louise was unable to bring in the name of Falla Lufa. This she was now resolved to do: keeping quiet about him to Mrs. Corryman had brought no useful result; it would be interesting to get a representative European group reaction.

When she finally succeeded the effect was mixed and striking, but not informative. "Oh, dear old Full o' Love! I miss him. Yes, I do, honestly. We can read the vernacular; we used to take his paper. A wonderful new grievance he had, every week." . . . "My dear, he's where he belongs. If Kenya'd had the sense to clap her agitators into jail, first chance—!" . . . "That's absolutely right; you can't act too quickly, my husband says, with Mau-Mau just over those hills out there." . . . "Not *those* hills, Moira darling! You've got no sense of direction." . . . "Full o' Love" . . . "Full o' Love" . . . "Wasn't he the editor or something who criticized Captain Hilbery?" . . . "Oh, well, we've got to admit, Tom H. is a bit of a high-handed soak, though mind you, I'm devoted to our genial Tom, like everyone else." . . . "As I remember, he criticized the prison administration as well." . . . "We can't let an Arab be rude to one of our own people in his filthy little paper, and tell the civil service how to run things! Especially after he'd been rude to the President —oh, ages ago." . . . "Full o' Love" . . . "He was rather a joke." . . . "I think it's a shame, poor little man." . . . "Tiresome little man." . . . "He was a lot more serious than that. These half educated natives, of course they don't even know when they're helping Communism without meaning to."

"Now I won't have you being unkind about educated colored people!" Mrs. Corryman was playful but firm at the same time, protesting that many educated colored women were her very good friends. "We've got to influence the men through the women. I say, educate them all better, and we shan't have so many Full o' Loves." Once more Louise received the impression that Mrs. Corryman had a gift for coming to respectable conclusions by dubious reasoning. But she turned vehemently on Louise who, if she had been forgiven on one count, was now temporarily in disgrace on another.

"I advise you, though, to leave Falla Lufa alone. Leave him alone! People who don't know anything about local politics shouldn't stir things up—interfering in what they can't understand—I'll tell you what comes of that, every time. More harm than good! If you're looking for something to write about, you can write about our wonderful welfare services. And wonderful they are. I tell everyone, England cares for her dependent peoples as no other country ever has—"

"Yes, I believe that's true, but I—"

"So much of it voluntary work, too."

"I didn't come to Africa 'looking for something to write about,'" said Louise. "I came—"

"I'm relieved to hear it!" said Mrs. Corryman, as though this settled the matter of Falla Lufa. "When you're up and about again, I shall take you to meet our organizing public health committee. You'll be amazed by the scope of the work." She outlined some of the charitable activities in which Arab and Indian women also participated. In her mind, it was as if Louise were decently amazed already. "—*dear* Mrs. Downes," she finished, and passed on to another guest. Louise was forgiven again, or almost.

The coffee drinking went on. Conversationally, it was like one of those parties in childhood where, Louise remembered, someone always seemed to be saying, "And now let's have charades!" as soon as a game of Oranges-and-Lemons was well under way. But these were children with huge responsibilities, playing cheerfully with issues of empire and the disintegration of social forces, with human liberty and misery. Also, like all the children's parties of her youth, it seemed to last much too long. "Shoo!" said Mrs. Corryman laughingly at a quarter to four. "Shoo, shoo! I've got a hospital board meeting which was supposed to start at three-thirty!"

There was a chorus of protests, and a hurried making up of faces. "Nobody but you ever dreams of arranging committee meetings in the afternoons! No doubt all the rest of the board are your educated colored friends, who feel they have to attend because you do! Well, they'll wait for you."

Someone explained to Louise, "You'll find, Mrs. Downes, we're all terribly slack here, except Mrs. Corryman. It's the climate. Men—our men, I mean—pretend to be in their offices by seven-thirty in the morning. Actually they get there at eight, look at their letters and go off to breakfast till about nine-thirty. And then everything, but everything, stops for the day at half-past one. Except, of course, the native shops and Mrs. Corryman!"

"That," said someone else, with an air of telling the truth in jest, "is why she's so tremendously influential. Because we all know that she's behind everything that really gets done. Where should we be without her?"

"Nonsense," said Mrs. Corryman. "And Mrs. Downes isn't running away from here yet. Not for many days. Till her wrist's absolutely mended and the plaster's off. So she doesn't need to learn about Zanzibar's disgraceful ways for quite a while! Shoo, everybody."

When her lunch guests had gone, she said, "Such a pity I have to go out now. And then on to dinner at the Resident's. But as Dr. Asaby hasn't turned up this afternoon, he won't be along now till tomorrow. I'll certainly be in to see him with you then. What a shame we never get time for our real long chat, do we? I'm so looking forward to hearing about Cambridge nowadays! What a charming coincidence that you turned up practically with the poster! So goodbye for tonight." With her hand on the door curtain she paused to observe archly, "D'you know, when I was your age, my hair used to be just the color of yours!"—waggled a minatory finger and waited for response.

"Well, it isn't now, is it?" was the only comment which rose to Louise's embarrassed, searching mind: in any case, Mrs. Corryman's hair was the kind of dun streaked with gray into which fair hair seldom or never turns. As this was obviously not a suitable reply, Louise fell back on, "Oh."

It seemed to be adequate: Mrs. Corryman withdrew, waving at her with fluttering fingers, as though she were a baby.

11

The Ramparts of Africa

While the afternoon drowsed toward dusk the drums were working up, far off in the town, and black laughter—high-pitched and excluding—drifted in from a street which must lie just below her windows, Louise judged, from the clearness of the passing voices. She had not yet looked out to see.

She rested, but not easily, her eyes on the picture of Cambridge until its details blurred in the gloom of the room; and the sweet silliness of Aunt Rose grew farther and farther away as King's College Chapel disappeared. Because Louise's damaged wrist had begun to trouble her again, and a general feeling of malaise was creeping upon her, that sweet silliness seemed unusually precious.

Nothing sweet clung to the silliness of Mrs. Corryman. There had been something sinister, not merely exasperating, in her latest alternation of graciousness and autocracy. In defense of the things she believed to be worth while, Louise realized, she would probably not be silly at all, but capable and determined. It crossed Louise's mind that Mrs. Corryman's opposition to any investigation an outsider wished to make in Zanzibar could be formidable indeed. ". . . and then on to dinner at the Resident's." A word in an effective quarter could put obstacle after obstacle between official records and a suspect inquirer. Mrs. Corryman would certainly not balk at keeping her immobilized here, by all means short of force—so much was evident already—but beyond this, she might be quite capable, if she thought it desirable, of getting any overcurious intruder run out of the place as a troublemaker. The last idea seemed fantastic, Louise thought, as applied to herself: but then Africa was a fantastic land.

The reflection of distant lightning flickered over the ceiling: it was a moment of uncomfortable magic when anything was believable.

She dragged herself out of bed, in an attempt to break the uneasy feeling laid upon her by the drums. The glory outside took her by surprise when she walked unsteadily to one of the three long windows—stopped her breath for a second, and brought the physical sensation of the acceptance of beauty into her throat and her eyes— the tightening and prickling which come before sudden tears. None of the women who had poured in and out of the room since she arrived had paid any attention to the view, overfamiliar as it was to all of them, except to point out that the mountains hid Tanganyika, not Mau-Mau land. But there stood the great ramparts of distant, sunlit rock, forbidding even in this mellow last light—both forbidding and enticing—guarding the approach to the myth-ridden, blood-soaked hinterland of Africa.

How far away on the mainland they were she could not guess: they reared up beyond the coastal plain, and between that and Zanzibar island lay a stretch of quiet water covered in thin mist. Floating here, a native fisherman in a dugout canoe—a half-naked figure suspended between air and water, a ghost belonging to no time, no element—paddled toward no imaginable welcome among living men, infinitely lonely and touching. He might have been actually within hail, or a long way out from the shore.

Hard-edged against the dazzling blue of the sky, the clouds carried inland by the southeast monsoon piled up on the horizon, rank upon rank of majestic invaders from the sea, and from their dark bellies the lightning crackled and blazed down on the mountains, revealing distant clefts which the sun had deserted, bringing them nearer for seconds at a time; yet all the while the sun shone serenely through the upper air. These evening storms in fine weather, though they were almost of daily occurrence while the dry monsoon blew, had about them a splendor to which she never grew accustomed to the point of indifference.

Giddiness increased. Much of the heat of the day remained but she was shivering. She dragged a sheet off the bed and, muffled in it, settled herself on one of the spindly gilt chairs which she had come to dislike intensely, with her elbows on the window ledge. For relief from glory she looked down into another world, the teeming street where Bantu girls bulged out of tightly wound cloth of violent patterns, giggling in groups as they passed among the slow-moving Arabs, and the lighter, more graceful figures of the Indians. A few of the Arabs were fierce-looking long-robed men with curved knives stuck in their belts, many more were Europeanized office workers, probably from the Sultan's staff, or the nondescript products of the docks, but even they carried themselves with a swagger which was beyond the Indians; and the white men. Seen from above, Europeans showed an unimpressive boiled-ham pink wherever their limp clothes revealed their skin.

This was the hour of the day when people came out to cool themselves on the coast road, along which the big stone houses of the wealthy had been built in the busiest days of the slave trade. Mrs. Corryman had been fortunate in securing the home of the most ruthless and successful: the walls were grandly thick and insulating from the heat. As Louise leaned on the broad ledge she was almost hidden from the street, but presently she grew aware that someone was smiling up at her. Dr. Asaby was approaching.

He was ushered into the Picture Room by Toma, who went round lighting the antique Arab lamps hanging on silver chains from the ceiling. "What did I say, Mem?" was muttered in Louise's ear as Toma passed behind her chair on the way out again.

"I like this Ali Baba atmosphere!" said Dr. Asaby, thereby deftly removing himself from it. "Not good light for doctoring by, but excellent for suggesting to patients that I might be a magician."

"The patient passionately hopes you are!" Louise told him. "Please make my wrist well enough at once to let me go away."

"Where?"

"I don't know yet. Somewhere in Zanzibar. Near enough for you to keep an eye on me and see I really am all right. All I long for you to say is that I'm fit to move."

"For that," he said, "your wrist is probably good enough now. Though I have no doubt it is hurting somewhat at the moment. I suspect you are one of those medical puritans, like so many of your countrywomen, who have an unrecognized objection to taking the full amount of any pain-killing drug prescribed for them."

Louise agreed meekly: after the first dose of aspirin, having resisted temptation to take a second too soon, she had in fact taken no more at all.

"Unfortunately there is also no doubt that you have a slight temperature. I shall at once take it officially—purely for reasons of protocol!"

"Nemesis," she said. "I pretended this morning to be feeling much worse than I was."

While she was silenced by the thermometer, he launched into his excuse for visiting her at this hour, and not at either of the times suggested during his earlier visit. For over an hour he had been—"ridiculously!" he said—locked out on his own balcony. He had gone out for a breath of fresh air, the long window had blown shut behind him, and the catch had fallen into place. Although his wife was in the house his cries had been unheard, the balcony overlooking a secluded corner of the garden. He had been released, too late for the afternoon visit, only when one of his small children returned from school through this part of the grounds.

"As to tomorrow morning—" Their glances met several times, in shared enjoyment of such virtuosity, but he persisted blandly to the end of the explanation, which in this second part had something to do with his son's birthday, temporarily forgotten, coinciding with

the Sultan's move to the Summer Palace. "So you see my coming
now was unavoidable," he said, and took the thermometer out of
Louise's mouth, scarcely glancing at it in the inadequate light. "A
fellow student of mine at Oxford—he was a West Indian, we were
at Rhodes together—said this to me when we qualified, 'Remember, you and I will always need to be more scientific, when dealing
with the English or Americans, than their own doctors. Faith healing
must be left to them, it's not for us.' So, on the evidence of this"
—he waved the thermometer and then put it away—"I am afraid
that you must stay in bed for another twenty-four hours. Stay in bed
and take what is prescribed. If not, I shall increase the dose. That,
your heart could stand without difficulty, but not, I imagine, your
conscience."

Confidence flowed from him. As a doctor he probably was a
magician, she surmised. "Dr. Asaby, if I do exactly what you say,
will you do two things for me? Send a written message, when you
get home, that I've got to be left absolutely quiet for those twenty-
four hours? That I simply mustn't be allowed visitors; in fact I
oughtn't to talk at all? And then tomorrow evening I'll manage a
miraculous recovery. After that, will you make it possible for me to
get away, by insisting I'm fit to look after myself?"

"Why? What is it you want so much to do? No, that is not a
medical question; there is no need for you to answer it."

"But I don't mind." It was in fact a pleasure, restful in itself, to
talk again to someone of her own mental age, or older. "I'd like to
see if I can make what I intend to do sound sensible to you. It
probably won't. I'm not even sure that it makes sense to me."

"Then if I may suggest, dear madam, return to bed first. But
also, please, without hurry." He took a string of amber beads from
a pocket and passed them slowly, soothingly, between finger and
thumb, waiting for her to settle down and marshal her thoughts.
"This is a habit I got into at Oxford," he said. "The friend I mentioned before advised me, when I first arrived—anxious, like all
young men, to be liked—'You cannot win English approval by
behaving as the English do, because they will think that you, as an
Arab, don't do it very well. So do, and be,' he told me, 'everything
they expect of an Arab.' At once I went out into the High and
bought this at Venables—you know the shop?—and today I doubt

if I could break myself of the habit without uncomfortable effort. But I had an excellent time at Oxford."

"I'm not surprised. But glad to hear it, all the same. Even though I spent six years of my youth in the Other Place!— You know Falla Lufa?"

"I know of him, yes."

"He's a man who seems to me to have suffered injustice. That is, he may have done. I can't be sure because everyone I meet who knows anything about his case tells me something different. If he has, he's still only one man out of millions who've met it. But there comes a time in many people's lives when for their own peace of mind they've got to do something which seems to them to justify itself, and them. An action good in itself. Perhaps it's only a gesture of despair or reconciliation they make toward their own souls—supposing they have any!—by accepting responsibility for someone else, chosen almost at random. Falla Lufa was chosen for me by the chance that his name cropped up several times at moments of crisis in my own life. Now I must see what I can do for him—if there is anything I can do."

"One moment. This sense of responsibility—is it perhaps greater because if injustice has been done, it has been done by your own people to someone who is not of your own people? Oh, technically he is, of course, 'British Protected Person,' as I am. But not of your own race?"

"Yes, I think so. It's hard to say. What I know for certain is that I must try to find out what has really happened. I can't investigate from here. I can only do that if I'm living on my own. Help me to get clear of this house as soon as possible."

He shifted his beads for a few seconds in silence. Their gentle clicking merged into the background of the drums, and the thunder now dying away in the distance.

She felt bound to add, Arab courtesy being infectious, "Not that I'm anything but grateful to Mrs. Corryman for her hospitality, you understand."

"Of course, of course," he said, and their eyes met briefly. "Mrs. Corryman is indefatigable. A remarkable woman. It is indeed fortunate for humanity that we have her here in Zanzibar, where she organizes the distribution of charity to the deserving poor." There was then the slightest pause, just long enough to separate the two sentences so that no continuity need be recognized. "Has it occurred to you," he asked, "that had she remained in Lyme Regis, she would by now have been a Justice of the Peace, possibly a Children's Magistrate, probably a Prison Visitor and on the Watch Committee, or the Board of Guardians? But we are wandering from Falla Lufa. If you will let me advise you, leave him alone."

"My turn to ask, 'Why?' " Coming so soon after Mrs. Corryman's attack, his echo of her words was deeply disturbing.

"Because I think—no, regrettably, I am sure—you personally are making the mistake always made by the British as a ruling power. You pay too much attention to bodies, not enough to minds. This surprises you, coming from a doctor?"

"It does!"

"Still, it's the truth. Here and in every place where you govern alien peoples. This man's body is in prison. You might be able to free that; I cannot say. But I doubt that you could free his mind."

"And one's not worth doing without the other? Is that your view?"

"Of course. But then I am not European—in spite of Oxford. Perhaps to me it seems much less important than it does to you, whether one individual human body ought or ought not to remain in prison, if his remaining there is to the convenience of a régime which on the whole I favor. I do not know where his mind is, or if it would be freer outside."

"I can't accept that. I mean, that his mind might not be freer if his body were freed. Will you take it as a compliment, and not rudeness, if I speak very freely, as if I had known you for a long time? And say that to me, this sounds like a meaningless bit of fantasy?"

"Somewhat oriental fantasy, at that? I knew, naturally, that it would be an unacceptable idea. To you, as to practically all your people. Now I will be very frank in return—also, you understand, as a compliment? 'Love us!' you cry, to subject peoples throughout the world. 'Or at any rate be less ungrateful, and don't actually hate us! For look what we have given you in material things! And more than material things—in notions of fair play and not taking corruption for granted in high places. All this we have given you.'

(You say.) 'What's that complaint? In giving these things we have trampled on feelings? Sometimes robbing the receivers of all manly choice and dignity? Oh, dignity—! But really,' you say, 'how can anyone be so blind to self-interest? Putting pride before safety from slave raids and starvation! My good Colonist, or Mandated Subject, or British Protected Person, junior partner in the great experiment of Commonwealth, you silly coon, you' (you say), 'surely you realize that your grandfather rarely had his stabbing knife dry from human blood, and lived in constant fear of his neighbors? Also he had hookworm. While you have a nice clean job as a waiter or porter, and if you pay your taxes, bury your faeces and keep quite quiet at all times, you have reason to be afraid of nothing under British Rule. Love us!' you cry. 'Or refrain from pushing us out, after we have so carefully taught you how to improve your cattle, even importing prize breeding bulls for you from England, regardless of expense. That is surely the least you can do!' But so often nowadays, as you know, dear madam, there is—less!"

"There is, indeed! Thank you. That *was* a compliment. Why aren't you a politician instead of a doctor?"

"Why should I be? Here, where my home is, I should be expected to work against the things I admire. I am in favor of the continuance of British rule precisely as it is at present in these territories. That is why I wish so much you would think less about bodies and more about minds."

"You're in favor—"

"It is an excellent working compromise, yours the real power, ours the comforting parade of it, the show. Our Sultan is useful to you, admirable to us. A most delightful old gentleman. Rightly concerned, at his age, mainly with his soul. But at the same time, very much a realist about his position! With our highly mixed population, what governing alternative could be better? Freedom? For whom to do what? Falla Lufa is a disturber. As I have heard, not one who wishes to upset the present régime entirely—which would be regrettable but at least make sense: no, instead, he desires merely that everything should always be a little bit different from whatever it is. The true fanatic. Leave him where he is, doing the least possible harm."

"In fact 'It is expedient that one man should die for the people'? Well, not die, in this case, but suffer a living death for considerable periods, at intervals? (I can't even find out yet how long Falla Lufa has been sent to prison for, this time. His first sentence was six months, of which he served about four, I believe.)"

"It will be much longer this time, no doubt, as he has offended before. I have forgotten, myself, exactly how long he has been given. That was a quotation from your Bible, was it not?"

"Yes. I'd forgotten for the moment that you said you were a Moslem."

"Certainly it is expedient. In matters of government I also think it is frequently quite right—which is not necessarily the same, even for one like myself, a descendant of a third cousin of that Sheik Loair in whose house you are sheltering, unwillingly!"

"Is that what you are? How interesting."

"Bodies! Bodies again, not minds!" His charming smile took the sting from the words.

"Well, you must admit, Dr. Asaby, it's incongruous, you and Sheik Loair being related. And incongruous, too, that feeling as you do about British rule and our pathological desire for appreciation, you should want us to go on ruling."

"Oh, I think not. Alien rule is bound to be often exasperating. When, as here, it is essential, then yours is the easiest to put up with. You are, indeed, incomparably better at it than anyone else. Your men in Whitehall are at times so stupid, it is hard to think they are not being so on purpose. In matters touching my own experience they have been clumsy, ignorant, provocative, again and again. They have let down your men on the spot—district officers and the like—who are usually among the best men by which any country can ever have been served. I have met a number of them —patient and understanding. Devoted to the people they look after, whether these are backward tribes or a town society like ours in Zanzibar. Sometimes at the cost of their own careers, they try to soften the worst stupidities of Whitehall for their charges. No other country, I think, has ever produced so many of such men. When this supply fails, it will be time to get rid of British rule."

Louise noticed with appreciation that Dr. Asaby's command of English grew, and his sentences became less mannered, as his interest in any subject increased. Thereafter she suspected that his lapses into Arab-English were merely more of his deliberate concessions to the liking of the English for Arabs who appeared traditionally Arab. A remarkable man. Her respect for him deepened moment by moment.

"Why did you say," she asked him, "that alien rule is essential here because of the mixture of races? Haven't you a growing educated class of young men who must want to take over?"

"Why should they? When on the one hand they cannot combine with one another, because of racial prejudice, and on the other, as individuals they are at the head of nearly all departments already, running the territory? For the moment, I doubt that many want more. And I will give you one illustration of why I, myself, am in no hurry for self-government in the hands of either Arabs or Indians. Or the Africans, or the Goanese, or any other large minority! Observe, there are three hotels in Zanzibar where only whites are admitted. Who owns these hotels, and imposed the ban in the first place against all non-Europeans? Upholding it so fiercely that if I went in to see a patient, unless beforehand I had made most careful arrangements, I should risk being treated with great discourtesy? Why, in each case, a colored man. Can you think I imagine that this sort of clambering on one another's necks would go out with the British? In Oxford I met no snobbery so strong as that among my own people, though with us it is a different kind, more American in feeling, based on money and possessions. But for all that, you should not think, wherever there are no riots in the streets, everything is satisfactory."

"Physical violence or its absence—is that really all we go by, as rulers?"

"Bodies, bodies!" He nodded. "Do you imagine that a few hundred miles away, Mau-Mau *started* with slaughtering? No signs beforehand, do you suppose? No warnings which might have been taken in good time, if you had considered minds? And the resentments growing in them from frustration, from the sight of too much privilege for two few men, all of them white? Look now at the Mediterranean. Look well, while there is time! My father was in England before the First World War, when your Governor's house in Cyprus was burned down. My family came originally from Persia. Persia, to many people in England, is practically next door to Cyprus! They said to my father, then, with anxiety, 'We are afraid there may be trouble there'—You see, something had happened physically. But then nothing else was burned down for quite a while. 'Oh, Cyprus is quite all right after all,' they said happily. 'It's a relief, isn't it?' And took no account of *why* that house had been burned. You think the time to take preventive action is *after* the police whistles have begun blowing, and then it is about bodies you worry. Falla Lufa is also a mind, which can do more damage than twenty bodies in a street out of police control. Officially, twenty unruly bodies out of doors make a Disturbance, you know. And this is serious. Not like a thought. Though both are infective. Myself, I am quite content to learn—as I did accidentally, the other day— that Falla Lufa has been quietly moved out of Zanzibar, but is still in jail."

"He's been moved! Where?"

"To Harmatta jail. Just outside the Protectorate. You did not know?"

"Of course I didn't! After all, I came all the way from Europe to Zanzibar in order to see him here. If possible."

"Well, he is still not very far off. Harmatta jail is in the Carran, that strip to the north of Tanganyika."

"But I can't afford to go chasing him about the country! Even if I could get permission to see him there."

"It was inevitable he should be moved. His second prison sentence was for attacking the conduct of police officers here where he served his first term, and also the findings of the Court which sentenced him—Contempt, expressed as strongly as he could word it. (Which is very strongly, but he is not very literate.) Plainly, he could not be left in the charge of the same men whom he had held up to ridicule. That would be to deal un-Britishly by bodies. Though I am sure they would really have been quite decent to him—Zanzibar has a delightful jail."

"How do you know?"

"From spending a night there." Only a faint twitch of a smile showed that Dr. Asaby was aware of having scored. "It was before I went to Oxford. Naturally I had read about kicking off policemen's helmets on Boat-Race night, and similar activities. It occurred to me, and to two friends who were not going, that with their help I should practice. Here they are less forbearing about youthful spirits

than in your University towns. But I was quite comfortable. I believe
Harmatta is still more so—even further from the barbarities of the
white-run jails in South Africa, where 'uppity' natives have died
overnight, mysteriously, when they went in only for forgetting to
carry a work pass— Oh, yes, indeed they have! As no doubt you
know. What a versatile people you are in government! But we keep
getting away from Falla Lufa. Harmatta is the place where there was
a scandal a little while ago, but of quite a different kind. Convicts
going freely to the local town on drinking parties, though officially
to buy provisions for the warders. And hiring out their labor at their
own price. Making trouble with the wardresses in the neighboring
Women's Prison. Writing themselves tickets of leave, those who
could write. I am sorry you are disappointed by his being there—"

"Dr. Asaby, you hardly look it!"

"No? But I am. And you should take comfort in thinking that
Falla Lufa is well situated, or as well situated as his mind permits."

"Please tell me something. Later, I'll have to think seriously how
this news affects what I do. Whether I now crawl ignominiously
back to England without seeing him. But now, because of the way
you said 'uppity native'—'silly coon'—I want to know if anyone here
has ever called you, an Arab with Persian blood, either of these
things?"

"Oh, yes," he said cheerfully. "I have once been addressed as
'you fortunate coon' by Captain Tom Hilbery. He was, I admit,
considerably drunk, and off-duty, on Christmas day."

"Captain Hilbery, the police officer Falla Lufa attacked in his
paper? I must meet him, at least, as soon as I can. Now will you tell
me all you know about the Falla Lufa case, so that for once I can
get the whole thing from one person? And," she added, gravely in-
clining her head—the blow about her quarry's whereabouts made a
smile impossible to produce, for the moment—"from a person whom
I can and do trust."

"Thank you! This is still part of our bargain, I suppose? You
will do what I tell you, medically, if I give you information I think
you are just as well without? What odd jobs one must undertake
if one wishes to make English ladies sensible about staying in bed
and swallowing aspirin! Here, then, is a story which has happened, at
one time or another—or something very like it—in every British

possession where there are various colored skins. Captain Tom Hilbery is a large, able, unorthodox policeman, who drinks, occasionally too freely. (Why should he not? He is a Christian, and in any case able to retire, because he has inherited enough money to buy himself cirrhosis of the liver quite harmlessly on a family estate in his own country.)"

"So much I knew," she said. "At least, not in those terms, but I had the facts."

"Yes, it is from here on that the story is a little different from your picture of it, I imagine! I have gathered that you see an unpopular little figure—Falla Lufa—undeterred by punishment for annoying Authority accidentally, attacking a popular figure—Captain Hilbery —by telling the truth about him. And getting no support. Because everyone has rallied round the popular man?"

"This is more or less what I saw. And that's why I came."

"Captain Hilbery is capable of speaking to me offensively when drunk, as I told you. He is also capable, at all times, of being a most useful police officer. Just because he is unorthodox, not concerned with rules, or promotion, and deals with any situation by the light of his own common sense, which is considerable."

"You are remarkably fair-minded," Louise interrupted, "after being insulted by him!" Dr. Asaby looked surprised.

"I cannot be insulted by such as Captain Hilbery, excellent public servant as he is, in his own way," he said, and Louise glimpsed the enormous Arab sense of superiority which made tolerance possible, a conviction so complete that, beside it, Mrs. Corryman's racial pride dwindled into a protesting parochialism.

"Storr, his former chief, you will not meet—fortunately he has gone. He was the good white man who does so much personal harm by living up to his princples, when these are unhappily before their time, in an unenlightened society. He made friends here with colored men, mainly Africans, who were not ready for his friendship. Any Negro he employed about his house, to dig his garden or clean his car, was ruined for life in this place by being encouraged to expect an equality he would never find again, outside that house. It was not fair on a simple colored man in a mixed society. Falla Lufa was one of those dazzled by this comradeship. He should not have been, an Arab! But he was. Hilbery would think nothing of

kicking 'a coon' in the tail, rather than sending him to prison. (This
may be always wrong but is often kinder.) There was friction between the two police officers, but when Storr was shifted away, that
was not the reason for his transfer. Falla Lufa, of course, could not
accept this. So came his insult to the Resident, the Throne, and all
that has followed. When he came out, he set about avenging his
friend. It is true that everyone out here sides with Hilbery, but not
on the grounds Falla Lufa supposes. It is just that Hilbery, out of
great experience of the tropics, knows when to shut his eyes!"

"What was the reason for Storr's transfer?"

Dr. Asaby's eyes disappeared in laughter. "A very typical Zanzibar problem. You will understand it better when you get out into
the town. Storr encouraged Falla Lufa to demand in his paper
the enforcement of an early closing rule which in fact is still law here.
But no one thinks of obeying it. Hilbery always knew better than
to do anything about it, and ignores it still. It is quite unworkable
in a place where whole families live in their shops, as well as by
means of them. With babies and cooking pots among the merchan-
dise. Friends drop in for gossip, at any time of day or night—you
have noticed from here, the drums never quite cease? If a friend
wants to purchase something while chattering, naturally such a
home is open to trade for twenty-four hours a day. To interfere
with the inevitable, on principle, is to become an intolerable nuisance."

"And it was as nuisances that first Storr, and then Falla Lufa,
were pushed out of the way?"

"Exactly," said Dr. Asaby with satisfaction. "Storr was an insufferable, upright man. Hilbery is neither. Or insufferable only when
he has overindulged. Also Storr, I am told, despite Oxford, my ear
is not quite sensitive enough to detect the difference—had a slight
cockney accent, and Hilbery has not. This actually kept Storr in the
superior position quite a while longer than he would have enjoyed
it without that defect."

"Did it? How astonishing. In a British Protectorate. Why?"

"Because, it was explained to me very seriously, everyone in the
white community was afraid, if Storr got pushed out of here into a
less attractive situation in the Colonial Police Service (which is what
happened) everyone else would say it was due to prejudice and

his not being a gentleman. Whereas in fact it was due to his being
such a nuisance. He was a nuisance through stupidity. Falla Lufa
is a disruptive one. Let him hug his chains in peace! If I—"

There was the sound of Mrs. Corryman's voice, shouting for
Toma, downstairs. Dr. Asaby leaped to his feet and began on an
explanation of an interesting surgical case which he should have
been attending some while ago. Louise shook his arm with her
sound hand. "Never mind why, Dr. Asaby, just go! But please, please
send that message about absolute quiet. No entertaining. I was
terribly sick last night after acting as assistant hostess for hours."

"Very well." He walked cat-like to the doorway and stood listening. Mrs. Corryman had only come in to fetch something on her
way to dinner, and did not visit the Picture Room. They heard
her, still calling directions, hurry along the passage to her own room
and close the door. Dr. Asaby sat down again, now frankly waiting
until she should have left the house in order to make his escape
unseen. They spoke in intimate, soft tones.

"What do you think of Karel van Epp?" Louise was moved to
ask, and was annoyed with herself for being so anxious to hear his
answer. She made herself add, casually, "I met him quite a long
time ago in England, and then by chance again this year in Holland."

"I have much respect for him as a scientist. He is doing valuable
work for Zanzibar."

"That sounds as if you don't like him as a man?"

"You are right."

"Why? Is it because of Cochi?" She was astounded to hear her
voice asking that.

"What do you know of Cochi? She is a relation of my wife's," he
said stiffly.

"I didn't know. I'm sorry I asked that, of course."

"How well do you know van Epp?"

"I've had two meals with him," she said, wondering that this
should really be the extent of their acquaintance. "Two meals with
an interval of years in between. One was a College lunch at which
I happened to be put next to him. And the other was dinner before
a comic circus when we ran across one another again by accident,
as I've said. In Walcheren Island. That's all."

"Yet you know about Cochi." She could feel his eyes boring into her mind as she looked away, exasperated to find herself coloring: he would not fail to notice that. "An imprudent, in some ways stupid girl," he said. "Her emotions are stronger than her reason. Unlikely, she is the responsibility of my family: particularly myself as the head of that family. Just as—you will have gathered from our talk about Falla Lufa—I do not share the modern weakness for believing the ruled are always right and the rulers always wrong (a peculiarly Western form of masochism!), so I cannot share the idea that the emotions of one person should be placed above the interests of a group to which that person belongs. In this case, a whole family. Therefore my sympathy and approval lie neither with Cochi nor with the man who has encouraged her to disregard all wishes but her own—and his. Nevertheless, the situations produced by emotions of this kind have to be reckoned with. Dear madam, if I may advise you again—though I doubt that you will take my advice about this any more willingly than that about Falla Lufa"—by now he had fully recovered the distant urbanity of their first meeting—"when you reach the place in Zanzibar where you will be, as you say, entirely on your own, I suggest that you should avoid sitting in the evenings with your back to a window, or door, with the light on the other side of you; or in any position where you can be seen more clearly than you can see. I should take quite a lot of care to avoid that, if I were you."

She stared at him. It seemed impossible, even by so much as asking him, "Are you serious?" to accept the idea that he might be.

As if answering the unspoken question, he said, "Please accept that I am wholly serious. I take it that you are the person whose existence is at least implied by the letter which my wife's niece received two days ago?"

"What letter?"

"From van Epp. Preparing her for—breaking to her, rather a change of attitude on his part. A stupid girl only in some ways, she is quite capable of realizing—as I did—that there was some obvious urgency prompting him to write ahead of his own return. These things are so much easier to manage by word of mouth. Presumably the reason was just arriving, or had already arrived, in Zanzibar. You are that reason, aren't you?"

She did not answer his question: what was the use? He knew. She wondered instead if he could hear her heart beating, very loudly; but was not sure herself if it were with pleasure or fear.

He said, "If you are thinking, 'No one else can know,' that, I assure you, is because you have been only forty-eight hours in this place! Now, if I fail to look in tomorrow evening, to note the miraculous recovery you promise, I should like you to come and show it to me at my surgery, when you can. Goodbye."

Mrs. Corryman had gone, in a crescendo of shouted instructions ending in a bang of the great outer door. Bowing himself from the room, Dr. Asaby ran lightly as a boy down the stairs.

The drums, and the laughter which shut Louise out of the African world waiting beyond the windows took over the stillness and emptiness of the room.

12

The Flitting

Morning and evening in Zanzibar rarely seemed to belong to the same day, they were so far apart in mood. Morning was relatively sane.

Dr. Asaby had been exaggerating for effect, if not exactly joking, Louise told herself twelve hours after his visit, when Toma wakened her by bringing in her breakfast. But even in the reasonable early morning light she knew that by dusk she would believe again, with a quickened heart, that Dr. Asaby had indeed meant, "I am entirely serious," when he said it. She must try to see him as soon as possible where they could talk freely, and get him to be more explicit; how did he envisage danger? Against precisely what means of attack should she be on guard? But she realized beforehand that trying to

142

pin down to a definite statement this subtle, alien mind would be extremely difficult, probably impossible if Dr. Asaby were not inclined to elaborate.

Whatever message about her health he sent to Mrs. Corryman proved remarkably effective. Toma pulled-to the shutters over all three windows when he came to take away her tray, leaving only a splinter of light between one pair: to Louise's protest that he was overdoing things, he replied firmly that this was by the Mem's orders.

All the morning, Louise was left to herself in a deep green gloom, as though her room were at the bottom of the sea, except for one interruption when Mrs. Corryman jingled in: she wore many bracelets which rang like bit harness. "What do you think, poor Colonel Callendar— Oh, bother," she said. "What a nuisance you mustn't talk! Here's something for you to mend. I've looked through your stockings: no holes there." She put down a reel of cotton with a needle stuck in it, and one of Louise's vests with a shoulder strap which would be the safer for a stitch or two.

She was about to jingle out again when Louise, feeling audacious, said, "Oh, Mrs. Corryman, if Dr. Asaby says I'm fit to leave here tomorrow—and I'm pretty sure he will—I really do want to go, you know. It's not that—"

"Fiddlesticks, dear, fiddlesticks." The chill in Mrs. Corryman's voice belied the warmth of the words. "Now I'm not having any more of that."

After this only Toma came near her, stepping soft-footed with her lunch tray, a local paper and a postcard, which he took to the window. "You permit, Mem?" he asked courteously, as though she were the person who had ordered the darkening of her room, before he opened the shutters enough to let him read it comfortably. "What does it mean"—he spelled out the foreign words carefully—" 'Goud-blond haar is mooi'?"

She sat up in bed. "What's that?"

"First it says, 'Just remembered what one species of parakeet says in Pemba.' Then"—he spelt out the words again—"Then, 'I always knew they spoke Dutch, but not how right they were.' Then nothing more. What is 'Goud-blond haar is mooi'?"

" 'Fair hair is pretty,' I think," said Louise weakly, aware that she ought to reply, "Really, this is no concern of yours!" However did Toma get on with Mrs. Corryman? Perhaps the mistress of the house had a human side which her guest had not yet seen.

In the elation of knowing that Karel van Epp had written again, she asked, "What do you think the parakeets say, Toma?"—half hoping he would tell her they spoke in ki-Swahili or Arabic. "Aren't there any words their calls suggest to you, in any language?"

He handed over the card, with a disdainful shrug: "I cannot imagine an Arab troubling to think what a bird might say! Mem, my wife is back. I come to tip you the wink, we go tonight. Two rooms in the Stone Town are taken in your name."

Apprehension leaped at her throat. She made herself ask, "How much rent do I have to pay?" as though this were the first thought in her mind.

"Not much, as I promised you. One pound a week, and the place is now taken for a week." (Later, she discovered that this was well above the current price: though rooms were scarce, when available they were very inexpensive in the Stone Town.) "These rooms are beside the shop of a cousin of my mother-in-law," he said. "So I come to look after you there. As otherwise you would be often lost, at first. It is a confusing part of Zanzibar."

"But, Toma, you can't. I only wish you could!" She would be far less frightened of the move if she could have beside her some-one who was not altogether strange to her, in the maze of the Arab quarter which she had just glimpsed, on the way to her encounter with the homali cart. "But you see, I can hardly afford to keep my-self. I can't possibly pay anyone to look after me."

"You do not pay me. I come only for a day or so. Till your hand is unwrapped. I tell Mem, now my wife is back, I send my oldest nephew in my place." He raised his voice—Mrs. Corryman was calling from along the passage. "Coming, Mem. And I am *not* disturbing this other Mem with my talk." As he went out, his hand rose again to his mouth to hide the absence of a smile.

Through the long, dim hours of the afternoon Louise lay and worried, tried to stop herself from worrying by working up pro-fessional interest in the format of the local paper, found that she was straining her eyes in the filtered light without taking in what she was looking at, and so gave herself up to worrying again in idleness. She had longed to get away on her own, but even before the talk with Dr. Asaby the prospect of living alone in the Stone Town had been alarming, though not alarming enough, however, to affect her resolution. She would be among the crooked alleys winding between listening walls, part of a squalid, raucous world teeming with unknown life. But now her nerve was shaken. She had less than her usual confidence that she could manage whatever came her way, or endure what she could not manage.

And apart from physical apprehension there was the growing fear that by this whole effort, this quest for justice for one man, she was merely making a fool of herself. If so, after a straight warning from someone as intelligent as Dr. Asaby, what a really remarkable fool she was going to look in her own eyes if she persisted! (To someone like herself, these were really the only eyes whose judgment mattered in the long run.) Listening to him, although she argued against his standards of judgment, she had become less and less convinced that there was anything she could do for Falla Lufa. Even if there were, it might be better left undone. "Leave him alone"—perhaps they were both right, for their different reasons, Mrs. Corryman as well as Dr. Asaby.

For the first time since Louise had made the gesture of throwing aside her job (and a more fatuous, embarrassing gesture seemed hard to imagine, in this dispiriting light) she found herself missing with absurd intensity the racket and stimulation of the office in London. Ten minutes in the reporters' room would have seemed to her delightful. Typewriters, Fleet Street gossip and telephones took on a nostalgic charm, against the everlasting soft pulse of drums, and laughter in which she had no part. Even the jokes of her colleagues became charming in retrospect; quick, allusive, and much wittier than they had sounded at the time—"Along the sky the line of the Downes—" Excellent. How could she have thought it a typical sample of Einarsen's silly facetiousness?

There was nothing to prevent her from taking the next available boat home! Once this idea had pushed its way to the front of her mind, it would not be pushed back again, to that part of consciousness where things known but not considered have a dim, separate existence of their own.

The only provident action she had taken before sailing for Africa had been to buy herself an undated return ticket, in order that she might feel free to spend, in Zanzibar, everything she had in hand. Just under twenty pounds remained, with which to meet all the emergencies of an indefinite stay, apart from the small monthly retainer checks, the first of which was just about due. But the stay need not be indefinite! She would get out of this house, certainly; but nothing, not even courtesy to Toma, could force her to stay for more than a night or two in the rooms he had found. The idea of retreat was now like a small snake, unpleasant but lively and joyful, wriggling about in her mind.

Once it was there, other ideas insinuated themselves alongside. Her editor would be delighted to see her back, accepting without further interest that she had recovered from a minor nervous breakdown—he was well used to this trouble among the more valuable members of his staff. The present assistant, ex-feature, editor, a brilliant Far Eastern correspondent in his day, had always had a serious collapse whenever the Concert of Asia quieted down sufficiently; he was absolutely reliable during crises. Louise began to imagine herself greeting acquaintances in London: it might be policy to force an interview with the assistant editor, and see if he could be made friendly again, after all this time.

Toma's wife came tearfully into the room, bringing not all Louise's belongings but an armful of clothes which she had evidently picked out herself as suitable escape kit: it included the one elaborate cocktail dress Louise had brought with her. Lalla knew almost no English, so that Louise could not discover from her what was the matter; she might be distressed at the thought of helping in this defiance of Mrs. Corryman's wishes; perhaps Toma had bullied or beaten her into complicity. But she cheered herself up by giving Louise a pantomime of how the escape was to be made; language was unnecessary for such a gifted mimic.

From about six o'clock there would be a cocktail party going on downstairs—the cook demonstrated the time on Louise's watch, and thereafter became a whole cocktail party by herself, making high-spirited noises under her breath. Toma would slip away from his duties and come to fetch Louise: his wife evidently considered him a fine figure of a man, for she grew dignified and important-looking when she became Toma. Louise was to steal downstairs with him, wearing her elegant dress; moving about on tiptoe, Lalla smoked her middle finger nonchalantly, swishing her hips around as Louise, in a rehearsal of what was to be done, supposing that by mischance Mrs. Corryman or any of the guests caught her on the way out. This was the point of the dress. First, saying "Wah-wah-wah," with appropriate gestures, Lalla was the trapped Louise explaining that she felt so much better, she had come down to join the party as a surprise; and then, with upraised hands, astonishment turning to pleasure, she was the hostess crying, "Wah-wah-wah-wah? Wah-W*ah!*"—"Oh, splendid. Now isn't this fun? First you must have a drink! And then I want you to meet—" She was all hostesses, all guests, willing and reluctant, the thinker and the thought. It was amazing how the rowdy imbecilities of a European cocktail party —the late arrival still sober, while others were further ahead in jollity—could all be conveyed by a babble of "Wahs."

After a few minutes' chat, Lalla conveyed, Louise was to watch for her opportunity to disappear from the gathering and join Toma waiting in the street, while the party wah-wah'ed on behind her, unsuspecting. But with any luck she would not be caught, with the conviviality at its height. Laughing helplessly despite her worries, Louise wondered how many white hostesses with Arab servants guessed at the perfection with which their mannerisms and those of their friends, exaggerated by alcohol, could be reproduced in the kitchen, where the staff, if Moslem, drank nothing but water, and looked on at those social antics with a keen eye, unclouded by sympathy. It was nice not to have Toma about; Louise could snort without reproof.

The cook dressed her in readiness, none too gently. She had brought no means of keeping up Louise's stockings, and no slip to go under the semitransparent dress, but having little talent for wordless communication herself, Louise decided to accept this and do what she could for herself later.

The fat little Arab woman forcibly pushed her down in the bed again as soon as the dress was fastened, spreading out the skirt carefully before covering Louise to the chin with the sheet. Louise got up as soon as Lalla had gone, to improvise garters with balls of newspaper twisted into the back of her stocking-tops. She made a petticoat, passable so long as she remembered to take small strides, by stitching a towel on to her vest: the needle and thread with which Mrs. Corryman had fobbed off her request for her suitcases came in useful after all. She must remember to see that Toma returned the towel in due course.

Toma's urgent whisper, "Come, Mem," sounded from behind her while she was watching, through the shutter slit, dusk encircling the ramparts of Africa, crowned once more by their private thunderstorm. Louise had been trying out her strength in walking, and was pleased to find that, notwithstanding anxiety, the day's unbroken rest had worked as she had promised Dr. Asaby that it should: she was no longer giddy when she stood up.

Toma did not wait for her to follow, but ran back to taking wraps and handling trays of drink on the floor below, leaving her to make her way stealthily down the stairs toward the noise. Silent movement was really unnecessary: guest after guest had arrived during the past hour, greeting one another with cheerful hails, and the hubbub of talk had reached its top pitch: but there was such a feeling of guilt in creeping like a thief out of a house where—on the surface at least—she had been given kindness and hospitality, that Louise tiptoed with all the caution which Lalla had imitated, and jumped with nerves at every fresh sound. No lamps had been lit on the stairs leading up to the bedrooms, and leaning over the banisters near the last bend, invisible in the darkness, Louise stood for a while having what was really a Moslem's eye view of a cocktail party. A few feet below her, people with glasses in their hands, in various stages of elevation, passed along the brightly lit passage between the two rooms into which the party had spread, chattering vehemently about very little, using the full power of their voices in order to be heard at all.

At the foot of the stairs, Toma stood with his back to her, watching for the moment when the passage should be clear for long enough to let her cross, unseen, the only obviously difficult stretch on her way out—the five or six yards between the bottom of the stairs on which she stood, and the head of another stairway leading down to the front door. Though he could not have heard her coming, he took for granted that she was watching him from close above; shifting his tray to one hand, he kept the other behind him with one finger raised, warning her to wait.

Someone momentarily distracted his attention by asking for a particular drink not on his tray. A vague woman with an affected manner, whom Louise remembered from the coffee session, edged past him, demanding loudly, "Now where's the Little Girls' room? I forget," and started up the stairs toward Louise. With an effort Louise remained quite still, knowing that anyone peering upward from light into darkness would only see her if she moved; and Toma, grandly unhurried, beckoned one of the other servants, directed him to get the drink required, respectfully attracted the attention of the vague woman as she paused on the edge of darkness, and shepherded her safely down toward a cloakroom on the party floor.

Mrs. Corryman bustled back and forth, in her most affable mood, making Louise feel guiltier yet. People did not behave like this in Lyme Regis: by its standards her action, as a guest, became not only disgraceful but perhaps wounding to her hostess, which was a deterrent thought. There was that uncomfortable theory about the pin which penetrated an elephant's hide hurting much more than an ordinary pin prick.

"Now, Mem, quickly. I meet you outside." Toma disappeared in one direction, Louise sped the other way, as he had indicated, running with tiny steps for the towel's sake. She reached the top of the lower staircase but stopped there, face to face with a couple arriving late for the party. The woman claimed her enthusiastically: "Oh, Mrs. Downes, you're not leaving yet! And I've been promising my husband for two days he should get you to tell him that wonderful story you gave us about Lord Beaverbrook!"

"Lord Beaverbrook?" Louise had not met this particular Press peer. She slipped, sideways, between the newcomers and the wall, round the angle of the stairs with the passage, and so out of sight from the party rooms. From the point of view of looking silly if captured by Mrs. Corryman, this was the worst point of all. Wearing her party dress would be no excuse for being on this staircase, leading only to the main door.

"Yes, and the wife of the American politician!"

"Oh, that." (No association stirred.) "No, I've repented about repeating that story; it's too malicious. Please forget it."

"But you made him out to have a heart of gold."

"Did I?" said Louise, in no way reassured about her tongue's

activities in her mind's absence. "But hardly the politician, would
you say? No, I really feel I oughtn't to pass on what's only hearsay
after all, and probably quite untrue. Anyway, I'm afraid I mustn't
stay now, because I've got someone waiting for me—" She hurried
on down, still remembering to avoid strain on the towel.

"Where are you living now?" the woman called after her. "You
must come and see us . . . dinner."

Louise put a few more steps between them. "Awfully kind . . .
so nice . . . delighted . . . Wah-wah-wah." The noise from above
made first-rate cover: they smiled and waved. Someone else was just
being let in by the watchman who sat there, all night long: the
huge, nail-studded door swung open. She was out.

13

Cochi

In the shadows Toma waited beside another figure, below whose
sleeves dangled Louise's suitcases. This man was a white-clad
ghost without face, hands or feet, where his skin—much darker than
Toma's—blended with the night.

"Go with him, Mem. I come later." Toma melted away toward
the back entrance of the house, and the ghost moved off so fast
that Louise was forced almost to run to keep up with him. In fifty
paces they were swallowed up by the world she dreaded: narrow,
crowded side streets led one out of another, alternately bright with
naphtha flares in front of the caverns which were shops combined
with dwellings, and patched with gloom for long stretches, in which
she stumbled over the uneven ground. Here she could smell the

life around her more easily than see it. The drums were rollicking. Over the entrances of almost all the booths were loud-speakers, some relaying Arab music, some Indian, and a few, European dance tunes.

In the lit places, heads turned and eyes stared at her, neither hostile nor friendly, but curious. In the dark, the going was so difficult, half blinded as she was with the contrast from the light, that twice she called anxiously to her guide to go slower; he took no notice. Alley after alley appeared to end abruptly in a wall, but always, diving down a sharp-angled passageway, they came out again among more booths and shops, more tumble-down dwellings with families squatting near the entrance. Children were everywhere, underfoot. An old woman, defecating by one of the rare lampposts, shouted something at her. Rocking in a chair alongside, in the corner of an archway, an old man with a bandaged head cackled with glee. A beggar on a trolley propelled himself along by his hands and clutched at her foot, pointing to his useless, trailing legs. Where a knot of men were bargaining round a stationary homali cart, indifferent to her efforts to get by without pushing them, she lost sight of her guide, who had forced his way through; by the time she managed to get round the obstruction which blocked the tiny street, he had disappeared. Frightened, she stood still in one of the better-lit stretches of an alley where the houses almost met overhead. All round, the din was prodigious. Yet miserable as it looked, this must be a more prosperous neighbourhood than the part through which she had just passed: the frontage of the shops was wider, colored cloth hung in festoons outside; it was probably a dyers' or weavers' quarter. An acrid, chemical smell mingled with the hot smell of humanity.

Children gathered round her, standing in a ring, eying her warily, imitating the way she carried her strapped-up arm across her chest, pretending that they too had scarves tied round their necks to support one hand. At the moment some detached part of her brain, an idiotic-secretary cell, produced the association which had escaped her on the stairs of Mrs. Corryman's house. The anecdote about the politician's wife was true, but not when grafted onto Lord Beaverbrook. It had happened in Cambridge, to a don friend of her uncle's.

Then I am less frightened than I think I am, her mind told her stoutly, yet knew at the same time that this was not so; the recollection was in every way an irrelevancy. What should she do if the guide failed to return? Attempt to ask her way back to Mrs. Corryman's house, and face the need to explain what she had tried to do? But whom should she ask?

She went through a fumbling pantomime, pretending that what she was stopping for was to get her empty cigarette-case out of her bag, and open the matchbox which happened to be still with it, but her serviceable hand was trembling too much to let her manage the matches: she spilled the few that were left, and felt unable to bend down and retrieve any of them from the filth of the street. She got the case back into the bag with difficulty, and stared at the children, as if keeping her watchers at bay by this means. A bigger boy, of about twelve she judged, appeared to be the leader. He pointed. She looked down. Part of the towel-petticoat had ripped free and hung below the side of her flimsy skirt. It looked ridiculous. With a great effort she made herself laugh. It was not a convincing laugh but it set off the children: they doubled up and then giggled, on and on, coming closer, losing their awe of a stranger. Suddenly the stinking street, even the terrible African night all round, infinitely capacious of evil, felt a little less menacing to her. For the moment, though probably only for a moment, the children were well disposed toward her. She had mastered her trembling by the time the guide came back, without her suitcases.

"Where are they?" she asked. He did not answer.

He was an ill-favored, angry-looking man, an Arab with evident African blood in him. He jerked his head at her to come on, to follow him. Not moving, she asked again, "Where are they? My cases?" feeling that she must keep the initiative if she could. He shook his head and she gave in, frightened once more. Never, during the risky moments in the riots in Tripoli, had she been quite so much afraid: she assured herself that the weakening effect of her accident was to blame.

The guide led her at the same unslackening pace for a few hundred yards, back along the way they had come, to the archway where the old man with the bandaged head sat and rocked; the children followed in a body. They went through the arch and across a courtyard. The hurrying man pulled aside a curtain over a doorway: here was a small, lit room, bare except for a lamp and a bed made of thongs stretched over a low wooden frame, and her suitcases standing beside the bed. He held out his hand for payment. Hesitating, she opened her handbag and took out two shillings. He pocketed the coins and held out his hand for more.

"No," she said, making signs that he should now go away. He turned truculent, shaking his open palm under her nose, protesting, not in English, though the meaning of his words was clear enough. She turned away, arranging her suitcases on the bed as though they were pillows, for something to do, and then looked round, feigning angry surprise at finding him still there. She took a bold, threatening step toward him, wondering what her next action could be if he stood his ground; but, grumbling, he backed out of the doorway, leaving the curtain half-drawn behind him as he went away. She pulled it across the doorway again: there were no windows to the room, only another doorway, leading to a passage. The children pulled the curtain back again, tittering. They bunched in the doorway, craning their heads into the room. They were as capricious as birds, and as predatory. They were no longer well disposed toward her. They had seen her bullied. She was alone, and injured in some way. They had seen her take money out of her handbag. Their eyes, unwinking, glistening, were fixed on the bag.

Hoping they might grow bored if she were quiet, and they did not see the bag, she lay down on the bed, propped up uncomfortably on the suitcases, her handbag tucked under her elbow, on the side of her body further from the doorway. Could they smell fear, she wondered, as animals did? Or sense it somehow?

They scuffled, pushing one another over the threshold, and then scrabbling back when she shouted at them menacingly. Menacing them with what? If they rushed her, there was nothing that she could do against them, one-armed: they were too many. More daring than the rest, one boy threw at the bed a piece of dried ordure from the courtyard. It hit her shoulder; she brushed off the fragments with an air of indifference. A very small, very dead bird followed, and then more dirt. About half a dozen of the children were by now inside the room, pushed on by those behind, who threw blindly, over their heads. A few pebbles rattled on the wall

beyond her. The lad who seemed to be directing the persecution
was working round toward the other side of the bed, and the bag. It
held all the money she owned, as well as her passport, ticket home
and other papers. She knew now that it would have been safer to
hide it in one of the suitcases. She called the boy to her peremp-
torily, trusting that he talked English.

"In five minutes, when my servant comes, I will tell him to reward you if you clear these children out of my room. They disturb
me. I wish to sleep. You understand what I say?"

"Yes," he said sullenly, measuring with his eye the distance to
the bag under her arm. "What will you give me?"

"Sixpence. But not I. My servant. For whom I am waiting."

"Give it to me now."

"You saw I could not give that other man more money because I
have no more coins with me. Not until my servant comes and brings
them to me. Only that paper money called checks, no good to anyone else, because I have to sign each one before it can be used."

"When your servant comes, you will tell him to give me a shilling?"

"Sixpence."

"Ninepence?"

"Sixpence."

He hesitated.

"But if the others are still here when he comes," she said, "I shall
tell him to reward you in quite a different way!"

He half grinned, but then his eye fell again on the bag. "Why
have you no more money with you?"

"Because sensible people keep it in a bank till they need it."

"In that bank you have plenty money? You could give me more
than two shillings?" He was still moving slowly, as if aimlessly,
toward the other side of the bed.

"I don't answer any more questions. You answer mine! What's
your name?"

"Ibrem bin Dowd," he said reluctantly. Another small shower
of pebbles was thrown over the heads of the children in the doorway.
One hit her on the leg but she did not move: one hit him and he
shouted angrily, not in English.

"Well, Ibrem—" She noticed with thankfulness that her voice

was steady. "Apart from what my servant will do, if your followers have not gone by the time I count ten, I shall give a particular description of you to my friend the police officer, Captain Hilbery. You know him?"

The boy nodded, looking worried. The introduction of Hilbery's name had been an even greater inspiration than conveying to the guides at the docks that she had been in Zanzibar for years. Also it was plain, from the way he turned and surveyed his companions truculently, that up till now Ibrem had not thought of them as "his" followers, and the idea was attractive.

"One—two—three—"

He threw her a grin, and fell with flailing hands and feet upon the other children.

When Toma arrived, immediately returning to her a shilling which he had taken off the angry ghost—"You gave him twice too much, Mem. It is bad for such men"—there had been peace in the room for some time, only Ibrem remaining, as a guard. It was difficult to make Toma let the boy have this shilling, but Louise insisted: she was not going to open her bag again in his sight to look for a possible sixpence lurking somewhere in it.

"Only half is for you now, Ibrem, you understand?" she said. "The other is payment for what I shall tell you to do for me tomorrow, if you turn up here in the morning. If you don't turn up, there will be no more sixpences, ever."

Toma gave Ibrem a hefty kick as well, to send him on his way, on principle, but thereafter Ibrem was Louise's messenger or guide whenever she needed service of this kind. The tariff was always sixpence, and Ibrem always bargained, in vain.

Toma cleared the loose dirt out of the room, with a brush which he had brought along with his own baggage; two cooking pots, a brazier and a clean turban scarf. "You do not sleep here, Mem. This room is for me, and we cook in it. Here is for you." He took her along the passage and through the back of a cloth shop, or booth, reeking with the sharp dye smell she had met outside, into a room almost as bare as the first, except that certain unlikely Edwardian knickknacks had come to rest in it. There were two china vases of the sort to be won at English fairs playing Houpla, a commode disguised as an ornamental chair—something Louise had read about but had never

seen before—and on the wall a framed, fly-spotted picture called
"So Big!" showing a roguish little girl standing on a thick volume
in order to be as tall as a sitting St. Bernard dog wearing a resigned expression.

For no one of Louise's generation, race and class—or almost no
one—was it possible to look with detached, critical, adult eyes at this
distorted artistic atrocity. Obviously the little girl could not be so
small, nor the dog, even a St. Bernard, quite so sentimental, but a
copy of this work had either hung in the nursery, or been admired
in the nursery of friends. It was firelight flickering on the ceiling,
observed from bed; it was Mummy, or Nanny, allowing cake before
bread-and-butter, on special occasions; it was security. To Louise, it
meant all this, far more than the poster of Cambridge; "So Big!"
had hung on the landing at the top of the nursery stairs, in her
parents' house. (It would never have been tolerated at the Farrants': Dorothy's taste was always precocious.) At the moment, finding it was nearly as comforting as a copy of "Lou Flap" would have
been.

Whether or not "So Big!" really affected her mood, Louise slept
all night with the corner of a filthy counterpane tucked round her
waist, to keep off the dawn chill, even more deeply than she had
slept at Mrs. Corryman's, despite the unremitting clamor of the
Zanzibar night.

She dreamed, just before she awoke, of being in the Master's
house: Dorothy was coming upstairs, determined to make her listen
to something she did not want to hear. Quite a long, elaborate sequence preceded this point in the dream, but the whole thing must
have passed in a second or two, in no more than the time taken by
someone to repeat what had set Louise dreaming that she did not
want to listen—"I am Cochi. Why are you here?"

Louise opened her eyes as the girl seated herself with a show of
assurance on the foot of the bed.

"Come to that, why are you here?" Through Louise's mind shot
the suspicion that Toma was not as trustworthy as he seemed: he
must have been bribed by Cochi for the girl to know so soon
where she could be found.

"I came through the shop—I know these people. I wanted to see
what you looked like—I meant to catch you asleep."

The girl was magnificent to look at, Louise had expected that: in feature Cochi strongly resembled the pale-gold girl in the Javanese restaurant at Middelburg, but she was handsomer, more vivid and vital, with slanting eyes and a thin, curved Arab mouth: she was darker too, unusually dark for an Indian-Arab mixture, with a wonderful, warm, glowing skin. What Louise for some reason had not expected was that Cochi would be so young, surely not more than seventeen; and so appealing because she was young and frightened, under the effrontery which was only partly natural. "You're not very pretty, are you?" the girl said.

Louise repeated the words she had used to the Polish woman journalist, "Not very. Just rather," and then added with truth, "Really not at all compared with you."

"I suppose someone must have thought you were, once. Quite a long time ago, I expect!—I can see the ring on your hand. You're married."

"I was, at one time. What do you want?"

"I want you to stay out of our world, Karel's and mine," she said stonily. "Get back where you belong." Then the stoniness broke. "Get out, get out!" she cried, beating her clenched hands on her knees. "You didn't need to come here."

"What makes you think it matters where I go?"

"He has written—" Louise could not hear the words through the storm of angry tears. Something about . . . over . . . to prepare . . . money. Suddenly the girl threw her head back, the tears stopping. "What fools they are, men, eh? To write that now!"

Some wry part of Louise's mind was also thinking that it was an unfortunate time Karel van Epp had chosen. "But he doesn't say this has anything to do with me?" she said. "He can't have told you that?"

"No. He doesn't say that. It was Said—you know him as Dr. Asaby—he told me Karel was in love with you. And you with him. European-fashion. In love! In love!" She was a creature of violently quick changes of mood: there was nothing but venom and self-torture now in her words, no reaching out to the gentleness in Louise for sympathy. "In love with you. A blown-out candle. A guttered candle of a woman. That's you. Someone else hasn't cared for you very long, has he? Maybe Karel won't either. In love!"

Louise understood what Dr. Asaby had meant in warning her: here was someone—in control a child: in feeling a woman—who would have a child's ruthlessness in trying to keep whatever she wanted; who would defeat her own ends, inevitably, though never counting beforehand the cost of any inclination she felt. In the distress of this interview, Louise's mind turned for escape to a small, unimportant bewilderment.

"When did Dr. Asaby tell you—you say, it was *Dr. Asaby?*—that I was the reason for that letter?"

"Last night. After he'd seen you. What does that matter? It's true, isn't it?"

"Last night. After he'd seen me!" She had not only liked Dr. Asaby, but trusted him. Had, in fact, told him so.

"Why not? He's the head of my family, isn't he? I've a right to consult him, I suppose! I came over from Pemba when that letter arrived— Oh, you're afraid to go to his surgery, to his house, are you, in case I'm there? I'm going back to Pemba, I can tell you. Going back to Karel's house, you understand."

"Listen. I'm making no promises," Louise said slowly. "No promises at all, remember. But it's quite likely I shan't be here long. I probably shan't be still in Zanzibar when Karel gets back." Pity stirred in her at the look of dazzling, incredible hope she was vouchsafed. Could the girl not realize that if Karel van Epp had decided to break with her, had told her that the affair was over, he was unlikely to change his mind because of anything Louise did now?

Tears poured again unheeded down the arrogant, touching young face. "You've got so much on your side!" Cochi said. "You don't even need to be pretty. You're strong. You belong to his world. You're white. Do you know what it's like, being shut out— Of course you don't!" Jumbled up, sometimes with resentment of all Europeans, sometimes with anger against her own family, came the story of being sent to school in England, and meeting there no color prejudice at all. "You're so stupid, so funny. Stupid, that's it. Back in your own country you don't mind. No one there made me feel it mattered, being darker. No one told me what it would be like when I came out here again. I was only small when I left here, and no

one minded then what I was. What was the sense of educating me
not to know? Letting me think I was as good as anyone else. When
here you're cruel. Why is it different here? You're so cruel! But he's
not. Because he's not English. He doesn't mind, anywhere."

Toma brought them both a cup of tea, in the midst of this out-
pouring. He appeared unaware of the charged emotional atmosphere, and fussed because Louise usually took sugar but he had forgotten to bring this with him. Cochi, lordly again, ordered him out
curtly.

She seized Louise's upstrapped hand and bowed over it her wild
sweet witch's head. "Don't take him away from me! You won't do
that, will you? Don't take him away."

"Cochi, no woman can ever take a man away from another
woman. Not unless he's ready to go!" Was that wholly true, she wondered? Like all such simplifications of human relationships—"I love
you because I am I, not because you are you!"—it had truth in it,
but truth that could occasionally be altered by circumstances. Even
if they had not met again in Holland, she and Karel van Epp, he
would probably have tired eventually of this seductive, ill-balanced
girl. Of what merely beautiful woman did a man not tire in time?
Or of what woman of any kind? But the bonds of the mind could
hold when those of the flesh weakened. The girl might have kept
her hold a while longer, though, if Louise had not offered a different kind of companionship. Louise knew, out of her own experience,
what one more occasion of love could mean, to a lover: she had
thought it worth everything earth could offer. How could she
measure Cochi's loss because, through her coming here, something
perhaps inevitable had happened sooner? "I don't want to hurt you,"
she said humbly. "Please believe this: what brought me to Zanzibar was an idea which really has nothing to do with Karel van Epp
or you." It was a strange feeling, being intensely sorry for this
dangerous young animal; and dangerous, Louise accepted that she
yet might be.

Cochi misunderstood her and flared up. "Nothing to do with me?
You tell me that, candle woman?" Her voice changed under the
stress of rage, losing what Mrs. Corryman thought its unsuitable in-
flections, growing singsong and shrill. "I'll say your coming here is
my business! Listen, get out. You'd better. And quickly!"

"It's a mistake to threaten after pleading," Louise observed, "if you want the pleading to work."

Before Cochi, small with hatred, crouching on the end of the bed, could find words in which to answer her, Ibrem was beside them, beaming at both in an ingratiating way.

"I come to earn my shilling, Mem."

"Sixpence," said Louise automatically, thinking how willingly at the moment she would have paid him anything she had, just for being there. Cochi could not get rid of him as easily as she could a trained servant like Toma.

"I'll want you to act as guide to various places in a moment, Ibrem." Turning to him, Louise ticked them off on an imaginary list. "First, the post office. The biggest one, if there are several. You know which that is? Where I can collect letters?" She heard a sob and a rustle, and Cochi had gone, running out through the shop. "And then the police station, where I can find Captain Hilbery?" This was to keep Ibrem well behaved. "And then a travel agent's. A place where people ask about ships going to England. You know where to find that, too?"

Sure. Sure. He knew where to find everything. "I am a good, trusting boy," he said, as though there had been no dirt throwing with his encouragement. "And my mother says, please pay me more money because she has other children. She is a good, trusting woman, too. Washes things."

"That might be useful. But you aren't going to get any money at all, this morning. Is that clear? You're going to work off the extra sixpence you got for nothing yesterday. Then when you do anything more for me, after this, you get another sixpence."

"Heigh-ho," he said with resignation.

"Good heavens!"

"Why you say that?"

"Because 'heigh-ho' is often seen in books written about a hundred years ago, but I've never heard it said."

"Then why they write it in books if nobody say it?"

"I haven't the least idea," said Louise. "Now go and wait for me, please, out in the courtyard."

"Why? I like to stay here. See what you do."

"Out!" said Louise.

"Heigh-ho to you, twice!" He gave her an impudent grin and sauntered away to the courtyard. She realized that if she stayed on in Zanzibar—at the moment this did not seem at all likely—she might get quite fond of Ibrem.

14

Hilbery

Toma brought her a second cup of tea and a boiled egg, both of which she feared came from Mrs. Corryman's stores, but as she had temporarily stolen Mrs. Corryman's servant it seemed trivial to balk at an egg. She ate thankfully, surprised to find that her first meal in freedom in Zanzibar tasted, not sourly of the scene which had just passed, but quite deliciously, of escape.

She had not dared undress for the night. Now, by devising a separate one-handed technique for each garment, she managed to take off enough to let her wash in a saucepan borrowed from Toma, and then dress again, in something more suitable than the cocktail frock. Water, which could be heated over the brazier, was the one plentiful luxury hereabouts. Although on the neighboring main-

163

land drought devastated the ground year after year, springs without number bubbled up in Zanzibar, Toma told her: it seemed that there were standpipes and communal taps even in the foulest alleys.

Her long hair was more difficult to do up without help. Eventually she succeeded in this by standing with the back of her head pressed against the upright of the doorway, holding the coil of hair in place, while she jabbed in her long pins with the free hand: the plaster casing round her wrist, though it allowed her to move the injured arm at the shoulder and elbow joints without the slightest twinge of pain now, still made her extremely clumsy in all automatic movements.

Not wanting to make regular use of the ornamental commode, which would probably be emptied seldom, she asked Toma to show her to a lavatory. He took her across the courtyard, Ibrem trotting behind, to inspect the communal washplace. She decided gloomily on the commode.

But when she and Ibrem emerged from the courtyard into the dyers' streets, Zanzibar's Stone Town had changed from the place of menace through which she had passed in the darkness, and become a realm of enchantment; there was beauty everywhere; dirty, unwholesome but overwhelming; beauty to banish gloom. Again, morning and evening showed separate worlds. Color rioted, crude but glorious. Here was still poverty, and the pervading smell of poverty: though the over-all sweetness of cloves competed with the reek of the dyers' materials, it could not cover the particular musky odor which means overcrowding in Africa. Disease, too, was abroad in the daylight; there were children with ophthalmia-clouded eyes which she had not noticed in the evening. The old man with the bandaged head was still rocking in his chair in the shelter of an archway; probably he had been there all night; but now he was sheltering from the sun, and the sun disinfected all things—the sun, and the huge purity of the clouds sailing through the bright sky, and a bustling wind bringing the reminder of other spices stored near the docks, carrying away much of the noise which went on and on and on. No one paid any attention to the white woman passing in the busy, laughing daylight. In the dust near the old man, a woman who was almost a child herself was playing con-

tentedly with her new toy, also a child. The shining, muscular backs
of the homali men were a splendid, living bronze. She could like
more than Ibrem here, if she stayed, thought Louise.

Coming out from the Stone Town on to the Maidan, a trampled
grass space beside a road crowded with cars, was another startling
transition, as though she had returned through time from the im-
memorial to the present day.

There were enough vehicles in the European quarter to cause long
traffic jams. Ibrem led her through these regardless of the hooting
drivers, whose rare chances of crawling forward a few yards he
destroyed with pleasure, but he paid ceremonial respect to the Sultan's Guard, padding barefoot and gaily uniformed through the
street, to relieve the sentries at the palace. As Major Deane had
warned her to expect, the innocuous red flag was flying in many
places; a mixed crowd of British and American tourists, off a cruise
ship which had put in for the day, kept pointing it out to one another with grave faces.

At the post office she lined up in a queue of these impatient,
sweating, red-necked visitors, determined to see all they could of the
island in six hours, after sending picture postcards home. It would
have been pleasanter to wait until they had finished their protesting and pushing and gone, but she must find out if her first month's
check had arrived without hitch. Throughout her captivity with Mrs.
Corryman she had intended to let Einarsen have an airgraph
from Zanzibar, as soon as she was at liberty, saying, "You see? I
didn't just do nothing! You were wrong for once," but it hardly
seemed worth sending now, with Falla Lufa out of Zanzibar and
herself almost decided to leave. She took the bunch of letters she was
handed, noticing that several were on the editorial stationery, and
moved aside from the crush, sorting the envelopes to find the important one from the accounts department first.

The dignified stiffness of the voucher between her fingers, small
as the sum it represented might be, gave her the sensation of being
relatively rich again. She opened the next: it was from MacAlister,
and even briefer than the crowing note she had intended for Einarsen: "What does it feel like to be out of a job?" The next told her
that the editor was dead, his going swift and unexpected, like most

of his actions. Emotion shook her: for the moment she did not read beyond the first paragraph. Someone irreplaceable had gone from her life. He had been old, but seemed indestructible.

As always, at the quick passing of a good friend, there was relief, following closely after the first shock, that for him there had been no long waiting, none of the indignity of decay. For this man of all men a brief ending was seemly. He had been mean, cantankerous, slave-driving, unjust, but what a whole, rare, rich human being! She stood with the letter in her hand, part of it still unread, flooded by the useless regrets that attend death. Had she ever made clear to this craggy figure how much she appreciated—indeed, loved him? Over the Norwegian witch trial he had given her the chance of her career, and she had taken it, made good and then thrown that career away. Oh, but someone as keen-sighted as that must surely have known how his staff felt about him. She wished, all the same, that she had risked his wrath and made this clearer in her own case; and was glad that she had asked him about the Voices, so that he could enjoy himself telling her personally.

A chirpy little tourist, dodging round her, said, "Well, dearie, if you don't want to buy stamps yourself, what about letting those who do have their turn?" She noticed distractedly that a second queue was forming behind her, because she had stood still in one spot for so long, and muttering apologies, moved out of the post office to finish reading the letter in the open air.

The writer was the Old Man's secretary, Louise's friend, who had been sacked. So had Louise. The assistant editor, once feature editor, was in full power now. What splendid chances he would have at last, she supposed grimly, of actually calling celebrities by their first names and not merely talking as if he did! Few would openly resent the familiarity from someone as influential as a London daily editor. And his own new assistant was a cautious time server who, as chief sub editor, had once killed a tangy story of Louise's for far-fetched political reasons. Louise's comment, which had reached him, was that he always acted as if his mother had been frightened by a Parliamentary Question. Her two well-earned enemies had not wasted much time. This first retainer check would also be the last. The Old Man's arrangement with her was canceled.

The Old Man's secretary was sincerely sorry: sorry to lose a great

chief, sorry to leave the office herself, sorry to be sending bad news
to a friend, but Louise glanced again at MacAlister's note before
crumpling it up and throwing it away. How reminiscent its wording
of the jolly-good-fun glee with which her colleagues had hailed her
apparent failure over the Middelburg report: how frightening it was,
that store of impersonal envy in human hearts, banked up against
the too successful, waiting to be used when they became less so!

"Now where, Mem? Travel shop?"

"Yes, Ibrem. Travel shop."

As she emerged from the post office he had been loudly bullying
two of his "followers," who had drifted by at the right moment; he
seemed disappointed that she did not appear more impressed by his
proclamation that every bit of this Mem's property was like his
property. No one else must even look at it. Scowling terribly, he
began shouting it at them all over again.

"Come on, Ibrem! Travel shop."

"No hurry, Mem. We take taxi."

"I don't think we do. How far away is this place?"

"Too far. Mem would be tired."

"Just where is it?"

"Down in the docks. Long, long way."

"That's not far. I've already walked here from the docks—and
carrying two heavy suitcases."

"But, Mem, I have not yet been in a motor car."

"Too bad."

He took defeat with Arab grace but never abandoned hope.
"Heigh-ho, heigh-ho, heigh-ho! Mem would not like to see Captain
Hilbery first? Police station is nearer."

"No. Travel shop." This news from her former office made her
return to Fleet Street urgently advisable. With a pen for sale she
should get back as soon as possible, before any of her reputation
withered. Reinforcing her inclination to abandon the Falla Lufa
project was the knowledge that journalistic memories are short; a
correspondent's fame is written in yesterday's edition; there is no ink
which fades faster.

"But if the police station is on the way?"

"What's the idea behind this, Ibrem? Has Captain Hilbery got
a car and are you hoping he might run us down to the docks?"

"Yes, Mem."

"Well, we're walking."

"Mem! There *is* Captain Hilbery," said Ibrem triumphantly. "Now you ask him. He likes all Mems your sort."

Her first impression of the burly man strolling toward her, in plain white clothes, carrying a horse-tail fly whisk, was that he looked like a tropical version of the Edwardian cad. The ironed mustache, the overconfident carriage, the knowing way he was eying her, all suggested that he was observing inwardly, "Dashed attractive woman, what?"—and her first intelligent remark would be answered with a drop in the social temperature, by a suggestion that she need not bother her pretty little noddle about that, whatever it was. On a more serious level she reflected that if this were the type her country still sent out to deal with colonial territories, everything Dr. Asaby said about minds and bodies was probably justified. (Dr. Asaby! She did not want to think yet of Dr. Asaby and that incomprehensible betrayal.) For a policeman, she decided, Captain Hilbery was almost vulgarly distinguished looking.

Their opening conversation seemed entirely in character with his appearance. He stopped close beside her, so close that it emphasized the difference in height, and his eyes twinkled down at her from his superior six or seven inches. Louise was five feet eight inches tall, and unused to having to crick her neck back uncomfortably to talk to anyone.

"Now, I know who you are, Mrs. Downes. In fact I was coming along to see you this morning in your hidey-hole. But you don't know who I am, so for once I have the advantage of a charming lady!"

"Captain Hilbery . . . presume." Unsmiling, she slurred the pronoun: it might have been "I presume," or "You presume." He was taken aback, but recovered his poise. The eyes twinkled down more quizzically.

"Anyone ever told you you're beautiful?" he said intimately, determined to put her at a loss.

"Frequently. I'm known far and wide as the Toast of Fetter Lane. What was it you wanted to see me about?"

Ibrem had melted away, having, probably, no more confidence in the police than the police had in him: if he were not going to get a

ride there was no sense in courting attention. But he was undoubtedly watching from somewhere nearby. Aware of this, Louise was
aware, too, of the wisdom of the move she had made, for her personal safety, in conveying that she was well acquainted with Hilbery:
she must be careful to keep up the impression. She smiled sweetly
upward, despite the crick in the neck.

The man roared with laughter and actually slapped his thigh—
something else Louise had met in books of the previous century,
but never before in life.

"You're a córker!" he said. "Woman after my own heart. How
we're going to miss you in Zanzibar!"

"Miss me?"

"When you go."

"When will that be?"

"Quite soon, I'm afraid." She found, suddenly, that she was
looking through the silly ogling eyes into a steely mind behind them.
This was not at all the man of first impression, any more than Karel
van Epp was. "That's what I was coming to see you about. Sorry,
but we can't have a white woman living alone where you are."

"Oh. How do you know where I'm living?" Did all Zanzibar
know, already? Hilbery, surely, could not have got it from Cochi, nor
was it reasonable to suppose that Toma would advertise to the
authorities what he had done.

"We have our ways of finding out," he said, twinkling again.
"And 'we,' you understand, means the police. Also, we understand
from Dr. Asaby that you had an idea of interviewing Falla Lufa in
prison. Apart from the fact that he isn't here, which Asaby says you
now know, I'm afraid we couldn't allow that either. All in all, I'm
afraid—" His voice tailed off, and he stood stroking his mustache.

There was for Louise the now familiar clutch of fear at the pit of
the stomach, an actual physical sensation, akin to the slight nausea
which had accompanied her spells of giddiness. This time she did
not say aloud, Dr. Asaby told you that!

She asked, "Do you mind telling me if Dr. Asaby came to see you
personally, to warn you about my intentions? Or about what I
might just possibly do—go on to Harmatta? So that I could be
stopped?"

"He's a sensible chap, Asaby. For a coon. Doesn't want trouble

here, I'd say, any more than we do. He didn't call on me, if that's
what you want to know. Saw my chief's secretary. Who—thank God
and his own guts, if you'll forgive the word!—has struggled back to
work with malaria, and a very game effort too. Till yesterday evening,
we'd no one in the office for three days but a half-witted filing clerk.
How's that for police headquarters? Fortunately, no one knew."

"Yes, I knew." But why had Dr. Asaby done this? Why?

"Did you, now! You journalists are a nosy lot, aren't you, my
dear?"

"It's what we're paid to be."

"You know too much sometimes."

"Sometimes. That's our occupational risk."

Keep talking! said the Voices in the back of her mind. She was
hearing them clearly for the first and only time in her life, exactly
as the Old Man had described. Keep talking and you can get this
man on your side. But only by matching steel against steel. You
need him.

"You're certain it was Dr. Asaby who went to police headquarters
about me yesterday, and not perhaps Mrs. Corryman?" When one is
very much alone, the act of trusting somebody is in itself important, out of all proportion to the confidences given because of that
trust. She must make quite certain of this double betrayal before she
could make up her mind how to accept it.

"Dr. Asaby it was, all right. If it'd been Mrs. Corryman she'd
have had us there talking yet!" He gave what Louise thought of as a
masher's guffaw. "Mustn't mind me. I'm retiring, you know. Have
retired, in fact. Just helping out because a couple of good chaps went
sick. So when I say 'we,' meaning the police, that's just by habit. I'll
be home in no time now. Meanwhile it's a wonderful luxury for a
policeman, saying what he thinks of the prominent citizens along his
beat, at last!"

"Yes, it must be. Though I understand you've been known to
indulge in it before. At Christmas and such times."

"Oho! Someone been telling tales about me? Well, I daresay my
shoulders are broad enough to carry that load! Now I don't mean
you to go running away with the idea, because of what I've said,
that we're all in cahoots here, wanting you to clear out of Zanzibar.
Far from it. You're an ornament. If I may say so without getting

my head bitten off? Stay around in that capacity, and you couldn't be more welcome. What we aren't keen on is having anyone from the Press using a whole lot of irresponsible imagination on our affairs. Why I said what I did, about your going, is that I've a notion about you—you're a lady who expects to get her own way! If you can't do what you like and live where you like—and I'm afraid you can't! You're a police liability while you're in that courtyard— Well, I fancy we shan't be keeping you as an ornament very long, more's the pity for Zanzibar. Am I right?"

Rage, an emotion alien to Louise, had been welling up in her slowly for quite a while. She had scarcely heard the last part of what Hilbery said. Blood was beating in her temples, an extraordinary and unpleasant sensation; she could feel the heat of it rising through her face. Too many people had been trying to stop her from doing as she intended.

"No!" she said. "If you mean, am I clearing out of here in a hurry, no, you're wrong!"

Once before she had been kicked upstairs by an incomprehensible betrayal of friendship: the leaving of her sheet of doggerel on the feature editor's desk had led to her rise as a special correspondent; Dr. Asaby's hurtful moves against her should defeat their own ends, in much the same way. "I shall stay in the Stone Town, Captain Hilbery—or anywhere else I choose in Zanzibar—for as long as I please. No doubt you can get me shifted out of one spot; I shall then move to another. I shall see Falla Lufa, by some means, and decide for myself if I'm going to do anything further. If I do, it won't be with 'an irresponsible imagination.' I'm not attached to any paper at this moment, which has an advantage I hadn't thought of before — From today, I've no contract preventing me from writing anything, anywhere, and what I write I can get printed. The only thing which will control what I say is the truth: not you."

She had been ready to run away again, but not now. He looked down at her appreciatively. "You're a bonnie scrapper, aren't you, sweetheart? Come and have a drink."

"No, thanks, I don't need one." She quoted the Old Man affectionately. " 'Best flavor in the world is the salt taste that comes into your throat before you launch into battle against skulduggery in high places.' Of course, I don't know if there has been skulduggery

here. In fact, so far everything suggests that there hasn't. But that's
what I'll find out. I've got just a bit of what might be that taste, now.
And I don't want to dilute it."

Attack! urged the Voices. It's your best chance with this man
(They had a slight West-country burr, she noticed with interest.
The Old Man had come from Bristol.)

"Besides, you drink too much," she said. "I've heard that on all
sides." She was amazed to hear herself being so rude to a stranger.

"Well, I—"

What he said was drowned by the hooting of cars beside them: a
more than usually massive traffic jam had developed. Into it dashed
the little man who had chivvied Louise in the post office. He waved
his sola topee in a beckoning fashion at the interlocked lines of
vehicles, in which several homali carts were mixed up. The sola
topee, Louise had already learned, was the sure mark of the day-
ashore tourist: no one else of European blood wore them in Zanzibar, and only a few Africans still affected them for show.

"Come on, come on—you there—Gray Car!" he bellowed. "Back
up a bit there, Black! More—more—that's right—more!"

"What the hell does Little Busybody think he's doing?" said Hilbery, at once the police officer again. Louise observed with approval
his instant switchover of attention to his job.

"Soon sort you out!" Little Busybody was shouting encouragingly.
"Come on, you there, move in behind Black."

"If I weren't off duty, I'd fix him!— It's the homali carts," Hilbery
explained, as earnestly as if his conversation with Louise had been
entirely friendly, and all about Zanzibar's traffic problems. "Never
can get the car drivers to realize that those chaps have just as much
right to the roads as the cars have. More. The homalis belong here."

"Now, right back, Green! Right back. Go on." There was a re-
sounding crash and a tinkle of glass. The owner of the topee walked
rapidly past them, making for a side turning, and as his short legs
twinkled by, he winked. "Too many cars everywhere in the world.
Always hated the bloody things!" he said, and disappeared.

Louise and Hilbery turned to one another agape. "The swine!
The wicked little swine!" he exclaimed. "Of course I ought to arrest
him, but I'm not going to. What a wonderful thing to do!" They

beamed upon one another, delightedly. The Old Man, who would have loved that incident too, seemed very close, to Louise.

"I will have that drink after all, please!" she said. "No, you come and lunch with me instead. Somewhere where we can talk." This was the habitual gesture of the journalist with the unquestioned expense account; she was not really thinking of what she said, while trying to hear the Voices whispering their final prompting: they were fading.

She was relieved when he turned pompous and said at once, "I've never taken a meal from a woman yet, and I don't intend to start. You will lunch with me." She must remember that her under-twenty pounds had got to last indefinitely, now that the vista of her life in Zanzibar was stretching out again, further than she could see.

"That's very nice of you, Captain Hilbery, in the circumstances! Thanks," she said, "I will. Where and when? I've got one or two things to do first."

"At the English Club. Seven-Zanzibar: that's local time. One o'clock to you. Meanwhile I'll have to deal with this mess!" There was a crescendo of angry voices from the stationary cars.

"Yes, I suppose so," she agreed inattentively. The message had come through, softly, urgently, and the Voices faded forever from her ears. As he turned away she asked casually, "Exactly when is Falla Lufa being brought back here from Harmatta? As soon as you leave, isn't it?"

He stared at her. From his expression she might have been a ghost walking in daylight. "Who told you that?"

"Professional ethics—never reveal sources."

"But it's not even officially decided."

"No, but it will be, no doubt."

"I thought there were only two people in all Africa who knew there was even a question of his being shifted again, to finish his sentence here. Falla Lufa and myself!"

"Well, now there are three of us," she said. "See you at one o'clock."

15

The Smell of Fear

Ibrem silently materialized beside her as Hilbery walked away toward the impacted cars.

The homali men were enjoying the rumpus enormously, doubled up with delight because only white property was involved. Hilbery swung his fly whisk good-humoredly, and short, at an African who capered backward in front of him as if Hilbery were a car to be lured on to destruction. Dodging the feint, the man fell over, and immediately became a dog, chyiking as he scuttled for shelter on hands and knees round one of the damaged vehicles, crawling under it and pushing his nose out impudently between the wheels to sniff at the police officer's trouser leg, and then draw back with a disgusted shake of the head. Louise watched Hilbery entering into this

174

lively pantomime, threatening him with the harmless horse-tail end of the whisk when the car was suddenly able to move on, leaving the "dog" unprotected. Intuition told her how fond Hilbery was of what he considered "his" people—"his coons": probably he did not really want to go home, to devote the rest of his life, as Dr. Asaby said, to the bottle. If so, there was more behind his resignation than the inheritance of money. There was always more behind everything, it seemed, in Zanzibar.

"Well, Mem, do we ride?" Ibrem was growing impatient.

"No, but we aren't going to the travel shop, anyway. First I've got to go back into the post office and shuffle through that queue again to get something." (Einarsen should have his air letter, now that she had decided to stay!) "And then, can you take me to Dr. Asaby's?"

"Then travel shop?"

"Not the travel shop at all. At least, not for a long time, I think."

"How you do chop and change."

When the defiant note had been posted to Einarsen, they plunged once more into the gay, deplorable and—by daylight—cozy slum of the Stone Town back streets, with Louise still leaping nervously into doorways at the first rattle of a homali wheel, or the rhythmical grunting of the crews. She thought despairingly, I shall never learn my way about here! And immediately found herself beginning to notice the angle of the sun on the top of the high, crumbling walls which enclosed them, and to gather from this in which direction they were walking.

Dr. Asaby was in, but kept her waiting for some time before he would see her. She wondered if he were trying to get in touch first, by telephone, with Cochi, or possibly Hilbery, to find out how matters stood, and whether or not she knew of his visit to Police Headquarters.

When she was shown into his consulting room at last he began, talking faster than usual, on an exposition of the difficulty of prescribing Western medical remedies in terms of water- and fire-omens: this, he said smiling, was what had delayed him in receiving her. He had that morning visited two African patients, who would certainly resent his showing that he thought they believed in superstitious rubbish, but at the same time would not follow his treatment for tuberculosis unless he conveyed that secretly he accepted, as they did, the local explanation of how the disease had been contracted: they must have passed water on a stone which had been struck by lightning. This was the prevalent belief throughout the African quarter of Zanzibar: the alternative means of infection was to smell a hut thatch burning. Instructions about hygiene had to be dovetailed into suggestions for avoiding these accidental risks in future: it had taken, he told her, a great deal of thinking out, as she might well imagine. While he talked he examined her arm and hand carefully, pressing the flesh on either side of the plaster, moving her fingers separately. He exclaimed with pleasure, in parenthesis, that she had been as good as her word: her temperature was normal; the bones appeared to be behaving well; by her color he could judge that she was free of shock. She drew in her breath sharply.

"That shouldn't have hurt," he said anxiously. "Does this?"

"No. Neither. I wanted to change the subject—Dr. Asaby, why did you—well—double-cross me? There's really no other term for what you did, is there?" Once the words were said, the situation was easier: it had been horrible, waiting to charge with this someone who had seemed a friend. "I came for an explanation because I must understand for my own sake, why you did it."

"Ah"—he produced his amber beads—"then you know I went to the police, after seeing you? Perhaps today you have been talking to Hilbery?"

"Perhaps. Well, why did you?"

"I should have said, dear madam, that this was obvious. If you think back over our conversation— But before we go any farther, let us finish with the medical aspect. I should like to leave on the plaster for at least a week more, to save the points of fracture from being knocked. It will help the wrist at this stage if you will exercise the finger muscles yourself, as much as you can without strain."

"To me it isn't obvious! When we talked I thought I was speaking freely to you as a friend. (How stupid this will seem to you, I suppose!) And that you accepted me as one."

"I was honored to do so." He gave her his formal little bow. "It is I who will be the loser if—how shall we say?—if I succeed in persuading you, one way or another, that Zanzibar is not a good place for you. I have few patients to whom I can talk as we talked, if not 'of Shakespeare and the musical glasses,' of almost everything else! A rare pleasure. I hesitate before saying this to a Cambridge lady, but it was like being back in Oxford."

"Your idea was that I should clear out quicker if I could be stopped, 'one way or another,' from doing what I came to do? Making mischief about Falla Lufa, as you and Mrs. Corryman consider it! That was your idea, wasn't it?"

"That was indeed my idea, but of course not for any reason connected with this tiresome little agitator. Bodies, bodies! No, frankly, my concern was, and is, purely a family matter."

"If you mean Cochi, she came to see me this morning."

"Really? So soon. Naturally I am anxious that nothing untoward should happen to you, through someone for whom I am responsible. This is what I should have thought obvious. Also—"

"One minute before you go on to anything else: Would you mind making quite clear the limits of what you think Cochi might do, out of jealousy? Would they include throwing vitriol, for instance?"

"Oh, in Zanzibar, and Pemba too, for that matter, there's probably no sulphuric acid to be bought in the open market," Dr. Asaby said soothingly. "I daresay the hospitals and the oil companies' laboratories keep some, but they'd be careful to see it didn't get into unauthorized hands. In fact I don't think I've ever heard of a case of disfigurement here by that means."

"But she would be capable of something of the kind? That's what I'm trying to get at."

"To do her justice, for she is after all a relative of my wife's, I think she would prefer to see you dead rather than disfigured."

"Dead by what means? I don't propose to move from here, unless you have me thrown out of your consulting room, until you stop being quite so evasive! I want to know what to guard against, because I'm telling you now, I'm staying!" Louise knew that losing her temper would not help her with this gently smiling man, but the nervous strain was very great.

"What a pity! Let us hope you will change your mind. About Zanzibar, I mean."

"You haven't answered my question."

"No, but then really"—he spoke as though she were a child making an unreasonable request—"how do you expect anyone to set a limit to what might be done by a jealous woman?"

"It was you who chose to make her that, so far as I'm concerned! You told her, for some reason I can't even guess, that Karel van Epp is in love with me. Something I'm not even sure of myself!"

"Not, perhaps, with your mind," said Dr. Asaby, the beads traveling faster between his fingers and thumb.

"What made you do that?"

"Kindness," he said unexpectedly. "Oh, kindness only to one connected with my family, I admit, but then if you knew more of Arab ways, that wouldn't surprise you. The only analogy which might help you to understand us in this matter is the clannishness of the Scots. Loyalty within the unit of the family, of certain definite degrees of relationship, outweighs any loyalty to a friend, even when the friend is greatly preferred to the relative. Still, a desire to shorten for her as much as possible the time of uncertainty—I think you would concede that is kindness? Van Epp's letter warned her, in the rather vague terms which a man generally uses on such occasions, that all is not to be as before. Naturally, being young, and not very intelligent as I told you, she hopes that when he comes back she can win him over to change his mind. The sooner she abandons that idea, the better for herself as well as for the family. I assure you, we dislike her liaison with a man of a different color quite as much as, were she white and the position reversed, we should undoubtedly disapprove of her consorting with an Arab-Indian mixture! Among ourselves we consider that it is Cochi's Indian blood, due to an equally stupid infatuation of her mother's, which accounts for her behaving in this reckless way. Still, once the episode is over, a reasonably good marriage can still be arranged for her. To be frank —I forestall your comment, 'What a pleasant change!'" He gave her his charming smile.

"Dr. Asaby, I'm far from the mood for making that kind of comment!"

"Very well, then, just to be frank—and this is the point I tried to make before, when you stopped me—there is another reason for my regretfully wishing you out of Zanzibar as soon as possible. Although I think the chance is almost non-existent that she can get him back, as things are, yet if you were not here and she improbably succeeded, he would be quite likely to marry her, the Dutch having so much less color-prejudice than the British or ourselves. Though in the ordinary way I am against mixed marriages, in the circumstances this might be the best solution for my family."

"Yet you said you did not like Karel van Epp!"

"As her unofficial owner. I should have much less objection to him as a husband. He is a young man of great ability, with good work behind him already, but more ahead, I think."

"And whether they would be happy, publicly tied together in a place where the wives of many white officials he is bound to meet would steadily refuse to recognize her, no matter how long she was married to him—that wouldn't matter? Only what would be best for her relations?"

"I have told you before," he said stiffly, "we do not put the pleasure of individuals before the good of their community—in this case, the family. Now you will, I hope, excuse me? I have to attend at the Palace. Can I rely on you to come to me in about a week, or before if you notice any discomfort, any loss of power in the fingers?"

"I doubt it. May I just settle my account before I go? I understand that I'm likely to be changing my address in Zanzibar quite a lot in the near future, so you wouldn't know where to send it."

"As you wish. Let us make it a nominal charge, because I have so much enjoyed talking to you, at Mrs. Corryman's. And because I see I cannot make you understand my action, and must therefore have hurt you more than—quite rightly—you would care to show me. (I like, don't you, your Lady Blessington's uncharacteristic remark, 'There are so few people before whom one would deign to appear other than perfectly happy'?) Shall we say, half a crown a visit?"

"Oh, but that's absurdly little," she was moved to protest, and then remembered that she could not afford this kind of pride. "However, thank you," she said, producing seven shillings and sixpence.

"Will you do two things for me?" he asked, escorting her to the door with unimpaired courtesy. "No, three? Will you try to accept that I acted with reluctance, not with malice? The second thing is, if you go to another doctor to have the plaster taken off—naturally I should prefer to finish the job myself, but there is nothing complicated about it, anyone can do it for you—will you please, for the following three weeks, rotate your hand like this, watch, six times every morning and six times every evening, without fail? I want you to lose no freedom of movement, and it is in the last stages of healing that stiffness can sometimes set in. The third thing is, supposing you eventually marry Karel van Epp, will you send me an invitation to the wedding, wherever it may take place—Holland, England, it doesn't matter? I might then get myself to take the long holiday I have promised myself for years, and go in search of my youth, and all its illusions, in Europe!"

"That seems to be a lot of supposing," she said. "But, yes, I'll do that. I'll do all three things. 'If.' Goodbye."

Ibrem was waiting faithfully outside, squatting in the shade of a palm tree a little way down the road. While he sauntered back to her she reflected with rueful admiration that she had got out of that remarkable man, Dr. Asaby, exactly what she had expected—almost nothing. An assurance that one of the most horrible forms of violence was probably, but not certainly, less likely to be used against her than some other form, still unnamed. The proof that, beside the traditions of his race, neither she nor Cochi counted at all, as human beings.

"Where now, Mem?"

"English Club. To meet *my friend*, Captain Hilbery. And then that's all for today. If you like to look in tomorrow morning—eight by my time, not yours and the Sultan's clock—and I've anything for you to do and you do it, you'll get another sixpence."

"That dress very dirty, Mem."

"No, it was clean this morning, and it'll have to be a lot dirtier before your mother gets a chance to wash it. Let's see if I can take us back to the Maidan—that's on the way to the Club, isn't it?—without your telling me unless I go wrong." He thought this grand fun, but after three turnings she was helplessly lost and gave up.

To keep her mind occupied, she tried to get Ibrem to explain Mohammedan time to her; she had noticed that the clock on the Beit el Ajeib, the House of Wonders near the Maidan, was six hours earlier than the time by which the local Europeans lived. The form of Hilbery's invitation to her convinced her that there was this awkward double-reckoning to be mastered. The boy's explanation was not easy to follow, because he could not imagine what there was to explain. "In truth, Mem, it is simple, because you can make one time into the other time on the fingers of a hand, if you borrow a finger from the other hand, and remember which way to count." Prodded by many questions, he conveyed at last that Mohammedan time concerned itself—reasonably, as he pointed out—with the hours of daylight when a man could work. Daylight, she knew, lasted from about 6 a.m. to 6 p.m., her time, all the year round in these latitudes, varying only half an hour with the seasons. With this help she worked out that "the end of the first hour," a phrase often heard from the Faithful, was called "seven o'clock in the morning" by the Infidel, whose midday was the sixth hour for the Sultan's more loyal subjects. "It is really most simple, for those who can count. All Arabs can count." Endless confusion, she realized later, was practically guaranteed to the town by the insistence of people like Major Deane on sticking to the European reckoning, as a matter of principle, without making clear that this was what they were doing, while they arranged appointments with those whom they tended to call the Nigger Lovers, who sided with the majority of Zanzibaris in using the Mohammedan system. And also on principle, forbore to say so.

Louise and Ibrem did rapid little sums in competition, as they walked in and out of sun and shade and radio-ridden filth, and then, all at once, of the chatter of innumerable sewing machines, clacking away in front of every shop in one street, before they reached the knife grinders' haunts, where everyone was sharpening something lethal. He was much the quicker.

He explained, too, that the House of Wonders, which carried the intelligent clock in its tower, was called by this name because it also contained the only lift in Zanzibar. Country folk coming into the capital were amazed by this room which rose and fell, and would watch it for hours, to the scorn of persons of his kind, who soon understood its working. To covet a ride in a car was one thing, he conveyed; a car could go all over the road, and in almost any street it liked; to be impressed by a cage moving forever through the same space was silly.

"Look, there is Toma's real Mem," he said, pointing: they were approaching the Maidan again. Louise dodged back into an alcove between two stalls as if a homali cart were after her. "She is not also a friend of yours?" he asked.

"Oh, yes. Yes. But you see she's talking to someone. I wouldn't like to disturb her."

Ibrem nodded and squeezed into the alcove beside her. The ways of Europeans were so peculiar that one oddity appeared little stranger to him than another.

Sooner or later, Louise accepted, she was bound to run into Mrs. Corryman face to face, inescapably. In this seething city everyone of every color met everyone else, or at least caught sight of them, two or three times a week, on the Coast Road or the Maidan; unless, like the Arab women, they stayed in strict seclusion—which made Major Deane's greeting, "Have you been here all the time?" seem more extraordinary each time Louise thought of it. But let the meeting not be today! She hoped this with the force of a prayer, and watched Mrs. Corryman pass by safely, her head turned away toward her companion, to whom she was talking, talking. The elderly Indian lady beside her seemed to be expostulating more and more feebly: no doubt Mrs. Corryman was urging something upon her which the white woman believed was inevitably for her companion's good— Louise had a sudden mental picture of her late hostess going through life helping unwilling lame dogs over stiles into fields containing bulls.

People observed while they were unaware of being watched always had a touching quality, as if they had been disarmed. If one happened to be fond of them they became, as Karel van Epp had said, very moving to see. Even when they were not lovable, they often seemed to the beholder unfairly pathetic. Louise felt her heart go out to Mrs. Corryman, now that she herself had got away from that oppressive house; and this despite her lively sympathy for the Indian lady, whose resistance looked to be wearing down—the sari'd head wagged slower, the agitated hands made trailing gestures of helplessness. So much goodwill was running to waste here. Somehow, today, Louise determined, she must find time to write to Mrs. Corryman, perhaps from the English Club, explaining her behavior, if it could be explained.

But at the English Club Louise forgot about this. She had been trying, in the last minute before her arrival, to decide whether or not to drop a hint to Hilbery of the fear which Dr. Asaby had implanted. The police were responsible for her safety, even if she chose to stay in the Stone Town: Hilbery had acknowledged that when he said she was a liability there. As she walked in, she decided against raising the subject; it meant saying too much about Karel van Epp; moreover the atmosphere of the club was so overwhelmingly provincial-English that the kind of vague threat which she would have to mention became patently absurd. Danger of the sort she had envisaged, while she talked to Dr. Asaby, simply could not seem real in the vicinity of the people she saw there.

Gathered in the lounge were many of the Europeans she had met, or glimpsed, at Mrs. Corryman's; but not, fortunately, Mrs. Corryman herself. At lunchtime this was an abstemious place: Hilbery, sitting in a corner with two male cronies, was drinking whisky with them; everyone else appeared to be sipping nothing stronger than iced beer or tonic water. She looked round at their faces, knobby or prematurely faded according to sex—Zanzibar's climate was notoriously cruel to women's complexions—and they all looked very mild and gentle. She had to remind herself that these were the people who were keeping Falla Lufa in prison.

Hilbery did not see her for a moment when she first arrived. He was talking with an anxious eagerness to his friends, as if holding off thought of the time just ahead when good companions might not be available, or none who shared the background of his whole life, and approved of him in spite of his weaknesses or perhaps because of them—when there would be no Club like a second home where he had a particular niche. What a tragedy retirement could be to such a man! Again there came to her the feeling of pity for someone watched unawares.

He saw her, jumped up and came over. "Now don't apologize for being late," he began jovially. "As you see, I haven't been bored while waiting!"

"I wasn't going to apologize, because I'm not late."

"There's my girl! You'd be surprised what a lot of people are put off their stride by that opening of mine!" The sparring match had begun again. "I know what you think of my habits, but would you like a drink yourself, or shall we eat right away?"

"Eat, please." He had plainly had several drinks, already.

"All right, you trot along and titivate while I finish my round with the lads. Meet you in the dining room in five minutes."

When they sat down together, he flashed his white teeth at her and said in his overconfidental manner, "Reverting to what I was saying—d'you know I've never been bored in my whole life? Simply don't know what the word means!"

"Then how do you know you've never been bored, if you don't understand what the word means?"

He guffawed, and ordered the meal for her, telling the steward, "We'll both have my Special. You let Ah-Ling know it's to be two special Specials, or else—!" She thought again, with sympathy, of what it would mean to this man that after he had left Zanzibar no one would know what his Special meant, in any connection.

"You're an intolerable lass," he said. "D'you know why I liked you from the first?"

"Yes. Because I stood up to you. Personally I think it's tiresome to have to kick people before they can be made agreeable, but with some it seems to be necessary."

"Well, that isn't the reason! Or maybe it's half the reason, but there's this other bit. The message you sent about the coons who ran you down."

"What message?" She had only the haziest recollection of the hours immediately after the accident.

"You didn't want them to get into trouble, remember? Not that they stayed around to find out if any was coming to them. One of them's not back yet from Malindi. I've just been hearing where he is—taken service with a friend of mine. One of the chaps I was drinking with just now. It was decent of you to bother about that. So I liked you before I saw you. Might even have gone on liking you if you'd turned out to wear glasses, and had thick ankles. As it is—! Well, it's done you proud, that message. I've got a bit of news for you about Falla Lufa."

"What is it?"

"It's officially agreed he comes back, as soon as I leave. We're all at sixes and sevens here, with the chief in hospital in England, and his deputy ill. Difficult to get decisions through, as things are. But I thought, Well, I'll only retire once. Might as well make it worth while for my friends. Went back this morning after I'd cleared up

Little Busybody's havoc, and pressed for the decision, and got it by cable. Back he comes in four weeks, when I leave!"

"What I don't understand is why he's coming back. As you gathered, I had an inkling he was. But not the reason for this second move. (Thanks, by the way, for getting this settled.) I thought he hated you, and everyone who could be suspected of any connection with Storr's departure; in fact, the whole prison administration. Why shift him again?"

"Because he's homesick!" said Hilbery, chuckling. "How's that for a damned silly reason? He's been begging to return to Zanzibar. The requests were sent on to me from Harmatta. Homesick for our nice little jail, out on the Mazzizini road. It really *is* rather nice," he added proudly.

"So I've heard. It does you credit!"

"Not me. Callendar. Asaby recommended it to you, I suppose?"

"Yes. 'Homesick'! Well!" Less and less would the story tally, except in outline, with the tale as told by Einarsen. And as if to emphasize this, Hilbery began talking in more general terms about the coons—the silly coons—his coons. All right if you knew how to handle them. Only people like Storr never did.

Each time the exasperating word "coons" came, she swallowed back a protest. What use would it be? He was leaving, he would never learn, and in his mouth it was a term of affection, not contempt.

She let him talk, and heard paternalism speaking, at its best and its worst. Hilbery and his kind—the old, passing order—loved with a jealous, angry and despairing devotion the former Africa whose people they could protect and master, under a régime in which "good" natives were those uncorrupted by civilization from a state of savage innocence. When natives lost their simplicity they ceased to be lovable. "Coon" included approvingly all primitive Africans, who laughed without cause and were cruel without cause, like children; and also those few Arabs with whom he was able to get on, despite their more sophisticated minds. Indians were not coons. He had never felt the same responsibility toward Indians. There was something very sad, she thought, in the acceptance of men like this one, that the youngsters who must succeed them soon would not care for their coons personally, as they did. Perhaps it would not really be a full compensation for this that the newcomers would be careful never to use that word.

Several drinks, and the prospect of going back to England, had loosened his tongue. In the hour they spent over lunch, Louise learned more of Africa as it used to be, and as it was at the moment, than she might have done through years of living in the Protectorate. But not of Africa to come, with cooperation between black and white inevitably, at last, on equal terms, or else not at all.

"This'll surprise you, maybe—I've helped get plenty coons a prison sentence in my day, but I've never liked doing it. Wouldn't keep even your subversive editor friend there if I could help it. Jail's no place for the colored. There's something in them that can't stand it. Rots them. Boot them friendly-like up the arse, that's all right, if I may drop into the vernacular. But don't send them inside, that's what I've always said."

"Yes, that's what I gathered, from Dr. Asaby."

It was hard not to like him more and more, while seeing at the same time how supremely hateful he could be to any educated non-European.

"Ah, well, I talk too much. I drink too much. (Though in the whole of my stretch out here I've never been the worse for wear on duty. A small matter for pride, you might say. Still, I'm proud of it.) And now I'm going home. Of my own free will I resigned, but perhaps only just in time. I wouldn't want the authorities here to have to kick me out." He smoothed his mustache and enveloped himself in his raffish charm like a cloak, but his voice was apologetic. "I've been a good man in my time."

"I'm already convinced of that," she said warmly, and meant it, adding silently with pity, But your time's over.

"But my time's over." So pat an echo of her thought, as though he had heard the words, fetched the easy blood tingling into her face—it was ridiculous that after years in a hard-boiled job she should be still at the mercy of her fair hair and fair skin, blushing like a schoolgirl whenever she was embarrassed. She was thankful to him for not being as observant as Dr. Asaby. "When I first came out here," he said, "all I had to do was to stop the coons sticking knives into each other. Now, well, no one can stop them sticking notions into one another. I'm ready to move with the times, as fast as I can.

But that's not as fast as Africa's moving. I'm lucky to go, I suppose, while there are still people here sorry to see the last of me."

So this was what lay behind his retirement: not only a growing weakness for the bottle, but the fear of tarnishing a record of love. It did not bear thinking of, the hole in the heart waiting for him when he reached what he called home.

She understood now why almost everyone—including the Resident, according to Falla Lufa—had preferred him to the awkward idealist, Storr. From afar, this preference looked so sinister: the forces of oppression standing together: from nearer, so human and inevitable, and probably justified by the relative worth of the two men to their community.

"Tell me about Storr," she said eagerly.

Already, looking back, she regarded with the indulgence of an adult to a child, the simple-minded indignation with which she had listened to Einarsen's account of Falla Lufa as the innocent victim, Storr as the underprivileged good white man, and Hilbery himself as the bullying, protected villain. Whatever the truth of the story, it was not that. She must have been remarkably gullible, she supposed.

"Oh, him!" said Hilbery tolerantly. "Not a bad chap in his way. Bit of an outsider. Selfish, 'enlightened' blighter. But whatever he did was from the best motives. He'd have been all right in some other territory. Where he is now, of course, and I understand he's doing fine! Trouble was, everything he did here from those splendid motives of his made certain that someone else would bash the poor coons over the head for having the ideas he gave them. Cruelest thing anyone can do to a coon, in my opinion, is to let him think he can have something that's—well—not right out of his reach, because then it'll stay just a dream. More or less harmless. But something about ten years ahead of what public opinion will stand. That's where Storr and I couldn't see eye to eye. We had five years of so-called working together, me under him. That's when I really started drinking! I'm sorry for old Full o' Love—silly coon. You know why I was so set at first to keep you from interviewing him, and maybe writing articles about him? I felt he'd got enough to bear, even if it is all his own fault, without a lot of sensational muckraking all round him."

"You have got a poor opinion of the Press."

"Yes," said Hilbery simply. Then he twinkled at her, by habit. "Perhaps I'm changing my mind about that, having met you!"

"I doubt it. Perhaps I'm changing mine about several things, having met you. Can't I see Falla Lufa earlier than four weeks hence? Can't he be brought back while you're still here?"

"Upon my word," he said explosively, "you are the most grasping, ungrateful woman! I move mountains of red tape for you, and all you say is, 'Can't it be done quicker?' "

"No, truly, I am grateful."

"I ought to have stuck to my original inclination to get you out of here as soon as possible, intolerable lass!"

"It's just that I'm so hard up," she admitted. "I don't want to wait around Zanzibar all that time. In spite of what I said this morning about staying as long as I pleased. Especially not with you chivvying me from place to place!" Now was the time to tell him that there was another reason for avoiding delay—that she was afraid. She looked about the dining room, even more cozily English than the lounge, with couples and foursomes eating not very hot curried chicken and not very well mashed potatoes with reassuringly nice table manners. Here was Zanzibar's daylight magic at work: if she spoke about Cochi, and the shapeless fears connected with her, what she said would sound absurd even to herself. The moment passed: they moved into the lounge for coffee.

"This chivvying around, as you call it," he said. "It's got to be! You realize you're letting down the whole Memhood of this place by what you're doing?"

"Do you mean, if a white woman lives alone in two rooms in the Stone Town people will assume she's a prostitute?"

"Of course. Your colored neighbors will, anyway. But that's not what worries us—the police. It's a pity if you get raped—bad for the coons. Still, it's your concern, specially after you've been warned. But if the local boys think you've got money, as well as being a tart, you're liable to get your throat cut, and that does matter to us. In fact it mustn't happen. So out you go." The steely look had returned. Of the two Hilberys in one skin, the aging Lothario who liked to have everyone at a disadvantage, and the tough, devoted policeman, Louise greatly preferred the policeman.

"Where to?" she asked.

"That's your affair. Not mine."

"How long can I have before I've got to move? I've taken the place for a week."

"Let you stay three days more. But I'll personally tell the people in the shop, who own the house, that if you're there after that, they'll lose their license to trade!"

"All right. Though I don't know where I'll go. Meanwhile, isn't there some superannuated native policeman I could hire as a watchman? Cheaply—it'll have to be very cheaply, I'm afraid! Don't you know one who might like to eke out a pension?"

"No. They live on their wives' work—yes, I do, though! Old Hamid. He gambled away the older wife, and his younger one left him because she wasn't going to do all the work by herself. He's pretty decrepit, but better than nothing. You know, that's not a bad idea. Not a bad idea at all. I'll make you a sketch map to help you find him. Then the pair of you can be chivvied about together."

While he was drawing for her, on the back of a menu, a rough guide to the old man's usual haunts, she thanked him both for the lunch and for changing his mind about letting her see Falla Lufa. He looked across the table at her with honest, weary eyes, and without the smirk which usually accompanied his personal statements.

"Don't be silly, intolerable lass! It's just as well I'm going. I could easily have fallen hard for you." The smirk came to his rescue. "Hopelessly susceptible type, that's Hilbery. I've taken it good and proper four times in my life, I may say, and each time I've made an unholy mess of things. As several people here could tell you. Yes, every way, it's just as well I'm going." When she left, he turned back toward the bar, saying awkwardly, "Want to make the most of the old place while I can."

Two people, met at Mrs. Corryman's, waylaid her with invitations to dinner on her way out of the Club. "We want to hear more about your exciting world!" Her heart sank, but she accepted both. They meant free meals.

Just outside she met Major Deane.

"Thought I might catch you here. Came on from Mrs. Corryman's and brought along a letter for you, just in case. Said I'd take it back if we didn't connect. How on earth did you get away?"

"Well, it wasn't altogether easy." She had no wish to explain. "Thank you for acting postman." Before the letter went unopened into her handbag, she had noted Karel van Epp's writing on the envelope. "But I thought you only came over from Dar-es-Salaam once a week?" she said. "It's not more than four days since the last time you were here—though, heavens, it seems longer!"

"Does it?" he said, brightening. "I say, does it really?" He seemed enormously pleased at what he took to be a compliment. She had not the heart to make clear what she had meant. "Awfully glad to see you're better. Came over today because it suddenly struck me— Left arm bashed up. Must have done in your wrist watch. So I thought, Can't leave the poor girl all that time in bed without a watch. You see, I imagined you were still laid up with *her*. And I brought along my spare watch."

"That was good of you. Really, a very kind thought. Kind action too, to come such a long way for my sake. But actually, my watch is this locket thing." (She wore it on a brooch, pinned to her lapel.) "And the homali cart didn't even crack the crystal. I haven't used a wrist watch for years. Still, that doesn't make it any less good of you to have taken so much trouble."

"Oh, not a bit," he said. "No bother to tote it back again. If people of the same party can't stick together and help when it's needed—" Because of her look of bewilderment he amplified, "Political party, I mean. Both anti-Commies, after all. Remember the tussle?"

"Major Deane—" She stopped. It was no use trying to counteract illusions from the past; there were too many in the present. "Do tell me," she asked instead, "did Mrs. Corryman say anything about my leaving her?"

"Rather. Says you're a ridiculous girl, but a nice one. You weren't in the least in the way."

"Ridiculous? Not rude or peculiar. Just ridiculous?"

"Why ever should she think you were rude? You left because you felt you really oughtn't to impose on her kindness any longer, getting fit again so quickly. Didn't you? That's what she told me."

"Oh, well, I was afraid she might think it was rude of me, not having written to thank her immediately I left." (This was wonderful. Here was a face-saving explanation to give Zanzibar, even if Mrs. Corryman could not believe it herself.)

"You'll find people don't bother much about that sort of thing out here," he said. "Very easy on manners. Look, don't want you to think I came over only about that watch. Mustn't get credit on false pretenses."

"No?"

"No. As a matter of fact, when I was on the way to the police with your message, I got an eyeful of a bint of these parts. And to be strictly truthful, I'm out on a recce."

"Oh, Major Deane, I do wish you luck. All the luck in the world," said Louise, relieved to find that she had been unduly flattering herself. "In that case I mustn't keep you a moment longer. Just start me off, if you can, in the right direction on this map." She showed him Hilbery's sketch. He insisted gallantly on escorting her all the way: there was no hurry for him, he said, until the cool of dusk brought everyone out on the coast road, or down to the docks to look at the shipping. In the end they had to employ a small street urchin as guide; he was as grasping as Ibrem, and more successful.

The negotiations with the potential watchman were easy, but not reassuring. He appeared to be drunk, a bad sign in a Moslem Arab, and even frailer than Louise had expected from Hilbery's description of him as decrepit. At everything she said he shook all over with soundless laughter, hiding his mouth behind a leaf-like hand and nodding his beautiful old head in agreement. But he asked for less money than she was prepared to pay, and perhaps, she thought, his mere presence, wearing a watchman's armband and carrying a watchman's staff—both of which, he assured her, he could borrow for nothing—might be slightly discouraging to people of evil intent. She took him on for a week, for the hours from dusk till dawn, and though it was still early afternoon he insisted on escorting her back to her quarters, with courtesy equal to Toma's. Like everyone else in the Stone Town, he already knew where a white woman was staying alone.

She said goodbye to Major Deane, wishing him luck again. He had no idea where his quarry lived, but went off jauntily to survey the popular promenades and work out a strategy, to cover them systematically at the appropriate time.

She was very much aware of the letter she carried in her handbag as she walked slowly beside the old man, but would not read it until she could be alone. On the way she discovered that he was in fact sober, but extremely deaf. Contact with Europeans, especially the joky Colonel Callendar, had cured him of the Arab belief that laughter was essentially rude, and suggested that it made a good disguise for deafness. As white people apparently like to be laughed at when they spoke, it was safer to laugh anxiously all the time, while replying at random. He was a pathetic but charming character, she found.

To her surprise, Toma disapproved of him less than of every other countryman of his on whom Louise had heard him comment. This man, he said loudly in the watchman's presence when they arrived at her lodging, was undoubtedly a rogue, a fool, and useless, but might serve her reasonably well as he appeared to have no other fish to fry. It was even convenient, he admitted, for the Mem to have someone, however incompetent, to look after her from tonight onward, someone at least older than the unspeakable Ibrem, for Toma himself must return at once to Mrs. Corryman's. The nephew was proving unsatisfactory; he broke things, and moreover claimed that when he consented to deputize, it had been understood that he should sleep with Lalla.

"You must not think of me as a ship leaving a sinking rat," Toma said, bowing formally over Louise's hand, while the watchman laughed his way backward across the courtyard, promising to return at nightfall.

"Indeed, no." Louise inclined her head equally graciously, shaking hands vigorously. She had already discovered that with Arabs she must shake hands at the beginning and end of every transaction. She assured Toma that she would always be grateful for the help he had given her, and wondered, wistfully, if it could possibly be anyone else who had informed Cochi beforehand where she would be going from Mrs. Corryman's. It would be good to be able to trust someone.

Before he left he had just time, Toma said, turning to practical matters, to teach her how to shop in the big native markets. This was essential if she were to go on living cheaply without him. For the next hour, with Karel van Epp's letter still unread, she was given a lesson in bargaining, learning a technique which she feared she would never be able to use so forcibly without Toma at her elbow, hissing in her ear, "Three pennies too much, Mem. Laugh, walk away, and then come back."

By the end of the afternoon she could manage the loud astonishment, the louder mockery (in English) at shameless efforts at robbery, which could be enjoyed by both parties to the bargain, and the few ki-Swahili words of blistering quality, which must be spoken low in order not to injure the seller's "face," lest the deal should be broken off: she was still not quite convincing when she strolled away disgustedly, and returned obliquely. Some dozen of the hands she was politely forced to shake, while filling a palm-leaf basket with stores, were palsied, scaly or filthy, or all three; but in the Zanzibar day mood she could not care. Over everything danced the gay, cleaning wind, full of sunshine. The pure reds and browns and gold of the markets, glowing even in the shadows, leaped into satisfying life at the touch of this light, where peppers and heaps of dyed cloth and corncobs were piled together anyhow in heaps; and in the sheltered corners, where the air was still, it was laden with spice and drumbeats. Unless I make efforts to remain a European prig, she told herself, I shall begin thinking that decay and disease matter less in Zanzibar than elsewhere. And I suppose that would be a pity, a misjudgment? In a burst of extravagance she bought for fourpence a sweet-scented jasmine bracelet, from the old woman who sold eggs while her grandchildren squatted under the booth, twining flowers into garlands.

The strong smell was grateful as Louise walked back alone, through the dyers' quarter, with her basket held like a baby in her sound arm, so that she could put her nose down to the bracelet at intervals. Toma had left her in the market with no further ceremony; she knew the way to her lodging from that point.

The jasmine scent in her nose hid for several seconds the new smell in her room, harsh, musky, sweaty. Louise looked round: the door between her room and the shop was still locked, as she had left it. This was the door through which Cochi had come; but anyone who knew or had been told the way could easily get in through the

room where the children had tormented her and, later, Toma had
slept. There was only the bead curtain to keep out flies between
this and the courtyard.

The visual memory which made her an accurate reporter assured
Louise that several small possessions of hers, scattered about, had not
been moved. But someone had been very recently in the room,
someone sweating with nervousness, as she was too, despite the
growing coolness of the approaching dusk. Someone who had been
waiting about in the room for a while. Subconsciously, some detached part of her mind had noted that same smell when the
homali men picked her up: a smell of fear, of black fear.

She forced herself to stay in the room long enough to search
through her belongings, not to get out quickly as she wanted to do.
Reason said that if this intruder had been only a sneak thief, the
visit was relatively harmless. But her two suitcases were still there,
under the bed, locked, and there appeared to have been no tamper-
ing with the fastenings. Her keys, passport and all the money she
had were in the handbag she had carried with her while shopping,
along with the unread letter. Nothing was missing.

She went out then, with all her will holding back her feet from
running in panic. She would stay away from this place until after
the watchman had arrived. The one complicated route she had so
far mastered in the Stone Town was the way from her lodging to
the Coast Road. This seemed, once again, marvelously of the twen-
tieth century when she reached it, and thankfully skipped across
between the honking cars, full of smart young Indians and Arabs,
driving to petting parties on the golf course. She followed the direction of the cars, aware with her eyes and ears, but not interested
for once, that the spectacular evening storm was flashing and growling
on the far-off mountains.

Lamps were leaping into moth-haloed radiance, over the doorways
of the big houses. She passed Mrs. Corryman's unobserved, and
where the lamps began to thin out, on the edge of the town, sat
down on the side of a homali cart which had been left conveniently
close to a light. Now she would read Karel van Epp's letter.

The relief from tension was so great that she found she was looking at the words through tears. "You are a pest," it said without
preamble, "and I am very angry with you. For look here, you have

ruined my climbing holiday, which as I think I told you, I expect to enjoy more than any other part of my leave. But there is no point in staying on here, and worrying about what might be happening where you are. So I will be back almost as soon as this airmail gets to you. Am I right in remembering that you have freckles on your arms, but not on the back of your hands? If so, why not?"

Crying in the lit street, where anyone might recognize her, became embarrassing, and getting up she walked on rapidly into the gloom, until she had control of herself again. Then the gloom turned menacing, and she came back into the lamp-lit area and sat down again on the homali cart, watching the distant flashes absently. If Karel van Epp were near at hand she would be much less afraid; fear would remain of human size, and not grow with the shadows, out of all proportion to daylight worries, into something vast and possessive like the Zanzibar night. She accepted the implication of knowing that with him beside her she would be brave in any circumstances, and having accepted it—having acknowledged like this to herself, almost incidentally, that here was a man she could love—she was able to think more collectedly of the intruder who had been in her room; frightened, she was sure, of what he had come to do, which was not to steal.

One of the local children could have been in, entering out of deviltry, daring Ibrem's wrath. All of them were dirty enough to leave behind a reminder that a hot sticky body had been in the place; but then the smell would have been of Arab skin, Arab dirt. Though of mixed blood, they were mainly Arab, and through thin, sun-cured garments, Arab skin had a pleasant odor to a European. Even Arab sweat, whether fresh or stale, was lighter and less rank than a Negro's. What she had noticed was without question the heavy African tang, intensified by excitement and apprehension. The Negroes said all Europeans stank to them of decay, either because this was true or out of revenge for the intolerable fact that the whites could certainly recognize the peculiar odor of Negro skin and hair. Louise thought suddenly of the one simple, acceptable explanation, and let out her breath in a sigh of relief. One of the sanitary men could have come round earlier than usual to the courtyard and, curious about the Mem living alone, taken the chance of an unauthorized look round.

These night-soil shifters were a strange, wild-looking lot, invariably
Negro like the homali men. Usually they did their work at dead of
night, their faces daubed with whitewash or splashes of color, wearing
crowns of palm leaves, coconut fronds or banana trash pulled low
over their foreheads, which made them officially invisible to their
friends, by showing that they did not wish to be recognized. The
disguise was vestigial; local courtesy had a charming inverted snobbery, which Hilbery had explained to her at lunch. A man doing a
menial job for money in Zanzibar should be cut, not because acknowledging him as a friend might drag down the recognizer, but lest
recognition at such a moment might embarrass the recognized on
any future social occasion. She had glimpsed two of these odd figures
in the courtyard, looking like participants in some fertility rite, when
she was following the guide, with the children after her. She had been
too preoccupied to pay them much attention at the time. Of course it
had been one of these harmless sanitary men! He would be afraid of
being caught spying. She had to believe this; she must spend the
night in that room, without Toma just along the passage.

The storm died away over the mountains. When an hour had passed
since full darkness came, she judged that the night watchman must
certainly have arrived, and began to walk, slowly at first, and then
faster and faster, back toward her lodging; if she loitered now she
might not be able to make herself go on. She thought that Karel
van Epp, coming by air, might arrive at any time; she thought, or
tried to think, about the nursery picture "So Big!" and the ways by
which it might have reached her room.

Ibrem, on the lookout for her, met her where the twisting side
roads leading off the Maidan plunged into the heart of the Stone
Town. Someone had reported to him which way she had gone. He
capered about with pleasure: "Mem, Captain Hilbery has sent his
car for you. I can ride in it too?"

"But why should he have sent a car for me? To go where?"

"I don't know, Mem. But the driver, he knows. Captain Hilbery
tell him to fetch you. Says hurry. Car not able to get near your place
because of curly corners. Waiting two, three streets off. Driver not
liking to leave it there, many bad children about. You know."

"Yes, I know about the bad children!" Perhaps after all she would
not have to spend the night in that room. This summons could mean

that Hilbery had found some safer place for her. Or it might be news about Falla Lufa. In any case she would see Hilbery and tell him, now, that she was afraid. She had been a fool not to take her chance at lunch.

Ibrem went bubbling on. "Driver says he wait for you to come back, but I go at once to look for you. Very hard to find. You walk a long way, not like most Mems. So that will be something more for me, as well as ride?"

"Oh, yes, you get another sixpence for fetching me," she said in thankfulness. "Has the night watchman come?"

"Long time. Old goat—doesn't hear. Goes, 'He, he, he.' Can play games with him."

"If you do—understand this!—if you or your followers try playing any tricks at all on that old man, Ibrem, you never get another penny from me."

He threw her a surly glance under his magnificent, sweeping eyelashes, and muttered something, but it was probably only "Heigh-ho." His interest was centered on the new experience; running on ahead impatiently he led her through several alleys she had not traversed before, wriggling into danker slums behind her courtyard, and on to a wider road where a smart young Arab scrambled out of the driving seat of a green saloon car, and saluted her. "You are Mrs. Downes?"

"Yes, where does Captain Hilbery want me to come?"

"English Club, Mem." The driver opened the door into the back for her.

For a second she hesitated. The distance was one she could have walked in a few minutes. Probably it would take considerably longer to cover in a car, which would have to go an extraordinary way round to avoid the turnings negotiable only by homali carts. But Zanzibar's white residents, she knew, behaved as if they were webbed to the knees, making a fuss if they had to walk anywhere, and they expected newcomers to do the same. She could not with dignity ask the driver why Hilbery wanted to see her; in any case, the man probably would not know. "All right, Ibrem," she said. "In you go."

"No, Mem. Not this boy also." The chauffeur stepped forward, still smiling, and barred the way, but Ibrem dodged in under his arm.

"Why not? I promised him the ride. Then he can walk back from the Club."

"I am sorry, Mem. Captain Hilbery would not like it."

"Oh, nonsense," said Louise amiably. "I'm sure—" She saw the driver's eyes flicker toward the other side of the car, where a man whom she had not noticed before in the dim light was standing. The only street lamp in sight was on her side, and some distance away: all she could see clearly of the other figure was a hand, resting on the spare wheel of the car. It was too blunt-fingered for an Indian's, too dark-skinned for an Arab's. "—he wouldn't mind, really, but it doesn't matter," she finished evenly. "The boy can come another time."

"Oh, Mem!" Crouched on the back seat, Ibrem protested piteously.

"I've just remembered, Captain Hilbery asked me to bring some papers to the Club, next time I had the chance," she said. "Out you get, Ibrem, we'll fetch them now." She was already moving back toward the narrow twisting alley up which they had come, where the car could not follow. "Just wait here for me a minute more, will you?" she called back to the driver. "I'll phone Captain Hilbery, as he's at the Club now, to make sure which he wants."

Ibrem remained obstinately in the car. She saw the driver and the other man hurriedly consulting in front of it as she retreated still farther up the alley. "Ibrem!" she shouted with all the authority she could achieve. He jumped out and came running after her, grumbling furiously.

"You said I could ride. You did. You know there is no telephone thing near your rooms, so how will you speak to Captain Hilbery before you go?—Oh, look, Mem, driver has not waited for you!"

As the car, with both men in it, passed the opening to the alley, gathering speed, Louise noticed that a piece of sacking draped round a box on the carrier obscured the number plate at the back. No doubt something else—caked mud, perhaps—hid the one in front. "I rather thought he mightn't," she said, leaning against the wall, feeling sick. "Now take me back, quickly, to the night watchman. And the next time I go to a bank to fetch money"—it would never be wise to admit carrying so much to Ibrem—"I'll give you a whole two shillings to make up for missing the ride. Then you can buy one for yourself in a taxi. As far as from here to the Club." He raced ahead toward the courtyard, shouting to gather his friends around him so that he could boast of the money he would have shortly. Louise had to run to keep him in view. There was no chance to ask him, casually, the question she must get answered. With a wave of the hand, a gesture as between equals, intended to impress his swelling group of followers, he left her as soon as they reached the archway into the courtyard, where the old man with the bandaged head was still rocking, like a pendulum to Time itself. Within the courtyard—a welcome sight, indeed—the night watchman was ensconced on a stool before her doorway, complacent in loaned regalia of brassard and staff.

She bent down and said loudly in his ear, "Do you know Captain Hilbery's car by sight?" As an ex-policeman he must have seen it, but she surmised that all cars would look much the same to him.

"Yes, yes." He nodded with satisfaction, showing her how he could make the heavy stick ring on the ground to frighten marauders.

She saw that only if she could get him to say No, or to volunteer some information of his own, could she be sure that he had understood any question.

"What color is it?" she shouted.

"Yes, yes!" He laughed obligingly.

The one advantage of Zanzibar's restless night life was that voices could be raised prodigiously without disturbing the neighbors. "Has Captain Hilbery a green car?" she fairly bellowed. Despite the background noise of the drums, and the wailing Asiatic music from loudspeakers, two of the garlanded night-soil men who were clearing the communal lavatory looked round at her in surprise, symbolic creatures caught in some act of evil magic.

"No, no, Mem. A black car, he has. A very fine black car. Twice since the Vuli" (Short Rains) "I have had the honor to sit in it beside him, going to see my young wife in a fishing village down the coast. He urged her to come back and work for me, as she should. He is a kind man, Captain Hilbery. But she is lazy and prefers to eat only fish. She would not come, for all he said. Many hearts, not only mine, will be sad because he is leaving us. We sat more than an hour, both to go and to come back, in his fine black car. Only Captain Hilbery would take so much thought for me. But now she has a baby by a fisherman there, it is no use."

16

The Falla Lufa Papers

During the night, she burned up the small store of candles bought the previous day in the market, in order not to lie in the darkness listening, wide-eyed. For once her great asset, her command of sleep, was as poor as Uncle Arthur persistently believed.

The ringing of the night watchman's staff made itself heard, toward morning, only at longer and longer intervals: her retainer, Louise supposed, cat-napped more soundly than she did, but his wraith-like presence in the courtyard was a comfort, and the hours passed and nothing happened.

Long after he had left, footsteps approaching down the passage between her two rooms set her trembling again. By this time Louise was

200

up and—thankful for the distraction—engaged on the slatternly job which passed for housework by Stone Town standards: soft dirt got trodden into the mud floor, anything hard was thrown out through the doorway, to wait for rain, wind, scavenging animals or nothing at all to move it farther from the threshold. For this, her inexperienced sound hand was adequate. Mrs. Corryman came in, finding her at work with a palm-leaf brush.

"Well, I'd no idea you journalists were so domesticated! So here you are, you naughty girl— Had to get on to Tom Hilbery to find you! Thought I'd catch you in if I came at breakfast time. I've missed you, you know! As if you were the least bit in the way! Not a thing to worry about. Always have my place full of people—you ought to have seen that. Still, I like pride and independence in anyone—if I hadn't got 'em myself I'd still be in England at you-know-where, bless it. Now, about tonight. I've got a friend of yours coming! You'll never guess, so I'll tell you who, shall I?"

"Do, please," said Louise without interest. It could not be Karel van Epp.

"A Mr. Einarsen. He's coming to dinner, and of course you must, too."

"Good heavens!" said Louise comprehensively. So this was how individuals, like nations, came to believe their own propaganda: Mrs. Corryman had taken less than two days to convince herself by the excuses she had made to cover her guest's embarrassing flight. The awkwardness was now all on Louise's side. She thought of her worry about the pain caused by the pin which penetrates the elephant's hide, and nearly laughed, despite a racking headache brought on by sleeplessness.

"Ah, you're wondering how I know he's a friend of yours? Old Mrs. Know-All, aren't I?" Mrs. Corryman asked, putting her head on one side, but mercifully this time not waiting for an answer. "Well, I'll tell you, I get all the passenger lists sent to me in advance. Through friends in the various offices. Same as I do the railway posters. That's how I knew when you were coming. Seems he's going on to Cairo after investigating conditions in Kenya. Mau-Mau I expect. Why on earth doesn't he fly?"

"I've no idea—oh, yes, sinus trouble. He hates planes," said Louise limply. The headache and the effort to keep up with the kangaroo-like bounds of Mrs. Corryman's talk brought back the atmosphere of her first evening in Zanzibar.

"Fancy that. Thought all newspaper people loved skipping about in them. I sent him an invitation by radio to the ship; couldn't wait to get acquainted here, because he'll only have one night in Zanzibar. I always find journalists so interesting. And he's radio'd back that he'll come if you do. Now how does he know you're here?"

"Because I wrote and told him—oh no, that was only yesterday, and I addressed it to his paper in Sweden!" It seemed far longer ago than that: weeks, months ago. "I don't know," she said, "except that it's never difficult for any journalist to find out where any other journalist is." Absently, with the reversed handle of the broom, she was scattering the little pile of rubbish she had swept up. Few social prospects could seem less attractive than an evening of Einarsen's unsparing questions.

"Shouldn't do that!" said Mrs. Corryman, as sharply as though she were speaking to one of her own servants. Meekly, Louise collected the rubbish together again. "Come any time after six, dear, for cocktails first. We'll make it an all-white affair in deference to your friend. Swedes are funny, aren't they? Not like the French. Don't dress, of course. You know, you do look peaky still. We'll have to feed you up."

"Tonight I'm dining with the Osbournes." Louise wondered if she would have remembered this engagement, without the formidable conjunction of Einarsen and Mrs. Corryman. "They asked me yesterday, at the English Club, and I can't possibly put them off."

"That's all right," said Mrs. Corryman with her neigh of satisfaction, retreating down the passage like a horse carefully backing out of its stall. "I'll simply ring them up and say we're all eating at my place, for your sake; it'd be a shame for you to miss your friend when he's only got this one night here. They'll understand."

In stupefied silence Louise watched her go. If it had been too difficult to mention fear at lunch with Hilbery, it was unimaginable to say to Mrs. Corryman, I am almost certain that last night an attempt was made on my life. Possibly there were two attempts. By men hired for the job.

Could such a statement have been tried, either Mrs. Corryman would not have listened closely enough to take it in, or she would have assumed control of the whole situation: practically speaking, the attempts would then have been made against her life. All the high-powered people in Zanzibar would immediately have been called in —the wrong people, from Louise's point of view. Karel van Epp, and the reasonableness or otherwise of Cochi's jealousy, would inevitably have been thumbed over, and Louise's tenuous relationship with him would have become a series of entries in police files. Telling Hilbery would be another matter—now. He was blessedly personal in his methods. It would be an advantage that he was no longer officially a police officer, but merely someone helping out ex-colleagues at a time of illness. Acting in a private capacity, he could mean salvation for everyone. She must talk to him with no more delay.

When Ibrem came round, eager to take her to the bank and collect his compensation, she made him accompany her first to the telephone kiosk near the Sultan's House of Wonders, from which to ring up police headquarters.

In any land, the inside of a telephone kiosk is a homely thing: here were the usual *graffiti*, with a strong family relationship to those in Cambridge, London and elsewhere, even though some of the captions were in flowing Arab script. The sound of the bell ringing was reassuring, too: it belonged to the normal, daylight world. But the answer, when it came, was unsatisfactory: Captain Hilbery was not expected in the office till the afternoon. A voice which sounded like that of Ralmi, the filing clerk, told her that she could make no appointment with him before four o'clock, and refused to divulge his private telephone number. Ralmi had evidently had enough trouble through indiscretion. "Very well, four o'clock at the English Club, please," she said, giving her name to the voice, and making the voice repeat it, and then repeating it again herself, and the message too, hoping that something would get through to Hilbery, without any fanciful trimmings by Ralmi.

Now the long, soft hours of the Zanzibar day lay ahead, pouring their sunshine and the jolly, spice-laden wind between her and the terror that waited for the dusk to loose it again. She was not unduly nervous while her shadow shortened under her, and she could keep Ibrem close at her side. Wicked little street urchin though he was, he evidently had some value and was feared as a witness.

After they had been to the bank, she armed herself with a trayful of frantic-colored Arab sweetmeats: Ibrem adored these fly-encrusted slabs of unguessable origin. She bought them from a street trader, bargaining for the man's whole stock, and the tray too, so fiercely and cleverly, in imitation of Toma, that at one moment Ibrem was helpfully afraid she was really not going to buy anything. While she doled out small, deliquescent lumps of the stuff to him, one by one, at irregular intervals, unmoved by his appeals for more, he showed no disposition to drift away to other, more exciting and nefarious occupations than waiting on her whim, wherever she chose to go.

This was to the Records Office: she must make full use of Hilbery's absence to browbeat whoever was in charge there, by using the ex-police officer's name ruthlessly, if necessary. Later she could tell him about it, and he would laugh and call her a still more intolerable lass. For the moment the obstacle to be got round, or through, or over, or under, by any means known to a journalist, was that all copies of the important issues of Falla Lufa's own paper had been confiscated as inflammatory matter; she could not consult them in the ordinary way, in the editorial files, and get them translated for her.

There were other little hills of red tape to be surmounted, too, she found. The records of the two trials which had sent him to prison could only be seen after application had been made in due form: the process would take about three days, she was told, with the chief of police and his deputy both away. Louise swept through the office like a hurricane, insisting on speaking personally, on the Records Office telephone, to the unfortunate secretary who had struggled back to work at Police Headquarters with malaria still on him. She battered down excuses that this was really not his business, that he was unwell himself, and suggestions that she should call again tomorrow, when higher authority could perhaps be invoked to waive the regulations about due notice. "Higher authority" might mean the British Resident, she surmised, and if the Resident said No to her request for special facilities, she would have little chance of getting a look at the confiscated papers.

"But Captain Hilbery assured me—" and "After what Captain Hilbery said, this is too ridiculous—" she threw about indignantly. She alternated flattery with bullying tactics, repeating—because appreciation always sounded sweeter at secondhand—what Hilbery had said about his colleague's heroic return to his desk in the emergency;

and then fulminated again about the lunatic obstructiveness of official ways. Einarsen, a master of this sort of thing, could not have done better.

"Has it occurred to you," she demanded menacingly, "what sort of report I'm bound to wire back to London—both to Fleet Street and to Whitehall!—if I don't get access to those papers today? Two public trials, on British-protected territory, of a British-protected person, and a British journalist is not allowed to see the official records. Why? That's what a good many people are going to want to know."

"But really, Mrs. Downes, no one has finally said you can't see the confiscated issues. Or any of the other papers. It's just that today—"

"I should hope not!" said Louise, as though a suggestion of the utmost impropriety had been made to her.

"—after due notice—"

"How do you suppose it'll look to the rest of the Commonwealth? Where there's pretty strong feeling about the freedom of the Press, I can tell you!" As she spoke, she pictured the unfortunate man at the other end of the line, his head resting on one hand as he nursed his malarial headache; but there was too much at stake for sympathy to be shown now, and she went on. "We in England are on the lookout for any infringement of that, whatever you think you can keep quiet about in Zanzibar. The Colonial Office—"

"I assure you, no one's trying to keep quiet about anything. It's only a question of the proper notice! Two or three days—"

"But this is monstrous. Simply monstrous. Call your filing clerk: he can tell you that it's now four days since I wrote to the chief of police, asking to see all the papers. Four days!"

"Yes, but Colonel Callendar was already out of Zanzibar then, on his way to England with appendicitis, and I was down with malaria and his deputy—"

"You poor man!" Louise warmed her voice with womanly understanding. "I do see what extraordinary bad luck it was—really, a frightful situation—all the responsible people going sick at the same time. Particularly for you, feeling you'd got to struggle back somehow. I believe one goes on being miserable for days, doesn't one, after getting up too soon with malaria? I haven't had that myself, but I have had appendicitis—" She gave him a gruesome, gaily irrelevant account of being operated on in a Balkan hospital, in daunting cir-

cumstances, and getting, for her first meal after the ordeal, an ome-
let in which she bit on something hard. With foreboding she recognized an unmistakable tooth filling: this was no place in which
to have further repairs carried out. Having swallowed the rest of the
mouthful she felt round with her tongue to find out which of her
fillings had worked loose, hoping that the cavity could safely be left
until she returned to England: but all her teeth proved to be in excellent condition.

She told this horrid little story well (its minor nastiness seemed
rather pleasant to recall, in contrast with the oppressive terror of the
previous evening). The deputy chuckled sourly, and then with better
grace. The rest of the conversation was conducted according to the
unscrupulous go-between method practiced by telephone diplomats
of all kinds, when people listening to one side of the talk are unaware
how much has already been agreed to by those at the other end. The
Records Office staff and Police Headquarters were both left with the
impression that all the concessions made to her had been made at
the other end. Half an hour after her arrival at the Records Office,
Louise was sitting at a table in a secluded room with the reports of all
the legal proceedings in which Falla Lufa had been involved spread
around her, together with translations of his editorials and his personal dossier; while Ibrem hugged his knees contentedly under the
table, making everything within his reach stickier and stickier. Once,
when he seemed to be getting restless, she let fall a sixpence, as if accidentally, in getting her pen out of her bag. As if accidentally, his
bare foot moved sideways to cover it as it lay on the floor, and both
settled down again.

She had taken some of Dr. Asaby's aspirin, and the headache had
lifted; but for a few minutes, though, she found difficulty in concentrating on the formal, legal phrases which concealed such a sad, many-
sided and slightly fantastic story, but the habit and discipline of
journalism proved useful here, in helping her to shut out of her mind
her own concerns. Soon she was absorbed without effort in what she
read, for the tale was not only of one cantankerous man but, in miniature, of almost every problem of colonial development, and the slow
delegation of power from the rulers to the ruled.

This was usually too slow for Falla Lufa, who managed to combine,
at the same time, a share of the aspirations of all subject races toward

freedom, and a curious kink for seeing existing regulations enforced—
an ambivalence which was always leading him into lawsuits.

He emerged from these documents as a much more endearing person than she had recently imagined him to be: fierily honest, and obsessed with resentment of the arbitrary inequalities of race and color,
but also as someone who made it impossible for authority to deal
with him leniently. Authority, in fact, had been very patient—patient,
but possibly unwise: in the end it had made a martyr of him, or allowed him, which was more satisfactory still from his point of view, to
make a martyr of himself.

She was surprised to learn that he had been involved not merely in
two but in seven court cases. Five prosecutions were at his own insti-
gation; he was an inveterate plaintiff. Not only had he called in his
paper, as she knew, for a stricter observation of the shop-closing regulations, which in Zanzibar were unworkable anyway, but he had
campaigned for the enforcement of several other orders which for
years had been generally disregarded, to the benefit of the majority.
With the practiced elasticity of British rule—known by harder names
in other countries—they were still kept in the penal code, so that they
could be invoked when violations became a nuisance. Falla Lufa insisted, in his editorials, in naming those who profited by this *laissez-
aller* attitude of authority, and suing them, generally for libel or
slander, when they protested overvigorously against his interference.
For these suits, which he lost more often than not, neither he personally nor his paper could pay: it had a tiny circulation, but was important, Louise realized, out of all proportion to its sales; because it
spoke continually to underprivileged readers about abuse of privilege. To those with little of either sort, good and bad privileges must
always look much the same.

Once, she read with surprise, he had come up against Karel van
Epp as an expert witness: Karel had probably forgotten all about
this, as he had never been interested in the fate of Falla Lufa: his
only concern in the case would have been to ensure that no one did
anything stupid about die-back disease. Before insect-borne infection
was suspected, an ill-considered order had been hurriedly passed for
the cutting down and burning of trees showing certain symptoms.
Had this been carried out, it would have dropped the crop produc-
tion by about a tenth for several years, thereby ruining a number of

the growers, who worked on small margins, without stamping out the disease. Falla Lufa demanded that the law should be obeyed, printing in his paper lists of plantation owners, mainly Indians and fellow Arabs, whom he accused of endangering the welfare of the community by noncompliance. Called in by the other side as a specialist in mold infections, the Dutchman had disposed of his case in five cold sentences.

Yet through everything the tiresome little man said or wrote, which displeased authority, in court or out, there shone integrity of a touchingly high order. He was honorable, and brave.

From the records of the two main legal cases which she had come so far to study—the trials for subversion, when the crown proceeded against him, and he was defendant, not plaintiff—she gleaned nothing factual which she did not know before. The outlines were as Dr. Asaby and others had presented them, as to the order of events, though not necessarily in their interpretation of what had happened. Apparently there was no limit to his partisanship for his white hero, Storr, who shared that graceless weakness of his for inflexibility at ill-chosen moments; nor, accordingly, to his hatred for Hilbery as the supplanter, the so-called "nigger-hater." (But Hilbery was so far from being this—how pathetic it all was!) The words in which he had accused the Resident of partiality for Hilbery were so wild and ridiculous that authority must have been hard pushed, she thought, to act on such grounds. Coming out of prison he had lost no time at all in continuing his tirade; the new attack against Hilbery personally and the whole Zanzibar penal administration began in the first issue of his paper to appear after he regained his freedom: he was only out of prison for a matter of weeks. (Yet now he wanted to come back to this particular jail for the remainder of his sentence, which was likely to run for another six months with remission for good conduct— Louise felt farther than ever from understanding the springs of his conduct.)

What emerged most clearly from these papers was that if anyone should have been accused of partiality for Hilbery as against Storr, it was not those in authority so much as the ordinary citizens of Zanzibar. They knew where they were, with Hilbery. They came forward with highly conflicting testimony, but it all pointed one way. Falla

Lufa's personal attack on Hilbery was based on the police officer's heavy drinking: hardly anyone in the town could have been ignorant of this, yet one witness incidentally volunteered on oath, while giving evidence about something else, that he had always believed the Bwana Mkubwa to be an abstainer, like himself; and he had worked as Hilbery's orderly for seven years. Laughter in Court had had to be suppressed. Awkward modernity had very little appeal, it appeared, to anyone in these parts except Falla Lufa. Poor Storr; he had obviously been a good man too, but with all the devastating single-mindedness of the born reformer.

"Don't we eat something more soon?" Ibrem was tugging at her dress with brightly stained fingers.

She looked at her watch, letting another sixpence roll down. "Oh, goodness, yes!" The morning had gone. She became aware not only of hunger but of sleepiness, with which she had been battling successfully for some time because of the interest of the papers. "You come back with me, and I'll get something for us to eat out of a tin. Maybe we'll open two tins." This, she knew, represented his highest ideal of luxury. She was not going alone into that inner room where, by now, the raw, vivid odor might have returned, might be waiting for her.

The sweetmeat tray was empty. On the way to her lodging she found another seller, and bought Ibrem one more smallish slab, of which she gave him half now, with the promise of the other half after lunch. She must keep him with her. If it were odd to be—quite possibly—buying her life with these insanitary sugar concoctions, she knew that hereabouts lives had been bought before as cheaply, or cheaper. The old slave market, the greatest the world had ever known, lay close to their route. Slaves who were dragged half-dead or dying from the holds of the dhows which drove in before the northeast monsoon, the "slave wind," used to be disposed of at once on landing, not kept for auction, if they looked unlikely to recover from the voyage. Two or three together would go for almost nothing to the more sportive-minded Sheiks in the trade—not to Loair; he was a businessman; he bought only sound bodies. If all of them died, the new owner lost on the transaction, being responsible for disposing of the carcasses by dragging them as far as the Great Ditch of stagnant water, which still bordered the Stone Town. It continued to stink, as it had stunk for centuries; it was interesting that ghosts seemed able to project a smell.

Conversation with Ibrem on the way to lunch was intermittent: he skipped from her side whenever he caught sight of any of his cronies, to torment them by showing the empty sweetmeat tray, and patting his stomach with satisfaction, putting out a multicolored tongue. Trying to find things to talk to him about, she discovered that there was a school which he should have been attending. But it could not be any good, he said, and his family said (which was why they did not care whether he attended or not), because it was free. Christian missionaries ran it—very fairly, Louise gathered—promising the parents of the Moslem children they taught that they would not proselytize. According, however, to Ibrem, unimpressed by their selfless war on illiteracy, if they had really been sure of the truth of what they preached to their own flock, they would not have kept their word. Difficult indeed, she thought, when she could wrest her mind for a minute from her immediate concerns, were the problems of the split administration in Zanzibar. On the whole, the Protectorate seemed to be tolerably well run: there was, quite plainly, nothing like the official corruption she had met in North Africa, in the former Italian colonies, where corruption was endemic in the ground; nor the fear and resentment of the white people by the colored which was reported continually, and more and more bitterly, from South Africa and Kenya: but if the bigger things were satisfactory, many of the smaller were not. Throughout British tropical Africa there was no compulsory education, no standard education of any kind for such as Ibrem, and the price of that lack was too high, humanly speaking, for any civilized community to go on paying complacently. It was, in fact, Ibrem.

It was while she was marveling at the human mind's ability to worry on two widely separate levels at the same time, that she came face to face with Cochi near the Maidan. So the girl had not returned to Karel's house.

Both women stopped, hesitating: they must pass within inches, hemmed in as they were by moving traffic. Ibrem had skipped off again, brandishing the tray, but they were not alone: around them were people who probably knew Cochi, and might have heard of

Louise. "How are you, Mrs. Downes?" the girl said loudly, in her cultured voice.

"Oh, I'm very well, thank you—" Louise was uncertain whether or not to add, "Cochi," and refrained. She did not know the girl's other name; it could not be Asaby, as she was a relation of his wife's. Did an attempted kidnaping, presumably with intent to kill, imply social familiarity in public, hereabouts? How absurd this was! Would it sound condescending, from the white to the colored, to use the girl's first name, while Cochi called her, "Mrs. Downes"? "And you, too?" she asked politely.

"I'm fine, thanks."

They went their ways, Louise with her heart shaken by pity. Cochi's beauty had affected her anew but more than that, once again, she felt the impact of the girl's youth and defenselessness. Some inner voice said unwillingly, In no circumstances can I rob that child! And added, still more unwillingly—that desperately hurt child!

Beaming, the fat proprietor of the cloth shop, to whom Louise's rooms belonged, waddled across the courtyard to meet her as she approached. Three men, he said, one white, one Arab and one Indian, had called to see her during the morning. They had come, the white man alone and the other two together, not long after she went out, and they had seemed very sorry not to find her.

Who were they? He said he did not know. She realized that this was likely to be a tactful pretense. Like the sanitary men, those in search of a woman, especially a woman not of their own color, would be officially invisible; white men were known to prefer anonymity on such errands.

"Perhaps they will soon come again," he said encouragingly. "It is a pity Captain Hilbery say you go from here. Business good, eh? But Captain Hilbery himself go very soon. Then you come back—and I put the rent up!" He shook with jollity. "Now I laugh only," he assured her, nudging her, pleased in a friendly way by her quick success. Hilbery had evidently been right about the conclusion the neighborhood was bound to draw from her lodging alone in this part of the town.

Not waiting while they talked, Ibrem had run in ahead of her, to get the brazier alight by "borrowing" glowing charcoal from the proprietor's wife, a woman fatter, more bawdy-looking and even more amiable than her husband, who had become so hideous that she was no longer kept in seclusion from such as Ibrem. By the time Louise could bring herself to go in, both rooms and the passage between them were full of charcoal fumes, too full for her to tell, try as she would, if any trace of the smell she had been sure she would recognize again were still lingering in the air.

She boiled a handful of the undersized local eggs, and let Ibrem open a tin of condensed milk and another of biscuits, on which to spread what was left of the sweetened milk when they had finished using it in their tea. This was made in the saucepan, with the water in which the eggs were boiled, by lifting out the eggs and pouring in the leaves—it was a highly concentrated meal, both in labor and in food: Ibrem thought it splendid. She was so hungry herself that she ate her share of the horrible jam substitute with relish, and immediately afterward sleep dropped upon her like a veil coming down softly, softly, between her and reality. She had slept hardly at all the previous night, and the Zanzibar climate allowed no such vigil to pass without taking toll of wakefulness by day. Hot food was stupefying, her eyelids grew heavier. She was back in the struggle of the first night at Mrs. Corryman's, but now it mattered much more that she should not sleep.

She moved into a less comfortable position, getting off the edge of the bed to sit on the floor. In a few minutes she was leaning against the frame, nodding off again: she woke with a jerk. If only she could have a cigarette! She must not let go now. While she had her wits about her, she could keep Ibrem by her side and be relatively safe. He was just finishing the last half of the ghastly green sugar slab. If she slept he would either rummage through her handbag and be off at once; or wander away, bored, whether she paid him to remain or not: and the men, whoever they were, might return. Perhaps they were harmless—Major Deane, possibly, and messengers from Mrs. Corryman and her other acquaintances. And perhaps not. She forced herself to her feet, half drunk with sleepiness.

"The English Club, Ibrem, and then that's all. I want you to take me there now."

"You know the way. I showed you."

"I might forget. I need to be shown at least once more." She would be nearly an hour early for her tentative appointment with

Hilbery, but she could pretend that she had made a mistake about the time. Though not officially a member, she might be allowed to wait in the lounge and use the women's room. In which case she could fall gloriously asleep locked in the lavatory. She turned Ibrem out, fumbled her way into her last clean dress, and brushed her hair.

"You go to meet Captain Hilbery?" asked Ibrem when he was allowed back.

"Yes. Why do you want to know?"

"Because when my mother say, are you harlot?—" Louise was surprised that he used the biblical term, until she remembered where he occasionally went to school—"I tell her, best kind have only one special man at a time. Captain Hilbery, very important man." He grinned ingratiatingly, and set about turning his implied compliment to advantage. "Now I take these few last biscuits with me? Plenty more children where I live. My mother most ignorant woman. But I tell you, trusting."

"I know. You told me that before. Leave those biscuits in the tin, all the same. It's more than half full and I want what's left."

"Captain Hilbery soon be going away from Zanzibar now. That a pity for you?"

"I gather it's a pity all round. But when I said he was a friend of mine, I didn't mean he was a *special* friend." If she had not been so drowsy she would have seen the advantage of letting Ibrem believe what he pleased.

"No?"

"No. Let's *start*, Ibrem! I want to get to the English Club."

"Those men the fat one tell me about in the shop, when I get fire —you think they come back?"

"How can I tell when I don't know who they are?"

"I get baksheesh if they do? Just a little?"

"Why should you?"

"Not tell Captain Hilbery!" Evidently her disclaimer had been unconvincing.

"I've already said, I don't belong to Captain Hilbery. I don't belong to anyone." This sounded, even in her own sleepy ears, less like a boast than a somewhat forlorn admission, and so Ibrem took it.

"You like I bring wealthy Indian here one day?"

"No. Now get going."

"I know another Indian. Not so much money, but very sweet
man."

"No."

He snatched up the biscuit tin, with a look daring her to try stopping him, and was away across the courtyard in a flash, laughing,
leaving Louise to find her own way to the Club.

She was fairly sure of this runway by now, but keeping her sense
of direction, by watching the lie of the light on the top of the walls,
was always hardest when the sun was high overhead, as it would be
for another hour yet.

She walked fast, through the relative hush and emptiness of the
siesta time, with only an occasional catch of the breath from anxiety
when a turn brought no instant recognition of the street. The alleys
of Zanzibar changed their features from hour to hour with the shifting of the light: it was not only that they looked different in different
degrees of shadow; booths which stood on one side in the morning
might be moved across to avoid the afternoon sun. But it was easier
to stay alert and wary if she moved quickly. It was also safer, or felt
safer. The difference in safety between the Zanzibar day and the
Zanzibar night seemed to her now an illusion. The last scrap of it
had blown away before the knowledge that men, whose names she
could not discover, had come openly to her lodging, sometime before noon, inquiring for her. No moment when she was alone appeared to be without risk in this city, where eyes and ears, unseen but
apprehended, waited with terrible patience behind the grilled openings in the walls. But if she hurried, she could hold back the veil of
sleepiness dropping, dropping dangerously, between herself and the
outside world. Even so, the figure at the other end of an alley into
which she turned was not real for a few seconds.

She stopped and drew back into the deep shadow of a doorway.
Between them, a net seller's wares hung flapping in the breeze. He
was something she had created by needing him. He was akin to the
fisherman she had seen on the lagoon, isolated in space and time, not
wholly human. Karel van Epp was separated by her weariness from
the dazzling light, the beggars and the dirt and the triumphant colors
of Zanzibar. He was in a world which held nothing but himself. He
was love, come again because at last her heart had forgiven her.

Walking toward her, looking upward under a sheltering hand, he was doing what she had been doing, finding his way through this labyrinth of openings and dead ends by the gilding on the sun-topped walls. He paused uncertainly by a turning, perhaps twenty paces away, considering its general direction. She saw the tall figure, the strong brown neck and the face half averted, clear-cut, intensely alive, and knew that he had been right in saying that it could be marvelous to see someone you loved approaching, before that person saw you; to watch unsuspected. Marvelous indeed; a sudden glory. How had she failed to know that of course this was the white man who had tried to find her before noon, and gone away because she was not there, and waited, and now was making his way back to her rooms? Who else could it be, this day, this superb day of the kind which for years the world had forgotten how to make?

He caught sight of her through the blowing curtain of nets and came running. "Louise—your arm—what has happened?"

"Nothing serious. Trouble with a homali cart. The plaster comes off in a few days. Oh, Karel—"

"You are a damned nuisance, like I said in my letter!" he told her, smiling, relieved, and took her in his arms and kissed her. "Aie, aie, goud-blond haar *is* mooie."

They stood close together in the Stone Town street, looking at one another, gravely now, saying nothing more for a while, and it seemed inevitable—there was no surprise for either of them, only great happiness in their coming together—that this was how they should meet, sure of one another, after that most perfunctory leavetaking when they had last seen each other in Holland.

"In future I will throw coconuts at the parakeets who say what only I am to say. But *what* a nuisance you are! And I tried so hard not to let you be—I wanted my leave undisturbed."

"Karel—"

He kissed her again, gently, his fingers prying loose strands of the sleek hair drawn back from her face; and round them the life of this quarter of Zanzibar, such of it as was not asleep at the ninth hour, shuffled and crept, or dashed past with homali carts which just avoided them, and took no notice at all. The shameless greetings of white men with white women in public were too well known to the local populace to attract interest.

"Oh, Karel. Karel!"

17

*The Road Through
Ngambo*

"I was trying to get back to your place from the Maidan," he said. "Already I have been there once, this morning—"

"I know." By now, in her enormous new happiness, the enchantment of being fully alive once more, it seemed to her that she had indeed known all along.

"But that was from the airport side. Which is not so complicated. Come. We will get right away from people for a bit. To where we can see only palms and mangroves instead. Perhaps, as a great treat, I will point out to you a clove tree with die-back on the way! Or find one for you where we are going—I have a borrowed car waiting on the Maidan to take us, because mine is still in Pemba."

"I doubt that at the moment!" she said, walking beside him in

216

the direction in which he seemed to want to go, which was not toward the Maidan. "Cars can be shipped direct from one island to the other, can't they? But not overnight, surely? Is it green?"

"My car?" he said, puzzled. "Yes. Why?"

She told him of the previous evening's incident, watching his face, seeing it grow grim and anxious.

"This is what I kept telling myself, in Austria, could not be happening! Of course not. Not today, in Zanzibar," he said. "In Zanzibar, where I knew well enough with the back of my mind that things like this can happen, any day! That was why, when I saw your arm in plaster—!"

He made her describe, with as much detail as possible, the two men involved in the episode, the driver and the figure she had only glimpsed by the car, but could identify neither of them.

"There would be no difficulty, though," he told her, "about buying men for such a job here. Do you know, I think that was partly why I wrote that letter to Pemba when I did—"

"You certainly didn't time it very well from my point of view!" she said mildly, too much absorbed in noticing the changes in his face as he talked to feel properly reproachful.

"No, and for what that has meant to you, I am sorry, indeed! Oh, I am sorry, too, of course, that I had to write as I did at all—sorry on account of someone else. Because of what it must have meant to get that letter." Instinctively they were both avoiding the girl's name. "Though you remember from Holland, do you, that I try not to feel sorry for anyone, more than I can help? Because it does no good, we both agreed—loose, pointless pity; and it is always a little insulting to be pitied. But I think I wrote that letter then because I wanted to worry, knowing what I know of Zanzibar ways. Wanted a reason, do you understand, for coming back here quickly from Europe? To *have* to come. So now I am here, and you must let me sort this out my way."

"Karel, I am not going to marry you."

"No? Well, I have not asked you—yet," he said, and laughed. "And won't, till I can see the way to let you live in Zanzibar, or Pemba, without fear. Otherwise" (this with the matter-of-factness which she found completely disarming) "I should have to give up my job here and take you back to Holland, to be safe. I think it

would be worth marrying you at that price. In fact I know it would
be, for certain. But I want to avoid having to do that if I can."

"Yes, I see. Do you think Dr. Asaby could be behind this? Of
course, I've wondered and wondered. In the little time there's been
for wondering! In a way, I'd rather it was Asaby."

He said, "Asaby might want you out of Zanzibar: he would
never go to this length. I accept—and I think you do, too—that if
you had got into my car last night, by now your body would be
floating up the coast. The current goes north, and there are enough
piranhas in the water between here and Mombasa to be sure you
wouldn't be floating recognizably for long. No, I'm afraid it was
not Asaby."

"Karel"—Louise made an effort to break the ban—"I've met
Cochi. She came to see me. When I first got away from Mrs. Corryman's. And I saw her again, accidentally, in the street today."

He gave an exclamation that might have been anger, or only
unwilling acceptance of the situation.

"She's so young," Louise said. "So pathetically young. How could
you—? I didn't expect to feel as I did, touched. That's why I said—"

"Look, I do not want to talk of this now," he said firmly. "Later,
yes, we will discuss everything. But first there are many more good
things to say. As this, that I see it is true you have freckles on your
wrist and your arm. Down to the hand and then, stop. In Austria I
looked up the English word for "freckles" through two dictionaries
because of this mystery—Dutch-German, and then German-English.
Arabs and Indians don't have freckles, so I never learned the word
here. But I was sure I remembered right. None on your hands!
Now why, *liefste?* And how did you get away from Mrs. Corryman?"

They walked, talking, arguing, each assuming that the other was
noticing the direction, until they heard the Koran being chanted
shrilly by the small apprentices in a silversmith's booth, and remembered passing it a few minutes ago, going in the opposite direction. They were wandering aimlessly through the heart of the Stone
Town. A child was rewarded munificently by Karel for guiding
them out of it.

"It would be possible to live ten years in Zanzibar and not
know the way about any part but your own," he said. "Many

Europeans here are like that. They can tell you how to find the
Residency, the Beit el Ajeib, the English Club, and where to show
visitors some interesting old doors. Have you yet seen Ngambo?"

"The African quarter? No, I only know there is one."

"And you a journalist. Who has been here four days. Should you
not be ashamed?"

"I expect so."

Suddenly the lunch party at Cambridge came back to her mind's
eye. Then it had been so hard to attend to what was being said.
Now it was wonderful to say the most ordinary things, and hear them
spoken. She remembered from the past that this was what it was
like to be in love. The least important opinion, or piece of information, passed from one to the other, gathered splendor from the contact it made between loving mouth and eager ears. It was no longer
opinion or information, but an airy bridge.

"Ngambo is more than an African quarter. It's another town,
lying side by side in space, and far away in time. So far away in
time, there's more difference between Ngambo and the part of the
Stone Town where you live—more hundreds of years of civilization,
you understand!—than between the Stone Town and the road
ahead." The road ahead was the westernized street by the Maidan,
with its crowds of European cars. "I'll drive you through Ngambo
on the way out," he said.

But almost as soon as they reached the thatched mud huts, standing at first in neat rows, sleep swept down on her again. It would
no longer be denied by the time they were in the outskirts, furthest
from respectable Zanzibar, where the dwellings were of flattened
petrol tins, huddled together haphazard, in a squalor more extreme
than anything in the Stone Town. "I'm so sorry," she muttered. "I
don't want to miss one minute of your return. Don't want to miss
this either. I'm sure it's terrible—disgrace to me as one of the ruling race—but"—she could not fit words to her thought: that the
Negroes' huts looked cheerfully fragile after the sinister permanence
of Arab buildings—"I can't keep awake any longer," she said, "now
I'm not frightened."

"*Mooi meisje*, I can't hear what you're saying! You're talking into
my shoulder." She had slumped against him while he drove.

"Doesn't matter. So sorry. Asleep." She slept with the deep abandonment of trust until they stopped, eons later, as it seemed, and in another world.

"Where's this, Karel?"

"On the east shore."

The quiet about them was startling after the clamor of the town: only a soft, continual clicking—sand crabs scuttling in and out of their burrows, he told her—mixed with the rattle of the coconut fronds high overhead, and the thump and hiss of breakers. A rough track ran down through a grove of palms to the sea. Ahead of them, at the end of this green tunnel, great slow-moving hills of blue water rolled in from the horizon, to smash in dazzling white foam on a protective reef offshore, sending on gentle ghost swells to whisper and vanish on the pale sand. Day was nearly done: a group of fishermen, dragging in a net, made long shadows which danced a solemn ballet over the wet shore. Karel's arm was round her shoulders.

"This is the most beautiful place in the world," Louise said with conviction.

"Good. Because I think you must stay here a day or so."

"Just as I am?"

"Just as you are."

"You, too?" She was grateful to have responsibility lifted from her for a while. Soon she would take charge of her own life again, but at the moment she was ready to acquiesce in any decision arrived at for her, in the deep security of love. She would do whatever he wanted.

"No, but I will come back. Tomorrow, I hope." He took her face between his hands. "I think we are not either of us ready for me to stay with you now. Do you remember telling me in Holland that going to another man had been 'an experiment. It didn't work'? Well, when you come to me, it mustn't be that sort of experiment." He kissed her, to stop her from beginning to speak. "Yes, yes, I know. You say you won't marry me. And in the end of course that will be your choice. But whether I will ever be your lover, that is really much more my choice! And I have already decided. But not for now. Now, well, we will be practical. Behind us is the village where one of your night watchman's wives is living. Hilbery told me her name, and the village I knew already. I can arrange for her to give you an empty hut, and look after you. I met Hilbery this morning at the airport, just after I arrived. He told me where you were staying in the Stone Town, too, and said you had got to get out. But for a different reason! He called you—"

"I know, 'an intolerable lass'!" Whatever he wished! This was joy in itself, to decide nothing more for a while.

" 'An intolerable lass—a grand girl.' "

"Hilbery!" She sat up, away from his arm. "I'd arranged to see him this afternoon at four!"

"Well, it looks as if you can't, doesn't it?" he said smiling, pulling her back to him. "Because now is after five. And anyway"—he hesitated and the smile died—"it would be no good trying to see Hilbery this afternoon, I think. Poor devil."

"What's gone wrong?"

"I will tell you—not in much detail. Because I have always thought Hilbery a fine man in many ways. And him above all I would not like to insult with pity. Oh, no, of course not 'him above all,' because you come first that way. But a man defeated by himself, at the end of a long, hard fight—this makes poor telling."

"He was on duty—he was taking duty for someone else, rather—and he got drunk? Is that it?"

"You know?"

"I know what would be tragedy for Hilbery."

"Well, then, there is even less to tell. When my plane landed this morning, all the passengers had to wait on the airfield a bit. The road was blocked by the Sultan's guard. That was when I first saw Hilbery, and he was all right then, and we talked of you. The delay was because His Highness was just going off to Mombasa—which he also rules officially, you know. At least, it's on his strip of mainland. Special guard of honor, and plenty fuss, and Hilbery on duty, because he'd asked to be, for the last time. Seeing to the police side of it. He has always done that sort of thing with the—how would you call it?—panache? —the flourish which the crowd loves. Then plans went a little wrong, I don't know how. The Sultan was not on time. It was very hot. And I saw Hilbery again. Not so good. He was cursing some 'coons' of his, who got in the way of the guard. He was pretty drunk. Afterward—I would not have thought a man who has fought the bottle so long could go down so quickly. But perhaps that was why. Because he has fought too long, and was too near release. I do not like thinking what that man must have gone through, these last years out here, since the drink got him, wondering if he could hold out long enough to do his job."

If it were true, Louise realized, that Karel van Epp strove not to pity, then this was because here was a man in whom compassion, when it struck through the protective shell over his feelings, struck deep. "You know he resigned because he was afraid of failing in just this way?" she said. "I found that out when I lunched with him. Oh, officially it may be because he's inherited some money. Actually, it's because all his pride is bound up in what he's been. In what he and his kind have done for Africa, in their time. Will everyone in Zanzibar know what happened this morning? I'm not asking for a description of what sort of fool he made of himself, but was it very noticeable?"

"In front of Moslems, who do not drink? Yes, it was very noticeable! And several friends of Mrs. Corryman's happened to be seeing off other friends—that is your answer, whether anyone in the English Club will know! People tried to help him, and he wouldn't be helped."

"Poor devil, as you say. The white police officer—the symbol of authority! What will happen to him?"

"Nothing much. Because his resignation is already accepted. He will go home a bit earlier, with his record spoiled."

"Even with your coming back—even after last night—I mind this so much for him."

"You like Hilbery? Somehow I would not have expected that. A man for men, or for very silly women, not you, I would have said."

"Karel, no one and nothing in this part of the world is what anyone could sensibly expect! Hilbery—Asaby—Falla Lufa too, the nearer I come to him, which isn't very close yet—everybody's totally different from what I believed at first. Hilbery—I can't bear the *vieux noceur* side of him. Nor the bit that has to discomfit anyone he meets so as to feel top dog. I can see that supposing there'd never been any trouble between him and the other white policeman, Storr, whom Falla Lufa loved, Hilbery was still bound to be the grievance of grievances to anyone legalistic in mind, like Falla Lufa. The official who administers British rule not by the written regulations but his own personality: and does it so well that the small people are fond of him, though not the Asabys! Yes, I like Hilbery, now. I thought him detestable when I first ran across him. And I like Asaby too—grudgingly. We've quarreled. There's a Zanzibar figure who couldn't really be more unlike the image of himself which he projects with such charm! And Falla Lufa—well, he's not here but in Harmatta, as maybe you've heard by now, from Hilbery. So I haven't reached him in the flesh but I believe I'll be seeing him shortly. And the nearer I get to him, the more contradictory everything about him grows. Heard of in Europe, he sounded unmistakably the good, wronged man. Then when I first arrived in Zanzibar he began to look fatuously self-important, a character with no real stature at all. And now, from here, when I've plowed through his dossier, his trial records and translations of his articles in his own paper—I just don't know! I can't even make up my mind about his loyalty to his well intentioned white friend, the one who did the right thing for the wrong reason, or else the wrong thing for the right reason, in treating all colored people as his equals and friends—I can't decide whether that sort of loyalty has anything to be said for it or not. All that's emerged for certain, from everything said by everyone else, is that good intentions, without intelligence, in rulers, is desperately dangerous to the ruled. I simply don't know what Falla Lufa stands for—it was all so clear, a long distance away! Or whether he really matters at all, to anyone except himself."

"And to you, Louise!" Karel said. "To you he seems to have given the thing he hasn't got, liberty."

"Yes. I don't really understand that either. I only know I'm thankful my heart has forgiven me. Oh, Karel, it's wonderful to talk again, without wondering if the other person will understand. To talk, and not be afraid." Gaiety bubbled up in her. "Do you think living in Zanzibar makes people peculiar, or do they come here to live because they are peculiar anyway?"

He was holding her so that his eyes could wander about her face, with the shadow of leaves flickering over it in the low light. "I don't believe you heard the last thing I said!" she told him. "It was a question."

"I did. Partly," he said. "With one ear." He made havoc of her hair, pulling the pins out, murmuring into it.

"Not in Dutch. I can't understand what you're saying."

"It is as well, if you still think you are not going to marry me," he told her lightly. Plainly he did not take this statement very seriously. "All right then, I will prove I was listening. In my short time in Holland and Austria, I read, oh, nearly not at all. But in Pemba, a great deal. And I have not yet found a book, in your language or mine, which gives an idea of what life in a British colony or protectorate is really like. I think maybe no writer could be loud and lumpy enough, and also keep a good conscience as an artist! But no, *liefste*, I can't tell you if people go funny because they come to Zanzibar, or come to Zanzibar because they are funny people. It could be both!"

They talked against time—absorbed in each other but aware that dusk, and another parting, were coming quickly—trying to say all that had been left unsaid beside the Walcheren canal. A bluish gloom gathered under the palm trees, and the sea ahead, with the spray flinging rubies and emeralds and gold on to the reef, reflected back a sunset flaring unseen across the sky behind them, hidden from them by the trees. Both of them, it seemed to Louise, were delaying putting into words something of immense importance to them both, the most important thing of all for them to recognize: Here is a love which could destroy both our lives if we came to it with reservations in our hearts. Not an easy love, but wholly demanding and wholly rewarding. There is still time to draw back, if either of us is not prepared to love completely.

Cochi was with them, like a ghost, in the darkness rising from the clicking sand, and among the shadows reaching down to them from the palm fronds, just ceasing to rattle in the evening calm. But not Louise's own particular ghost, who was laid.

The fishermen coiled their long net into two of the outrigger canoes lying pulled up on the beach, dragged these into the water, and paddled them away, side by side through a gap in the reef, riding the swells outside as though the boats were a pair of tethered horses jumping together, the men standing poised high on the net, exquisitely skillful in their balance. The first firefly streaked through the gloom, and the two in the car could no longer pretend that night had not come.

"Karel, you said this place was 'on the east shore,' but how far from Zanzibar town?"

"About twenty miles, only. You will be safe here, though. Zanzibaris don't much like fish, and that is lucky for us. Bless the climate, which makes it bad in a few hours. Anything caught in a fishing village like this must be eaten nearby. There is no regular trade between here and the town. The worst you will suffer, my poor Louise who likes good food as much as I do—you will have to live on fish! Till I can get something else to you by car. Now we should find the huts, and hope all the people have not gone to sleep with the sun."

He turned the car and drove back a few hundred yards, stopping where a narrow path ran off the main track, among trees which by the smell were no longer coconut palms: the air was full of a light, sweet scent. "This is 'mother-of-cloves,'" he said. "Not the bud, which is dried to help make cigars, and stop toothache, and put in the world's apple pies! The full flower. I think women should wear it, instead of what they do wear. To me this is one of the nicest smells that can ever be."

They got out, and he left the headlamps burning, to guide him back to the car. He gave her a torch and took one himself. Looking back when they had gone a few steps and Karel, pausing, was running the light along a glimmering white branch, Louise saw thousands of insects dancing already in front of the powerful car lamps. They were dancing, she thought, for her pleasure in hearing him say, with superb single-mindedness, "Now here is your first clove tree with what the planters call the sudden-death disease. Myself, I am not much interested in the sudden death, because there is nothing to do about it, but see now, this next tree is starting die-back. Look, where that branch is part-broken from the trunk. What a pity it is so dark, and you can't see it well. But you must promise to come and visit it in the morning!"

In the small ring of lean-to shelters and rondavels at the end of the path, a few people were still standing about, staring curiously at the green glow of the headlamps through the leaves. Among them was the former wife of the night watchman, suckling her new baby. A town girl, she was delighted by any break in the monotony of village life. Lazy she might be, as a wife, but giggling a welcome, she was willing to move her family out of their hut, which was one of the bigger rondavels, for the handful of silver Karel offered her, and to do anything else for Louise that he might suggest. Already unoccupied,

however, were several of the small lean-to shelters, belonging to the
men who had paddled away in the dusk. Their trip was expected to
last many days, and prompted by Karel, Louise chose one of these.
In a community where the staple diet was fish, every dwelling big
enough to cook and eat in fairly reeked of it. The shelter was only a
place to be crawled into for sleep: in this benevolent climate, while
the dry monsoon blew, no more protection was needed from the
dawn wind and the things that fell from the trees—overripe fruit,
insects, or bird droppings—than hurdles of woven palm fiber fastened waist high round the trunk of a living sapling. Turning domestic, Karel whittled her a native toothbrush with his pocket knife.
"I shall like to think of you sleeping here," he said. "Now I must go,
Louise. Walk back with me a little way."

But first, out of courtesy, they had to drink a bitter but not unpleasant native brew, by the side of a hurriedly resuscitated fire, from
two china cups of honor, one marked "Peninsula and Orient Line"
and the other "Bovril," and to eat quantities of half-raw fish. For this
they were both hungrier than they expected. In the village, only the
watchman's former wife spoke a little English; he had still been in
the police in her time, but Karel spoke ki-Swahili, "ki-settler" as he
called it, the bastard tongue of the coast. He was recognized with approval by several of the fishermen; a plantation area lay inland, some
of it experimental ground which he visited several times a year:
long-standing feuds existed between the fishermen and the wild,
roaming gangs of pickers who brought in the clove harvest. This was
the young white man who appeared unexpectedly to rage against
their enemies, with words of vivid abuse which all could appreciate,
when the pickers were mangling the trees more ruthlessly than usual,
wrenching down whole branches to speed the gathering, making the
fatal breaks in the bark through which ants carried in the spores of
disease. "Ki-settler," Louise had already learned from Hilbery, was sig-
nificantly composed very largely of terms of exasperation, reflecting
the European's helplessness against the slow-changing ways of Africa.

Too soon, still unwilling to part, they were standing in the scented
darkness, as far as she was to come with him along the path from
the huts, with the car's eyes lowering at them like some jungle beast's
through a screen of trees.

"Remember this is an old village," he said. "I'd forgotten, there might be something more for you to worry about than getting tired of fish! There are probably jiggers in the ground. Also hookworm around. And Bilharzia where water stands. But if you don't put bare feet on the soil, and fetch water yourself straight from a spring—there are bound to be many springs, deep ones, wherever you go—well, you can come to less harm here, certainly, than where you were. My God, if I had not come back!"

"What are you going to do? I must know."

"Find out all I can. About how my car got to Zanzibar. If it was my car—which unfortunately I don't doubt. And who drove it. And try to make her understand—as later I shall have to work to convince you, I can see!—that the past is past for me. Whether you live or die. There is no way back to it."

"Karel—"

"Yes?"

"Be kind. As kind as you can."

"You are a funny person, Louise. Dear and funny. Someone plans your death, quite cleverly. Just failing by luck. And you say, 'Be kind.' Yes, all right. I will hurt as little as I can. But sometimes it is not to be helped, that people hurt each other badly. I am grateful to you, though—very grateful—because you did not tell Hilbery, or someone like him, about the car-that-was-not-his. Anyone else would have gone to the police at once."

"You've no need to be grateful," she said. "I was going to tell him this afternoon, if I'd seen him. Tell him everything!"

"Then I'm just grateful you couldn't!"

She was strangely glad that he still had some tenderness for Cochi; was anxious to save her what he could: and at the same time she was afraid of the strength of the ties which two years of living together could fasten between these two people. In a few hours he would be seeing the girl again. Both Karel and Louise were intensely conscious of this.

He said, "Whatever I find out about the man who drove my car, or the other man with him, I am not going to report to—I was going to say, 'to Hilbery,' but of course it couldn't be to Hilbery, as he is now. I think he will be on a blind for days, after realizing what he's done. Maybe I would be too, in his place! But those men, I want to know who they were, for my own satisfaction. What they did

—what they tried to do—that wasn't their idea. So there's no sense in letting the police hear anything about them. And Cochi—well, I am the only person who can convince her you might as well live."

"If you leave her, it mustn't be for me! Not wholly because of me!"

"Louise, be sensible. I would have thought you too intelligent—"

"You aren't talking to my intelligence," she interrupted vehemently. "Karel, you're talking to my heart, and we both know, hearts are stupid things. Sensible people's are as stupid as anyone else's! More stupid, sometimes, I suppose, because they're the sensible people's only outlet from living and thinking so reasonably all the time, on the surface! This *is* the justice of the heart we talked about. I've carried a load of stupid guilt for years, trying and trying to run away from it. For a lot of complicated reasons, I'm free now. I'm not going to take on another load. Not going to buy my happiness with everything someone else has in the world. When hers is a poorer world than mine, even without you. Yes, even without you!"

"All this let us consider when you are safe, Louise, and not before! Safe anywhere, not just hidden away here. I am trying—without much help from you, *liefste!*—to look at one worry at a time. I must see her, tonight if possible, in Zanzibar if she is there still. In Pemba as soon as I can, if she has gone back to my place. And make certain she believes without hope what my letter only made her fear, I think—that we are at the end of the shared road, she and I. Whether you come with me on the next bit or not. This is what I meant when I said, you must let me settle this my way."

"You think she can accept that? Will it make her resent me any less if she does?"

"Any other woman, and 'No,' I would say. But in Cochi there is something—I liked it—something down to earth. She can see facts when they become facts. It is what I liked best in her, that way of looking at things as they are, not to be changed by wishing. Oh, she will fight while there is hope. But not without it. That is what I liked best, that earthiness, apart from her looks, I would say! Can *you* accept this for now: the day I was riding toward Veere by the canal, already I knew, I promise you, before I saw you again, the end of that shared road was just ahead? No, this is not quite true—was not very far ahead: that is better. I am not pretending I am sorry I met her when I did. It had good patches, that road. She is lovely. Because she is so young—which you mind so much—the most lovely thing I have seen. Did you notice, I wonder, when you met—"

"That she's like the glorious-looking girl in the Middelburg restaurant?"

"Louise, what an uncomfortable companion you could be! Trained to notice and remember too much. Everything! Well, I am lazy about emotions, like most men, I think. I had so many things nicely arranged in my life when you came along. My work, which all this doesn't touch. My leave with friends fixed up. Soon there would have to be a break, I knew, and all the trouble connected with it, but not yet—so I hoped. I told you, that morning in Holland when you said on the telephone you were coming here, most of me just didn't want the nuisance you were bound to be, if I let you become anything at all to me, beyond a fine person to take to a circus and talk to afterward. I think this way I must be specially lazy."

"Also specially honest!" Louise said.

"Do you know that is the first nice personal thing you have said to me? Since you offered to get rid of the pudding!"

They laughed together softly in the listening darkness which was suddenly streaked with fireflies for a few seconds, as if these living sparks were thrown off by their change of mood. One by one the floating lights went out. He took her by the shoulders.

"But I do know now," he said, "on every level I live on— How shall I say this, to avoid the words 'I love you,' which both of us have used before to other people? You with truth, and I, not so much! Well, then, I will say I wish to put up with you, damned nuisance as you are at the moment, and I wish it more than I can wish anything else! Tomorrow, if I have straightened things out by tomorrow, I will come back. Tomorrow, or the next day, or day after that, or maybe even the next one after that, if I have to cross over to Pemba, which takes time."

She clung to him then, shaken with emotion, sobbing out the thing to be said which she had put off saying. "Don't come back unless you're sure we belong together, for more than just a little while. Because there's been too much saying goodbye in my life. I can't believe now that anything can last, except the habit of running away. I know that can, for years and years! I've grown afraid of letting myself take hold of anything I really want for fear of losing it again. I could stand the disappointment if you didn't come back now. You've got to see her, I accept that. And she loves you. You may change your mind again. She'll try to change it, of course. If you aren't to hurt her more than you need, you can't stop her from trying to remind you of the fine things you've shared, in two years. If you come back to me, it must be because you're sure you've found what you wanted. Not for a little time, full of more goings-away, mind or body. Ending as this affair is ending for her. It mustn't be like that for us."

"It will not be like that. You worry about Bilharzia," he said, feeling very solid and gentle in the darkness. "Also about hookworm and a little about jigger fleas, which lay horrible eggs under your toenails. Not about me. I am sure. Quite sure enough for two if necessary." He brushed her cheek with his lips and turned toward the car.

Anticlimax came upon them relievingly with her gasped, "Oh, Karel, Einarsen!"

"What is that?"

"I forgot Hilbery this afternoon. And now, at this minute, I ought to be dining with friends of Mrs. Corryman's, in Mrs. Corryman's house, along with an ex-colleague of mine, a journalist from Sweden. Einarsen's the man who started everything by telling me about Falla Lufa."

"Well, it looks as if you can't, doesn't it?" he said reasonably, and she could hear by his voice that he was smiling broadly. "Because now it must be after ten, our time, and it will be getting on for midnight when I reach Zanzibar, with the roads as they are. I could telephone then and say, not to wait—if they are still waiting! But I shall not do that thing. I would rather no one else knew where you could be found."

18

Fishing Village

There began for Louise an interlude of extraordinary, indolent happiness, of anxiety temporarily suspended; three days outside normal living, when she listened to her senses, not her mind. And her senses told her, over and over again, that this was indeed, for her, at the moment, the most beautiful place on earth. The surprise, the shock of perfection came half a dozen times a day or more, in the chance grouping of people, of palms, of clouds trailing their purple shadows over the sea, and her eyes were open to beauty; open, it seemed, to nothing else.

Occasionally her thoughts whispered, in the worried fashion of other days, other places, that somewhere in Zanzibar town, or Pemba, the future course of her life was being shaped. And that

231

many women, from Dido onward, had waited by beaches as enchanted as this for lovers who did not return. But the breakers shouted down the whisper, and the transparent sand crabs clicked away the warning, like old women going "Tck, Tck, Tck" disapprovingly, at the very idea of almost everything.

Visiting the clove tree with the beginnings of die-back disease (which she dutifully went to examine soon after it was light, her first morning in the village) was a little like seeing Karel by proxy. She approached it laughing pleasurably, inwardly at herself and him; then a flock of birds screamed a phrase over and over again from neighboring bushes, and they were evidently of the same breed as the parakeets of Pemba who proclaimed that "Goud-blond haar is mooi," for the words seemed to her ear unmistakable, and excellently articulated. She could envisage Karel, with his face half lit by the torch turned on the tree. Standing where he had stood, before the stricken branch, she was no longer alone. This, said her senses, is the way of his mouth; his hands and his eyes are like that. He stands, so. He is tall, lean, dark. But "tall," "lean," "dark" mean nothing now, for they are qualities he shares with other men, and he is no longer of the same flesh as other men. He is Karel, and his body has turned into magic.

Reason tried to reassert itself against her senses as she strolled back to the village, which was just stirring. This new man of hers was one of whom she really knew very little, except that anyone who was with him would always need to share him with his work. She had said, and meant, that she would not marry him if this involved damage to someone much younger, much less armored against life than herself. This is how the hair feels, at the back of his neck, her fingers recalled, and reason and compassion were silent. Neither found much opportunity to make themselves heard during the day. Primitive time, during the light hours, is always very full of pressing duties—fetching water, feeding fire, observing portents and talking politely, with many gestures and smiles. At night they had even less chance, during the few minutes in which Louise could keep awake, lying on a pile of soft banana trash in the shelter. Tropical nights are urgent, fire-streaked, filled always with a strange atmosphere of promise, of tormented waiting, as though something for which all the days of the earth had been preparing were imminent and might

happen now—now—from one second to the next: they are not reasonable, nor kind.

The fisherman who had taken on the watchman's young wife invited Louise to come out in his boat, along with his woman and
baby, in order to do for pleasure, after his night's work, what he nor-
mally did for a living, which was multiple trolling. Louise accepted
with delight: the boat was an outrigger: they sailed at speed across
the wind, with several lines out on whippy bamboos fastened like the
spokes of a fan to the mast; and through the clear water, in which
their movements could be watched, the silly, gorgeous-colored boni-
tos dashed alongside the boat, racing with one another to swallow
the lure, which was no more than a tern's feather used as a spinner.
Cutting a tooth, the baby chewed with interest on a little live mack-
erel-like thing which plopped aboard when the boat drove through a
rippling silver shoal on the surface, scattering the white flurry of
terns crying and diving over it. An imperturbable child, he breathed
fishily at Louise when she held him while the mother unhooked a
catch and tied on a fresh feather: they were all entirely content in
the boat, except the mackerel.

When Louise landed, a car was standing under the palms, near the
end of the road to the sea, and her heart raced, slowed, and then
plodded on cheerfully, as the man it had brought came forward and
presented himself nervously: this was Karel's Indian assistant, sent
over with a load of tinned food. "Mijnheer's left hand," he described
himself imaginatively. Mijnheer van Epp, he said, looking at her out
of the corner of his eyes, had gone on to Pemba. The assistant appeared terrified of being questioned, uncertain as he was whether
either of his chief's women was aware of the existence of the other:
in his case it was plain that the left hand thought it knew all too
well what the right hand was doing. He had bought exactly what he
had been told to get, in a hurried midnight telephone message from
Karel, and had not risen on his own initiative to the idea of including a tin opener. The gift, though well chosen, was useless: in the
village there was not even a coconut cleaver, which might have
served to break open a tin. Eager to get away, concerned only with
the letter and not the spirit of the order he had been given, he piled
the tins neatly in her shelter, and firmly regretted that he could not
possibly take it upon himself to drive out again in Mijnheer's ab-

sence. He had been told to come once only, and tell no one where
he went. Perhaps, he said as an inspiration, someone else would pass
by with a tin opener. Louise let him go, and went on eating fish and
nothing else, but with diminishing enthusiasm.

Soon it was night, and she laid her sun-soaked body and wind-
lulled mind to rest on the thick bed of trash in the shelter, and almost at once, it seemed, dawn was creeping through the holes in
the woven hurdles on a sweet breeze, and another long, busy yet idle
day had begun.

The people of the village were friendly, and interesting-looking,
from a mingling of blood more complicated than anything she had
observed in Zanzibar town. Malay stock, carrying delicate features
and heads set well back on wiry bodies, had been added to the more
usual Arab-Bantu-Indian mixture, and in some a far-off dash of
Persian blood gave an aquiline cast to proud faces. There was occasionally a trace of Chinese ancestry in the set of the eyes. They were
used to white people coming among them, Government officials on
their way up or down the coast, anthropologists or medical inspec-
tors, and were not in the least curious to know why she was staying
in someone else's lean-to, eating fish, fish, fish.

To wear while she washed her dress, and dried it on a bush, the
women lent her a kanga, a length of bright patterned cloth to wind
round the body, from just below the armpits to half way down the
thigh, when she went with them to the particular spring where all
the communal washing was done. Several sources of clear running
water were nearer; but only one, half a mile from the huts, might by
custom be used for drinking and another, still farther off, for cleaning anything.

When Louise succeeded in making the ex-wife of the watchman
understand her question, why none of the nearby springs could be
used, the woman appeared shocked but vague, conveying that if this
were done the children would certainly get colics and the women
miscarry, while the men caught no fish. Louise realized that the village must have been founded farther down the coast, perhaps centuries ago, and had shifted gradually with the altering of the passage
through the reef, on which the fishing depended. Living coral insects built out a shelf under water, making one entrance more dangerous for the boats, while elsewhere the gales pounded a wider gap

where the coral had died. New generations of men had put up their huts, and rebuilt them after the destroying Masika, the Long Rains, farther and farther from those springs which alone remained sanctified by tradition. Slipping easily into local life, into acceptance of whatever the day brought, Louise walked without protest the proper distance, to slap twenty guineas' worth of French silk lightheartedly against stones worn flat by the hands of gossiping women, through uncounted years.

And when her dress dried, she still wore the kanga, buying it to keep with twelve assorted tins and the promise of something to open them with before she left. While closed, they were already of value as playthings for the children, who adored the pictures on the labels. A kanga, she discovered, was the most convenient of all cool garments, adjusted by one wriggle and discarded by another. It could be slept in, and was also admirable for going down to swim, off the steeply shelving part of the beach where the white sand frightened away sharks. The owner could walk into the water, holding the kanga higher and higher, roll it into a ball on reaching a certain depth, and throw this up the beach to someone—and there was always someone —willing to wait there as an excuse for doing nothing, in order to throw it back at the right time. Louise's kanga bore a pattern of R.A.F rondels of varying size, the two largest designed to be worn, back and front, where local wit considered a target most endearing. Decorously, wondering again how long she would retain any Euroean prejudices in this climate, she hitched the kanga slightly to one side, so that the main target areas were on the left buttock and the right hip. Giggling, the other women tried several times to rearrange it, but finally desisted.

Sharks, it was conveyed to her, were rare in these waters, but she must keep inside the reef, for safety, and to the part of the shore clear of dark coral patches. Brilliant light on all sides of her colored her skin swiftly; she was one of the few fair-haired women who turned brown without discomfort. Even sitting in the shade under the palms, through the heat of the middle day—watching the fishing pelicans, so grotesque and clumsy on the ground, so graceful in the air—she was subject to the play of powerful reflected sunshine, and by the morning of the third day there were no freckles still noticeable on her wrists and arms; they had merged into one, covering every part of her left bare by the kanga. Her face, shoulders and legs were, if not of the same hue as the villagers', to be considered white-skinned only by courtesy, and her hair was rapidly bleaching into tow. She was aware of immense, indolent well-being, very little lessened by mild hunger. (It was possible, she found, to develop a kind of second wind for fish eating, but not to go on eating quite enough.)

The moon sank into the arms of the dawn, at the end of her third night in the village, and Louise came out into the open to savor the sweet, fresh moment of change from night to day, along with the amiable little fruit bats which flew at this hour, after hanging since dusk in her sapling. The air still tingled with the expectation of the night. One half the world was black or faintly silvered, and the rest, gold turning to flame, as the sun came up in glory behind the sea. Karel will be back here today, she told herself with certainty, for no reason except that the first rays touched her like a caress. But the hours went by, bringing no visitors, until noon had passed.

The midday meal, eaten communally in the largest hut, seemed sumptuous to her, but to no one else: the night's catch had been unusually poor, and the villagers fell back on bananas, a matter for grave apology. The local self-sown variety were small, hard plantains which required cooking: Louise had been wanting to try them but had not liked to roast them for herself: raw, they had bested her; they were less appetizing than fish. The villagers looked on them as the English country people she knew round Cambridge regarded blackberries in due season—as food fit only for children, or adults in embarrassing necessity. The ember-roasted fruit tasted like bread with chestnuts.

After the meal she walked toward her shelter—chosen for its isolated position on the outskirts of the village—humming with well filled pleasure, carrying a new pile of banana trash for her bed, and trying to envisage this place in the downpour of May, when the dry monsoon ended and the children were said to roll about from one collapsing hut to another like balls of mud.

Terror stopped her. A smell brought her again the unforgettable tightening of the muscles of the throat which meant fear almost beyond control. The flavor of a cigarette hung in the air near the shelter.

Karel smoked Dutch cigars while his supply from home lasted, and then nothing: he had been too preoccupied to lay in a stock on his last leave. No one in the village used tobacco in any form. It was nearly three weeks since Louise herself had smoked.

The toe of a town-shod foot protruded from the opening of the shelter. She stood paralyzed, a few yards away, while seconds went by. From the movement of the foot, the person who had crawled in now turned on one side to watch her. Through the loose-woven walls she could be observed, but from where she was, she could not see in, beyond the foot. She made a movement to run, and then checked it: where could she go—to the sea, the palm trees, the other huts, in a village on which she had really no claim?

"I frightened you, didn't I!" said Hilbery's voice with satisfaction.

"Yes," she said stupidly. "Yes, you did," and hated him at the moment for his need to see everyone in an inferior position before he could be kind.

He crawled out. "Well, I've got you what you wanted. Falla Lufa's back in Zanzibar jail. And I go home by the next passing ship. If you want to see him, you'll have to come at once."

She could not hate him any longer when he stood before her shakily, the effects of a prolonged drinking bout still pathetically evident. This was a beaten man.

"I'll have to think about that," she said, passionately unwilling to leave this good place. If Karel came today, and she had gone—

"There's gratitude for you. Intolerable lass that you are. I pull myself together—for you. Out of the biggest bat ever. Pull all the strings I can still get my hands on—for you. Get a special escort sent racing up to Harmatta by truck—quite illegally, too—to bring him down into this territory. And then you say, you'll have to think about it!" He was not now drunk, but not entirely sober. So much alcohol in the blood took a long while to drain away. "Well, sweetheart, you'll have to think quickly, because no one's going to let you in and out of the jail, against regulations, when I'm not around any longer! My, my, you have gone native." He looked her over, smirking, tugging at his mustache with an unsteady hand, the sad specter of an Edwardian masher. "Suits you, doesn't it?"

"I expect so. Sunburn usually does. I haven't looked to see." This last sentence was untrue; of course she had looked, in the still water

of the pools round springs: she would be comely when Karel came
to her.

"Unusual little love nest you've got here. *Is* it a love nest?"

"No, it's not," she said, angry again, not at the implication of the
question but at the impertinent curiosity of its asking. The world
must keep its shabby paws off her and Karel. The thought shot
through her head that if she did not marry Karel, but lived with him
—as in the dawn, longing for him, she had more or less accepted
that she would—this was exactly what the world could be relied on
not to do. Here stood the world, ready to paw and guffaw at a guess.
"I'm here because you were quite right," she said, "about my not
being able to live unmolested in those rooms! I was taken for a prostitute."

The laugh he gave seemed to be dragged up from afar, from the
depths of the man's obsession with his own burning self-contempt.
"Well, well, what did your Uncle Tom say!"

"And, incidentally, this is just about the best possible way of
studying local life if one is a journalist without an expense account!"
she said. Long ago she had learned, professionally, that a true but
irrelevant statement made the best concealment for another truth,
which must not emerge. Karel wanted no mention of the episode of
the car which should have been black, not green. Then however thin
any other explanation of her presence here might sound, she must
stick to it, and Hilbery could believe what he pleased. Except about
her relations with Karel. At least the fact, already known, that she was
very hard up, did go some way toward backing up her preposterous
excuse for living like this.

But Hilbery was too deeply sunk in his own concerns to pry farther. "Well, make up your mind, wench. You coming, or aren't you?
My car's on the beach road, and I'm starting back now."

She was torn between the desire to stay; to wait here until Karel
came to fetch her, if all went well, as he had promised; to prolong
for a few hours more, or even a whole day and night, this lovely time
of indecision: and all the promptings of common sense, of professional habit, of caution, which spoke on the other side. Plainer still
to Hilbery, if she insisted on staying now, would be the conclusion
to be drawn from her odd way of life.

She temporized, raising objections, trying to think of a method of leaving a message for Karel with the watchman's ex-wife, which would not be overheard by Hilbery. "If I come back to the town, where can I spend the night? I can't go to that lodging. Three of my would-be clientele called the last morning I was there! I've even less money for a hotel than I had when we first met, and there'll be no time to look for another cheap room today, will there?"

"You are a silly lass," he said, rousing himself slightly. "You don't seem to realize you're quite a big frog in quite a small puddle, in these parts. There's not a white house in Zanzibar that wouldn't give you a shakedown. It needn't be Mrs. Corryman's."

"I wish I'd realized that before!" she said. "Who told you just how to find my shelter?"

"Tamil helper of that Dutch botanist fellow with a name like a hiccough. Caught him speeding back to town through Ngambo. He said he'd brought you a lot of tins, and told me just where he'd stacked them."

Louise made a mental note never to repeat this to Karel, by whom the nervous young Indian seemed overawed already to the point of imbecility. Karel would probably want to sack him for carrying out one order too literally and another not literally enough. She had by now a warm sympathy for anyone who desired to hang on to a job.

"Now, how about it? Yes or no? Because I'm off."

"Yes, I'll come. It'd be idiotic not to, wouldn't it, when I traveled all the way from Europe for the chance of seeing this man? And thank you—belatedly! Thank you very much. It was good of you to bother—as things are," she finished awkwardly.

"Oh, so you've heard, too. Even out here! Well, everyone knows everything in this island. I suppose it'll take quite a bit of getting used to at home—privacy! By the way, sorry I couldn't turn up at the Club to meet you that day! Anything special you wanted? Hope you didn't wait too long."

"No, that's all right. I was going to ask your advice, meekly, about getting out of my room!" So everyone did not know everything in Zanzibar, she thought, and was thankful. He was unaware that she had not reached the Club after all. "Look, I don't know much about that incident out at the airfield," she told him. "And I don't want to. Only that things went wrong for you in the way you always hoped they wouldn't. Only enough for me to feel really sorry. Deeply sorry. Sorrier than I can say. I mean that."

"I believe you do. Intolerable lass—grand girl. I said that about you to someone else—and it was about the last cold-sober thing I said!"

"Well, you start back for the car," she suggested, "while I crawl into a dress, clean if crumpled."

"You can come in a kanga, if you like. Anything so long as you drive. You can drive a car, I take it?"

"I can, but I haven't a driving license for this part of the world. And I've no intention of appearing in the town in a kanga."

"Perhaps you're right. About the dress, that is. Doesn't matter about the license." To her dismay he insisted on waiting while she changed, talking to her through the shelter wall. "After all, I'm still thought of hereabouts as a policeman—wrongly. No one's going to stop us and ask to see your license when you're with me! The point is, I made a pretty wobbly journey coming this way. Scared the daylights out of a few homali cartmen. Dented a palm, I fancy, and maybe the car—I haven't looked to see. Because at least it still goes. Drink improves some people's driving, but it never has mine. I'd not like the last thing I did in Zanzibar to be squashing a couple of coons. You'd better drive."

He ambled along behind her when Louise went to say goodbye to the watchman's ex-wife: there was no chance of leaving a personal message for Karel.

"I am going back to Zanzibar town with Captain Hilbery. With—Captain—Hilbery," she said as clearly as possible, hoping that the name, which the woman already knew, might be repeated to Karel in due course and reassure him about her disappearance. If not, she wondered, would he jump to the conclusion that she was running away again, at the last minute, and this time from him?

"Captain Hilb'y not get me back to first man. This one better. Very sorry no fish." Nothing could convince the troubled woman that Louise's departure from the village was unconnected with this scarcity.

The leaving-brew appeared in the ceremonial cups, and Hilbery lapsed into gloomier silence beside the hut fire. By so many others he must have sat, in his long life of service out here, saying goodbye on happier occasions. Louise begged off him his elaborate pocket knife, as her farewell present to the village, and showed the watchman's ex-wife exactly how to use it to open tins.

"Oh, God, let's get away from here quickly!" he muttered, as soon as they were clear of the hut.

Louise climbed with reluctance into the driving seat of what the watchman had described as "a fine black car. A very fine car." It was not so fine now. There was considerable damage to both fenders. She started the engine and sat for a moment, getting the feel of a strange machine; she had never driven this make before.

"How I don't want to go back to an England I haven't seen for twenty years!" Hilbery burst out suddenly. "And I wouldn't be admitting that to anybody if I wasn't still a bit under the influence. Consider yourself lucky this day that you'll be doing the driving!"

"I do," she said. "And I also consider myself lucky for a lot of other reasons." Hilbery's car was standing exactly where she and Karel had talked, under the palms. She looked round, taking leave with her eyes, obscurely aware that, although she had been happy here, she would never wish to come back to this place.

19

The Awkward Saint

Hilbery spoke only three times of his own accord on the journey, and after a while she gave up trying to talk, wondering if she had already been, like Major Deane among the desert flowers, tiresomely persistent.

As if to make it harder for him to wrench himself out of this setting, the road to the town was jolly with song, and with sights which he would expect to remember all the rest of his life as typical of the island. Asleep against Karel's shoulder, she had seen nothing of the plantations on the way to the coast village. Teams of pickers were at work in the coconut groves on both sides of the road. Negro climbers, with a loop of rope twisted round and between their ankles, swarmed caterpillar-like up the tall, bending trunks, and threw down

242

nuts to be collected, in a leisurely way, by a very fat Indian accompanied by a very thin donkey. As usual, it was the Indian who had the best of it, but it was the climbers who chanted all the time, loudly enough to be heard above the engine of the car—old, endless-seeming ditties, some on the Asiatic scale, some on the African, and jumbled up with them, modern song hits from the West, learned through the radio, probably at second or third hand, for they were only recognizable at intervals: Zanzibar curlicues and grace notes had changed their woeful, sagging harmonies into something exotic and cheerful. The men's voices floated down from the waving plumes of the coconut palms, making tents of gay sound, even out of "I Don't Know Why I Love You Like I Do," and when the wind blew strongly, the tents of song behaved like real tents loose at the foot, bellying out on the leeward side, so that voices from afar stretched across the road to her, while near at hand, downwind, the song was pushed fluttering back against the tree: she could see a man singing close overhead, but the noise streamed away unheard.

Hilbery said suddenly with no context, "Plenty men out here would think nothing of it. Incapable in public—what's that to hard-bitten chaps in bigger positions than mine? You hear them boasting of it. But everyone has some special sort of odd pride. People said, 'Old Tom's always all right when he needs to be.' "

"An odd pride or an odd shame. Yes, I know." She found it hard to think of any comfort to offer him. "Out here, you're going to be remembered by a whole lot of unimportant people, with various colored skins, as someone who made sense to them. Whose standards they could understand. I've heard the scalawag of a boy who acts as my guide in the town saying it was a pity you were leaving. Isn't that going to matter to you, when you look back, more than one isolated failure?"

He grunted without replying, or possibly when he spoke again, minutes later, what he said was meant as an answer, his acceptance of her consolation.

"Well, glad to be able to do just one more thing for just one more silly coon!" he said. "Old Full o' Love. I told you I'd got him brought back in a hurry for your sake. So it was, but also for his. Because it's Zanzibar he loves, and so do I. While I'm still here, if visiting hours and regulations interfere with the times you want to see him, you can have him taken outside his cell, and talk to him in what used to be my old office, if you like. Now turn right here, for the jail."

Just before they reached the unpretentious-looking building which housed the prison, he said, "By the way, fine old hue-and-cry there's been after you, because you vanished like that. Friend of yours— Swedish journalist or something—arrived and made no end of a fuss. He wanted to see Falla Lufa, too. Lot of officious people told him he'd better go up to Harmatta for that. He'd only got twenty-four hours to spend here anyway, so he dashed straight off for Harmatta, and got there just about when Falla Lufa was arriving here. Funny, really."

"Very, very funny," said Louise. "Funnier than anyone could possibly understand without knowing Einarsen. Is he coming back?"

"No. He said he wouldn't have time."

"Nicer and nicer," said Louise ungratefully.

She felt extraordinarily nervous, for a practiced interviewer, as she got out of the car and walked up the path beside Hilbery. This was the end of a quest.

"I shan't come in with you myself, for his sake," said Hilbery. "Queer to think he still hates my guts over Storr, after all this time, or so I'm told. I haven't seen him since he came back. Poor old Full o' Love!" He handed her over to another police officer, an eager, pink-cheeked boy. "See you later, at the English Club—perhaps!" he added, and winked at her. "If I'm not too loaded again." A wink, she thought, can be the most depressing of all human gestures.

An impulse to delay the meeting with Falla Lufa took hold of her; she wanted to plead that she really must have time to clean up, and change out of this unironed dress before seeing anyone. But there was nothing more respectable left in her suitcases; in any case they were in her rooms some distance away across the town, and surely it was not necessary to make-up carefully to talk to a prisoner she had traveled thousands of miles to see? She stifled the impulse, and her feet carried her forward, beside the pink-cheeked English lad, who asked for her autograph, having once seen her name in a paper.

Two white-robed Arabs were being ushered out of Falla Lufa's cell as she approached. They bowed, murmuring her name in passing— she was back in the frightening urban world where everyone knew who she was, without corresponding knowledge on her side. Then a door was unlocked and locked again behind her—she would be allowed twenty minutes' talk alone with the prisoner, on Hilbery's recommendation, she had been told—and a small, shriveled figure was rising from a sleeping-ledge spread with (of all unsuitable things in this climate) a lion-skin kaross by way of bedding.

He, too, bowed, and then held out his hand: it was like a monkey's paw to touch, hot and leathery. She felt an uprush of affection and concern for this will-o'-the-wisp of justice, who had led her back to life. Whether he now turned out to be something of a mountebank, or of the stuff of which true martyrs were made, she would remain permanently in his debt. She was even ashamed of having been so mean recently about Einarsen, who had mocked her on toward this quest, with accidental benevolence.

"Ah, Mrs. Downes, you are a journalistic colleague? Except that you are not, I think, an editor but a reporter?" Falla Lufa's good but pedantic English flowed out very fast on a shrill, carrying voice, always as if he were addressing an invisible audience behind her. "I hope you have not come to liberate me?"

"You don't want that?"

"I joke, of course. I know that you have not the power."

"Except possibly in an indirect way," she said. "By drawing public attention in England to any slip-up of justice there may have been. Through an article or a series of articles in one of the London papers."

"Which London paper? Because I have no wish to waste my time. Some of them are aimed at entertainment only, and are without serious influence."

She had not thought of time, for a man in prison, as something he would not care to waste over any chance of deliverance, and was charmed rather than otherwise by his attitude. She explained her present position to him quite fully, and the possibility that she might not write anything at all, if the facts did not seem to her to warrant the effort. Falla Lufa, like Hilbery, was someone with whom it paid to be blunt, almost rude.

"Quite so," he said. "In our world you have made a name for yourself. I have heard of it. As a free lance you should be able to choose a reputable paper. I am willing to leave that to your common sense, and talk of my case. But I must disabuse you of a misconception at the outset: there has been no 'slip-up of justice' as you call it." He looked at her disapprovingly, like an adult correcting the slovenly speech of a child. "I have incarcerated myself for a principle."

"Yes, so I imagined. Could we discuss the principle?"

"But first," he said, "you will surely wish to take in the details of my surroundings here, for your descriptions. You notice that this is a light, airy, whitewashed cell. I am fortunate in getting back my old room, for which I acquired some regard during my first sentence. Here are books, and fruit, which my good friends have just brought me as evidence of welcome, along with this magnificent kaross to sleep on, and other presents."

Irrelevance being strangely catching, Louise heard herself asking, "Why a lion's skin? Won't it be terribly hot at night?" which was not what she had come so far to learn.

"The lion is the king of beasts. Truth is the king of virtues. And will prevail," he said, seating himself with composure on the sleeping-ledge, to await her next question. As this was not immediately forthcoming, he motioned to her to sit beside him and went on, "I am glad to be here once more. Very glad. Where my friends can visit me, consult me, find satisfaction in showing me their esteem. In Harmatta there was liberty amounting to license." (Then Einarsen would have got hold of some excellent ammunition for his paper's anti-imperialist campaign, she thought benignly.) "Here, I will not say there is peace, for me, but at least I am not wholly wasting my time. I can study, keep abreast of local affairs, even influence them perhaps through advice given to my friends."

"Could we—"

"In fact, you might say I am an awkward saint," he suggested, and gave her a smile which was both unexpectedly sweet and disconcerting. One of his middle front teeth was missing; he had probably lost it in early childhood because the other, much longer than the rest of his teeth, had moved into the gap, and the effect was neither rabbity nor human but unfortunately enthralling. Louise found it impossible not to watch eagerly for each glimpse of this irrelevant, long, central tooth. "Should you not be taking this down?" he asked.

"No. I never make written notes while interviewing."

"I have always insisted on it, as an editor. It avoids inaccuracies."

"The London Press is not so particular."

"Your joke," he said, as a bridge player might say, Your trick. "Tell me, was your first impression of me that I looked like Gandhi?"

"No," she said, and could think of nothing to soften this. His only likeness to the Mahatma lay in the unimportant outward fact that whatever Falla Lufa wore—at the moment it was a weary white prison-suit—was always likely to look too big for him. There was no Indian guile about his coiled-spring excitement of manner.

"That is most clear-sighted of you, for I am not really like him. Though some have thought so. And I admire him, mind you, but the parting of the ways comes for us when he says that violence is always wrong. No, there are times when it is necessary. To rid the world of evil. I should myself be prepared to have recourse to practical action, for that purpose, if the occasion arose. You could say"—he gesticulated at her with a forefinger as though he were directing her to write this down, and then, remembering, gave her his distracting, winning smile—"that I am really more like Dr. Albert Schweitzer. A believer in implementing decision."

How far could overweening vanity go, she wondered, when it was fostered by weeks, months of lonely brooding? Yet this dauntless little creature was not contemptible, even at his most absurd.

"Could we," she asked, "get back to the principle behind your deliberate provoking of the law for the second time? Why did you do it?"

"Ah, you see it was deliberate, then? Good, good." He seemed to think it in some way a triumph of his own that she had realized this.

"Well, naturally I do, when you started abusing one of the police officers, and the whole of the prison administration, in your paper, and saying your first trial was unfair, the moment you were free from your first sentence! The authorities had no choice but to act. Or do you think they had?"

"No, they had no choice. As the law stands."

"You knew that you were bound to get a second period in jail for contempt of court, when you wrote as you did?"

"I knew that."

"Perhaps you did it because you disapprove of the law as it stands?

You wished to protest in that way, to make clear that the law should be amended? Or administered differently?"

"Oh, dear no," he said, sounding shocked. "On the contrary, I always desire the law to be firmly upheld. It makes for order. I appreciate order."

"Then, *why*—?" This was the most difficult interview she had ever tried to conduct. As it went on, less and less clear became their respective roles: which of them was interviewing the other?

"Do you worship a God, Mrs. Downes?"

"Mr. Falla Lufa, has this any bearing on what I'm trying to understand? On why you did what you did?"

"Certainly it has. And remember, please, I did not ask you to try to understand!" Like a lecturer with his subject well in hand, he was clearly enjoying, in a melancholy way, the presence of his invisible audience.

"Very well. (I accept, of course, that you didn't invite me to come here and talk to you. In fact, thank you very much for seeing me.) I recognize that there's more in the universe than matter, but I can't believe in any sort of semihumanized intelligence behind it, of the sort which could be said to 'like' this, or 'disapprove' of that, or take a friendly or otherwise interest in living creatures. Certainly I don't expect personal survival in any form. Is that what you wanted to know?"

"I asked you if you worshiped a God, not if you believed in one."

Louise opened her mouth to protest, shut it again and swallowed. She had interviewed many elusive subjects, but hitherto the most elusive had always been women. "All right, though I can't imagine how this can possibly be relevant! Before I could worship a God I should need to be convinced not only that this God existed, but above all, that this God was worthy of worship. A God only partly in power seems to me unthinkable, but a wholly powerful God, responsible for the cruelties of life—or indifferent to them, to the point of allowing them to go on—only interfering arbitrarily, when prayed to sufficiently—well, this is such a foul idea, to my way of thinking, that I'm thankful my reason doesn't require me to consider it. Now does that satisfy you?"

"Quite. Quite. We see practically eye to eye. Except about the use of prayer. I am in favor of people praying, even though there is nothing there to be prayed to; it does them good just the same. But otherwise we are in agreement, and I am so glad. It makes this interview worth while, in any case. We are in accord that there are mystical values, which are independent of faith. I am a man who longs for pattern in the universe. Who longs—oh, with a great loneliness!—for spiritual things to have meaning. So if they have none, ultimately, then it is I who must give them meaning myself in my own, smaller universe. By loyalty. By courage. By fighting on, even when outgunned. Because I have no faith, in the religious sense of that word, the things in which I do believe are all the more precious to me. Can you understand that?"

"Oh, yes."

"Then I will tell you what these are: order, law, friendship. Mrs. Downes, I have only had one white friend—true friend—in all my life. I leave it to you to judge if this friendship was important to me. Do have a grape."

"What?" His high voice had run on without pause. "Oh, I see. How nice. Thank you." He had picked up a small bunch of grapes while talking. She had been attending only to his words, and the unfathomable passion behind them. Now he divided the bunch carefully in half, gave one cluster to her and began to eat the other.

"This is an amiable jail, is it not?" he said. "No wonder I longed to return to its quiet from the farcical laxity of Harmatta. This is more like a monastery. Though to be sure, I have never been in a monastery." He laughed, quite merrily, with fanatical thin lips separating round the tooth.

"You would hardly be left alone in your cell with a woman in any monastery of which I have heard. (I joke again.) Look, Mr. Falla Lufa, you say this is an amiable jail. But in your paper you set about it, and everybody connected with it, pretty roundly. Was this because the former police officer, Mr. Storr, had been wrongly relieved of his job, you felt?"

"That is so. Do not hesitate to finish my grapes. Overjoyed at my return here, my friends—my *colored* friends, as some would carefully call them—delight to bring me gifts. Oh, all sorts of gifts. Have a mangosteen?"

"No, thank you. Just three more grapes." (After so much fish they were a revelation of how grapes should taste.) "But when you made this gesture," she said, "your friend Mr. Storr had already left the Protectorate and taken another post elsewhere, hadn't he? There was no chance of his being reinstated here, whatever you said or did. By lashing out at his supplanter, in print, what did you hope to achieve?"

"Nothing." He was enjoying himself again.

"Oh, dear!" Soon the twenty minutes would be up, and she would be no nearer, she thought despairingly, to the heart of this cantankerous little mystic. "Surely if a man sacrifices himself publicly for a cause—practically forces the law to victimize him, as you've done—he must want the world to know what his cause is, and what purpose he has in mind? This is what I've come a very long way to try to get at—your motive."

"If you had put yourself to the bother of reading my legal cases—all my legal cases"—he looked at her sideways, mischievously—"only then would the principle underlying my actions become apparent to you."

"Well, I read them and it didn't," she said flatly.

"You have read them? All? You can say, all?" He was overwhelmed with astonishment and satisfaction by the fact that she had taken so much trouble on his behalf—far more impressed by the time she had spent in reading about him than by the distance she had traveled to see him. The vanity of the man which ran hand-in-hand with the intransigence of the saint showed in his increasing excitement. "Mrs. Downes, I am confused! You, a busy white lady. I did not think anyone but myself had quite such devotion to the task in hand, whatever that task might be. And I have met only one other white person so concerned with what befalls the colored—the 'coons'—the 'niggers'—I need not name him to you. You do mean, all, not only the two chief actions?"

"I read the whole file on your activities in the Records Office—and I may say I got to it with considerable difficulty!" If this flattered him, let him have such small pleasure. "Now that we've talked—round and round—I've got some slight idea of the value you put on sacrifice for its own sake." He made as though to interrupt, and she hurried on. "Yes, yes, I know! When nothing more practical in the way of a tribute presents itself as an alternative. But I wouldn't have got even as much as that from those papers. I doubt if anyone else would, either." She had a vivid impression of Karel, at that moment, searching for her through the village down the coast, growing frantic because she was not to be found, and missing the woman who had the message about Hilbery—the whole family might well be out trolling. The picture did nothing to help her keep professional patience with Falla Lufa.

"And I don't see there's anything—" She hesitated, uncertain whether or not this would be a blow to the extraordinary, obsessed man looking at her expectantly. "I don't see at present," she said, "that there's anything useful I can do about what I've learned. Anything I can write."

There was silence. The set half-smile on his face did not waver. When he spoke, it was in a tone of indifference, real or well assumed. "Remember, I did not ask you to."

"Oh, indeed, as I told you before, I accept that. My difficulty is still that, rightly or wrongly, you forced authority's hand. So there's really no case I could put up, for revision of your sentence. At least I can't at the moment think of one."

"I understand, Mrs. Downes. I wish to correct a misstatement. I think I was not quite accurate at one point in our conversation—which has been interesting to me, whether anything comes of it or not; and to you, too, I hope? I said I was glad to be back here because I could be in contact with friends, and through them with the life of Zanzibar. And of course that is true. But also—I wonder if this is something which will appeal to you?—the drumming! There is nowhere like Zanzibar for the sound of drums at night. If you have been brought up with it, you miss it inexpressibly. We are some way out of the town here, but when the wind is strongest—or perhaps I only imagine that the throb carries to me. I am supplying the beat with my blood. Still, it is easy to imagine that the drums are talking to me, now that I am back."

"But if you feel like this," she cried, all irritation forgotten, "liberty must mean so much to you! It must!"

For a few seconds understanding seemed to hover near them in the air. " 'So much'?" he repeated, surprised. "Oh, you cannot possibly know *how* much."

"Then *why*— Look, there's a lot more I'd like to get at before making up my mind if I can help. Captain Hilbery—"

"Captain Hilbery! Captain Hilbery!" All at once Falla Lufa was shaking with anger. It was as if finding that someone had considered his unsuccessful legal cases important enough to study had destroyed a barrier between them, and with it, his control of emotion. He reacted trigger-fashion to Hilbery's name.

Out poured a jumble of abuse for the arch enemy of his friend Storr, and therefore his own; and extravagant praise for the one white man who had treated him as an equal in every way. Nothing could persuade him that Hilbery had not plotted with other Europeans to remove Storr for his own advancement, using Storr's familiarity with such as Falla Lufa as an excuse. She tried to stem the torrent of loathing in vain.

"Listen, please! As a fellow journalist I want to know what's happened to your paper. It was officially suspended at one time, I understand, but that's over. Now you're back in Zanzibar, can you make arrangements for it to appear again?" (I should hardly be surprised, she thought, with this amenable jail as it is, if it were run editorially from here.) But he waved the question aside.

"Michael—Michael Storr—he wanted me to call him by his first name the day we met! As soon as he was off duty. Expected me to. He lent me a shirt—fancy, he lent me a razor, too. One of his own razors—when I was caught by the early rains, and had to stay one night at his house. Just after he arrived. 'Take one of my shirts,' he said. With him, it was not just that being of different races didn't matter. He made me forget that it was so. Actually forget."

For the first time Louise realized with her heart, not only her head, what the subtler forms of color prejudice could mean to a proud, touchy spirit like this. The politer, colder distinctions which an Arab or Indian would meet could be no less wounding than anything an African was likely to experience, in a mixed society. And Hilbery stood for all the loneliness and frustration Falla Lufa had endured, every humiliation of his kind before the arrogance of the self-appointed elect: but above all, for the loss of his sole friend.

The twenty minutes were up before the ranting ceased. A warder came in, a slow, benign, silly white giant who had looked from time to time through the spy hole in the door. "Now chuck it, you," he said, and Falla Lufa subsided, turning away to the grated window, gripping the bars with trembling hands.

"He gets worked up!" said the warder, as if he were discussing an animal which could not understand. "Remember that all right from the last spell he did here!"

Louise, too, knew indignation, and longed to protest furiously, "What do you know of the agony of another human being?" but within his lights the warder was, plainly, a good fellow, and she asked instead, "Can't I stay a few minutes more? There are just one or two more questions I want to ask."

"Sorry. No one from outside allowed in the jail at mealtimes. Besides," he added with an unexpected nursery touch, "it's bath night. Still, it's been arranged—you know—for later. In *his* old office. If you want it."

She walked over to the small figure by the window and spoke to his back. "Mr. Falla Lufa, as a colleague I'm grateful for what you've given me, quite apart from whether I can make use of it or not."

"You realize I can only accept release," he said without turning round, "if the authorities recognize, when remitting my sentence, that less than justice has been done, not only to me but to my friend?"

"I'm afraid it's very unlikely they could be made to take that view. Or that I'd be the right person to try to make them, by way of public interest. Because I'm not convinced enough, myself, to be persuasive. But I would like to go farther into your case, because I'm immensely interested. It's been suggested—without consulting you, I'm afraid—that I might see you outside your cell, later today. Captain Hilbery offered to lend me the room here he sometimes used as an office, so that we could talk again. But you mightn't be willing to come there, and I certainly don't want pressure put on you, to induce you to agree to anything distasteful to you."

"The office Michael Storr also used?"

"Yes, I suppose so. That's partly why I wondered, would you be willing to come?"

He swung round, in the grip of tremendous excitement, his face working, and stared at her silently.

"Now come on, Full o' Love," the warder said plaintively. "The lady asked you a question, didn't she? Hurry up and answer." He had probably not bothered to follow what the question was. "You got to go now, Miss. Sorry and all that."

"Would Captain Hilbery be there?" Falla Lufa asked. His excitement seemed if anything to be increasing. He had reached a stage which appeared close to exaltation.

"I shouldn't think so, from what he said to me a little while ago," Louise told him. "But of course I can't answer for that. Clearing up papers, or fetching something he'd left there, he might walk in. Would you prefer not to come?"

"No!" he said, surprising her by his vehemence. "No! I am willing to come, as you wish." He bowed to her ceremoniously as she left.

Hilbery was waiting for her outside the prison, sitting in his car, smoking. "I thought you were going on to the Club?" she said, glad to see him there. Menace still seemed to her to be lurking in the sunshine which filled the Zanzibar streets. She had not been looking forward to making her way from the jail to the English Club alone.

"I found I couldn't face people," he said frankly. "Not yet. Come and have tea with me somewhere else. You'd be doing me a favor if you would. I'm not exactly good company, I know. But I can't take my usual cronies. All about to be bloody sympathetic, or else say, 'Hell, what's it matter? Lot of bother about nothing!' The way I told you. How about it?"

"Yes, of course I will, if you like. Where shall we go? It'd better be somewhere quiet where my dress won't be noticed. I'm rather conscious of looking as if I'd been put through a mangle in it."

"There's a place near the Beit el Ajeib called the Cantonese Tea Bower," he said. "Very dim lights, and the owner doesn't bar any colored skin. Just as well, seeing the way you've burned! Well, what did you make of Full o' Love?"

"I hardly know!" she said. "I'm still a little stunned. In some ways, perhaps he's the most impressive person I've ever met, because of his terrible power of devotion. And in some ways, one of the silliest. Thank you for making it possible for me to talk to him. And for letting me see him again, later on—I certainly want to do that. He's obsessional, incredibly brave, in an odd way humble but wholly devoid of modesty, emotional, incorruptible—in the sum of things, I suppose, rather a magnificent, futile little figure. He called himself an awkward saint. Perhaps that's the best description."

"It's not bad," he said. "All right, I'll bring you back here to see him again when we've had tea. Maybe you'd better not be seen driving my car through the middle of Zanzibar, after all, and I've still got the shakes. So we'll leave the car here and cadge lifts. And before we get back, I'll fix up somewhere for you to sleep tonight. Worst comes to the worst, I'll inform on you for driving without a license, and we'll lock you up in the jail. As you've seen, it's quite pleasant."

They went part of the way by police jeep, which was going in to the town for supplies, and walked the last hundred yards or so. In this distance Louise met two people she knew: one was Ibrem, who darted aside and out of sight in an instant. She surmised, rightly as it proved eventually, that he had now appropriated all her small store of food, though he took nothing else and allowed no one to touch anything in her lodgings, where her suitcases still waited safely. The other was Mrs. Corryman's Toma, who was amazed by her transformation into a brown-skinned woman, to the point of losing his dignified courtesy. "Mem! Can it be you? I would not have believed you could look such a warm slice of sweet potato!" He clapped his hand over his mouth, as though guilty of laughter, and hurried on.

In the Cantonese Tea Bower the newcomers from the glare outside were blind for a few seconds. The illumination was deliberately so dim that no one coming in could make out who was already there; but those inside, whose eyes had adjusted to it, could recognize the new arrivals in time, if necessary, to let down the looped curtains of bamboo and beads which hung beside each table: all the tables were in separate alcoves. Only at the moment of entry was it necessary for anyone to be visible. Everyone made use of these places, Hilbery told her, at some time or other; and everyone disparaged them as tawdry, unnecessary, and likely to give a wrong impression of Zanzibar to the tourist.

An amiable voice hailed them both by name. Her eyes grew accustomed to the gloom. In a split second of social horror she foresaw how inexorably one genial person was about to force three other people, with the utmost politeness, to sit together, against their strongest inclination. There was Major Deane, waving at them vigorously, and beside him sat Cochi.

"Hallo-hallo, Mrs. Downes! Treat to see you obviously so fit again.

Wonderful. Ah, Hilbery, glad to catch you in time to say, 'All the best.' Hear you're slipping away from us any day now. Come and make a foursome."

Hilbery scarcely troubled to disguise his unwillingness; Louise would have given a great deal, and Cochi probably more, to avoid the encounter. But Major Deane was already busy borrowing chairs from other alcoves. In no time they were all settling down together, ordering more tea, and plenty-plenty cakes, and for Hilbery, who pleaded the need for a hair of the dog, a chaser of whisky.

Major Deane did nearly all the talking: he was bursting with pride and pleasure in his companion. "Fair cop—got to admit it!" he said. "Remember the last time we met, Mrs. Downes? When I told you I was off on a recce? Well, *this*"—he beamed at the bent, dark head beside him—"was what I was recce-ing for! Only no luck for me *that* day."

Cochi looked up and the two women stared at each other, and smiled and smiled, hiding their love and their hatred behind their eyes, the hopes of one and the gallant despair of the other. For Cochi's acquiescence in Major Deane's proprietary manner sprang from something other than brutal practicality—Louise was immediately aware of this, through some heightened understanding produced by the tension between them. Karel had said, "A queer girl . . . down to earth . . ." But it was pride—a fierce acceptance of unalterable defeat—which now dictated Cochi's equally proprietary air: "Alan says . . . *We* like . . . Alan, do make the boy bring more hot water." Jauntiness was wrapped about her like a tattered fancy dress. Sometimes, only the rents were noticeable, Louise thought, in the long silences the girl kept, while Major Deane chattered on.

Louise's heart went out to her: almost all her heart. One part, the selfish depth below every level on which sympathy could exist, was jubilant with relief. Cochi and Karel had met, had talked already. They must have, for the girl to have transferred herself to this dull, good-natured little man. With honesty, Louise looked and marveled. In terms of flesh alone, nothing she could give to Karel could make up for what he lost, in relinquishing Cochi: jaunty and withdrawn by turns, this girl was lovely beyond all praise, in any mood. Karel had been sure; quite sure, he said; but Louise had not dared to believe it until this moment.

Smiling, smiling till cheek muscles ached with the effort, Louise remembered herself standing in the bow of the ship which brought her, watching the harbor lights in reflection scything away the ties with the past, and wondering with whom she would sit in the houses where lights beckoned to her across the water. Life was consistently less probable than any picture of the future supplied by her imagination; she could not have expected, at that time, a courteously conversational occasion with someone who might, or might not, have paid a small sum to have her killed.

The two women passed one another sugar and milk, and Louise ate insubstantial little cakes ravenously, despite pity and thankfulness. With no idea how they would end, she heard her own voice embarking on fatuous sentences, making talk about sunburn, and how lucky she was in not scorching, though she was of the same coloring as Major Deane, whose nose had skinned in what looked to be a highly painful fashion. She was embarrassingly bright, she felt; and could think of nothing else to be.

Hilbery remained morose, growing if possible more so under the other man's irrepressible efforts to draw him out. Major Deane had just enough tact not to refer openly to the debacle at the Sultan's departure, of which he had evidently heard, but was equally plainly of the think-nothing-of-it persuasion. He talked pointedly of the fuss people made about trifles in Africa; although some of what he said was directed at Louise, not Hilbery: he was shocked to hear that she had actually seen Falla Lufa after all.

"Recollect what I thought of that idea when you got me to help you write a letter about it? Not impressed, I was. Definitely not in favor. Surprised to hear you persisted. But of course you did get an awful shake-up from that homali cart. See you've still got the plaster on your arm."

"Some of it." Part of the supporting band had cracked, worked loose and come off, through the combined action of sun, sea water and rubbing, when the skin underneath started to irritate with prickly heat. "I'll be rid of the rest in a few days. But I assure you my continued interest in Falla Lufa isn't due to my being knocked silly in an accident!"

"Oh, rather not. Never meant to suggest that for a minute," said Major Deane jovially. "Still, it was a rotten start for your visit. Hope Zanzibar hasn't been too unkind to you since then?"

"No. Thanks. It hasn't."

Needing to take no part in this exchange, Cochi let her disguise slip momentarily, and her face was naked in its misery. Louise felt the stricture of tears tightening her own throat; sadness and fear were strangely alike in their physical effect. She forced more pointless questions and rejoinders, ate more food, laughed at nothing. It was the most macabre party at which she had ever been present.

"Oh, come on," said Hilbery, unable to stand any more bonhomie. "If you want to see Falla Lufa again, make it now."

"And matter of fact, pretty soon *we*'ll have to be thinking about the boat to Dar!" said Deane fondly. "I'm in luck, Miss Cochi here, and her cousin for chaperon, are coming to stay with me for a week. Wish you people could look in. We'll be quite a household." There was no getting out of shaking hands all round.

Cochi looked up once more into the taller woman's face, her eyes searching it, contemptuous and wondering, as if studying the lineaments of disaster, trying to find solace in understanding. Hatred could couple with resignation: had done this already—Louise grasped that she was safe, and again her unashamed heart sang. But rarely could victory in any human contest have brought so much compassion to the victor.

Outside the Cantonese Tea Bower the day was fading, and in the coming night the streets of Zanzibar would be full of shadows, but no longer of terror for her. There would be no further attempt at violence: Cochi, she knew, had accepted that it was useless.

"Cousin-chaperon, my foot!" said Hilbery as they emerged, blinking again, into the remnants of daylight, and watched the other pair walking away to find a taxi near the Maidan. "Does that half-witted little soldier think I've just arrived out here? That girl's a man-eater. Like most men in the neighborhood, I've had a shot in the same direction myself," he added, cheering up slightly, "but I didn't happen to be lucky. Or else I was, very: depends which way you look at it —Deane'll find he's married to her before he knows where he is, if he isn't careful. And probably even if he is."

"How can anyone—how can 'most men in the neighborhood,' as you say!—be so cruel?" Louise asked, relief finding an outlet in a gust of anger. "Spoiling that child's life without compunction, by seeing how far they can go, 'without paying for it,' as I suppose you'd call it?" When she was with Karel, and they had talked briefly of Cochi, she had not been able to finish the phrase, "How could you—?" with the open accusation of cruelty. Hilbery bore her reproaches vicariously.

"Cruel?" he said, genuinely surprised. "I don't think that's fair. Have you any idea what life's like, for an Arab girl of good family, when she's respectably married? As Asaby would have liked this one to be, just as soon as she came back from school? He's the head of her family, did you know?"

"So someone told me." Louise was giving nothing away.

"She's kept shut up in her husband's house, most of the time. Goes out veiled, with an attendant, when she does go out. Sees practically no one but her husband. Who treats her as of no account, except for breeding. Oh, she might also be allowed to see his close relations occasionally, and a few married women carefully chosen by them to be her friends. With all the old ladies from both families giving tongue against any liberty for her which they hadn't had in their youth. It's always the old women who hold back progress of any sort, social or medical. What they couldn't enjoy let no one have. Any pain they've borne, so much the better for their daughters and daughters-in-law: do them good. Specially daughters-in-law. That girl —as things are, she's lost caste with Mrs. Corryman and such. And with Asaby, naturally. But she's known something better than she'd ever have had if she'd stayed conventional. She's met—well—affection. Along with other things! Rare thing to meet, let me tell you, for an Arab girl, affection. Or for a high-caste Indian girl. Rarest of all for a bit of both, probably." He used the word "affection" awkwardly, as though afraid to admit the importance of something in which his life might soon, he believed, be very poor.

"No, I hadn't realized what respectability would have meant for her," Louise said. (And for her, particularly, it would have been very hard, she thought.) "I take back some of what I said about your callousness."

"Don't be so grudging, pet!" He was recovering his old form rapidly, with the hair-of-the-dog's help.

"All right, all of it, then."

"That's better."

Her heart leaped to exonerate Karel; her puritan reason told her
that she was a hypocrite, accepting Hilbery's view because she needed
so badly to be able to believe in its comfort. Of course it was biased,
and only true in part. Of course Karel had hurt the girl appallingly.

A passing car jammed on its brakes, backed and stopped beside
them. "My dear, where did you get to? We wondered and wondered!"
Here were the forgiving Osbournes, with whom she should have
dined at Mrs. Corryman's with Einarsen.

"I'm awfully sorry—" she began.

"You'd better not ask where she got to!" said Hilbery, smirking,
conjuring up a thin semblance of his exasperating personality. "I've
just retrieved her from a village down the coast where she'd apparently
gone native. Says she was living there alone! I should leave it at that,
if I were you."

"I have been living there alone! As the villagers could tell you."
How tiresome facetiousness could be! She turned away from him
and spoke only to the Osbournes. "About that evening, I was going
to write and apologize, or come round to explain—" But with easy
Zanzibar hospitality they insisted that her failure to turn up had not
really mattered, they had dined at Mrs. Corryman's and met Einarsen, and only he had fumed. "Let's fix up another night instead.
Come Tuesday?"

Obligingly they drove Hilbery and Louise the three miles to the
jail, protesting that this hardly took them out of their way; they were
going to play golf. The new links, conveniently watered and rolled by
the convicts, as exercise and employment, were practically an exten-
sion, they claimed, of the prison. "But look here," Mrs. Osbourne
said seriously, "you interviewing Full o' Love! What a very odd thing
to do, if you don't mind my saying so. I'm sure my husband
agrees, here we feel we've heard more than enough of him and his
views."

"That's right." Osbourne sounded still more earnest. "Personally
I'm sorry to learn the fellow's back with us, even in jail."

"You two had better give Mrs. Downes a bed for the night," Hilbery suggested on the way. "I've practically turned her out of her
lodgings down in the dyers' district. Not safe for a white. In spite of
the local color she's taken on so thoroughly."

"Of course. We'd be delighted," they said. It was as easy as that.

But now—what a nuisance Hilbery was being! Louise wanted this accommodation no longer. Since the meeting with Cochi, all she longed for was to be left on her own.

"It's extremely good of you," she said, guarding her voice from irritation. "Especially after the shocking way I've behaved to you. But actually I don't need a bed tonight, thanks very much. I'm all right."

"What d'you mean, all right?" Hilbery demanded, reasonably enough. "You said earlier on, you'd nowhere to sleep tonight. Nowhere to go except those rooms, and for once we saw eye to eye—you can't stay there."

"We'd love to have you. Honestly. You'd be no bother. This isn't England. Anyone can have a shakedown without fuss."

"Yes, I know— It's so kind of you—but—" How could she explain, or be convincing without explaining, that in the last hour fear, like a weight inside her, had been dissipated by a look, by another woman's air of beaten acquiescence under a pretense of gaiety? Against the real danger which had shadowed her, alone in the Stone Town, the minor risks of the night which Hilbery foresaw seemed nothing at all to face: merely those of being mistaken for a prostitute. But Karel knew the whereabouts of her lodgings: not finding her in the village on the coast he would return to look for her there. She must be waiting for him this time. She would not run away again. Time seemed to be pressing toward some signaled meeting. The sky was reddening for a sunset of fantastic beauty: the benevolent thunderstorm was rolling punctually round the horizon, over Africa. She must be alone with Karel this evening; somehow, anyhow.

"I thought you were getting sensible at last about what a European woman can and can't do, on her own, in this place!" Hilbery grumbled.

"I was—I am. But I've been thinking things over. I know I'll be all right till tomorrow. Then I'll clear out." Really, a journalist should be able to improvise better than this! "I've just remembered," she said, "I arranged to pay off the night watchman, and the boy who runs errands for me, sometime this evening. If I don't go back there, they'll both be waiting around till all hours. And I've got to pack my things. I'd love to take up your invitation for another night, if I may, Mrs. Osbourne? Tuesday, perhaps? But not tonight. I'll be very busy, very late," she finished lamely, looking almost appealingly at Hilbery. "Struggling to get everything into suitcases. Isn't it queer how one's clothes seem to swell?"

Hilbery, who enjoyed embarrassing people, must surely be aware, she thought, that it would take her about five minutes to clear her possessions out of those rooms. Would he press his advantage? "Oh, let her do as she likes!" he said, almost rudely, to the kindly husband and wife who were fairly pestering her to run no risks. "She's mad. So am I. Zanzibar will be well rid of the two of us. But hardly anything ever happens to the mad! Well, here we are. Thanks for the ride."

Overhead, unnoticed by anyone else as she and Hilbery got out of the car, a wedge of small, screaming birds told Louise, "Goudblond haar is mooi—is mooi—mooi!" She was thankful for her little triumph: in an hour, perhaps—or less—surely in two hours' time—they would be together, she and Karel.

Inside the prison, Hilbery led her along a bare stone corridor which took her back in memory to an English boarding school: the domestic smell of oniony stew mingled with the steam and soap of hot humanity on bath night. Then they came to the administrative block and the school atmosphere faded. "In here," he said, and ushered her into a small room furnished with filing cabinets and a wide table, much less cheerful than Falla Lufa's cell. "I'll send for the awkward saint."

He went out, and she heard him calling an order down another echoing corridor: then he was back. "Now, Bonnie, let Uncle Tom hear just why you're suddenly so anxious to be alone tonight! I'm not so easy to put off as your would-be hosts."

The lifting of his alcoholic depression was complete, and made him again the man she had first met. He was showing the side of his complicated nature which she most disliked: she wondered if he had somehow got hold of a few more hairs of the dog without her noticing, that he was so quickly and thoroughly restored.

"I'm telling you nothing more than I told the Osbournes," she said, still in an amiable tone. "Please go. You said I could have Falla Lufa to myself."

"Not till you tell me what's up."

"Please go," she said, less amiably. Feet were approaching down the passage. "He hates you. You know that. I like the little man. I don't want him distressed."

There was another door out of the room, presumably leading into a different passage or other offices. "Plenty of time," Hilbery said annoyingly. "He's had two other visitors since you, I hear, though that's supposed to be against the regulations—outside visiting hours. Members of his family. They've been bringing him presents all day. Probably smuggling in a whole lot of things he's not supposed to have. Well, we turn a blind eye, in his case. So in the circumstances it won't hurt him to hang around in the passage for a minute, while I find out, what's behind all this, eh?"

"Captain Hilbery—" She was not sounding in the least amiable at this stage. The feet were coming close, near enough for two sets of footsteps to be distinguished. For her this had been a long, emotionally exhausting day. "I've told you I'm grateful to you for getting Falla Lufa back here. And for letting me see him here. But I don't understand why I should account to you for anything I choose to do when you're no longer responsible for my safety. Please do go. Surely we can talk later—if necessary?"

He came and sat on the corner of the table nearest to her, and looked at her with his practiced twinkle, head slightly tilted. "Remember I guessed at first glance you're a pretty lady who expects to have her own way, and if she doesn't get it—!"

The door opened and a warder came in, saluting smartly. It was the same good-natured oaf whom Louise had seen before. "The prisoner, sir."

"Wait outside." Hilbery was able now to snap back instantly into his official demeanor. "This lady will let you know when she's ready to see the prisoner—by herself." Briefly, he flashed over her his caressing, masher's smile. "Then bring him in and leave him here for twenty minutes, fetch him and take him back to his cell. I shall be waiting outside in my car—you might send somebody out to check the air in the tires."

"Very good, sir." The warder turned to go. Hilbery moved toward the other door.

"You see?" he said, twinkling again over his shoulder at Louise. "Everything your own way!"

His voice must have carried through the open door to where Falla Lufa stood. The little man darted in, past the slow-moving escort, before the latter had time to reach the door into the passage.

One glance at Falla Lufa's face, which was shining with a greenish tinge—the only form of pallor possible to a colored skin—warned Louise that he had worked himself into a mood far beyond the state of near exaltation in which she had left him.

What happened in the next few seconds seemed to take quite a long time, yet waiting as if paralyzed, she did nothing to warn Hilbery. Looking back it was as if she knew from the instant Falla Lufa came in what must follow.

Hilbery hesitated, and evidently decided that the ex-editor, the peculiar prisoner to whom special indulgence was allowed, had not heard the order to wait outside the office. He put on an affable expression as the little man hurried forward. "Well, old chap, back among us to give Zanzibar the benefit of your advice again? What's the next grievance going to be?"

Falla Lufa stopped, steadying himself with a hand on the corner of the table between them. "I have come, Captain Hilbery"—his voice was so shrill and breathless that it was scarcely audible—"to give Zanzibar all I can. An act of cleansing." He came quickly round the table, close to the big man, and stabbed him twice in the belly, under the heart, wrenching the knife upward.

Louise did not see the blade in his hand, nor from what hiding place he drew it, only the swift double thrust and the jerking action. The warder was staring, open-mouthed. Then Falla Lufa was bowing to her: "You will understand. You only, perhaps. And my friend. With all my heart I wanted my freedom. But for friendship—" and then the warder had grappled with him, shouting for help, had disarmed him and was starting to drag him out. Other feet pounded along the passage.

Red hands pressed to the wounds, Hilbery was keeling very slowly off the table, looking incredulous. "Silly little coon," he said before he died, an hour later.

20

A Letter from Cambridge

"Maybe this is the worst thing you do, you superior English people. Not taking the hatred you rouse seriously. Till too late."

"That's about what Dr. Asaby said. But what happened this evening doesn't make sense, Karel! None of it makes sense. Hilbery, who really loved 'his coons,' going out like that—because one of them was an awkward saint, and really managed to believe that Hilbery was a cunning devil! And Falla Lufa, poor fantastic little Full o' Love—"

"Who wanted something to sacrifice himself for. Do you remember, *liefste*, talking about 'the hole in the heart'? Well, from what you say, he filled it with Storr. (One of the most boring men I have met in all my life, I think, but of course that has no bearing on

265

what he could mean to someone else.) Falla Lufa makes sense all right. Only you are still too close to this horror to see."

"If only I hadn't interfered—if only I'd never come here." Over and over again, in the hours of darkness through which they talked, her mind came back to this. Shocked, appalled, she had returned from the jail to her rooms to find Karel waiting for her there. "If I hadn't come to Zanzibar, hadn't asked to see him, this ghastly thing wouldn't have happened."

"Then everyone would have been better off, you think? No, love, not everyone!"

"Hilbery. He'd have gone home."

"I wonder—that particular man—would he have been better off? Maybe just in the way that being alive is better than being dead, because being alive can always be turned into being dead, but not the other way round. Not much better."

"Falla Lufa. Oh, Karel, he'd have been released eventually. With or without my doing anything. Now he'll hang. For Hilbery!"

"And for his friend, remember. All you have told me says that part of him must have wanted that. Listen, Louise, we are adults, you and I. We know that there is only a limited responsibility that one person can take for another."

"If I hadn't tried to help— It was a kind of arrogance, you know. That belief I could put the world right for someone else, if I chose. They were right, those people who said, 'Leave him alone.'"

Karel shifted her head gently on his shoulder with his free hand, turned her face toward his and kissed her. His other arm was under her shoulder, holding her close to him, because to hold her and patiently let her talk the misery out of her mind was the kindest thing he could do for her. They lay together on the strap bed in her lodgings, and outside in the courtyard the old watchman nodded and dozed on his stool, and the pitch of the throbbing in the noisy Zanzibar night varied continuously.

"You are not to blame, Louise. You tried to help. Yes, of course you can say truly, 'If this—if that—' then you are the cause of what happened. I agree, if Falla Lufa had not been brought back from Harmatta, before Hilbery left, just to suit you—if you had not insisted on seeing him that second time, which gave him the chance to get a knife off some admiring relation of his, when he realized he

might meet Hilbery—well, then, Hilbery would be alive now, and
Falla Lufa could not have made certain for himself that he will
never be free again. (I think they may not hang him: he could be
found mad. But in any case, he will never be free.) If all these things,
still you are not to blame. You must understand that. For there are
always so many other 'if's.' If Hilbery had not always been a law to
himself— See, in any human action, you can only judge fairly how
much is your doing if you can weigh all the 'if's' which were settled
by you, against all the other 'if's' you could not help. Such as Hilbery
being what he was. And that you can never do. Not in this case, not
in any case."

Later, when she was calmer, he said, "If you had not tried to interfere—tried to help—you would still have been running away. Very
successfully too. But now, instead, you are going to marry me."

"No."

"Yes."

"Am I?"

"Yes, quite soon."

It was a strange night, their first together, very different from the
fusion she had imagined in the dawn beside the lean-to shelter,
when she had first longed for him as a lover. For hours they talked,
he keeping her close to him, arguing with her for her happiness and
his own, being tender and understanding, letting her live through
the day's events until she had mastered them in her mind, and could
think without shuddering of the sequence in which they had led up
to tragedy: earlier, her mind had picked at random at isolated facts
of horror, the slowness and pain of Hilbery's dying, while she stayed
beside him, waiting for an ambulance to come out from the town,
bringing a doctor; but there had been nothing that anyone could
do: her own inertia in the critical few seconds after she had realized,
as it seemed to her now, exactly what Falla Lufa was going to do,
and there had been time to shout a warning, yet she had made no
sign. Karel's nearness was consolation, his steadiness something to
which she could hold when waves of revulsion swept through her
mind. Then, suddenly, from one second to the next, the storm of
physical passion took them both, the leaping infection of the blood
ran from one to the other, and the horror of the day was blotted out,
till they slept, from exhaustion. In her dreams she cried out, fright-

ened by images of terror and violence, and he roused her. Finding
him within reach, she was comforted and slept again.

In the morning, able to face the world once more, she said,
"Here's something more that doesn't make sense. Nothing has
changed in your situation, only in mine. Cochi still loves you. You
know that. So do I. I've always said I wouldn't rob her, in any circumstances. But I know now that I am going to marry you."

"Good. Now I know it too! Though really I knew it quite some
time ago, remember? In Holland. And was not at all pleased. Such
an unwelcome upset it looked, that morning, from Veere!"

"I need you so much. That overrides everything for me. It
wouldn't, I suppose, if I had a more than life-sized, splendid character. But it does. One says, 'I will never—' and then gives in, to
something stronger than a good resolution. Wrong, I suppose, but
human."

"Yes, Louise. Very human!"

"Also," she said, for once groping for words, "I know this sounds
fantastic. I'm not even sure that it's true. But it's as if Hilbery dying
like that, by that stupid, irrelevant stabbing which I ought to have
prevented—which I could have prevented if I'd called out!— No, no,
I won't start on that again!— But it's as if this canceled the last part
of a bargain: oh, a most obscure sort of bargain I made, nearly six
years ago now. With guilt. I'm free, today. Entirely free. You said,
on the beach, that Falla Lufa had given me what he hadn't got himself, freedom. It was true, he had. Almost complete freedom. I felt
free then, except for one thing. A debt of pity. For Cochi. Hilbery
paid off the remaining bit of the price of freedom, for me. It doesn't
make sense," she said again.

"I think it could! You say, it was a kind of arrogance, your idea
that you could choose to put the world right for other people. But
Louise, you have always been arrogant in guilt. For *you* to do something which was not right—this was much worse than for anyone
else to do the same thing, wasn't it?"

"Yes!" she said, surprised. "Yes! Perhaps I'm not really so unlike
my Cambridge uncle as I've always hoped. He's arrogantly humble."

"You are not in the least like him," Karel said decisively, "in any
way but this. That you are arrogant, just a little."

"I have been," she said. "I don't think I am now! That attitude of

mine—I will not stoop to rob someone like Cochi—quite a big part
of it was the feeling that for me to take someone else's leavings was
not good enough. Well, I know this morning that it's much, much
more than good enough! Having failed Hilbery—I promise, this is
the last time I'll say that!—I don't feel that I'm quite such a special
person. From whom everything should be expected. Too fine to accept love gratefully on any terms. But I still don't see why recognizing that I'm no worthier or less worthy than anyone else should
have brought me such an enormous reward. What good have I done
here?"

"All that you could, Louise. Surely this is what matters? That you
came, willing to help. That you tried to help with everything you
have, your heart and your mind."

Ibrem put his head round the door, saw them and fled. Like the
fireflies down the coast, the brief apparition changed their mood.
Day had come, and the light filtering down the passage fell on the
picture, "So Big!" Karel got up and stood before it, naked and
happy. "Louise, what is this terrible thing? It is not yours, I hope?"

"No. It's the landlord's. But I like it! There was a copy on the
stairs at home, when life was safe and smelled of milk and biscuits.
Did you have a nursery with a fire, where you could see the reflection on the ceiling from bed? There are so many important things I
don't know about you. A lot to learn."

"Heaven prevent—is that the word? No, 'Heaven forbid.' Dutch
children are not shut away in nurseries; they live with the family. But
we had an English picture, 'When Did You Last See Your Father?'
How the worst English pictures get about! I shall not buy this one to
take to Pemba, as a wedding present for you. It would not fit there.
'El Huthera, the Green One': I told you its other name. More beautiful than Zanzibar. Windows in my house are built low down, for
you to lie in bed and watch the dawn come up over the sea, each day.
Always the same time, but always the clouds in new shapes and the
colors, not quite like yesterday's. You will find that as good as flames
on the ceiling for safety, I think. Will you be bored on Pemba? I
have two years more there. No, I think not. You have resource in
yourself." He had come back to sit on the side of the bed and stroke
her face with one finger. "What a lovely, lovely color you are!
Down to the kanga line. In Pemba you must become the same, all

over—nearly the same, nearly all over. There is a pool between many trees which is only for us. Do you think you will be bored?"

"With you? In a place where I can try my hand at writing to please myself, not other people, for the first time in my life? No, I don't think I'll be bored!" She added with friendly malice, "I'm surprised you can even imagine a woman being bored when there's die-back disease among the clove trees nearby, for her to consider."

"I am as bad as that, you think? But as a matter of fact," he said, almost apologetically, "I have pretty well stamped it out, just round us."

"Darling Karel. Do you happen to have plenty of money?"

"You mean, a big enough salary for two, or in my pocket now?"

"In your pocket."

"A few pounds only."

"But that'll be enough, won't it, for a very large breakfast? At the tourist hotel I couldn't afford to look at before. (I've got so tired of counting not just pennies but ha'pennies.) And will you buy me several packets of cigarettes, so I can chain smoke while we eat. Just at first? I can't get the taste of fish off the back of my teeth, and I'm still hungry. I'd forgotten how hungry."

"I believe this is not how the bride is expected to feel, after the first night. But I have always been so glad you like food. When we are old, we will each see that the other is disgustingly fat, maybe. But while we are both sure that we are both thin—come. You have had nothing since yesterday's tea, and I not since midday."

"I shall disgrace you at the hotel. Part of my sunburn is probably ingrained dirt, and I've nothing clean to wear. You can't shave, but you'll look relatively decent." They were dressing while they talked.

"Never mind. You have a way of appearing *glatt*—sleek—all the time. Even now."

"If Mrs. Corryman sees us, or her friends—"

"I am unshaken that St. Augustine *was* a Negro. Therefore Mrs. Corryman will never approve of me again. Therefore she will not approve of you for marrying me. But Mrs. Corryman does not come to Pemba."

They carried Louise's suitcases out into the courtyard where the old watchman, long after his time to be gone, was sleeping soundly, having allowed himself to slip from his stool to the ground, as an off-duty luxury. He said, "Yes, yes, yes!" cheerfully when they wakened him and paid him off: only as a tip was added did he realize that this was the end of his job, and he would have no further right to spend his nights in that comparatively peaceful spot: he began to mourn, wagging his head from side to side.

His regrets, expressed by a shrill "ai-ai-ai" sound, brought out the landlord from the shop at the back. Smiling with every fold in his face, he came waddling across the courtyard waving some letters, calling upon them to stop as Karel picked up the suitcases. Would the gracious white lady reconsider this matter of leaving, now that there was no longer any reason why she should go?

The news of Hilbery's death must have flashed round the Stone Town. Unusually obsequious for an Arab, the man poured compliments upon Louise, while observing Karel out of the corner of his eye creases. Here was a well dressed foreign client, one of those who had called before: business must indeed be brisking up for his tenant. As a kindly fellow at heart, he was pleased for her, as well as by the prospect of more rent. Never had he known an occupant of these rooms, he said, who was less trouble, more saddening in her going out, more delighting by her coming in. He assured her that he had personally looked after everything belonging to her in her absence, and kept the thieving children away, in particular one Ibrem. He had given the watchman something extra to stay awake in the darkest hours. In the last few days he had refused several offers for her rooms, offers which scarcely another house owner in Zanzibar, with such premises to let and no questions asked, would have dreamed of refusing. Compliments to himself began to flow even faster than those to his ever welcome tenant and her ever welcome friend. Would they honor him by taking coffee with him in his shop, and perhaps inspecting his unrivaled stock? Reluctantly, when they refused, he handed over to Louise the mail which he had taken it upon himself, officiously, to collect for her from the post office: among the envelopes there was one from Cambridge, in her aunt's writing.

Karel cut him short when he started, more aggressively, on a second round of self-praise, paid over the sum which was supposed to have been given to the night watchman, and the pair went on their way.

"That was rather nasty, but it doesn't matter now," said Louise, passing under the archway and into the street where the old man with the bandaged head was still sitting in his chair in the angle of the wall, as though he had never moved since she had first come by; and the old woman was again using the gutter, and a horde of children played in the dust, watching them like a pack of hostile little animals, only intimidated for the moment. The gorgeous morning light of Zanzibar lay like a benison on them all.

They swept into the hotel as though they were a couple of the stray locusts which sometimes blew over from the mainland, tattered but with undiminished voracity, to attack everything edible within reach. Red-faced tourists of the wealthiest class, toying in the heat with a traditional, heavy English breakfast, eyed them askance, not knowing what to make of a man in passable clothes but a two-day growth of beard, absorbed in a woman whose neat, distinguished head was set off by clothes in a deplorable condition, both of them ordering second helpings of everything, in an absent-minded way: kidneys and bacon, toast, fruit and coffee: while the woman smoked luxuriously all the time, with a glow about her crumpled appearance which aroused instinctive envy. A north-country English voice became suddenly audible in a lull in their eager talk: "Artists or no artists, if you ask me, Mother, people who don't keep up white standards oughtn't to be let in 'ere." The speaker received a stare of bemused benevolence from them both.

"Chake-Chake will be your nearest town," Karel went on. "There is only one other, Wete, in the island."

"Chake-Chake. Wete. Mevrouw van Epp, of Chake-Chake. There couldn't be better names, could there?"

"You think so? Woman I am not yet sure I have cured of running away, why have you not opened that letter which you say is from Cambridge? I want to hear more of that uncle, him with the no-way-through-stuff. But mostly I want to be sure that for you Cambridge has become a long way off! Please open it."

She did not tell him that in this hotel, full of plush and Edwardian furniture, designed to make the British feel at home if uncomfortable in the tropics, provincial England could not seem far away. With absurd trepidation, afraid again of the old spell, she opened and read the letter, because he insisted. From the close-written pages rose at once the familiar atmosphere of well mown lawns, of decorous life, and a throb of heartache, from habit alone.

"It's all right, Karel. My uncle has scribbled a note at the end, hoping I'm sleeping better. And Aunt Rose is worrying again about Dorothy; this time it's that perhaps she isn't eating enough. If only I were handy, she feels, for a good, long talk—" She put the letter back in its envelope and looked up smiling, certainty sweeping through her. "Oh, love, I can't forget Hilbery and Falla Lufa, and what they've done for me, instead of my doing anything for anyone, as I intended. But I do know that I am going to be enormously happy on Pemba."